ALL THE LIVES HE LED

ALL THE LIVES HE LED

BOOKS BY FREDERIK POHL

*A TOM DOHERTY ASSOCIATES BOOK

FREDERIK POHL

ALL THE LIVES HE LED

A TOM DOHERTY ASSOCIATES BOOK

NEW YORK

This is a work of fiction. All of the characters, organizations, and events portrayed in this novel are either products of the author's imagination or are used fictitiously.

ALL THE LIVES HE LED

Edited by James Frenkel

A Tor Book
Published by Tom Doherty Associates, LLC.
175 Fifth Avenue
New York, NY 10010

www.tor-forge.com

Tor® is a registered trademark of Tom Doherty Associates, LLC.

Library of Congress Cataloging-in-Publication Data

Pohl, Frederik.
    All the lives he led / Frederik Pohl. — 1st ed.
      p. cm.
    "A Tom Doherty Associates book."
    ISBN 978-0-7653-2176-3
    1. Vesuvius (Italy)—Fiction.   2. Volcanic eruptions—Fiction.   3. Terrorists—
Fiction.   I. Title.
PS3566.O36A78 2011
813'.54—dc22

                                                   2010036667

First Edition: April 2011

Printed in the United States of America

0 9 8 7 6 5 4 3 2 1

CONTENTS

1

INTRODUCING MYSELF

The first thing I remember is learning to duck-and-cover at Mme. Print-emp's École et Académie, though I didn't know why I was doing it. Of course I knew something was wrong, because it made my mother very sad and my father angry, and I was glad when what they called the Treaty of Spitzbergen was signed with the Stans and we could all go back to being happy. Of course, I didn't know anything about a treaty. In fact I would have had no idea what a "treaty" was and I don't think I had actually ever heard the word "Stans." Then it was all peaceful days for quite a long time, until they weren't.

Well, I'll tell you all about that, though it gives me no pleasure. I'm not sure I should. What I know for sure is that it certainly isn't going to make me look good.

Come right down to it, there isn't very much of my life that does, is there? Robber of old people as a teen, worker at all sorts of illegal activities as a grown-up. No, I'm not proud of myself. If there's a reason to do this experiment in Telling All it isn't because I want everybody to know what a great guy I am. Anyway, let's get on with the introduction.

My name is Brad Sheridan. The year I want to tell you about is the summer of '79, which is when I was working at what they called the Giubileo.

When I say Giubileo, you know what I'm talking about, right? That is, to give it its full name, L'Anno Giubileo della Citta di Pompeii, or, as I mostly called it when I had to call it anything, the Pompeii Jubilee.

That's where I was, that summer of 2079. If you were a tourist then I might not have to tell you much about the Jubilee, because if you were rich enough to afford it you were probably there yourself. Some thirty or forty million of you guys from the wealthy countries were. You came from places all over Europe and in both of the two Easts, the Near as well as the Far, plus the Pacific islands from Tahiti down to Tasmania, and just about everywhere in the world. Well, from some parts of the world, anyway. Not from the American Midwest. For sure not from some of the most heavily populated chunks of Canada either, especially from around Toronto and southern Quebec. Even there, there were a few surprises. Some people from North America did show up at Giubileo, at least from the lucky places like California and British Columbia.

Anyway, wherever you came from, you all seemed to enjoy the Jubilee. At least you did until everything went rotten at once, but we haven't come to that part of the story yet.

You should have enjoyed it. You got your money's worth at the Giubileo, because whatever you liked, the Jubilee had it for you. If your thing was sports you could watch the chariot races. If you liked thrill rides you could go to the Ferris wheel that gave you a four-minute overview of the whole city, both as it really was or as the Giubileo's virts had improved it. Or you could pay to get into the simulation chamber where they reproduced the whole bloody eruption of Vesuvius, exactly as any unfortunate AD 79 family would have experienced it, except that it was all virts and you didn't get killed. Or you could go for a ride on a slave (read: Jubilee-employee-) carried litter. If you wanted gore and brutality, you could go to the old Roman amphitheater, where they had plenty of both of those things. Twenty or thirty pairs of gladiators, a few of them real, would hack each other to death every afternoon for your sporting enjoyment. (Well, not all the way to death. Not for the real, live gladiators, anyway, and you could tell easily enough which ones were real. Those were the ones who worked for the Jubilee and never actually got a scratch, being mostly college kids enjoying a paid vacation in Italy, or Indentureds from poor countries, like me, trying to support family members in the old country on what we could send back. The gladiators who you could see really getting chewed up, of course, couldn't actually feel any of their ghastly wounds. They were all virts.)

If you weren't all that into sports or spectacles there were plenty of other ways to spend your Pompeii sestertia, that is, the counterfeit Roman coins that the sidewalk money-changers sold you as you checked in. You could buy a meal in the Refectorium, where you would get approximately First Century Roman food, although at Twenty-first Century prices. If you wanted more authenticity while you were eating, that was available too. All you had to do was find seven other people who were willing to pay to eat with you, and then you had it made. To those seven you added in yourself and the "host"—or actually, more often the hostess, because, screw historical authenticity, the tourists liked having good-looking young women presiding over the meal they could make themselves imagine might turn into a regular Roman orgy. That would make up the right number of diners for a traditional nine-person Roman dinner party. Then the eight of you "guests" would get a more believable Roman meal. Exactly how believable depended on what you were willing to spend. Boar stuffed with kid stuffed with goose stuffed with lark didn't come cheap, and, so they told me, tasted lousy anyway, though it was, I guess, authentic. For the price of that meal you got heavy doses of atmosphere as well. You ate in one of the restored villas, all as authentic as anything, or at least looking that way, and you ate triclinum style, also adequately authentic. This meant that the nine of you diners lounged on three great couches and practiced the art of eating with one hand while you were resting your head on the other elbow. "Slaves," by which of course I mean volunteers (Indentureds rarely got jobs where there might be good tips), served the meal and watered the wine and stood by with bowls to catch the end product of all that ingesting in case you, as many couldn't help doing, puked it all right up again.

Or you could strip down and try the baths. They were a reliable crowd-pleaser. There you could get yourself oiled and scraped clean by another "slave" using a copper thing like a dull straight razor, called a strigil. Or, if your tastes went that way, you could visit one of Pompeii's second-story whorehouses.

You couldn't actually get laid there, though. What you could do, for a little extra fee, was watch one of the whores, male or female, going at it with one or more of their customers, also with a choice of genders. That was pretty exciting, I guess I myself never wanted to see it enough to pay for even a reduced-rate employee ticket. Of course you knew going in that they would just be virts. It wasn't that the Jubilee couldn't have recruited live men and women for the job. They just weren't allowed to. Union rules.

Or getting closer to present cases you could've bought a cup of really bad "Greek" or "Roman" wine, and sat down to drink it on a bench beside one of those open-air Pompeiian wineshops—maybe the one I myself wound up running, halfway down the Via dell'Abbondanza—while you watched other tourists giggling to each other as they poked their fingers through the strolling virts of what were claimed to be historically accurate First Century Pompeiian citizens.

It was actually not a bad show. I might have enjoyed being there myself if I hadn't had to work so hard, both on the job the Jubilee paid me for as well as on the less legal ones I organized for myself. I didn't do those extra scams just for my own personal greed, you know. I did them because they were the only way I could send enough money home so that my mom and dad could keep on living some kind of a life in the Staten Island refugee village.

I think it must have surprised my parents that I was being such a dutiful son. Well, it surprised me, too. For most of my life I had been a long way from dutiful, parent-wise. But then, once I was out of the refugee villages, I decided I didn't care, I might as well be nice to the old farts. They were far enough away that they didn't bother me much anymore.

Taken all in all, working at the Jubilee wasn't the worst way to make a living. Some of my colleagues used to go on and on about how much they hated their jobs, and how different their lives would've been if only they'd been born to rich parents.

I didn't join in those sessions, though. I couldn't. I had been rich, I mean, or my family had, and look what it got me.

The thing about my parents having money was that they stopped having it at the same time everybody else did. I'm talking Yellowstone National Park.

I was about eight years old when Yellowstone happened, and pretty perplexed by the whole thing. I knew it was possible for people to lose their money and have to move away. I'm not just talking about my Uncle Devious (that crook) now. Sandy Stearman's family had had to do that when I was four, something about stock fraud that took his daddy away and left the rest of the family broke. But it wasn't even what happened when dear dishonest Uncle Devious was caught swindling that did our family in. That was bad enough—IRS agents, FBI, all kinds of people looking for that notorious swindler, my mother's brother-in-law—but we got past that (though somewhat poorer, because one of the people he swindled was my mom). But the real ruination of my life was done by Mother Nature herself, the old bitch. That was the Yellowstone ka-boom.

So by the time I was in my teens I hardly remembered what prosperity had been like.

I don't mean I hadn't noticed any changes. I certainly saw the difference between the eight-bedroom house overlooking the Missouri River where I'd lived since I was born and the tiny, shared-bath hovel that the government provided for us refugees on Staten Island. I did notice such things as, for instance, that Mom began looking older, and that she cried a lot. My father didn't, though. He not only didn't cry, he didn't even seem to care much one way or the other. He just sort of lost interest in wherever the hell we were, or whatever the hell we were doing. I couldn't help noticing that I wasn't going to a private school anymore, either. I was by then going to the Staten Island public schools, where the children of the old-time local families really hated us refugee kids from the villages, and showed it by beating us up after school. That is, they did until the refugee villages got completed. Then a couple thousand more of us refugees moved in and we began to outnumber the locals.

We didn't beat them up as much as they had done us, though. We couldn't afford to. The Staten Island cops were also recruited from the families of the old settlers. We quickly found out that whenever there was a fight we were the ones who were going to get slapped around, no matter whether it was us or the locals who started it.

Then, when the time came, I signed up as a freshman to go to New York A&M.

I guess I should explain what NYA&M was. Its full name was New York Agricultural and Mechanical University. It was not the kind of university that was intended for the academically gifted. Its purpose for being was to turn as many as possible of New York's wildblood youths into reasonably respectable citizens, capable of holding such minimally skilled jobs as waiter or, well, faculty member at NYA&M. I guess it was more or less a success. That is, when we wildbloods were in class we weren't out mugging tourists.

Anyway there was a good reason why I was there, and the reason was that no other college was going to give me a scholarship.

Well, to be truthful I should admit that I didn't really go to NYA&M, exactly, at least not in the sense of showing up for very many classes. I didn't have any reason to. NYA&M wasn't teaching anything I wanted to learn. I didn't have to know how to plant a Recovery Garden in my backyard; we didn't have a backyard. I wasn't going off to run earth-movers in Ohio or Kentucky for the Citizens Recovery Corps, either. It didn't pay much, and, anyway, who wanted to breathe all that lung-choking dust? So I attended classes at NYA&M just often enough to keep my scholarship, with its pitiful little stipend.

I did, once or twice, make the mistake of confusing NYA&M with some kind of actual institution for learning, like when I discovered that the recreational drug somadone had been invented in the Stans. You see, the Stans had been a fascinating mystery to me since childhood. Nobody would talk about them, but they were the people that manufactured the terrible drugs you could buy on any street corner that my mother said if I ever took I would turn into one of those haggard wrecks you saw in the government's "Don't Say Yes!" commercials. That was about all I did know about them, too, except that they were the reason we had the duck-and-cover drills at Mme. Printemp's, although my father said that if the talks broke down and the Stans started firing off those illegal nukes they were supposed to be hiding, a kitchen table wouldn't help. And where did these Stans live? Oh, somewhere in Europe, everyone said. Where exactly in Europe no one could say. Couldn't even confirm or deny my childish guess that maybe it was near the North Pole part of Europe, maybe floating around with Santa Claus in his great candy-striped houseboat.

So then I was a teen, and got into NYA&M. I had almost forgotten about the Stans because nobody wanted to talk about them, but one of our professors made me think of them. Well, sort of. He greeted us all, old fart pretending to be our friend, though he was at least fifty. He gave us a big smile and told us if we ever had any problems or questions we could always come to him. So I did. It took me five or ten minutes to come up with that nearly forgotten question about the Stans. So Professor A. Adrian Minkis turned away from the whiteboard and gave me another big grin. "Yes?"

"It's something I've always wondered about. What are the Stans?"

The smile didn't go away, but it shrank a bit. "Can I ask you, uh, Mr. Sheridan"—looking at his locator chart—"why you want to know?"

I was ready for that. "Well, Professor, uh, Minkis"—glancing at my locator card—"all anybody ever says is that it's better not to talk."

"It is," he said, looking around the room and obviously getting ready to ask, "Any other questions?"

I wasn't letting him get away with that. "But I thought it was important. Like having any contact with the Stans was against the law. Weren't they like threatening the whole world once?"

Mr. Minkis scowled at me, but then shrugged. "The Stans," he began, swinging into full lecture mode, "were a group of republics—Kazakhstan,

Uzbekistan, Turkmenistan, and Kyrgyzstan—that had been part of the old Soviet Union, long ago. They had been used by the Soviets to relocate important military and research facilities far from Moscow, and when the Soviet Union fell apart the Stans still had all those enormous facilities. Nuclear weapons, biowarfare research installations, all sorts of things. The rest of the world didn't trust them with all that weaponry and demanded they give it up, and they refused, and things looked pretty dicey there for a while, oh, fifteen years ago or so."

I said, "I remember! Duck-and-cover!"

"Yes, Sheridan," he said heavily, "exactly. It was an intolerable situation which was solved by the world expelling the Stans from all international organizations and forbidding anyone from going there."

He looked up at the big clock on the wall as though getting ready to end the session. I got one last question in, though. "But then how does stuff like somadone get out?"

"Oh," he said, "not everybody obeys the law, do they? Class dismissed." And never would he talk about the Stans again.

So NYA&M was a washout, but I didn't really care. I had better things to do with my time. Specifically, I spent most of my time on the street, hustling bucks in the Big Apple.

I don't like to talk too much about that period in my life.

That isn't conscience speaking, exactly. I was doing a lot of illegal things, sure, but so were the ten thousand other kids, refugees like me or even the local-born, who roamed the city's streets, working pretty much the same scams I was. Panhandling. "Guiding" the tourists, or anyway the dumber ones among them. Hanging around the side-street bars to roll the most nearly paralyzed of the drunks as they staggered in the general direction of their hotels.

That wasn't particularly profitable. Even drunks didn't carry much actual currency, and what can you do with cash cards that are keyed to the owner's sweat chemistry? There'd be jewelry, maybe, if you could find a fence who wouldn't cheat you and then turn you in anyway. But at best the profits were small.

But I did what I had to do to get them.

Let's face it. I was a mean little turd. The only thing that I can say in my defense is that I hadn't chosen that life. It was just the only life that was available for me. When I watched those old-time kid shows on the screen—that is, the pre-Yellowstone ones, all of them about well-washed boys of about my age who had moms who packed them lunches and went to parent-teacher meetings for them, and, especially, had dads who went to the office and brought home presents for their kids—well, while I watched those old shows I really wished I was in one of them.

But I wasn't. If Yellowstone hadn't happened I might have become one of those kids once, but Yellowstone did happen and I wasn't. And at least I had the sense to stay away from the kid terrorist groups that were getting organized about then.

Well, all right, maybe I didn't always stay totally away, because there was this one time that happened when I was about eleven. That one was a biggie, all right, although it wasn't actually about anything that was going on in the city of New York itself. What it was was this terror bunch that called themselves the Crusaders for the True Bishop of Rome. I had no idea what that meant, but I knew what they had done. They had fire-bombed the Sistine Chapel when the cardinals were supposed to be electing a new pope there. According to the news, they killed three of the cardinals, but it didn't make much difference. Old Jerome II got elected anyway. So, going home that night on the hydroferry, about six of us kids were talking about it, and one thing I said must have rung a bell.

A neighbor kid named Artie Mason pulled me aside when we got to the Staten Island dock. "You sound like a man with principles," he told me—an assessment that really took me by surprise. I don't just mean the bit about having principles; it was also the first time anybody had ever called me a man. "Would you risk your life for something important?"

"Depends on the money," I said, being a smart-assed kid with, really, no detectable principles at all. It was the wrong answer for Artie, I guess. He dropped the matter. And a couple of weeks later he was missing from class. From all of his classes. Permanently. It wasn't until nearly five years had passed and I heard he was in the Southeast Alaska Correction Center—residence limited to suspected terrorists—that I figured out what the question was that he had been going to ask me.

That's the way it went. Petty crime is what kept us going. I didn't do as much as some of the others. I didn't sell drugs, especially the old harmfully addictive ones like heroin or cocaine. There wasn't much of a market for them when somadone came along, but I didn't actually sell even that. Well, I mean I didn't sell it myself. I did stand lookout while dealers sold any amount of their somadone smokes or salves or licky sticks or whatever the fashion was at that moment in those remote and mysterious places called the Stans that nobody seemed to want to talk about, where the somadone and all kinds of other strange things came from.

Actually somadone is what put the Afghan and Colombian drug lords out of business—as good at making you feel good as the hard stuff but with no harmful physical effects at all. Unless you stopped taking it, in which case you got all the withdrawal symptoms of any cold-turkey quitting. Of course everybody knew that, which is why the only people who got hooked voluntarily were addicts to one of the older, harder drugs who were having their health totally destroyed thereby. This was a problem for our local drug dealers, which they dealt with in various ways—by giving away free somadone-laced lemonade, or by handing out somadone-enriched jelly beans at kindergartens. That's when I learned never to take anything edible from a stranger—or, for that matter, from most of the people who weren't strangers to me at all. The person I learned it from was my poor old aunt Carrie, but I'll tell you more about her later.

Anyway, the cops didn't bother with the likes of lookouts like me. The dealers did bother, though. The one or two times a cop did succeed in getting past me I got a pretty good working over from my employer of the moment to remind me to be more vigilant. That was bad enough but what was hard work then was trying to keep my mother from looking at me too closely for a few days, until the bruises lightened up. (My father wouldn't have noticed anything as trivial as a few dozen black-and-blues. Maybe if I'd turned up with an ear missing.) Oh, and I never pimped anybody, either. I might have tried, before I got good at other skills, but I was only fourteen years old then and the girls just laughed at me. Besides all the good-looking girls had gone off to be nanas or au pairs—or hookers—in Kuwait and Madagascar, and it was only the homely ones that had stuck around New York.

So those were the things we did. Since they couldn't put all of us in jail, we kept right on doing them.

Actually the cops were a lot more worried about terrorism than our kiddy crime. They had all the reason in the world to feel that way, of course. I mean, you just had to look down Fifth Avenue at the stump of the old Empire State Building to see what kind of thing they were worrying about. That had been the Unborn Babies Are Worth More Than Living Sinners attack, back in '47 or so.

I don't want to give the impression that it was all one-sided. The news said otherwise. They'd rounded up and convicted everybody involved in chopping the top off the old Empire State, and in our civics class at NYA&M the teacher bragged that the government had finally got positive proof that the master terrorist of the age, somebody named Brian Bossert, had died of his wounds after his attack on the city of Toronto, Canada.

It was the first time I'd heard the name Brian Bossert, and, oh, how I wish it had been the last.

I didn't really care what terrorists did, you know. Why then did I spend time watching terrorist actions on the news channels? Simple. They were doing something interesting, which the other news wasn't. It was of no interest to me that the king of England had to face a parliamentary committee of inquiry because it had been alleged that he was considering turning Catholic, or that the vice president of the United States of America, or what was left of it, was having an affair with the president's wife. None of that had anything to do with me.

I did wonder sometimes why the US loonies didn't employ their own gangs of terrorists, doing things like maybe going around and setting off bombs to punish the rest of the world for not—I don't know—maybe for not somehow preventing Yellowstone? It wasn't that Americans didn't have the skills for terror. I mean, look at all the home-brew nutties who showed their annoyance by blowing up a building here or there, or taking the occasional computer net down, in the old days. New York was still a pretty good target for the crazies, too, though usually on a smaller scale. It was a slow day when we didn't hear guns going off somewhere or see smoke coming out of a building. Some days it was a relief to go back home at night, because back in Staten Island we weren't much bothered by terrorists. Once, I remember, a bunch of descendants of the old Lenni Lenape Indian tribe got liquored up and shot up a police station in Freehold, New Jersey, because they wanted their ancestral lands back. But even if you counted the one-eighths and the one-sixteenths among them there weren't enough authentic Lenni Lenapes left to signify.

Anyway, I knew very well that there was nothing in New York for me. Nothing anywhere else in North America, either, it looked like, because even the parts of the continent that had been spared by damn Yellowstone were full of young people exactly like myself. Even the native East Coast kids couldn't find jobs at any decent pay, because us refugee kids were taking any jobs there were for practically nothing.

It wasn't much of a life for a growing boy, and that's a fact.

I did manage to stay out of jail most of the time. The reason for that was because when the cops did happen to pick me up, they mostly preferred to deal with whatever municipal ordinance I had infracted by punching me out in some alley to save the paperwork. So my life was pretty much crap.

I did know how I might be able to make it better, though. I knew where the money was, and I knew it wasn't anywhere near Staten Island.

As a kid, like every little kid, I had fantasies of running away, maybe to what was left of the Amazon to start a career as a highwayman, or maybe as a sheriff who put the highwaymen away, or running off to the semi-mythical Stans, those rogue countries that had faced down the whole rest of the world by the threat of starting World War Last.

And maybe I had another reason for venturing out into the wide world—like maybe looking for my Uncle Devious, who was more appropriately known, though not by us, as the Reverend Delmore DeVries

Maddingsley. And maybe then making him cough up whatever he had left unspent of my mother's trust fund that he had embezzled.

That wasn't realistic. I knew that. But what I also knew was that any place would be better than Staten Island.

2

HOW I BETTERED MYSELF

You have to be twenty-one years old to wear sex-preference jewelry or to sign the Indenture for foreign employment. I didn't care about the jewelry but I signed the Indenture the day I made the cut.

My mother went to the Egyptian consulate with me. My dad wouldn't. He wouldn't have anything to do with it at all, because he was still pissed about the fact that the well-known Kansas City real estate firm of Daniel S. Sheridan & Associates was never going to turn into the firm of Daniel S. Sheridan & Son. Certainly not back in Kansas City. It would be at least another twenty years before they cleaned Kansas City up. And not anywhere else, either, because who needed a real estate business anymore when most of the country's real estate was buried under a gazillion tons of ash and pumice from the eruption of the super-volcano at Yellowstone National Park?

So I left the consulate's office in the old World Trade Center Memorial Building owing somebody in Egypt 2.5 million US dollars for airfare and training.

All right, that sounds worse than it was. When you translated that into euros it only came to a little over €18,000, but it was still a lot of money. It was more money than I and my dad and my mother put together could hope to earn in the rest of our lives in the refugee villages. But it was a good investment for us to make, because a week later I was being airsick on a four-decker en route to Cairo.

I don't know if you've ever crossed the Atlantic, but if that was what you wanted to do then you had four options: hardwing, zeppelin, four-decker, and surface ship. The hyperjet hardwings were a long way the fastest but they were also wildly expensive; only governments and the hugest of corporations could afford them. The zep liners were by far the most luxurious, but costly and not very fast. For most trans-Atlantic passengers the four-decked, sixteen-engine turboprops were the crossing of choice. In maximum seating configuration, and nearly all their configurations were for maximum seating, four-deckers could carry some 2,650 passengers apiece. They weren't fancy, of course. Mostly the passengers bought Meals RTE at the airports, and the use of the toilets was by appointment only. But they got you there and you didn't have to pay an arm and a leg. (Well, just a leg, maybe.)

The four-deckers weren't the very cheapest way of crossing the ocean. That was the surface ships. They were also definitely the slowest—up to ten or twelve days, and depending on the weather, especially for the wind-aided ones, sometimes even more. No one who could possibly scrape four-decker fare together ever chose supercargo status on a surface freighter. But halfway across, in my six-abreast seat in the bowels of my own four-decker, *The Spirit of Juneau, Alaska*, sitting five meters from the nearest window and fifteen from the nearest toilet, I almost wished I had. But then it was over and I had arrived at the Gamal Nasser International Airport on its island in the bay of Alexandria.

What should I say about my four years in Cleopatra-land? Probably not much. It was interesting, kind of, but it was also a long time ago. Years've gone by, and God knows how many innocent deaths, and besides you're expecting me to tell you about Pompeii, not Egypt. Well, I'm doing that, but think it through. I couldn't sign up for the Jubilee in 2075, could I? It didn't exist until 2079, so there was this detour along the way. Four years of it.

I spent those years mostly guiding German and Russian and Bolivian tourists around as many of Egypt's historical sites as they had finished making into theme parks. That was most of them. And they were big, big business for a country that had been dirt poor for centuries.

I never got to some of their biggies, like Saqqara and Tutankhamen's tomb and his personal city, Amarna. Or to Karnak in Luxor, with its obelisks that the ancients had clothed in pure gold. Well, the modern Egyptians did their own cladding—only with them the gold, of course, was only virts.

The police were not much of a problem, as long as we weren't selling fake antiquities to tourists (which most of us were on the side, but we were generally good at not getting caught). Egypt in general loved having us there. They were used to having foreigners come to admire their ruins as far back as the time of the ancient Greeks. Then that Twentieth Century invention called the theme park taught them how profitable those ruins could become, and they had all the raw materials they needed standing idle there—sixty-two tombs in the Valley of the Kings alone, not to mention the temples, the pyramids, and that greatest of all tourist traps, the hoary old Sphinx itself. And when zeppelin tour cruises began to carry passengers in comfort to destinations far from any seaport, why, then the money really began to roll in.

So it wasn't bad in Egypt. Sure, the pay was crap, especially after they deducted the regular installments on the Indenture, but the tips were all right and I had a sideline or two going. Those wasted years on the streets of the Big Apple weren't altogether wasted.

The main thing that was wrong with Egypt was the inadequate supply of women. I did make contact with another guide, name of Patricia Hopper, and we shared a bed now and then. (Of course that was a firing offense. We weren't even allowed to wear sex-preference jewelry on the job, but we did well enough in the old-fashioned ways.) Patty and I also shared a few buck-hustles, but then she got caught doing illegal currency exchanges and the Egyptian police in their fezzes took her away. So, apart from paying one of the Cairo pros for half an hour's rental of her bod now and then, I was womanless for the next year or so.

On the good side, in Egypt we guides weren't bothered much by terrorists. That wasn't surprising, because who would be dumb enough to try to blow up a pyramid? Naturally the Egyptian cities were crawling with secret terrorist militias, Islamic ones and secular ones, more flavors of them than I could count. Sometimes we heard talk about some village that had been put under martial law. But in Cairo on my days off, although I occasionally heard gunfire or explosions or emergency vehicles screaming around, I didn't have much personal worry. The Egyptian terrorists didn't bother civilians much. They were usually too busy trying to assassinate each other's leaders.

Not always, though.

There was a new breed of terrorists, the Neue Fur—they pronounced it "noya foor"—who had been spotted in the Valley of Kings and were said to be active near the pyramids and the Sphinx. So I paid the right bribes to get away from those areas, and got myself posted to Siwa, the place where, a long time ago, Alexander the Great had worshipped a few ancient Egyptian gods. It had a good reputation among us guides. That is, it was said to be great for tips.

Probably it was. I never found out for myself, in fact I never actually set foot on that ground. While I was on my way up there the Fur did their thing. They weren't really mad at the Egyptians, just at their own government back in Sudan. But they worked a lot of Egypt over because there wasn't that much left to blow up in Sudan.

See, like I said, no terrorist with an IQ over forty was going to bomb the pyramids. The Furs didn't. They found a better target.

The big thing about Siwa was the temple of their head god, and it had an inner temple that was a really big Egyptian deal. In Pharaonic times only priests were allowed inside it. By the latter Twenty-first Century the rules were changed and now the only congregation for any of those gods was rich-country tourists. They came to spectate rather than worship and admission was now restricted to anyone who was willing to pay for a ticket.

What the Fur did, they quietly removed the government ticket-takers at the inner temple one day and replaced them with their own guys. Then they sent barkers around to announce that, for the next thirty minutes only, admission to the inner temple would be free. And then, when the inner temple was packed solid with wealthy Arabs and Europeans and Asians, they blew it up.

As I say, I wasn't there when the killing happened. I was fat and happy and airborne in my short-haul blimp, enjoying my free (free!) cup of Egyptian coffee that the stewardess handed around to all us passengers, and looking out the window (imagine having a window of your own to look out of!) at the sands and the occasional scrub and the even more occasional glimpses of the Nile no more than a couple hundred meters below us, and thinking about all the money I was going to make.

Of course the pilots heard about what was going on at Siwa right away over the radio. They didn't tell us, though. Didn't want to start a panic, I guess. But then it got onto the news, and the first-class passengers that had their sets turned on heard all about it. Then the pilots had their panic, all right.

By the time we got there the airport was packed with Intersec and Egyptian Air Force hardwings, and you could smell the deaths.

I took the hint. I didn't even get off the blimp, just stayed where I was until—hours later, because they were one by one security-screening every passenger coming to or leaving Siwa—we finally lifted off for the return flight to Cairo.

All that gave me plenty of time to consider what I wanted to be doing there. By then I had got the Indenture debt down to about €7,000, but those street hustles were beginning to attract the wrong kind of attention. And then there was the religion thing.

The Egyptian Muslims were beginning to throw their weight around again after the big suppression of 2065. It was getting on toward Christmas, and one of our Indentureds, Francine Robles-Espada, made the mistake of deciding to have a little traditional kind of a party. You know, mistletoe over the doorway and eggnog to drink. She'd been having a pretty good year selling fake funeral dishes and *ushabti* to gullible rich people from Peru and Madagascar—actually it was originally Patty Hopper's scam, but Francine inherited it, that and the far-away old flat where Patti kept her inventory, when Patti was taken from us. Francine was smarter than Patti, though. She never sold the stuff herself. She would be taking a tour group around and she would tell them how no decent ancient Egyptian would have allowed himself to be entombed without a crew of *ushabti*, the little ten-centimeter figurines made of the glazed quartz powder that the French call faience. Hers were made of baked clay, actually, but the tourists didn't know the difference. Then she would turn the group loose for free time just where one of her associates, usually an old drunk named Mohammed, was waiting, who happened to have a couple of the things in his pocket. Mohammed might get arrested, but Francine never would.

Until the party, anyway. It turned out not to be a merry time for Francine. The religion police stormed in and carried her away, on the charge of proselytizing Christianity. How? Through her heretical lights-covered Christmas tree, which affronted every true believer who passed by. Or would affront him anyway, if he happened to climb onto a neighbor's rooftop so he could see through the windows of her third-floor flat.

I had a problem about then, too. I had been manufacturing papyrus copies of that old Egyptian best seller, The Book of the Dead, and took on one of our drivers, a man with a modest police record named Faroukh, to do the selling for me. He did it very well, too, and even immediately turned my share of the cash over to me. Only after a number of profitable weeks he informed me that, while our seventy-five/twenty-five split was fine with him he wanted the order reversed so he got the seventy-five. Or else, he said, he would turn me in for the reward.

And so, taking one thing with another, the writing on the wall was clear. It was time for me to be going somewhere else.

Trouble was, I didn't know where to go. I checked into all the employment openings I could find, but most of them were terrible—manual labor in unpleasant surroundings, the kind of job none of the natives would touch, so they had to take on desperate Americans.

Then a different one of our Egyptian drivers showed me an advertisement in one of the Cairo papers, and that was when I heard about the Anno Giubileo della Citta di Pompeii.

The Jubilee sounded good. I was pretty sure there would be a shot at as much off-the-books business for me in Pompeii as there was in Egypt, and there would be a better climate, and not so much sand in my underwear at night. And, if I made the right connections, possibly a chance at moving up to something better than Pompeii later on—maybe even becoming a *gastarbeiter* in Germany, which, if I was lucky, could possibly even turn into a lifetime career.

And one other thing.

I know it doesn't sound like the kind of thing that a person like me would do, but I had been faithfully sending money back to the old folks at 16-A Liberty Crescent, Floor 15, in the Molly Pitcher Redeployment Village on Staten Island. The Jubilee gave its employees free health insurance. That wasn't the thing that caught my eye. I was just twenty-five at the time. I was already thinking of getting out of Egypt, and what twenty-five-year-old thinks he'll ever get really sick? But there was also life insurance. You needed it to protect your dear ones, the ad said coaxingly, and whose dear ones needed protection more than mine?

It was tempting. The more I thought about it the more it seemed to me that Pompeii had everything going for it, except one thing. When I checked they flatly refused to assume the remaining €7,000 on my Indenture. They said the term they would need me for was only the one season and they didn't think I could work the whole debt off in that time.

I fixed that, though. I let them make the Indenture even bigger—a thousand euros bigger—so if I didn't earn out at the Jubilee they could sell me to somebody else when the season was over. When I also put up another thousand out of my privately acquired funds, they grudgingly took me on. I was on my way out of the country in forty-eight hours. I was pretty sure that would be well before the Egyptian tax people might catch up on their double-entry bookkeeping and discover the rather significant discrepancy between the amounts of money I'd been observed to spend or send home and the considerably smaller sums I could have earned legitimately as a guide.

Then, when I was turning in my keys and IDs to the chief of Security, Fazim Ineverdidgethislastname, he gave me a scare. He studied my file for a long time, and then looked up and gave me his false-toothed grin.

"Hah," he said, and, "Ah." I thought he was thinking about arresting me for God-knows-what, but he was just having fun. "So this change is for out of frying pan into fire, is that how you speak of such things? Is danger attracting to you?"

I didn't know what he was talking about. Then he told me about the thing that had happened that morning in the Vatican. The truck that blew up in St. Peter's Square was driven by a member of the group that called themselves True Original Child of Christ Catholics, and what they were protesting was the ordination of married bishops. Their bomb was a pretty nasty one, too. They had wrapped twenty or thirty kilograms of chemical explosive with ten times as much of whatever radionuclides they could get. Most of that side of the basilica wasn't going to be useful for a long time.

But Fazim finally got tired of his jokes, and stamped my exit visa, and I was on my way.

3

BUON GIORNO, BELLA ITALIA

I couldn't afford airfare, so I had to take a surface ship to Italy. I didn't mind. I was happy to see the gangplanks go down and the ship begin to chug its way out of the Alexandria harbor, en route to Naples.

The vessel that took me out of harm's way had once been a cruise ship called *La Bella Donna di Palermo*, back in the days when things like cruise ships still sailed on the world's oceans. It was way better than the four-decker that had brought me to Egypt, though the *Bella Donna*, like all those old local cruise ships, wasn't very luxurious anymore. It wasn't very full, either. Near as I could tell there were maybe two hundred or so of us aboard, Ghanians and Sudanese, Palestinians and Tibetans, Cambodians and Tierra del Fuegans. And Americans. Male Americans and female ones. Young and old. The one thing we had in common was that we were all poor, well, that plus the fact that nearly all of us spoke some kind of English.

That was a hangover from the days when the US of A still amounted to something in the world. I guess the reason the language survived all the troubles was that Argentinians and Japanese always needed a way to talk to Moroccans and Finns. What with aviation lingo and the American troops that had once been stationed all over the place, the English language filled the bill.

My father had a joke about that. He used to say our language was the last thing of ours that anyone in the rest of the world had ever wanted, and if we'd only had the sense to charge them some kind of a license fee for using it we could all be living on the profits. Jokes about money were about the only kind of jokes my father made anymore. They were usually grim.

I put in a few hours trying to find as much about Pompeii as I could in the ship's pathetic excuse for a library. At least it made the time pass pretty quickly. When we got to the port of Naples it was late afternoon.

Most of the passengers left us as soon as we were disembarked, presumably for better jobs than mine. But there were a couple of other new Pompeiians on the ship, too, two young men from Ghana and a girl from Myanmar.

At the foot of the pier, just past the customs people who had waved us through without even looking up, a hydrovan was waiting, along with a youngish (but also beginning to lose his hairish) man who was carrying a cellboard. He clicked it four times, checking the pictures of each of us while we studied him. He was older than I, and a good bit plumper. He had a heart-shaped stud in his right nostril, so he wasn't gay, but nothing in either eyebrow, so he wasn't actively looking, either. When he'd given us a chance for a good inspection he looked up and grinned. "Welcome to the First Century AD, folks. I'm Maury Tesch, and I'm the one that came down to get you because the Welsh Bastard's got something else he'd rather be doing than meeting you. Throw your bags in the back and get in." As we climbed aboard, though, he made the Myanmar girl sit in back and patted the seat next to his own for me. "You're Bradley Sheridan? Nice to meet you. Tell me, do you play chess?"

He didn't wait for an answer, just kicked off the brake and stepped on the gas, and we were off through Naples's horrible rush hour traffic, a couple dozen kilometers down the coast, right to a traffic circle before a clutch of not very attractive dormitory buildings. A taffy-haired man with the build of a professional wrestler came down to look us over. "That's him," Tesch muttered. "The Welsh Bastard, only you better not let him hear you call him that. He's your boss."

The man looked like a boss, too. He waved Tesch away, then watched us unload our gear before he lifted a hand in a sort of greeting. "I'm Jeremy Jonathan Jones," he informed us, "and I'm the one you'll be taking orders from. You will live here in the transient barracks until you get your jobs lined up, then you'll be with the rest of the migrants. Now take your crap inside and leave it there, and then, the first thing we do, I'm going to take you all on an orientation trip inside the gates."

He turned and got behind the wheel of the van. He waited just long enough for us to obey his orders and not a moment longer; one of the Ghanians was just getting up out of the entrance well as the Welsh Bastard pulled the lever that closed the door. Over his shoulder he called, "You guys got a great opportunity here. Don't louse it up."

He sounded like he was doing us a favor, or, anyway, trying to make us think he was. He did impress me, though. So did the ancient city itself when we came to it.

On the ship's library machines the city had looked like a total wreck, the old buildings nothing but ruins. The ones that had ever had a second story didn't have one anymore, because the last two thousand years had removed it. The hundreds of little shops that had lined the stone-slabbed avenues were now nothing but cubbyholes with bare stone shelves, or more usually with no shelves left at all. Even the villas that had belonged to the rich people were junk. There was nothing remaining in them, or for that matter anywhere else in Pompeii, that looked like a flowering tree, a formal garden, or a lawn.

That was what it had looked like in the opticles of the ship's library. But the place the Welsh Bastard (as I learned to call him from everybody else who worked for him) showed us didn't look like that Pompeii at all. This city wasn't in the least empty, and it wasn't ruined. Although the hour was getting late it was a whole, live city, full of whole, live people.

The people on the streets of this reborn Pompeii came in two kinds. One kind was flesh-and-blood. Those were tourists who were coming from every country in the world that could afford tourism, wearing shorts and slacks and gowns and kilts and monokinis and burkas and headdresses, or any combination thereof.

The other kind was the Romans. I hadn't yet found out that some of them were plain Indentureds, like me, only dressed up in Roman costume, while others—well—weren't. To me they all looked the same: like people who were real, authentic Romans from two thousand years ago. Some were wearing slave gowns, working in the (now again well-stocked) shops or carrying goods of one kind or another in yokes on their shoulders. Some were in togas, gravely strolling the streets.

The buildings all had their upper stories back, too. Through the street doors of the villas we could see what the Bastard told us were called atria, with reflecting pools and flower beds and caged birds singing away. And—well, here's the thing. I knew very well that what I was looking at was all virts and not anywhere near real, but it all looked pretty damn good anyhow. It looked like a place I might even have been willing to pay my own money to visit, if I weren't going to be paid to work there, that is if I could ever have hoped to have the kind of money that visiting the Jubilee would cost.

We weren't there just to gawk at the sights, though. The Bastard had things to teach us. When we passed one undistinguished-looking alley entrance he hustled us by with a finger to his lips. Then, "Did you see what was in there?" he asked.

I had. There had been an open three-wheeler parked down the alley with a man and a woman having some kind of an argument inside. They were both wearing big, fly-eye goggles that glowed in a kind of muted purplish light and covered so much of their faces that I couldn't tell whether they were kidding around with each other or really mad. "Right," he said, when we had all indicated that, sure, we saw the vehicle. "Those two guys are from the Ufficio dell'Antica. They're here to make sure nobody damages any of the real old stuff that's around—not that you probably could, really, since whatever didn't get ruined by now isn't likely to, ever. All the same, don't fool with them. The Antica people are almost as bad as Security. Don't make jokes about bombs or stuff, they've got no sense of humor. And they're all over the place, and a lot of them don't wear the uniforms. Oh, yeah, and there's UN people around, too. They're the ones that wear the blue helmets, but they're only really worried about possible, you know, international criminals. Big ones, I mean. They won't usually bother people like you." He explained to us that Pompeii was blessed with three separate police forces, and they didn't necessarily cooperate with each other. "So the best thing you new fish can do is stay out of the way of all of them. Got that? And—well, that brings us up to the real deal."

He looked around to see if anybody was paying special attention to us, then muttered, "Look over there. You see where I'm looking, right behind the fountain where those Roman soldier virts are loafing around. See that thing that looks like part of the villa wall, only there's no ivy on it?"

"It does not look like any particular thing at all," the girl from Myanmar said.

"That's the way it's supposed to look. That's Security, there. They don't want people looking at their offices. They've got weapons carriers and guys in full battle gear and all kinds of stuff inside there. That's just in case. And they're the ones you specially don't want taking any kind of an interest in you. The Antica and the UN guys could toss your asses into jail, sure, but Security can kill." He looked to see if we had appreciated the importance of his advice. Then he said, "Okay. Now look here."

He marched us across to another alley, this one wide enough for a wagon. One wagon was rattling toward us over the paving stones, mule-drawn. Its driver was an elderly man in a slave's smock, hair unkempt, waving a whip. He didn't look like the dressed-up college kid I might have expected. He looked pretty convincingly ancient Roman, and then the Bastard showed us why. "Watch this," he said, grinning, and planted himself right in the way of the vehicle.

One of the Ghanians couldn't help shouting a warning, and the Myanmar girl swallowed hard. The Welsh Bastard just kept on grinning as the mule kept plodding right at him, its slobbery muzzle almost touching him—

Then it actually did touch him—

Then it kept right on going. It looked like the whole shebang went right through the Bastard, or the Bastard went through it. Anyway mule, driver, wagon and all kept right on going as though he weren't there at all. The Bastard got sort of fuzzily hard to see for a moment, and then reappeared behind the wagon as it rattled on away.

He laughed out loud at the expressions on our faces. "Simulations," he explained. "We've got the best virts in the business here; you won't see any better than these anywhere in the world. You're going to see a lot of these, you know, simulated guys marching around all over the city. Just pay them no attention. They aren't there. They're just images, really, except they also got sound, right?" He looked at the timekeeper on his opticle. "Wait a minute," he said.

It wasn't just a minute, it was like a long five or ten minutes, and then I nearly jumped out of my skin. From somewhere not too far from where we were standing came one of the most horrible shrieks I have ever heard. The woman from Myanmar whispered a little prayer, I think, it wasn't in English. I said, "What the hell is that?"

He was grinning. "It's the elephant."

"Elephant? What elephant?"

"What you're hearing is the last show in the arena. That's the one where large animals are getting killed and Christians are getting crucified and so on. Oh," he said, looking at the expression on my face, "they're all virts. You think the Jubilee is going to pay to kill a whole real elephant three times a day? That'd be stupid. Now let me show you the refectory where you'll mostly eat."

Once I got over that elephant's scream I began to cheer up. In fact, I have to say that at that moment I was feeling pretty pleased with myself for having the intelligence to come here. Pompeii made those old Egyptian rock piles look sick. Taken all in all, I thought that it was going to be a good place to build up my stash, or anyway I thought that until I met with the folks from Security.

4

BAD NEWS FROM THE COPS

I think I already mentioned that in Egypt if you stayed out of the cities you didn't have much of a problem with terrorists. Even better, you didn't have a problem with the kind of heavy-duty police presence that came when the authorities were worried about terrorists—and, given a choice between a lot of bomb throwers and a lot of cops, I might have preferred the bomb throwers. At least they wouldn't have thought their best target was me.

It's true that even in the Valley of the Kings every now and then some splinter group might try a drive-through tourist shoot, spraying fletches and bullets at the crowds in the Valley, just to show that they were still pissed off about Basque rights or the subjection of the Turkic Uighurs to the Han Chinese or the secession of French-speaking Canada. Or whatever. There wouldn't be any big, scary stuff, though. The powerful and well-financed terror groups didn't bother with Egypt.

The Italians, however, weren't taking any chances. That very first night, just as I was getting ready to think that sleeping would be a good idea, even in the tiny bunk beds that were in the dorm the Bastard showed us to, a plainclothes woman (whose name, she said, was Brigitta) showed up. Us newcomers weren't ready to go to sleep yet, she informed us. Instead she was taking the four of us to a Security office.

It wasn't the office the Bastard had pointed out to us. This one wasn't even located where the other administration offices were. It was all by itself, a low, unmarked building at the far end of a gated cul-de-sac, with nothing else nearby. (So no outsiders would hear the screaming, somebody joked. I was pretty sure it was a joke.) There wasn't any sign on the door and Brigitta wasn't any help; as soon as we arrived at the building she turned around and pointed at me and at a door. I got the message. I took one last look at my colleagues, huddled together and looking both scared and kind of happy that at least they weren't the first to go in, and turned to the door.

I didn't get a chance to knock on it. It opened as soon as I got there, and inside was a bare hall. Nobody was visible, but from somewhere a voice track said, "Wipe your feet and go to the room at the end of the hall."

When I did, two people were waiting for me there.

My interviewers were a man and a woman, neither of them particularly good-looking or, actually, distinguished in any way at all. Neither of them was American, either, I was pretty sure, but I couldn't tell from their names—Yvonne Feliciano and Johann Swinn, their badges said. Maybe Eastern Europe? Maybe not. The one who took me on first was the man, and what he did was ask me a long list of pretty personal questions. Had I ever owned a weapon? Did I ever take part in any demonstrations? How did I feel about the way the United States was treated since the Yellowstone accident? Had I ever known anybody who advocated force and violence as a solution to social evils? Did I have a police record anywhere?

That was where I got into trouble. I said, "No."

That made the two of them look at each other, then go off in a corner and jabber, their voices too low pitched for me to hear. Then they came back and bracketed me on either side, both of them looking as though I had betrayed their trust. "Why do you lie to us?" the woman demanded, and the man asked, "Are you not Bradley Wilson Sheridan, formerly of 16-A Liberty Crescent, Floor 15, Molly Pitcher Redeployment Village, Staten

Island, New York, arrested by the New York metropolitan police, Fifty-fifth Precinct, on May 26, 2065, for stealing with threat of violence certain cash and vouchers from one Terence Vincent Youngblood, a minor aged seven, of 16-B Liberty Crescent of the same redeployment village?"

That was a nasty moment. Nobody had mentioned to me the name of that little snot, Terry Youngblood, in years. I hadn't expected that anybody ever would. Anyway, when I caught my breath I pointed out to the two of them that I had been only eleven years old at the time myself, and the value of the stuff I stole from Terry's locker—the threat-of-violence business came later, after he said he was going to report me and I said I would pound him seriously if he did—was less than $10,000 American. So the whole business wasn't even a crime, just a misdemeanor. Besides, the charges had been dropped and the arrest expunged from my record—it was what they did for kids who didn't ever get caught doing anything more serious.

"Facts are never expunged from the record if one knows how to look for them," the woman informed me, "and a crime is a crime regardless of its magnitude. Continue standing here. Do not sit down."

The two of them went back to their corner for more inaudible jabbering. Then, without comment, they came back and instructed me to take off my clothes. All of them.

I'm not easily embarrassed. I'd been undressed in mixed company often enough before then—you can't get a passport in the US of A without a strip search, or a work permit in Egypt. Some of the officials at those little events, too, had been female. So it wasn't gender shyness. It was the way this Feliciano woman looked, more than anything else—not at all pretty, but not worrisomely ugly, either. Mostly she looked sort of like the product of a mating between a human dad and a mom who was some kind of a venomous snake. But they weren't going to let me off because I didn't like their looks, so I did what I was told.

Then the man attached sticky things all over my scalp, the back of my neck, my spinal cord, the soles of my feet, and several parts of my torso. Then he paused to look at what he had done. He was wearing a faint scowl. "What?" the woman asked.

"It is not important," he said. "I simply wonder if it mightn't be better to open him all the way up."

She gave him an unfriendly smile. "If employment of the amphiprobe should prove to be indicated," she informed him, "I will make that decision myself and will then request the colonel's permission to go as deep as necessary. Now you, Sheridan"—she was turning to me—"let us cover this matter again, this time without omitting important facts."

Then the woman asked me the same questions all over again. This time I acknowledged my juvie crime spree. Then the two of them went to the corner and talked for some time, again too softly for me to hear.

Then the woman came close to me, looked me straight in the eye—her eyes weren't hard little reptilian dots, just normal brown eyes, but I still had the feeling that she was just waiting for the right moment to stab her poison fangs into me—and said, "You are Bradley Wilson Sheridan—let me see—175 centimeters, 93 kilos, eyes blue, complexion pale. Born 2054, so now you would be twenty-five." I couldn't deny any of that, so I just nodded. She didn't seem to care whether I agreed or not, but went on without a pause. "In spite of my instruction you failed to disclose essential information about yourself, Sheridan. Why did you not tell us of your mother's sister, the one who for a time before her marriage actually lived in your parents' home, Mrs. Carolyn Sheridan DeVries Maddingsley?"

"Whose husband was known as the Reverend Delmore DeVries Maddingsley," her partner added. "The one who raised money to fund terrorists."

Right then I figured I was out of luck for good, and the best thing that might happen to me was that they'd put me on the next ship back to Egypt and its tax authorities and religion police and sand. Even that might be better than staying here. At least the Egyptians had been forgiving enough, or incompetent enough, to never mention Uncle Devious.

I said, "I don't know what you're talking about."

Of course I did know. I knew all about my Uncle Devious's secret criminal side, because of all the things that my father and mother had said to each other when they didn't know I could hear. It was pretty clear that I didn't know as much as the Security people did, though. After I told them, over and over, that I had truthfully answered every question on the Giubileo employment application, they reluctantly admitted that, no, there hadn't been any question that asked if I had an uncle by marriage who was accused of funding terrorists. Then they just began asking, fairly civilly, or almost, for me to tell them everything I remembered about my Uncle Devious.

Which was easy enough. I'd done it often enough for one American law enforcement body or another. So I told them yes, my uncle was Delmore DeVries Maddingsley. Yes, he was married to my mother's older somadone-head sister—swept the poor woman off her feet and married her, against my mother's advice and pretty nearly over the dead body of my father, but Aunt Carrie wasn't listening to her family. She was listening to her glands. Uncle Devious was a studly-looking man with a document from a Tennessee Baptist college that said he was a full-fledged minister, though at present without a congregation, whose current good-doing ran to raising money for poor Tibetan children. While Carrie was, and knew she was, a sickly somadone-hooked old maid. Sure, he had turned out to be a criminal, but we hadn't known that at the time. How could we? He had all those diplomas and certificates of awards for being such a wonderful guy. Plus all those before-and-after virt pictures of raggedy and starving Tibetan kids who became well-scrubbed honor students with the help of his charities.

So I told them everything I remembered, until they began looking bored. I won't say that satisfied them. It did send them back to the corner to mutter at each other again, though. Leaving me standing there to wonder, a. how much deep shit I was in, and, b. what this meant to my never quite abandoned hope of finding Uncle Devious myself and squeezing my mother's money out of him.

When they came back they answered one part of that. "Let me show you something," the man said. He touched parts of the keypad on his tunic. Across the room a screen lit up. What it was displaying was the face of a handsome man with a pencil mustache and just a few glints of gray in his neatly brushed hair. "Holy shit," I said, "that's Uncle Devious. DeVries, I mean."

The woman said, "Yes, this is how this Reverend Mr. Maddingsley looked when he went underground with his stolen funds."

"What he swindled out of my mother plus my aunt's three-million-buck trust fund," I agreed. And that $3 million was in real 2062 dollars, before the post-Yellowstone inflation.

"Oh, more than that," the woman said seriously.

"Very much more than a minor embezzlement from members of his family," Swinn agreed. "We don't really know how much. But, yes, quite a lot. At any rate, that is how he looked when the search began"—more *pat-a-pat* on his blouse keypad—"and this is how he looked on April 25, 2059, when this other picture was taken. He had just recovered from his plastic surgery."

The new picture on the screen didn't look anything like Uncle Devious anymore. For one thing, the smiling man it displayed was black, or coffee-cream color, anyway. He was also nearly bald. He wore neatly trimmed sideburns with a tiny sprout of white beardlet coming out of the dimple in his chin, which was nowhere near as manly as Uncle Devious's.

"That was taken at his estate near Ocho Rios in Jamaica," the woman was going on. "Three days later the local police found him, but someone else had found him first. Then he looked like this."

I've seen plenty of sickening sights in my life but never one more sickening than that. The man was now naked and on a morgue pallet. He didn't have any genitals. They had been hacked off. He didn't have any eyes, either—gouged out, nothing left but bloody pits over where his nose, too, had been cut away. There's no point saying how many other places on his body had been cut, stabbed, or gouged. I didn't count. I didn't vomit, either, but it was a close call.

"It was definitely Delmore DeVries Maddingsley," Swinn told me. "DNA match. Such matches are commonly made in America, where police have more freedom than we have with the do-gooders in Euro-center in Brussels—"

The woman turned to look at him. She didn't speak, but the male swallowed hard and abandoned the subject of do-gooders in Brussels. He said, "We think we know who did it to him—Brian Bossert, the guy who did the Boston Tunnel and San Francisco BART blowups. He's dead, too. He got it in the Lake Ontario oil attack later that year. But we never found the money."

"What was left of it," the woman said.

"We did find the surgeon who rebuilt Maddingsley into that rather good-looking Negro," Swinn said. "All the surgeon got for it, though, was a year in prison. Should've thrown the key away. There were some money judgments, too—he had to repay what Maddingsley had paid him, and of course we sold Maddingsley's estate and all his stuff. We think Maddingsley had a lot more squirreled away, though. We're still looking for it."

"And we're not the only ones," the woman said. "Some appear to believe that the funds were banked with the Stans."

"Which is of interest to us," Swinn added, "because of Mrs. Maddingsley's use of somadone, which comes from the Stans, and we wonder whether your uncle made trips there to secure it for her."

I thought they were beginning to get silly, but I just shook my head. "I don't know."

Swinn sighed. The woman gave him another reprimanding look, but after a moment she sighed, too. "Very well," she said, "you can now go."

That was it. They pointed to the door. As I opened it, the woman said, "You have displayed a very sloppy attitude toward providing the Security force with essential information, Sheridan. Do not do this again. Be sure you attend your antiterrorist orientation sessions. Do not miss any of them."

And the man said, "You're very lucky in the employment you have been offered here, Sheridan. You don't want to lose it. The soft-coal distillation mines at Krakow are always looking for new Indentured workers."

And the woman said, "You've made a bad start, Sheridan. You can repair it. If you observe anything suspicious among the people you will be working with report to me at once. My name is Major Yvonne Feliciano. To reach me use any communications facility in Pompeii and ask for my code name, which is Piranha Woman. Do it."

That was the end of the interrogation.

On my way out I saw my former fellow passengers sprawled out in the waiting room and eyeing me with malice as I passed through. Obviously they had been made to wait while I went through my own inquisition. I was a little sorry for them. Maybe a little sorrier for myself, with the news about Uncle Devious. I hadn't expected that information to come out of this particular interview. But there it was.

I tried to put it all out of my mind. For a while I succeeded.

5

THE CITY THAT CAME BACK TO LIFE

When you talk about Pompeii you have to remember that two thousand years is a long time. All those years had made significant changes in the way the city of Pompeii looked.

What had happened to that old AD 79 Pompeii was pretty obvious. You could see the cause of it, sitting right down the road from the city itself, and what it was was that humongous neighbor mountain named Vesuvius. And AD 79 was the year when Vesuvius blew itself up and cooked Pompeii in the process.

That was the bad part of that ancient event. Looked at from an AD 2079 viewpoint, it had a lot of good about it. All that rock and ash the volcano dumped on the city had the unexpected and fortunate effect of preserving its bare bones for us two-thousand-years-later people to see.

(When I say "fortunate" I don't mean that it was good luck for the actual Pompeiians who lived there at that time, of course. They didn't get any pleasure at all out of being preserved.)

So then, two thousand years later or so, the world is getting close to AD 2079 and suddenly somebody comes up with a great idea. They realized that they could make a pot of money out of having a two-thousand-year birthday party for the ancient city. So they did. They turned it into a kind of a theme park and they called it Pompeii's Jubilee Year, or L'Anno Giubileo della Citta di Pompeii.

Well, I said that already, didn't I?

When the mountain did blow its top, back all those twenty long centuries ago, it took everybody by surprise. It hadn't done anything of that sort in quite a while—in enough of a while, that is, that those old Romans figured it wasn't ever going to do it again. So they started building summer homes in and around Pompeii. It was very desirable real estate, especially if what you had been used to was Rome's cold, wet winters.

The situation wasn't all gravy for the Pompeiians, though.

The city did have a now-and-then history of pretty bad earthquakes. As a matter of fact, the city had still been rebuilding from one of the worst of them, a big one that had knocked down several temples and public buildings, when the big blast from the volcano put a permanent stop to the repair program. That was the end of that chapter in the history of Pompeii.

Nobody saw the city again for a long time. Not until some workmen, with their minds undoubtedly on other matters entirely, accidentally dug up a piece of it almost two thousand years later.

People are stupid, you know that? For instance, you'd think the old Pompeiians would have figured out that this was not a really safe place to settle down in.

They didn't. Still, hey, I'm not in a position to criticize them. We Americans weren't all that much smarter. It wouldn't have taken a genius in, say, 2000 to figure out that all those geysers and hot springs in old Yellowstone Park might just mean that something on a large bad scale could be getting ready to happen there.

Nobody did figure it out, though.

I knew how those old Pompeiians felt. I had felt the same way, back when I was a kid and Yellowstone happened. The big difference between us was that Yellowstone was a couple thousand kilometers away from our house in Kansas City, while for the Pompeiians Vesuvius was right next door.

So when Yellowstone began to do its serious premonitory shaking and rumbling, around 2055, the Americans had the sort of warning that you really shouldn't ignore. That didn't stop them. They ignored it anyway. According to the seismologists, Yellowstone only did one of those really big eruptions about every 600,000 years or so, so why worry? They didn't worry. Not even when other scientists pointed out that the last eruption had been about 640,000 years ago, so a better way to think about it was that it was kind of overdue.

Anyway, in America the people in charge of such matters didn't choose to do any worrying until it was quite a lot too late. By then the dust from that giant-sized eruption of what they began calling the Yellowstone super-volcano was already two meters deep in Chicago and St. Louis and Milwaukee—and right on top of my family's house on the old Missouri River as well.

I wondered if, a few thousand years from now, people would reconstruct Kansas City the way the Italians had Pompeii.

Probably not, I decided. Pompeii was pretty much one of a kind, while those thousands-of-years-from-now archeologists would have a large selection of ash-buried cities to choose from, since Yellowstone didn't stop with Kansas City. Actually it had buried nearly half of the land mass of the old USA's lower forty-eight before it was over.

So now let's get back to present time. We're up to the summer of AD 2079 now and the dead city has come back to life.

I don't know if some ancient Roman, just waking up from a two-thousand-year nap, would have thought the Giubileo's restoration of Pompeii was authentic. I guarantee, though, that he would have thought it was gorgeous. And I know there's one thing about it that would have surprised him a lot. Unlike the AD 79 version, our AD 2079 Pompeii didn't stink.

Well, didn't stink much, anyway. Especially if you stayed away from the public latrines, or the barrels of urine outside the laundry—see, the way the Pompeiians cleaned woolen tunics was first to soak them in human pee. For that reason every passerby was invited to relieve himself in one of those barrels so the laundry could have the raw materials it needed to get on with its work.

That was the kind of tourist guide fact I had been trying to fill my head with on the ship from Alexandria. I thought I'd made quite a lot of progress. That seemed to me as though it might justify giving me some preferential treatment, so I asked the Welsh Bastard to let me take one of the tourist groups out as a guide.

He laughed at me. "Asshole. You got to know something before you can tell the customers anything, don't you? Half of these tourists've read the same book you did. Why should they pay to hear it from you?"

However, he promised, they had a job for me that I could handle just the way I was. I could work in the bakery.

That didn't sound bad, right? Working with that great fresh-bread smell all around me? Chatting with the tourists as they bought their little souvenir loaves to take home? And making sure not to tell them (another fact I'd picked up) that because of the way the flour was ground, between huge millstones, there were tiny crumbs of rock in the ground-up wheat. I even thought that maybe everybody had been wrong about the Welshman's bastardness, because it certainly looked as though he was being fair with me.

Then I started work, and learned better.

Those sweet baking-bread smells? I never got to smell any. They were probably somewhere around in the air, but where I was they were drowned out by considerably worse ones. The bakery ground its own flour. After you've grated the flour out of the original wheat berries what you're left with is bran. That isn't a plus. Bran's worthless. That is, the only thing it's worth is that you can feed pigs with it if you want.

The Pompeiian bakers wanted. At my bakery their practice was to throw the bran out into the street so their herd of pigs could grow fat on it. Interesting fact: Did you know that bran is a laxative? Not that the pigs really needed one, but it certainly did enhance their natural capacities, and the resultant smell.

That was an example of the Bastard being bastardly, all right. It didn't stop there, either. The opening he had for me at the bakery wasn't in the sales department. It was nastier than that.

One of the ways our AD 2079 present-day Pompeii was different from the original was that in the Twenty-first Century we had plenty of electrical power to make the city run, a lot of it geothermal energy from shafts dug into the slopes of Vesuvius itself. Ancient Pompeii hadn't known how to do that. To run its industries it hadn't had steam engines or water power or windmills, either. For the energy they needed to make things move what they had was organic beings with organic muscles. So in order to grind that grain into flour the bakery had installed a big turn-table that was pushed around and around by played-out horses or mules. Or by slaves.

Slaves were cheaper.

Of course, I wasn't exactly a slave. There wasn't much difference, though. I owed the Jubilee the balance of that Indenture money, and until it got paid off I was theirs to command.

I hated the bakery job from the first minute, but not nearly as much as I came to hate it after a day or two. I even hated what I had to wear. They wouldn't let me keep my own clothes on. They gave me a kind of scratchy woolen smock (which I didn't really want to put on, because remember what I said about those barrels of urine they cleaned wool with) that came down to about my knees. They wouldn't even let me wear my own underwear.

I had been kind of expecting being required to wear some kind of native costume. After all, even the Egyptians had sometimes put me in long cotton gowns and sandals while I was guiding there. But the Egyptians hadn't cared what I wore underneath the gown. The Welsh Bastard did. "What if you bend over?" he asked, grinning. "You got to wear something there, don't you? And it's got to be right." And the undergarment they gave me to wear in case of bending too far over looked pretty much like a grown-up-sized diaper.

There was plenty of other unpleasantness to hate, too. I hated the day-long choking smoke from the ovens. I hated the fact that my stupid dream of ever finding Uncle Devious had blown up in my face. Especially, I hated Pompeii and everything around it, but that was before I met Gerda Fleming.

Actually, I must admit, working at the Giubileo wasn't all awful. They had given me a reasonably clean room to live in. That was in the Indentureds' tower flat, though that particular place was a good long trudge up the hill from the bakery. It wasn't all mine, either. I shared it with somebody— Scandinavian? Dutch? I never did find out—named Jiri Kopthellen. Still, the place had its own little bathroom, which was a step above most of what I'd had in Egypt. Or what I'd had on Staten Island, either. It also not only had a bed—all right, a cot—for each of us and a multichannel wall screen to share, but even a little fridge that Jiri kept filled with Italian beer. And, maybe best of all, I lucked out in having that same Jiri Kopthellen for a roommate. Or, more accurately, in that I usually didn't have Jiri there at all. He had a wife with an apartment of their own a couple of stops down the electric toward the city of Naples, and he much preferred to spend his off-duty time there.

In my own off-duty time I was kept pretty busy learning how to be a First Century Roman slave. Mostly that meant learning the "Roman" currency that was the only kind of money you could legally spend in-side the walls of the Jubilee: The silver denarius was worth sixteen asses or four sestertii; the sestertius, which was made of oricalchum (a kind of silver-copper mixture) was worth four asses; and one copper as, at the Jubilee's extortionate money-changing rate, equaled one euro.

That part I was interested in, because I was confident that there would be some good fiddles possible with befuddled tourists trying to make change. And apart from that all I really had to learn was to get out of the way of any free Roman, especially if he wore the toga that meant he was of senatorial rank. And also meant that he was invariably a virt, since there weren't any live Roman senators still around. And, of course, to consider the tourists as honorary senators, since it was their money that paid our bills.

The job itself, of course, continued to be lousy.

I suppose I would have liked it better if I'd managed to make a few friends. I hadn't. There didn't seem to be a lot of friendship on offer at Pompeii that year. And twice, in the first few times I tried striking up a conversation with a stranger, I discovered that some of the rest of the world really disliked Americans. They blamed us for letting Yellowstone happen.

There were a lot of people working at the Jubilee. Eight or nine hundred of us at least, including the ones who would be in public view, like me, plus the ones who worked behind the scenes to keep the whole thing going. (For instance, the guy who had picked us up at the dock, Maury Tesch, had something to do with the city's water supply system.) The workers came from all over the world. From Munich and Liverpool and Kiev and Buenos Aires, and also from places like Boston and Addis Ababa and Toronto and Cleveland and Tannu Tuva—that's in Outer Mongolia, if you didn't know. There was a big difference between the two groups. Indentureds, like myself, were there because there weren't any jobs back home. We needed the Jubilee's pay, pitiful as it was. But the other guys—

Ah, the other guys. They were the volunteers. They were college students on vacation, or maybe teenagers from well-to-do families in un-Yellowstoned countries having their first adventure away from home. Rich kids wondering how the other half lived. They didn't need the Jubilee's miserly pay. They all took it, though—hey, you never knew when you might want to buy an extra pack of somadone stim-gum. And they certainly didn't want to be friends with the likes of us Indentureds.

In fact it looked like nobody wanted that. Oh, I got to chat a bit with the man who met us at the dock, Tesch, now and then. He had a good job on the Jubilee waterworks, and, curiously, Tesch wanted to be friends.

All right, maybe I worry too much about being hassled by somebody—some male somebody—who's really only looking for cheap, quick sex. All I can say about that is that anybody who had been a punk kid working the streets of New York City when I was there would learn to be careful about that. Or maybe he would come to like it. (I didn't.) So when, once or twice, Maury Tesch invited me to join him for a hit, a puff, or something stronger in his own room I said no. See, the operative word there with Tesch was "guy." He wasn't the gender of friends I wanted to find.

That gender of potential friends did exist. I saw quite a few of them every day at quitting time. The employee dressing rooms were unisex, so every day there I got a look at thirty or forty reasonably good-looking women wearing various amounts of clothing, sometimes hardly any at all. None of them seemed to mind being looked at, either. Some even cast interested looks my way as I was unwrapping my diaper and pulling on my flexshorts. But they just looked. When I tried to strike up a conversation they gave me short answers and strolled away.

One of them, formerly from the olive-growing country along the Adriatic, was really nasty about it, too. (That's when I found out that there were a lot of people in the rest of the world that disliked Americans for not preventing Yellowstone, though that was pretty unfair. Really Yellowstone's blowup was fairly trivial compared to what it could have been, like plunging the whole world into another Ice Age instead of just causing a few poor harvests.)

I should admit that I wasn't totally frozen out. A couple of the women did finally let me know that they might be willing to take the electric into Naples with me some night, or check out some of the Italian clubs along the shore.

I didn't encourage them, though. Not only were those things expensive, but the women offering them weren't the pretty ones.

And then, wonder of wonders, one was.

I was sitting by myself in the game room playing, I don't know, Dust Robber or Intersec and Terrorist, when somebody sat down next to me. "Hi," she said. "I'm Gerda Fleming. You're Brad Sheridan."

I switched the game off in the middle of unexpectedly coming across a nuclear weapons cache while I happened to be holding a pulverizer bomb on a five-minute time delay. "Pleased to know you," I said, and shook her hand.

That seemed to amuse her. She said, "How do you like the bakery?"

That was definitely the most other-sex friendliness I'd been given since I arrived in Italy. I would have liked it even better if it had come from someone a little prettier, but she wasn't bad. I wouldn't say she knocked me over with her gorgeousness—hair pulled back in a sort of accidental-looking scrunchy, her really quite adequate figure camouflaged in middle-aged schoolteacher shorts and shirt. I might even have called her mousy, although she did have a sort of thoroughly female look that I appreciated, even if she wasn't wearing much in the way of makeup. Or much in the way of sex jewelry, either—no nostril studs, for instance, which I interpreted to mean that she wasn't urgently seeking.

She was nice looking, of course. What young woman who could afford an occasional makeover wasn't? But I wouldn't have said she was anything radical. I mean not the kind of woman who could change my life completely. Could even *be* my life. You see how wrong I often am?

Since she had asked, I told her how little I liked it, in detail. That also made her smile and offer me a stick of gum. Anyway, I found out from her what she did for the Jubilee show. Most days this Gerda Fleming person put on a blond wig to play a Pompeiian prostitute, but now and then they let her be a matron showing tourists around her villa and explaining the pornographic murals to them.

When I mentioned that I wouldn't mind my lousy job quite as much if the people were a little friendlier, she put her hand over mine sympathetically. "It's not you, Brad. The reason is they're too scared," she told me. "Strangers might be terrorists. Then, if the terrorists got busted, the Security goons would go looking for everybody who knew them. Can you blame people for being careful?"

I opened my mouth to say that, yes, I could, but she didn't let me do it. She squeezed my hand. "Don't worry, Brad: a. things'll get better, and b. listen, I think there's going to be an opening in the tourist *ristorante*, so maybe we can get you off the flour mill." She lifted her hand to look at her thumb watch, then grimaced. "Shoot. I have to run."

I stood up, looking her over. She looked pretty good, at that, maybe a little better than I had first thought—reddish hair, very goodish figure—except for being a little taller than I was and a lot more muscular. "One thing," I said. "How did you know I'm not a terrorist?"

She shook my hand, grinning. "You passed Security, didn't you? I mean, all but that early bit about swiping the kid's lunch money, so what's to worry about? And, hey, who can be responsible for what their uncles might be up to? Anyway, ciao."

She didn't say how she knew what happened in my Security interview, especially how she knew about my Uncle Devious. She just went out the door, and I didn't see her again for three weeks.

I didn't fail to think about her, though. Partly about the things she knew that she shouldn't have . . . but mostly, I have to admit, about the fact that she was redheaded, and tall, and, I ultimately decided, with a really good figure. And friendly. And, oh yes, female.

6

MY LIFE AS AN ANCIENT POMPEIIAN

I can't say I got used to the bakery job. Pushing that heavy damned wheel around wasn't the kind of thing that grows on you. But there were other things going on in my world, and, surprisingly, some of them almost made up for the crappy job and the paucity of friends.

I was, after all, sitting right there in the middle of the world's number-one tourist attraction. A lot of it didn't interest me—the "thrill rides" like the chariot races in which you could ride one of the chariots, racing against the other daredevil charioteers who looked at every second as though they were moments away from crashing into and maiming you, but who wouldn't have done much damage if they had, because they were all virts. Or the giant Ferris wheel that towered over the old city. Or the virt lake with its virt biremes and virt rowers. They all looked like the kind of thing you might want to take a girl on if you had one. But I didn't.

True, for us employees, it was almost all free. (Not counting, of course, those extra-ticket special attractions like the whorehouses and the fish ponds where "slaves" fed living, screaming other "slaves" to the "slave owners'" favorite mullets. All virts, of course, but as they were being eaten alive by the fish they didn't sound that way.

One thing I have to say for the Jubilee is that they did have about the

best virts I ever saw. I got to talking to one of the virt experts before opening one morning while he was finishing replacing some circuits in the
projector of the bakery's upper floors. He was proud of his work. The
basic science behind the things, he told me, had been invented back in
the Twentieth Century when a man named Dennis Gabor had developed
the hologram. Once that was done it was obvious that scientists could
make bunches of photons do just as they were told, which included standing alone and moving. The sound—what they called "Pompei sound,"
spelled with one "i"—came later. I had heard of it when I was hitting the
books in the library of *La Bella Donna di Palermo* but assumed it was
named after the city. Wrong. It was somebody named One-i Pompei
who'd invented it, more than a hundred years ago.

Dealing with that sort of system was one of the kinds of things I wished
I had learned back in good old—or I should say bad old—NYA&M but I
hadn't. As the technician was packing up his probes and meters I mentioned politely that I sure would appreciate the chance to be somebody's
helper long enough to learn how to do what he did.

That was the end of the casual chat. He gave me a freezing look, said,
"Don't get your hopes up," and left me standing there.

I got the message. He was willing to chat a bit with his social inferi-
ors. But when one of us talked about rising to his level the politeness
disappeared.

What kept me from total despair was that, no matter the bad parts, there
was still a lot to do and a lot to see in Pompeii, and quite a lot of it didn't
carry an extra charge. I saw as much of it as I could.

The Welsh Bastard had put me on the morning shift on the bakery
treadmill, six in the morning until two in the afternoon and—after a long,
hot shower to get the kinks out and a change into my own clothes—I had
the rest of the day to explore. I explored. I walked the old streets, being
jostled by Scandinavian and African and Japanese tourists, and wishing I
was one of them. I splurged for swims in the baths—the one bath, right
across the street from the villa with the "Beware of the Dog" mosaic, that

was the only fully reconstructed one, that is. The other baths were all virts. You could see a batch of ancient Romans eating, reading, bathing, whatever. But you couldn't touch them because there was nothing tangible there to touch. I ate peculiar cheese and weird fruits sold by the vendors in their little cubbyholes. (That would have been expensive if we Indentureds had had to pay full price for them all. We didn't.) I even watched a show in the amphitheater once—the little amphitheater in what they called the Triangular Forum, that is, not the big one at the edge of town that was too ruined and too far from the tourist areas to dress up. Those shows were okay if you liked a lot of blood, even make-believe virt blood, squirting out of the virt gladiators and the equally virt wild animals in the arena. But sitting through a whole show meant an hour or so of resting your bun muscles on those cold, hard stone seats, and that took a lot of the joy out of it. Besides, sitting in one place for very long gave me time to think, and I had more time to think pushing the damn wheel around than I really needed.

What I mostly thought about, of course, was my troubles. Especially my dashed hopes of finding, and collecting from, my rotten old Uncle Devious.

It was funny how those hopes stayed with me. I wasn't stupid—honest—and I was generally a realist. I don't suppose I had ever really expected to run into some tourist face, brilliant blue eyes peering out of a ruddy complexion, and immediately recognize my Uncle Devious. I had always known that that wasn't going to happen, because how would I have recognized him? Until Piranha Woman had showed me her scenes from Uncle Devious's last days I had had no real idea of what he might have been looking like by then. I'd always known that with all the money he stole he could buy himself any look he chose—like the one he actually did buy, according to Piranha Woman's photo, or any other slim or stout body, choice of hair and skin color, even gender, if he wanted badly enough to look that different. Whatever you wanted the cosmetic surgeons could supply, given that you had, and were willing to part with, the astronomical amounts of cash required.

So there had been no real chance that I'd have identified Uncle Devious even if I'd stood next to him at a men's urinal. But that hadn't stopped me from looking and hoping, and I did truly resent the fact that now even those slim hopes were gone.

Six hours a day of pushing that damn wheel around weren't all the Giubileo wanted from me. There was also the compulsory, and I do mean compulsory, Security briefings.

They weren't just the Jubilee's idea, either. They were Italian law. The Italians had had their share of terrorism, notably the fairly frequent attacks on the pope. Well, those and also the occasional secular kook group that came along, like the ones who called themselves L'Esercito Nuovo del Risorgimento, whatever that meant, and to further their objectives, whatever those might have been, firebombed the Ponte Vecchio in Florence one Saturday morning. That was a shock for the Italians. Even the Nazis hadn't touched the Ponte Vecchio, back in WWII days when the retreating German army was pulverizing just about everything else it left behind. In Florence they had merely demolished all the buildings for four or five blocks on either side. So it was the law that every Italian resident, citizen or not, had to put in one hour a week on training to resist terrorism.

Of course nobody really could do much that was useful about resisting it. But there were motions to go through, so we went through them.

The sessions weren't really all that bad. Oh, numbingly dull, sure, but they were something I could be doing with other people. Some of them were almost friendly. Well, noncommittal, anyway. There was Abukar Abdu, from some little town somewhere in Africa. And of course my chess and general conversation pal, Maury Tesch. There was a good-looking, dark-haired woman named Elfreda Something-or-other whom I might have had some faint hopes for if she hadn't been hanging on the arm of a large, Italian-looking guy I'd never seen before. There was also another Italian, this one named Vespasiano Gatti, who, it turned out, wasn't friendly at all. In fact he didn't like me even as much as the average other person.

Gatti made that clear one night when I spotted an empty seat next to him and sat down in it. He gave me one look—a really nasty look—and then he got up and crossed to the other side of the room. Why that was I had no idea. Gatti was middle-aged, or maybe a little more than that, and at first I thought he was too rich to be an Indentured because he carried a silver-handled cane and wore an old-fashioned three-piece suit made out of expensive cream-colored flannel. But then I got a better look. His cuffs were frayed and the ferrule of his silver-handled cane had been broken off and lost. He was at most a formerly rich man. Not unlike my dad.

A nice touch with the antiterrorism classes was that our teacher passed out little cups of espresso and those rock-hard things they call biscotti that I didn't care much for but appreciated the thought of. The person who provided the biscotti was our instructor, an old fart named Professor, or sometimes Colonel-Professor, Bartolomeo Mazzini. When I say "old" what I mean is really old. That is, about as old as an old man can get, with a bumpy old skull as bare as a baby's bottom. Mazzini hadn't even bothered to get his hair reseeded or to remove the wrinkles in his face or in fact to do any of the things that everybody else in the world did to keep on looking respectably young. When I came in early one evening he was sound asleep at his desk, and when the rest of the class got there and woke him up he stared around at us as though he wondered who we were and what we were doing there.

He didn't seem like a totally bad guy, though. Once all the coffee cups and cookies got handed out he would turn on the wall screens and show us everything that was going on, terrorist-wise. Like firebombing department stores and butcher shops in Argentina, which, he told us, was probably a push of native Indians trying to get the European Argentinians to go back home. But, he said cheerfully, we probably didn't have to worry about it spreading to Pompeii, or actually anywhere off the Argentine pampas, because already a couple of thousand Argentine and UN troops were systematically deploying rockets and artillery to pulverize a little town across the river in Uruguay because that was where the ringleaders of the terrorists had unwisely assembled.

Old Bart filled us in on stuff like that for ten or fifteen minutes in that first session I went to. Then he showed us pictures of a bunch of individuals—a Pole, an Ecuadorian, a couple of Filipina women—who were known terrorists and might just possibly be somewhere around our area (but, he admitted, probably weren't). Then he snapped off the screens, took a hit of his cooling espresso and beamed at us. "Any questions?" he asked.

So the actual Security briefing had amounted to, what?, maybe fifteen minutes or so? That was a pleasant surprise. We couldn't leave that early, though, so we looked around at each other to see if anybody had a question. Finally one of the Ghanians who had arrived with me raised his hand. When the professor pointed to him he had trouble getting his English going, so he leaned over and whispered to the man next to him. Who said, "Hamel says these class ordered by Italian government, okay? But you not Italian government. You Intersec Security person, Hamel say."

At the word "Security" the temperature in the room dropped a couple of degrees. It didn't change the amiable old-fart expression on the professor's face, though. "Hamel is very observant," he said, sounding more like an admirer than a threat. "Yes, Intersec is a global agency, but its personnel are often recruited from the country where they will serve and as it happens I am indeed Italian by birth. Are there any other questions?"

Most of the class had the look of not wanting to get into any conversation that included the word "Security," but finally a woman in the first row put her hand up. It was the good-looking one named Elfreda. She asked politely, "Is it true we will all have to work overtime for this Vespasian thing?"

I was sort of curious about the answer to that, too, since my readings on the ship hadn't given me any idea of what a "Vespasian" thing was, outside of being the name of Pompeii's current (as of AD 79) emperor. The professor included us all in his friendly look. "Afraid so, Elfreda," he admitted. "We're expecting big crowds on the anniversary, and we'll have to accommodate them." I guess I must have let some of my ignorance leak onto the expression on my face, because he was looking right at me when he said, "Maybe some of our newer people don't know what the anniversary is all about. Anyone care to tell us?"

Three or four suck-ups tried to answer at once, but it was a thick-necked American whose name I didn't know who got the nod. "It's about the Emperor Vespasian, the guy who was the twelfth Caesar, and—what?"

The professor was waggling a finger at him. "Not the twelfth. Anybody?"

He was looking right at the Italian with the frayed suit, but he didn't get a response until he said, "Come on, Mr. Gatti. You're named after him, aren't you?"

Gatti said briefly, "Vespasian was the tenth of the Caesars. If one looks at the virts in the refectory hall one will see this for himself," and that was all he did say. He went back to resting his chin on the silver handle of his cane.

The professor sighed. The same bunch of would-be teacher's pets began calling out supplementary information, but the professor stopped them. "Counting from Julius Caesar, Vespasian was the tenth, and what's special about him is that he was the Roman emperor who built the Colosseum in Rome. He died just before the time when Pompeii got snuffed. Specifically, June 2079 is the two thousandth anniversary of the date in 79 when Emperor Vespasian died and was succeeded by his son, Titus. That made a big holiday in First Century Rome, and so the Giubileo's going to mark the date with a celebration of our own. All clear? Any other questions?" None appeared immediately and he turned to me, beaming again. "What about you, Mr. Sheridan? You just got here. Isn't there anything that you'd like explained?"

Well, sure there was. In fact, there were a lot of things, and so over the rest of the hour some of the holes of ignorance in my head got filled. Not just by the professor, either. Most of my classmates got involved, and by the time the professor let us leave I had actually learned quite a lot of useful stuff. Like the fact that almost everything in the Giubileo gift shops was free for us employees. ("Because we'd steal it anyhow," somebody said from the back of the room. The professor just smiled.) And if there was anything I didn't like about my job or my accommodations I had the right to report it to my union, the Confederazione Sindacale Lavoratori del Giubileo. Which I hadn't even known existed but would have found out, it was explained to me, when I got my first pay and saw the deductions for union dues.

When the class was over and I was bending over the drinking fountain in the hall I heard Maury Tesch's voice from behind me. "You don't want to drink that stuff, Brad," he said amiably. "Don't you know fish fuck in it?"

Actually I'd seen the sign on the fountain that said "Aqua Potabile" and figured out in general what it meant. "It says it's all right, doesn't it? Are you telling me it would make me sick?" I asked.

"Maybe, if you drank enough of it, but you wouldn't do that. Tastes terrible. All the fountains recirculate, and by the twentieth or thirtieth time around it ain't fresh anymore. How about a beer?"

I considered that, wiping my lips as I straightened up. I wasn't much interested in making him a bosom pal, as he seemed to want, but there was always the chance that he might be able to introduce me to somebody more interesting. Like, say, a woman. But it was getting late, and I had that early-morning session on the wheel to think about. "Maybe another time," I said. "Something I was wondering about, though. What's this union we're all supposed to be members of?"

Tesch took a quick look around, then grinned. "What?" he said. "You never heard of the Confederazione Sindacale Lavoratori, otherwise known as the Mafia? Tell him about it, why don't you, Vespasiano, since one of your jobs is working there?"

Old Gatti was just passing us in the hall. He looked us both over, but he didn't exactly respond. "I do not want to talk to you," he said, and this time he was definitely looking me in the eye. He pushed past, leaving Maury staring after him.

"He's really mad, isn't he?" he said. "I was only joking."

"Maybe Italians don't like Mafia jokes," I offered, but I had something else on my mind. "Tesch? What was it you called him, Vespasian? Does that mean he's like royal blood or something?"

Tesch gave me a grin. "Him? Not likely. It's a common name, like all the ones that once belonged to one of the emperors, but actually I have heard that his family did have money at one time. They don't anymore."

I let it go at that; I only sympathized with families that had lost their money when they were my own. When Maury repeated his offer of a beer I told him I was too tired. "But listen," I said. "I've been wanting to ask somebody why they call my boss 'Bastard.' Do you know?"

He gave me a probing look. "Can't say," he said at last. "I think I heard once that he didn't hire any pretty girls unless they'd go to bed with him. But I don't know for sure."

And he walked off, leaving me pretty well convinced that he did know, but just didn't want to say.

Then, all alone in my lonesome little cot I lay awake for a while thinking about why Maury didn't want to spread some gossip my way. And thinking, too, about old Vespasiano Gatti. It wasn't the Mafia joke he had been mad about. It was Tesch who had made the joke, but the one Gatti had looked right in the eye of and said he didn't like was definitely me.

By the next morning I had pretty nearly forgotten about old Gatti. I woke up feeling almost cheerful. There definitely were good parts to working for the Giubileo, and one of the best was just looking out of my window when I got up in the early morning and was getting ready to go to my goddamn wheel. I could look down on that ruined old wreck of a city the way it really was when the virts weren't beautifying it, jaggedly broken buildings that sulked in the moonlight, more shadow than substance. But then, before my jaded eyes, skeptical, cynical, exhausted from the long hours and the bullying Welsh Bastard, old Pompeii would be born again.

To get ready for the day's customers, every morning, they turned the city on.

When they did that everything of the old city that age and disaster had destroyed was suddenly made whole. Buildings that had been no more than stumps for two thousand years suddenly got back their upper stories. Walls flashed into being where there had been nothing but rubble. From my window I could squint into some of the residential areas of the late Pompeiian well-to-do. I could see lush flower beds exploding into light-generated existence, reflecting pools that magically filled with sparkling clean water and captive birds beginning to sing. They even generated the people. There was this villa that said it was the home of a bigwig named Paoulous Proculus, and when that magicked itself into virt shape it was a big hit with the tourists. They couldn't get into the atrium, because that was roped off, but the virts of P. Proculus and wife could be watched through a doorway as they endlessly nibbled on apples and peaches brought by relays of virt slaves.

It was all holos, virts, and simulations. But it was splendidly done, right down to the bright curtains that flapped in some of the unglazed windows and the unreal, but convincing, pair of drayhorses that pawed the ground before my very bakery.

From a distance it was absolutely convincing. Was from pretty close up, as well, unless you tried to touch it. Of course, there was nothing there, just some cleverly deployed photons.

It was damn well spectacular, though. It almost made working there a pleasure, as long as you didn't count in the smells, the lousy pay, the suffocating summer heat and, of course, the Welsh Bastard.

I did like just to wander around on those streets that ancient Roman people had walked on two thousand years before. (All right, they weren't exactly the same streets. In AD 79 they would have been ankle deep in all kinds of crap the old Romans and their animals regularly dropped into the street. The Giubileo couldn't quite duplicate that feature of old Pompeiian life in 2079. The Board of Health didn't allow it.) But so much of what was there looked really real, especially in that great open space they called the Forum. I mean the real one, the one with the Temple of Jupiter at one end, still under repair from what had happened to it in the AD 62 earthquake, and the sort of town hall place that they called the basilica at the other. Plus all those old statues and all the people. The tourists liked the Forum, too, so it was always crowded with people strolling around and chatting and pausing to buy some nice ripe figs or simulated ancient Roman jewelry from one of the Indentured peddlers who had staked out claims on the flag-stones.

You understand that when I say "people" I don't mean only the flesh-and-blood ones. There were plenty of that kind of people—tourists and employees of the Giubileo, working at their assignments as fruit sellers and souvenir vendors and whatever else might make a euro's profit for the Giubileo. But there were also the virts. There were always a dozen or more virtual Roman citizens—copies that the Giubileo swore to its customers were of actual, specific First Century Pompeiian notables. The one who was always carried in an open litter was named Umbricius Scaurus, and his claim to fame was that he was the guy who owned the factory where slaves manufactured that horrible stinky fish sauce they called garum. Sometimes sharing the litter with him—and thus no doubt making life a real living hell for the Nubians who had to carry them, or would have if they hadn't all been virts anyway—was a man named Modestus, whose claim to fame was that he was the baker I toiled for around that wheel. Then there was Marcus Vesonius Primus—he was a fuller of cloth; evidently in ancient Pompeii tradesmen were treated like gents, at least they were if they were rich enough. And there was Caius Munatius Faustus and, oh, yes, Lucius Veranius Hypsaesus and, well, there were a lot of them. They did look quite real as they strolled and chatted with each other in what the Giubileo's staff linguists claimed was authentic First Century Latin.

The whole scene was pretty, with all those rows of columns and monu-mental Roman structures—and all of them brightly painted in red and yellow. Why all those colors? Because the experts had decreed that the place should look just the way it had looked two thousand years ago, and those were the colors the real First Century Romans had enjoyed. Those paint jobs were a surprise to most of the visitors, but not so much to me. The way the restored Sphinx looked in Egypt had been just as unex-pected, for the same coat-of-paint reasons. I can't say I liked the idea of smearing paint over the marble, but then I wasn't a First Century Roman. Or an ancient Egyptian, either.

Behind the columns the buildings were all two stories high, with togaed

Roman men and gowned Roman women gazing benevolently down on the crowd below. Mostly they, too, were virts, of course, though not all of them. The ones that were visibly Asian or African or blond weren't going to be virts. They were organic real people like me, although they were the particular kind of organically real people that got all the best and easiest jobs, which is to say the volunteers.

It was the hucksters that put ideas in my head. Those were mostly Indentureds, just like me. They set up their wares here and there around the Forum, selling food and wine and trinkets and fortunes told while you wait. Some of the trinkets were sort of authentic, being at least modern copies of real Roman cups and vases. Some definitely were not, like the souvenir maps of the Giubileo's Pompeii. They charged for all this. Wouldn't take genuine euros, though.

I took an interest in the money changing. That had been one of my best sidelines in Egypt, and even if I couldn't wind up any better than, say, a fig merchant in the Forum I could see possibilities. Like if some person paid me with a silver denarius, say—and if nobody who looked to be any kind of law enforcement was near—I could "accidentally" give him change of a sestertius—and apologize like crazy for my mistake if he caught me at it. Or I could change euros into asses myself instead of bothering the official money changers. But when I asked the Welsh Bastard if I could get one of those jobs he laughed in my face. "What do you think, you're an Australian?" he asked, sneering. "You stick to the job you're assigned."

But in the long run I didn't have to.

Surprisingly, the next day the Welsh Bastard called me in to his dispatch room, and what he had to tell me was that that *ristorante* job that Gerda had talked about had actually come along.

I kind of had hopes for that one—well, at least partly because I liked the idea of a reasonably good-looking woman doing things to help me. Besides, the *ristorante* looked like a good prospect for getting cash tips from the customers. On the negative side, it's true that the smells bothered me, because some of the dishes were authentic Pompeiian, which generally meant that they were smothered in more of that horrible rotten fish sauce. Not to mention the six or seven kinds of cheeses, all smelly—cow's milk or sheep's milk or goat's, sometimes smoked or aged, but always highly odorous. We Indentureds didn't get that kind of luxury food in the employees' mess. Or, to put it differently, even we Indentureds weren't forced to swallow that crap.

For a little while I was actually feeling optimistic. The decorations in the *ristorante* were pretty neat—virt-animated murals of all kinds of famous Romans and their famous (or a lot of the time you'd have to say their pretty infamous) wives and daughters. I thought that was a plus because working there meant getting a history lesson every time I walked through the room.

The work, though, was harder than I expected. When you're carrying breakfast for a table of six the dishes get heavy, and I had to take orders from six or eight different cuisines—standard international (steaks, orange juice, scrambled eggs, and the like), Chinese (what they called the dim sum menu), Middle Eastern (couscous), Scandinavian (a hundred kinds of pickled herring), Slavic (borscht and a lot of sour cream), and, of course, the alleged First Century Roman that everybody wanted to try once but hardly ever twice. I figured it would take me a month just to learn the menus.

I didn't have a month. It turned out that I didn't really have waiterly skills. What convinced the manager was when I spilled some of that Roman fish soup on a tourist from the Argentine Republic.

I should point out that it wasn't my fault. Argentinians aren't that crazy about fish to begin with. She shoved it away when she got a whiff of how it smelled, and it landed in her lap. There wasn't really anything I could do about that, was there? I even had a witness, the Somali named Abukar Abdu who was bussing my tables; he saw the whole thing and took my side. But the Bastard wasn't interested in that. For him, the customer was God and I was just a damn Indentured. (I guess the Bastard did pay attention, in his own fashion, because when I ran into Abukar a day or two later he'd been fired from his busboy job and reassigned as a

Nubian litter bearer, carrying rich tourists around in the brutal Italian heat. The Bastard said Abukar just happened to be the right color to be a Nubian so he was underutilized in the *ristorante*. He didn't mention that Abukar had unwisely stuck up for me.)

The first thing I thought of was my wannabe friend Maury Tesch. So next time he caught me outside the Bastard's dispatch room I asked him straight out about getting a job in water management. I expected he might turn me down, but not that he would be unpleasant about it.

But I was wrong. His expression froze. "You?" he said. "In hydrology? You don't have the training."

"What training do you need to turn a damn valve?" I demanded. "Okay. If we were talking about something like running virt displays maybe I don't have the background—"

Now he looked offended as well as irritated. "You're just proving my point, Sheridan. You can't compare hydrology with entertainment. If the virt crews get something wrong it's just an annoyance, but if something went wrong with the hydrology it could make people sick." He stood silent for a moment, and his expression changed again, more worried than anything else. "I'm running late," he said. "Talk to you later." And he was gone. And the next time I saw him he was back to wheedling a chess game or two.

Anyway, the way it turned out I didn't have to go back to the flour mill. The Welsh Bastard was unexpectedly unbastardly enough to try me on a couple of other jobs. I was a trainee at the gladiator school on the outskirts of the city for four days, until I got a little carried away when the audience clapped for me. I had forgotten that those disappearing daggers didn't disappear unless you pushed the button in the haft.

One sort of good, or almost sort of good, thing came out of that. Good-looking Elfreda What's-her-name had been coiffed and gowned and was leading a party of tourists in the audience when I stuck that guy's belly—fortunately not very deeply—and while the tourists were getting into their litters she came up behind and patted my shoulder and said, "Everybody makes mistakes at first. Don't let it get you down."

That sounded almost like code for, "Why don't you buy me a cup of coffee sometime and we'll see how it goes?" I made a mental note to follow up when I got a chance. She was right, too. The thing really wasn't my fault. I couldn't help my reflexes. Back in New York City if somebody came at you with a weapon, and you had a weapon of your own, you responded really fast, or you never got another chance. But after that little episode none of the other gladiators would perform with me. And the Elfreda thing fizzled out; next time I saw her she was heading for the Naples electric with a rich-looking, Asian-looking tourist, and when I said hi she gave me a Do-I-know-you?-and-if-I-do-I-wish-I-didn't look. So that came to nothing.

Then I was a male whore on the Via Nola for a while. We flesh-and-blood make-believe whores didn't actually have sex with each other, we just faked it, but then one of my audience members became interested and kind of really got into the spirit of the performance—he'd been drinking, of course—and I punched him out.

The Welsh Bastard didn't give up on me even then. He even let me guide a group of Californians around the city after all. He figured, I guess, that they'd be tolerant of a fellow American's incompetence, but I had bad luck. One of the tourists was a history professor from UCLA. I couldn't fool him. He complained to the management. That time the Bastard swore at me a lot, but he didn't send me back to the bakery even then. He gave me still another chance. I couldn't help wondering why, but I didn't ask. I just took the new job.

What he did was to put me in business for myself, selling wine in one of those hole-in-the-wall shops on the street they called the Via dell'Abbondanza.

When I say "hole-in-the-wall," I mean it just about literally. The shop was a room just big enough for a quarried-stone counter, a bunch of wine tubs, and me, with three featureless walls at the sides and back, and on the other side nothing but the street.

It wasn't a bad job. Relatively speaking, I mean.

Well, it wasn't really a good job, either. Those summer days in Pompeii were pretty hot. You might think I'd be used to all that, having just come from sunny Egypt. But the tombs in the Valley of the Kings were air-conditioned. The Via dell'Abbondanza wasn't.

Then there were the smells. It wasn't just the pee buckets or the latrines in the street. It was those vats of wine, too. The hotter it got the more vigorously they poured their stale-wine smells into the air. Sometimes I came close to getting a contact high off the fumes.

The pay was no better, either. In the beginning I had some idea of making it up on tips, but what kind of tips can you expect when the most the customers ever buy is a single cup of wine, which they mostly hate?

But I had thought up a list of such matters ahead of time. On my very first day at the wine bar one of my customers, an already fairly tipsy one, ran out of the Jubilee's fake-denarius tokens. He hadn't run out of thirst, though, and when he ordered another round he tried to pay me in actual euros.

Taking real money from a tourist was absolutely against the rules, as the Welsh Bastard had made sure I knew before he let me out of his dispatch room. On the other hand, real money had its attractions for me. The denarii were the Giubileo's own fiddle. They looked like silver, but weren't, and the beauty part of it for the Giubileo, as I had figured out for myself long since, was that quite a few of the unspent ones got taken home to Sydney and Bangkok and Zagreb for souvenirs.

So why shouldn't I have a little fiddle of my own? Making change from euros to tokens offered all kinds of possibilities.

There was one thing about the job that really ticked me off. That was the way the tourists would poke at me to see whether I was real or a virt. That's what nearly all of the children did, that is, but even a fair number of adults, particularly the Koreans and the Australians, gave me the occasional prod.

At least I didn't have to push that damn wheel. And I no longer had to make believe I was being buggered by somebody I didn't even know.

The Via dell'Abbondanza was pretty much peripheral to the major restored parts of Pompeii. To the west of my grog shop was a laundry, where you could see virt Romans washing tunics but fortunately couldn't smell them, then nothing much before you got to the red velvet ropes across the road to keep tourists from going any farther in that direction. There really wasn't any farther to go to, anyway, except to where the old amphitheater and a bunch of other structures had been left in the shape that time and Mount Vesuvius had given them.

Of course no velvet rope was going to stop a customer who had loaded up on my joy juice. That wasn't a serious problem, though. Security was ready for such things. If a drunk tried to push past those ropes a phalanx of virt Roman legionaries—breastplates, helmets, short spears, and all— would close ranks before him. If the customer persisted, confident that virts could never hurt him, a detachment of real, live and muscular Security guys were stationed just around the corner.

Those imitation legionaries weren't the only virts around. That far down the via they didn't bother to give us very much of that kind of window dressing, certainly nothing like the clusters of imitation citizens that strolled around the Forum. But from time to time a couple of those simulated ancient Pompeiians would walk by, appearing deep in their conversation, or a couple of simulated slaves would show up as they carried some simulated rich person's litter. Then, of course, there were the customers. They weren't simulated. Neither was the wine they poured into themselves, though it certainly wasn't exactly authentic, either.

All the virtual stuff was astonishingly convincing. Early on in my wine-selling career I tried to figure out just what parts of my own little cubbyhole were physically real and which were just insubstantial virts. I wasn't always right. The counter and the vats beneath it—they had to be real, or at least they had to be physically real Twenty-first Century copies of the two-thousand-year-old originals, because when I stretched out a hand I could feel them. Anyway the wine in my vats didn't spill out all over my feet as soon as the wine tanker came by with its replenishments.

On the other hand, the walls were visually virts. What the designers had done, they took those ancient walls with cracks like somebody'd gouged them with a chisel and pits you could hide a grapefruit in, and painted a fresh layer of trapped virt photons over it. And there it was, all egg-yolk yellow and coal-ember crimson, with wall paintings of ancient Romans in a heavily sloshed condition, looking as good as new . . . as long as you didn't touch them.

The wine, of course, was really as fake as the walls. I was instructed to tell the customers that the first vat was imported Greek, and the second Falernian, and the little one at the end held something that was made out of fermented honey, called hydromels. (I didn't get many calls for the hydromels.) What they all really were was tap water and grain alcohol, with a bunch of artificial colors and flavors to make them taste more or less the way that Twenty-first Century tourists would expect that First Century wine would. Every morning before the Jubilee opened for business the wine tanker would rumble up the via to my shop—a physically real cart, pulled by a real, animate, living, even smelly mule—so I could sign out for as much wine as it took to fill the vats from the driver's giant wine boxes, and then I was ready for business.

That was about all there was to my place of business. There was an upstairs, too, probably meant for the real First Century barkeep to sleep in, but that part was all virt.

To the tourists I was just furniture. They would point at me and take pictures of me, but as long as they didn't actually talk to me I didn't have to pay much attention to them. Which meant I could go through the motions of wiping off the counter, while what I really was doing was listening to the Italian-language lessons on my earplugs, or to the English-language channel for news and gossip. Or to the historical stuff. Or, when I got really bored, to whatever the Naples soundradio stations were broadcasting, which was mostly last year's Latin American poprock or those Neapolitan songs they call canzone. And, when I had the opportunity, I made change for the customers who hadn't converted their euros into the fake Roman stuff, and screw what the Welsh Bastard had ordered.

What with one thing and another, I had pretty nearly forgotten that anybody named Gerda Fleming existed.

That's what I used to tell myself, anyway. Except when I was feeling particularly lonesome. Or trying to get to sleep on that sack of pebbles they called a mattress. I remembered then, all right. Because have I mentioned that not only had this Gerda woman tipped me to the *ristorante* job but my estimate of her physical attractions, on second thought, had gone up a few stages. Actually (I was beginning to think) she wasn't bad looking at all.

If I didn't have a Gerda, there were at least a few sparse and tiny compensations. Little by little, some of the other Indentureds were beginning to thaw toward me. Cedric Mimsley, for instance, nodded to me across the Via dell'Abbondanza the third or fourth morning I saw him there.

The via wasn't a very wide street. You could spit across it if you were any kind of a spitter at all, but still, he didn't come across it to visit with me, perhaps because he felt that a person in his position couldn't afford to be seen with some lower caste person like me. Cedric's position, actually, was ticket taker for a virt whorehouse. That annoyed me for a while. Then I found out a little more about Cedric and I switched from annoyed-at to sorry-for. None of us Indentureds had any money to speak of, but Cedric had to be the poorest of the lot. He was a double-dip. Well, so was I, because of those extra euros I'd taken onto my debt to get out of Egypt. What Cedric had borrowed his way out of, however, wasn't anything that was merely hopeless, as Egypt was for me. His last job had been way lower on the totem pole than that. He'd been a decontamination worker at the old Soviet nuclear submarine base at Murmansk, and what kind of Indenture he'd had to sign to get out of that I shudder to think of.

And sometimes a few of my colleagues didn't get up and leave when I sat beside them in the mess. They didn't talk much, either, except to each other, but they didn't make me stop listening.

So gradually I was making a kind of a not unbearable life. And I hadn't forgotten that I was part of a family.

I wasn't all selfish, you know. Honest. I gave quite a lot of thought to old Dan and Marilyn Sheridan, sitting around with nothing much to do back in 16-A Liberty Crescent, Floor 15 of the Molly Pitcher Redeployment Village on Staten Island.

At least now and then I did.

I guess I bring that up to show that, never mind my fiddles and my history of occasional minor felonies, I still had enough common decency to have feelings for my parents' problems and needs. It wasn't their fault that Yellowstone had blown its top. Or that Uncle Devious was never going to give back Mom's mad money. Or that the US government was so drowned in emergency expenses that the treasury didn't have enough left over to give the refugees a decent standard of living.

I was doing my usual how-much-can-I-spare-for-Staten-Island arithmetic when more customers showed up and I had to hide my cell in my diaper. (The Welsh Bastard didn't want us to be seen with anything that was less than two thousand years old. Especially not with anything high-tech. Would spoil the illusion, he said.) But I needn't have bothered. These particular customers didn't seem to know I was there, maybe just another virt, but one with skills enough to take their asses and pour their drinks. These were cheap bastards, too. They kept on telling each other, in English and loud enough that I couldn't miss a word, how outstandingly lousy the wine was . . . while they were drinking it down, every damn drop. They sounded American, but were not my kind of American, anyway. Maybe Australian? Or Canadian maybe from the Maritime Provinces and thus still rich?

I don't know how long they would have gone on dissing my wine, and me, but they caught sight of somebody approaching along the via, a dark-skinned youth in a gray slave tunic like my own. "Real or fake?" one of them said to the other. "Beats the hell out of me," the other said. "Let's go stick a finger in his eye and find out."

I watched them go (their cups left totally empty on the counter), sort of hoping they would try it. The guy they were looking at was named Jamie Hardesty. He came from Springfield, Illinois, and he was as flesh and blood as I was, about twenty kilos more so, actually, and every gram of it pure, hard muscle. The ceramic pots that hung from the yoke across his shoulders would be holding food. Mine, among others.

The maybe Canadians must have got a better look at him because they veered off and wandered away, just glancing back at him now and then over their shoulders. Jamie set his pots down, rubbing the base of his neck where the yoke had bitten in. While I was filling the eating bowl I kept under the counter he said, "Oh, by the way, Brad. Gerda's back."

Now, that was the kind of news that rolled the clouds away. I guess my subconscious had been processing more, and hornier, thoughts about Gerda Fleming than my conscious was aware of. What I wished I could do was call her up on my pocket screen, right then, but there were too many tourists hanging around.

I don't mean I was consciously looking for a special boy-girl relationship with her. I hadn't been dreaming about the woman—not so that I remembered it when I woke up, anyway. I hadn't even tried to find out where she'd gone. I just remembered that she was the one I owed the *ristorante* job to, even if the job hadn't exactly panned out, and I thought I'd like to say thanks. I couldn't do it just then, though. First Century slaves didn't have Twenty-first Century phones.

So I had put Gerda out of my mind for the moment and I did the job I was being paid to do, gobbling down my food between serving cups of wine. That seemed to entertain the tourists, because, of course, I was eating the "lunch" with my fingers, as any Roman slave would naturally do, and they probably could tell from the look on my face what I thought of it. That day my lunch was a salty, fishy-smelling porridge. That's to say, it was just another bastardly little surprise from the Welsh Bastard who was my boss, with the fish in the stew right on the margin between kind of all right and really, truly, inedibly spoiled.

By then there were maybe twenty tourists clustered around my shop, treating themselves to a cup of wine or just enjoying the spectacle of a slave gobbling down his pitiful excuse for a meal. I was glad enough when I'd finished the last foul-tasting fingerful and some of the tourists began to drift away.

The only ones still dawdling at my bar were a pair of middle-aged men who were having a ferocious low-toned argument in what I supposed was Spanish. They showed no signs of leaving.

Then the two men exchanged a particularly nasty-sounding couple of sentences and did finally leave, in opposite directions. Now pretty much alone, I was reaching for my phone when something attracted my attention.

Down the via a quartet of slaves were carrying a litter in my direction. A flash of red hair from the occupant made me think for a moment that it was Gerda inside.

It wasn't, though. I caught a glimpse of the face and realized it was some other staffer in the blond wig of a Roman prostitute. Or, I realized on second look, it wasn't a staffer at all. It wasn't anyone alive. Palanquin, passengers, and bearer were all simulations.

I couldn't always tell the difference, unless maybe it was raining and I noticed the figures of the virts weren't getting wet. This time there wasn't any doubt. The side of the litter changed color to a sort of ripple of green and violet. Then it bulged out, and the figures of a young Asian couple jogged right through the palanquin.

Tourists were always doing that kind of thing, just to show off. Virts were as tenuous as air, and they didn't care what the customers did to them. What I myself minded, though, was that this couple, once they had crashed their way through the phantom palanquin, hurried right over to my wine bar, where they stopped, giggling to each other, and stood without speaking.

I remembered I was supposed to be unloading wine on them. "Wine?" I asked. "*Vino? Vin? Wein?*" That was about as far as I could go with European languages, and didn't know any of the Asiatic ones that might have been more useful. It didn't matter. The youngsters did not seem interested in wine in any language. What they seemed to be interested in was a man slowly approaching down the street.

He was kind of interesting, at that. He was middle-aged and wore a data opticle in his right eye. He was less stylishly dressed than the young people, but the wristscreen on his right arm was set with diamonds and he wore big, jeweled rings on all the fingers of his left hand. He wasn't alone, either. Eight or ten others of scattered ages followed him. "Good afternoon, sir," the man said to me, holding his unadorned right hand out for shaking. "I am Dr. Basil Chi-Leong, hello, and you are?"

"Brad Sheridan," I said, shaking his hand because I couldn't see any way out of it. Then I was surprised when this Dr. Basil Chi-Leong didn't let go of me at once. "Now that we are friends," the old man said sunnily, "I may ask a favor, I think? To be photographed by my family members with you? If I may? All right? Then thank you," he said, and threw one skinny arm around my shoulders before I could get out of the way.

At that point he changed his tone, and his language, and began issuing orders to his family.

Each one of the adults immediately began snapping pictures of me with one variety or another of camera, still, motion, stereoscopic, and who knew what other kind, as they took a picture with one instrument and then let that one hang from its neck strap as they reached for another. They only stopped when Dr. Chi-Leong raised his hand commandingly. He dropped half a dozen random coins in my meal bowl, still sticky with the remains of my revolting lunch, and said, "That was most enjoyable, Mr. Bradley Sheridan. Allow me to introduce my mother, Madam Katey Chi-Leong, who speaks no English, but is an avid taker of pictures. These others are my three sons and the wives thereof, with grandsons and grand-daughters. We are from the Republic of Singapore, perhaps you have visited it? No? That is too bad. But you will not mind if Madam Katey Chi-Leong, my mother, takes some additional pictures of you? And we will each have a cup of your best wine, if you please."

They did, too, every damn one of them. Even the children. I thought for a moment of refusing to sell wine to the littlest ones, no more than three or four years old; but the pleasure of selling fifteen asses' worth of wine in five minutes decided me against asking for IDs.

Actually, none of the children drank any of the stuff anyway. They carefully held their cups at arm's length, to avoid spilling them, or perhaps to avoid the smell of their contents, then set them down untouched on the countertop. Even their parents drank very little of the wine. A sip or two was plenty, and then they each made the same face and drank no more.

I didn't mind that a bit; there would be more to put back in the vat when they left. What I did mind was that, to get out of the hot sun, all dozen-plus of them had crowded into my tiny shop. It did not have room for such a mob. Three of the little ones had hopped over the counter to share my less congested side, and all three of Dr. Chi-Leong's sons were sitting on the counter itself.

The old woman, who had been more or less continuously photographing me, said something peremptory to Dr. Chi-Leong. He nodded deferentially and addressed me again. "You are American, is that not true? And of course, if I may say so without giving offense, Indentured? If that is the case please answer me this question, so that my mother's interest may be satisfied: Is your income from the Giubileo sufficient for your needs?"

No tourist had ever asked me that before, and I was caught without a good answer. "Yes" for the sake of my pride? "No" in the hope of a larger tip? "Mind your own business" as the most appropriate?

I was saved the trouble. An immense black shadow was passing over the Via dell'Abbondanza.

The youngest daughter-in-law, the one who hadn't been given room in the wineshop and so had been partly out in the sunshine, glanced up, shading her eyes. Then she cried something in that singsong language that I had no hope of understanding. In a moment the shop emptied out of Singaporeans, because they were all photographing the sky.

Dr. Chi-Leong glanced back at me, pointing upward. "That airship is named the *Chang Jang*," he said proudly. "It is given that name after a major river system in the country of our ancestors, which is the country of

China. It is this ship which has brought us here from Berlin and Moscow and other tourist places of that sort."

By leaning over the counter and craning my neck, I could see what they were looking at. The *Chang Jang* was one of those giant lighter-than-air cruise zeppelins that turned up in the air of every interesting cruise destination, Pompeii definitely included. The colors this one flew from its tail said that it was a ship of the Cathay Pacifica line. It surely was a monster. I'm not talking here about something like the little air-yachts that rich people sometimes flew, or the blimps that do inter-city transportation. I'm talking large. Zeps in general were usually two kilometers long or so. This one, hanging less than a kilometer above the city wall, was even bigger. It filled the sky from horizon to horizon.

The old lady spoke, Dr. Chi-Leong said something in agreement, and the family began to move away. The doctor pulled out a roll of euros—actually ink-printed-on-paper euros, I mean—and scattered a selection of them to cover their bill. "We wish you a good-bye, Mr. Bradley Sheridan," he said over his shoulder. "I hope that we shall meet again."

"Sure, fine, thanks," I called after them. I even meant it. The tips had been impressively good and they'd left at least a liter and a half of wine undrunk in their cups to replenish my vats.

When I finally got away from the wine vats it didn't take me long to find Gerda. She was in the refectory, waiting for me. Looking healthy and well rested, too, as she sat by herself at a corner table, picking at some fruit salad the kitchen staff had made up for her. She gave me a welcoming hug, just as though we'd been old pals. Or even in fact old going-to-bed-together pals. "Things all right with you, Brad?" she asked. "Care for some pineapple?"

I took a piece of the pineapple and sat down before I answered her question. "Fine," I said. "And you?"

"Well," she said, thinking it over, "I guess you'd say I'm really well, Brad, only hungry. Want to eat here? Or shall we go out and get a pizza?"

There it was, another installment of that old-pals-togetherness. I played it as dealt. "Pizza," I said, and that's what we did. We took the long walk around the outside of the Jubilee area to the Porta Marina train station, where all the little food and trinket shops had sprung up. I noticed that somewhere between the refectory and the entrance to the grounds we'd begun to hold hands as we walked. I also noticed—very carefully observed—that Gerda's earlobes were bare and teeth all uncapped. I knew what that meant. Well, sort of. I knew it meant either that she had no special sexual demands and was not currently in a formal relationship . . . or else that she didn't want to advertise her sexual tastes, as most young people did, because she didn't think it was anyone's business but her own. Anyway, we ate pizza from the first shop we passed, or at least she did. I didn't have much appetite. I was too busy looking her over, especially when she was looking the other way, and wondering what she'd been doing on the old *Chang Jang*. Not to mention that that fishy rice was clumped like a lead weight in my belly.

And then, when she had finished devouring her pizza, she exploratorily ran her tongue over her teeth a time or two. Unsatisfied with the result, she unwrapped a coat of ruby-red foil from something she pulled out of her bellybag and popped it in her mouth. I guess I was really enjoying watching her chew, and showing it, because she grinned and pulled out another stick of the stuff for me, this one wrapped in green foil. "Cleans your teeth," she informed me. Maybe it did. That wasn't why I enjoyed it so much, though. It was the taste of the gum itself, I guess, that really got my little buds tingling, fruity and flowery and, I think most of all, just a tad warmed by the flesh of Gerda Fleming.

What I was basically doing at that time, you see, was falling in love.

I didn't talk much. I mostly just listened while she told me that, boy, those zeppelins were really something, weren't they? And she'd taken passage in one on the spur of the moment to go to Munich to see her sick old great-aunt Mirabelle, who wasn't really an actual relative (Gerda explained, though I hadn't asked) but had been her granddad's live-in girlfriend when Gerda was little and they'd kept in touch. When she let me know that it was my turn to talk a little she was sympathetic (demonstrated by little hugs) as I told her how boring the wineshop was. Then, when it was getting late I walked her home. She lived in volunteer quarters, a lot nicer than mine, in a building that had once, I think, been the Italian equivalent of a pretty comfortable motel. She invited me in for a drink and we wound up in bed. And by the next day she was my recognized girl. And, short version, kept on being my girl for the next week, and the next, and the next, and, for all those weeks, we never did get around to visiting the Jubilee's gift shop or Ferris wheel. Never had the time.

7

MY GIRL

Was I surprised that all this happened?

You bet I was. Not so much by the way I was feeling about Gerda—which really was not totally unlike the way I'd felt about, say, Tina Gundersack, back in the processing camps in North Carolina, right after the evacuation or, for that matter, eight or ten other nubile young girls one time or another. But none of which, when you came right down to it, had ever showed any signs of feeling that way about me. I could only suppose that what was going on was some totally unexpected case of the "L" word.

You know the word. Love. The word that had never accurately described any relationship of mine before.

And why was I graced with this new thing now? I couldn't think of a reason. The old Romans (it had said in one of my readings) explained it pretty well. They thought that love was a kind of lunacy. Probably the old Romans were right. But when Gerda and I did things together it didn't feel like lunacy. It felt fine.

So Gerda was a whole new continent for me to explore. For one thing (but not the only thing) I hadn't had much particularly fine screwing before Gerda came along—the New York teenagers and the Cairo pros were rarely creative, so maybe I wasn't the best qualified judge. All the same I would have to say that in bed Gerda was—let's not let the truth scare us off—well, awesome. She knew just where to touch and how to squeeze and when to do the unexpected what. And she was right every time.

I thought she read my mind.

Of course, there was really a different explanation, but you couldn't have convinced me of that at the time.

So we enjoyed ourselves, we two kids (only Gerda was definitely not a kid) in love (or in something a lot like it, anyway). We would rent a three-wheeler, that is, I would rent one, and go down the coast or up it just to see what we would see. (Usually bars.) She didn't like to drive, though. She turned the driver's seat over to me, although she made up for it in criticisms and advice. I didn't mind. I didn't mind much of anything. We were having fun. Once or twice I talked her into hiking the lower slopes of Vesuvius, where the virt installers were setting up the projectors for the big sky shows to come. And one time she insisted on taking the chair lift all the way up to the lip of Vesuvius's deep, hundreds of meters deep, crater. She was the one who talked me into that one. She mentioned that if we wanted we could go down closer on rope ladders, but she didn't say it as though she was really suggesting we do it. All she said was, "Just look at it, Brad! Isn't it gorgeous?" I looked. But I didn't think it was all that interesting, not to mention that it was smoky and hot and generally unpleasant. And I didn't much like thinking about volcanic eruptions, because Yellowstone had permanently taken the fun out of that kind of thing for me.

We took the electric in to Naples a couple of times. Drinks in the Galleria. The compulsory museum visit so Gerda could stand rapt before fifteen or twenty old oil paintings. (I didn't mind. Gerda looked at the paintings, I looked at Gerda.) Maybe for a decent meal of something like those baby shrimp that they fry head and all in a deep-fry kettle. (The shrimp imported from somewhere along the Dalmatian coast, of course. Nobody in his right mind would eat anything that came out of the Bay of Naples.) We took one weekend in Ischia, soaking in the hot springs and losing as much money as I could afford, and maybe a little more, in the casinos.

That was where our only identifiable problem was.

It was kind of a big one, too. I'm talking about money. Gerda, being a volunteer, got to keep all her basic pay and her tips each month, and thus had about ten times the disposable income of an Indentured with a debt to pay off, not to mention a family to support back home, like me. That didn't signify for her. Gerda was an old-fashioned girl. To her that meant that when a man and a woman went somewhere together it was the man who picked up the check.

Quaint, right? Not to say sexistly offensive? But there it was.

On the other hand Gerda was, after all, Gerda.

The one thing that didn't cost us an as was about the best part of the summer. All it took to be wonderful was a bed. Or, in the case of my room, a cot, but Gerda's room had a really big bed and that was a lot better. That was even true of the view. Gerda's room looked on basically the same things as mine, but as it was up higher it saw a lot more of them. It wasn't only bigger than mine, it had its own private bathroom, and old-fashioned wicker furniture and carved wooden screens and shelves and shelves of these and those personal possessions. There were, it's true, a few puzzles, notably a framed photo of a good-looking woman of maybe thirty or thirty-five next to her bed, but she explained that right away. "My cousin Mary Elaine," she said. "She pretty nearly raised me after my mother got divorced and moved away. I wish Mary was still alive. You'd like her." Which I had no doubt was true. And Gerda's place had one big advantage over my own digs. Although Jiri was a roommate who was seldom present, Gerda didn't have any roommate at all. Except, quite a lot of the time, me.

All in all, it was turning out to be a pretty good summer, not to say absolutely the positively best summer of my whole entire life, and its name was Gerda Fleming.

.   .   .

I didn't spend all of my time with Gerda. I got the same weekly allowance of 168 hours of time as everybody else, but Gerda, at my very luckiest, didn't ordinarily fill more than twenty or twenty-five of them for me. I did still have to work. So did she, and sometimes the Welsh Bastard would schedule us, I honestly think out of pure meanness, so that I would be off while she was working. Or vice versa. Then I was thrown on my own pre-Gerda resources, which weren't much.

Of course, there was always Maury Tesch.

He was almost always up for a game of chess, which I almost always wasn't, or a gape at whichever Chinese zep happened to be blotting out the sun that day. "Holy Jesus, Brad, you know what that thing can do? A couple hundred kilometers an hour, sliding right over the ocean or the desert or the cities, it doesn't matter to a zeppelin, does it? And the size of the damn thing! They can easy hold two, three thousand passengers with swimming pools and restaurants and who knows what else?" But when I asked him if he was hoping to fly in one of them sometime he just scowled and wagged his head and said, "I wish," and wouldn't talk about it anymore.

He had some funny little ways, like the time in the staff refectory when I went to get a fresh glass of water and brought Maury one, too. He waved it away indignantly. "Drink water from the municipal system? Me? No way! Do you have any idea what the lining of those old pipes looks like?"

"Well," I said, finishing my glass and reaching for his, "I like it. It's about all I can afford."

"You can afford your health. If it has to be water, get the good stuff. Sparkling water, in a bottle. All those bubbles keep your juices flowing." He paused, looking up at me with that kicked-puppy expression. "Actually," he said, "I've got some up at my place. And maybe a little chess, if you're in for it?"

Actually I did give it a moment's thought, but then I shook my head. "I think I'd better——" I began to say, intending to invent some time-consuming and unavoidable errand, but he was ahead of me.

"Or," he said, "how about a little picnic in my pine grove? It's really a part of the Giubileo's water supply system. It isn't open to the public, just our people and their guests, and there's a little wine bar that makes sandwiches."

I had never heard of a grove of pine trees that had a wine bar. Maury didn't let me mull over it. "Yeah," he said, getting enthusiastic, "that's what we want. We can pick up a three-wheeler at the gate."

So I didn't argue. The three-wheelers were where he said they would be, the pine grove was a couple of klicks farther up the slope, and when we got to the razor-wire fence around it, the Security man at the gate glanced at the card Maury held up to his face and waved us through.

It was pleasantly coolish under the pines. A couple dozen men and women were at picnic tables scattered around the trees to enjoy it. What Maury was enjoying, I was pretty sure, was the expression on my face as I took all this in. "Nice, isn't it?" he asked. "We like it. Right here—under the ground, I mean—is where the basic water intake treatments are done for the whole park. Let's get our sandwiches."

There was a third class of workers at the Giubileo besides the Indentureds and the volunteers. Maury filled the gaps in. "It has to be like this," he told me. "They have to have technicians, don't they? Trained ones. You think they'd let, oh, say, Elfreda or what's-his-name, Abukar Abdu, run the hydro systems here? They'd have pee coming out of the showers and God knows what in the drinking water!" So the Giubileo hired trained hydrologists like Maury, with certificates from three schools and about a dozen cities around the world. And equally trained virt operators, power engineers, dieticians, medics, machine tenders, technical specialists of a dozen kinds—all of the skills that kept our little town safe and functioning. Even Maury—only a second-floor technician, nowhere near the penthouse elite in pay scale—still drew down a hell of a lot more than either Gerda or I.

He had it made.

We talked. He asked after Gerda, and didn't leer or make jokes about her, either. And he was interested in my family. He listened patiently—no, not patiently; as though he was really interested—to how tough it was for me to keep sending them money. "At least," he said, "you do have parents."

That was right out of left field. "Don't you?" I asked.

"Not anymore. They died. I'm alone in the world." Then he sort of shook himself and gave me a grin. "But enough of this depressing stuff. How are you getting along with the Bastard?"

The subject was definitely changed. I did my best to be noncommittal about a person I really disliked. I thought maybe I could get him to answer the question that had been nagging at me. "Oh, he's not so bad. Why do they call him that, do you know?"

He looked surprised at the question, as though it had never occurred to him. Then he shrugged. "Seems to me I heard it was because he demanded sexual favors from the better-looking female employees. That sound right?"

It sounded right enough. It also sounded like something I might want to ask Gerda about first chance I got—although Gerda wasn't Indentured, was she? She could've simply told him to stuff it if that sort of thing had ever come up.

I must have looked a tad too concerned about something trivial because Maury was giving me a curious look. "Is something the matter?" he asked.

That aspect of Gerda was not a matter I wanted to discuss with Maury. I changed the subject. "I was just thinking about funny nicknames. Like that female Security officer they call Piranha Woman."

Maury picked right up on that. "Oh, that I know. She isn't Italian. She started out in South America, pacifying rebellious native tribes who cut the throats of dairy cattle that settlers brought into the Amazon. But don't say I told you. She doesn't like that part of her life talked about."

Then he seemed to run out of conversation. He glanced at the sky, where evening was beginning to become night. He stretched and began picking up our trash. "Sorry for bending your ear with my troubles," he said over his shoulder.

"Not at all," I said, for lack of something better to say. It was getting toward the time when Gerda would be free again. I was thinking of leaving when he opened his backpack and took out what looked like a pair of stuffed Christmas stockings.

They weren't though. "I need to ask you for a favor, Brad. These," he said, setting them down on the table before me, "are some sausages that my uncle Rob sent me from Turkey. I won't open them. I guarantee you wouldn't like them, not even the smell, but I have to admit I'm very fond of them. Only Mordecai isn't."

I guess he could see I wasn't quite following. "Captain Mordecai Glef," he amplified. "My UN roommate. He's just arrived and they've billeted him with me. Only, you see, he's very religious and he thinks my sausages are traif—not kosher, in fact extremely nonkosher—and he doesn't want them in the fridge we share. So—I hope I'm not pushing my luck with you—I wonder if I can ask you for what I need. Do you think you could keep them for me?"

It was a pretty huge windup for a pretty tiny request. I told him my own roommate wasn't religious and sure I'd keep them. And so that was why Maury was being so nice.

Then, as a different three-wheeler was taking us back in through the Vesuvius Gate, Maury silent, me thinking that he was pretty weird but maybe, after all, I wasn't the one who had had the lousiest childhood after all, there was something else lousy going on right down the graveled walk. It started with yelling. We pushed our way through a knot of other Indentureds and what we saw was our fake Nubian friend from Somali, Abukar Abdu, being dragged away by a couple of those brawny Security thugs, with a fly-eyed Antica woman giving the orders.

So what had happened? An African sweeper-service woman who was crying gave us the answer: Abdu had been caught stealing loose mosaic tiles to sell to the tourists so he could send the money back to his kids in Mogadishu. "You won't see him around here again," she said, sobbing.

And that was that. I looked at Maury. Maury looked at me. "See you later," Maury said, and I said, "I guess you will."

8

SHARING

So in general I was happy. Relatively speaking, I mean. I was even getting along better with some of the people I hadn't been getting along with at all before Gerda—even with Elfreda, who seemed to have dumped the Somalian she'd been going around with for the last week or two in favor of a short and fairly homely Indentured from Sierra Leone. I supposed she had some criteria in mind for her boyfriend of the week, but I couldn't guess at what they were. I was getting along particularly well with Cedric the Pimp, but that wasn't because of a sudden efflorescence of native charm. It was what I had, more than who I was, that charmed Cedric. Sometimes he would stop by my wineshop in the hope of drinking the unfinished dregs cash customers had left behind, and once in a while I would let him. (That was because sometimes what was left was too little to be worth the trouble of pouring. But not too little for Cedric.) Most surprising of all, I was even—a little bit, anyway, or almost—getting along with the Welsh Bastard. Oh, I don't want you to think that the world was suddenly a wonderful place. But both things were definitely improved. (Of course at this time I had never heard of Pompeii Flu, or a lot of other unpleasantnesses. But then nobody else had, either.)

Basically, the good parts were the parts right around Gerda and me.

The other parts weren't necessarily good even then, and some weren't good at all. According to the news, somebody, or somebodies, had set fire to ten of Sao Paolo's biggest skyscrapers at once, killing hundreds of people, and some other bodies had blown a hole in the side of the Straits of Gibraltar tunnel, drowning other hundreds, and someone closer to home had dropped a hand grenade into one of the women's toilets at the *ristorante*, not causing any serious mayhem but making a couple of days of unattractive labor for Maury Tesch's water supply workforce, and thus for him, as well. And then, just when personal things were going so well, all of a sudden they got just that little bit better.

Like the afternoon when, finishing up for the day and looking forward to a dull evening because the Bastard had put Gerda on a late job, I was just turning the grog shop over to my second-shift replacement when I heard my name being yelled. Cedric the Pimp, running across the street as he called, his cell to his ear, grinning all over because he had a surprise for me. "What, did you turn off your phone?" Which I had, because I always did at change of shift because I didn't want the Bastard coming up with some new orders, but Cedric didn't wait for an answer. "So get yourself into a toga, Brad! Gerda had a cancellation! You're going to make her ninth dinner partner, only you have to get there fast!"

I made it. I was sweating from trotting there in the hot Pompeiian sun, but I arrived minutes before the string of litters that brought the paying guests did.

The villa where Gerda was doing her hosting was the one right across from the Forum that was marked as "The House of the Tragic Poet" on all the souvenir maps. It got its name from a big mural showing a rehearsal of a drama, but Gerda and I didn't call it that. We called it the Doghouse be- cause of its mosaic of a barking dog, with the words "*Cave Canum*." (Meant "Beware of the Dog." Even I knew that much without checking out the guide chips, because what else would you say to scare people away from a mean mutt?)

All seven of the paying guests were inspecting the dog, and the wall mosaics, and the decorations on the ceiling (virt) and the flowering shrubs in the atrium (real) with the self-conscious tittering of customers who know they're paying way too much for an obvious tourist trap, but have made up their minds to go along with the gag. This lot was all Korean, five grown-ups and a pair of ten-year-old twin girls. Who, when Gerda came out to greet them, turned out to be a lot more interested in what she was wearing than in her memorized lecture on First Century Roman dining customs.

I didn't blame them. Gerda was looking particularly gorgeous. It didn't hurt that she was ten centimeters taller than the tallest of the Koreans, but what the girls were murmuring over were the clothes she wore. I hadn't ever seen her in her lady-of-the-villa outfit before. She was worth looking at. Her gown was silk, and it clung nicely to her, entertaining the three male Korean grown-ups as well as me. She wore gold rings on all eight fingers of her two hands and on one of her thumbs. There was more gold around her neck, and on her ears and in her hair, and some of the gold was set with nearly marble-sized gems—rubies (maybe), emeralds (I thought), possibly opals, pearls, and what looked like carved amber of several colors and many shapes. I assumed the stones were all fake. They didn't look fake, though, and Gerda wore them like a queen.

Then the eating began.

I can't say what we ate, exactly, because a lot of it I couldn't identify. There wasn't any of that sheep-stuffed-with-bunny-rabbit kind of thing, but there were almost a dozen each of various sorts of flesh, fish, and fowl. The original Pompeiians appeared to have liked to stew tiny songbirds in honey, but I didn't, and the hamburgery mess some of the poultry was stuffed with smelled almost as bad as Maury's wursts. I didn't eat any of that. All the adult Koreans gamely at least tried it, though, while Gerda, chatting us all up while we ate, kept busy enough giving orders to the servers that the Koreans probably couldn't tell she was just pushing it around on her plate. Anyway, whatever they were giving us there was a lot of it, served to us by pretty young "slave" girls. They were Indentureds, of course, and I knew one of them. She had sold the tourists those little over-the-counter loaves of fresh-baked bread at

Modestus's enterprise, while I was heaving that damn wheel around. There was wine, seriously watered down for the little girls but tastier and in more varieties than the slop I peddled on the via. There were a dozen kinds of fruit—what looked like authentic First Century Roman varieties of fruits, too, all lumpy and tiny by modern standards, but tastier, too.

The meal went on for hours. Like a good hostess Gerda directed the conversation along appropriate First Century lines.

Did they think the new Flavian amphitheater in Rome—what we moderns called the Colosseum—would be finished in time for the games? And if the Emperor Vespasian should pass away, the gods forfend, would his son Titus do as well as the old man? And how had they liked the morning's gladiatorial displays? She impressed me. I found out later that one of her earrings concealed a tiny radio, feeding her facts and topics, but she still impressed me. It was a wonderful job. The Koreans apparently thought so, too, in spite of the fact that one of the little girls seemed to have hit her watered wine a little too hard. She puked fish soup and stewed pears all over the floor mosaics of food and flowers and one of Gerda's sandaled feet. Never mind. I, at least, was having a good time, and I hoped the Korean family thought they'd got their money's worth.

And then it got better. I don't mean for the Koreans. They tipped Gerda and the slave girls really well, shook my hand (but didn't tip me), and then went off to whatever the next thing in their lives was meant to be. I mean that it was better for me because then we had the rest of the day together, just Gerda and me.

Gerda hadn't known when the dinner would be over so she'd made no plans for the evening. Nor had I. So after we were back in our own clothes and her feet washed of ten-year-old throw-up she had an idea. "It's a nice day," she said. "Want to walk around the Jubilee? We could use our passes, maybe see some of the virt shows—there's a good crucifixion, or the one where they throw the slaves into the water to be eaten alive by the fish."

I'd heard about those shows but hadn't had any burning desire to see them. I said, "Not my kind of thing. But if you want to I'll go along for company."

She shook her head. "Saw them. So let's just walk up to the dorm."

We did, with glowering old Mount Vesuvius frowning down at us from the far hills and, high on the slopes, the distant figures of virt technicians setting up the projectors for gigantic displays to come. Not many of the other volunteers were about, so when Gerda said it would be nice to just stretch out on the grass by the dorm's tiny swimming pool we did, her head on my arm, our shoes kicked off and our bare feet touching. She yawned and said, "I wasn't sure it would be a good idea to have you there for the dinner, but it was fun."

I didn't exactly answer. I yawned myself. When I finished yawning I opened my mouth to change the subject—to mention, for instance, the fact that her bed was only a few dozen meters away and why weren't we getting into it?

But she changed the subject first. It turned out that it wasn't sex she was interested in just then, it was conversation. "Brad," she said, leaning back to get comfortable for a good, long chat, "you know what? You've never told me much about yourself. So how about it? What were you like as a kid?"

I turned my head to get a better look at her. Her eyes were closed, but she had the appearance of someone settling in for an extended period of listening. I thought that plan could possibly be changed, so I kissed her ear and murmured into it, "I guess I was pretty much like any other kid. Why don't we—"

She pulled her head away. "Please, Brad," she said. "I want to know."

That was pretty definite. I didn't have any choice anymore, so I told her how we'd been rich, then poor, and then I came over as an Indentured.

That wasn't enough. She was shaking her head. "More," she said. "What was your family like?"

I could not really imagine why anybody would want to hear about Mr. and Mrs. Dan Sheridan, but I tried to oblige. "Well," I said, "when do I start? My father was a real estate dealer in Kansas City. My mother——" I did my best. I gave her a fairly complete, if concise, history of my father's business and my mother's social concerns, but when I finished she wasn't satisfied.

She shook her head. "You didn't mention your uncle DeVries," she said.

That got my full attention. "Oh, hell," I said, "do I have to go on talking about him all my life? How'd you know I had an uncle DeVries?"

"Security isn't as secure as you might think, hon. What was it like, being related to a terrorist?"

I wasn't really satisfied with that answer, but I didn't really want to prolong the idle conversation part of our evening together. So I told her how Uncle Devious had courted and won the hand of my mother's kid sister, Carolyn. "I figured that was charity on his part, really," I told her. "Aunt Carrie was the homely one of the family, and sickly, too." So sickly in fact, that they were married less than three years when her immune system finally collapsed entirely and she died—of which particular disease I didn't know, because she had half a dozen or so of them at once. So Uncle Devious gave her a fine funeral and a four-ton marble headstone, with space for his name to go under hers when the time came, and everybody said how much he grieved for her. Of course, he inherited her trust fund. But he wouldn't keep any part of it, he said. He immediately donated the whole amount to the Tibetan orphans. He said.

"Which meant to his terrorist buddies, right?" Gerda put in. "Was that all the money he raised for them?"

"Oh, hell, no." So I told her how good Uncle Devious had been at talking the older and foolisher members of my parents' set into donating chunks of their surplus capital to his fund.

"Not so much Dad, though. He did get my dad to give him a ten-hectare parcel of unbuildable floodplain that he'd acquired in a package deal and had no other use for. But that was a scam for my father, too." So then I had to explain the United States tax code to her, and how my father turned over the land and took his charitable-deduction tax break—not for what the land was worth, but for maybe ten times that.

Gerda objected to that. "But didn't the tax people do their own appraisal?"

"Would've, sure. But it was out of their hands." So then I had to explain how Uncle Devious sold the land to a dummy corporation, which sold it to another, and so on until there was just too much paper to untangle. "The value of a thing, after all," I informed her, "is what you can sell it for."

"And your father wanted to help the Tibetan orphans?"

"My father didn't give a pig's fart for the Tibetan orphans. Or for Uncle Devious, come to that. He did like to screw the tax people, though."

She was silent for a moment, but I didn't give her a chance for more questions. All this talking about my past life had started me wondering about hers. So, "Enough," I said. "Now it's your turn."

She made a little face, but fair was fair and Gerda was conspicuously fair. Well, not when it came to picking up a check, I mean, but mostly. She thought for a moment, then said, "Did I ever tell you that I was overweight as a kid? I was. It wasn't fun, either." Then she began to tell me what it had been like to be a fat little girl in a prosperous family in a rich city, namely Munich. And how frequently her brothers kept getting arrested for being drunk and disorderly at the Oktoberfests, when you had to get really seriously drunk and disorderly to attract attention from the Oktoberfests cops, all thoroughly busy with several thousand other disorderly drunks. (Not just drunk enough to throw up, her brother Gerhardt had been, but drunk enough to throw up into the lap of a priest who was also a cousin of the mayor. And then punching out the priest when he complained.) And how she had always loved skiing down that gentle hill outside of town that had been bulldozed together out of ruins—no, not from some terrorist attack, or not exactly, she told me, but ruins that had been the result of bombing missions by British and American planes way back in World War II. And what it had been like for her and her family, those February days in 2062, when all the news was about nothing but the terrible volcanic explosion in America, millions and millions dead, famous cities buried, the whole world's commerce, travel, finances disrupted as a result. And—the part she remembered best—the spectacular sunsets that they had all those winter days, as the millions of tons of dust that once had been parts of Wyoming, Idaho, and Montana filled the air as they circled around and around the globe.

And then she did say, finally, "Let's go to bed." So we did. Only as I was getting out of my slacks something rolled out of my pocket, and it was the great big, fake-gold thumb ring that had been part of my costume for the dinner. "Shit," I said, looking at it.

"What, that thing?" Gerda asked, getting nicely close to naked. "Don't worry about it. You can just turn it in to Jeremy Jones in the morning."

"Sure," I said, but I didn't mean it. I didn't want to spend any more time with the Bastard than I had to. Anyway, I was less interested in conversation than in getting into that bed where Gerda was already waiting.

As I climbed in, she said penitently, "Did I bore you with all that talk about my family?"

"Not a bit," I said, which was true. But even as I was reaching out for her I was thinking that, funny thing, apart from the Yellowstone thing none of her reminiscences had any dates in them.

But really, what did I care if she didn't want to let me know how old she was? I had been pretty sure all along that she had to be more than my own twenty-five. Late twenties, at least. Or thirty, or perhaps thirty-five—hell, I didn't care if she was forty! She was still my girl.

If there had been any chance that I'd take Gerda's advice it didn't last. When Gerda's opticle woke her up it was to tell her that she'd been assigned to the evening shift at the live-action whorehouse, but when I checked my own it was business as usual at the wine bar. So when I'd got myself dressed for the job I barged into the Bastard's dispatch room. "Could you do us a favor?" I asked, my tone really polite because he'd been talking on the speaker and the way he looked at me showed that I was interrupting. "If you could just see that Gerda and I are on the same shift as much as you can—"

He didn't do that. He blew his top at me instead. "Jesus, Sheridan! Haven't you been enough of a pain in the ass already?" Which was just his way of saying, "Gosh, I'm afraid I'll have to say no to that," but it was enough to chase any idea of returning the ring to him right out of my head. So I went off to do the job they paid me to do.

It was a swelteringly soggy day, the only kind of Italian summer day that's worse than the blazing hot ones, and Cedric the Pimp was giving me that I-can't-live-without-a-shot-of-your-lousy-wine look from across the via. I made believe I didn't see him. When I took advantage of my lack of customers to bend down to my eyepiece there wasn't anything good on it. I don't know what I'd been hoping for. Maybe (listen, I was still at the cute stage of being in love) for some little I-can't-wait-for-tonight message slipped in from Gerda before she went off to be a housemaid moonlighting as a whore. There wasn't, though. There wasn't even any very exciting news when I clicked over to the public channels. More terrorist stuff, sure, but I could get pretty sick of one more batch of derailed trains and burned-alive hostages.

There was, of course, the usual begging letter from my mother:

> *Brad, dearest,*
> *Your wonderful gift just arrived and was gratefully received, as always. The estimate for repairing the community shower just came in, and we were trying to figure out where we would get the money to pay our share, so it got here at a wonderful moment, although it's only about half the bill.*
> *All my love, dear. Your dad is well, but still kind of depressed.*

Well, that gave me something other than Gerda to think about. Like wondering where I was going to get the cash for the next remittance. However much I watered the wine the customers drank and how vigorously I reused the leftover fractions they didn't, there just wasn't enough action around the wineshop to keep me, and my parents, solvent. I was having a serious cash flow problem. And Gerda was it.

I took another look at Mom's letter, in case I'd missed some crumb of good news. I hadn't. There wasn't any. My dad was depressed, was he? That wasn't a surprise, and another thing that wasn't a surprise was that she sent me her love but he didn't. I hadn't expected he would.

Across the street Cedric the Pimp was still giving me imploring looks. He was huddled away from the rain under the icon of his calling, the plaster penis, two meters long, that hung above his doorway to let customers know what was for sale inside. It wasn't really keeping the rain off. It wasn't drawing customers, either, because there were hardly any customers along the via to be drawn just then.

Even in good weather, Cedric's wasn't the most profitable enterprise on the via. It couldn't compare with the "real" brothels around the Stabian baths, where at least the "whores" were flesh and blood, even if not touchable by the paying customers. Not that that stopped those bastards, though; last time Gerda worked there she came back with little pinch marks on her butt. That didn't seem to make her very mad—mostly she thought it was a little bit funny—but what it made me feel was something else again.

Cedric's whores, of course, were all virts. I'd been inside the place just once to look it over—tiny cubicles with a narrow platform set against one wall, like a cot in a prison cell—and each cubicle's door marked with a painting of whatever specific variety of sexual act its occupant claimed to be particularly good at. I went once for a look, had no desire to go back. Cedric's was one of the few jobs in the Giubileo that I thought were more boring than my own.

And right there is when I heard Cedric's sad little whine from behind me ("Uh, Brad, I was wondering, could you spare a drop of your joy juice for a friend?"), and realized that I hadn't been discouraging enough. Cedric was right behind me, having taken advantage of the rain to sneak across the via.

Of course that wasn't the first time Cedric had come begging. Begging was what he did. He'd never had a euro to spare that whole summer, and until he got that whopping Murmansk indenture paid off he never would.

But I gave him a cup of wine all the same, and while he was lifting it to his lips I slid the ring out of the fold in my diaper where I'd been carrying it and displayed it to him. "Look what a dumb thing I did," I said.

When I explained what the dumb thing had been Cedric was reassuring. "That's"—swallow, swallow, most of the wine already down his throat—"no problem, Brad. Just turn it in to the Welsh Bastard when you're off this afternoon. Say, do you think you could spare a little more—?"

I didn't let him finish that. "I'd rather stay away from the Bastard," I said. "We aren't on such great terms, but, hey, you don't have that problem, do you? How'd you like to give the ring to him for me?"

"Aw, no, Brad," he said, his tone both sorrowful and apologetic—and his now empty wine cup held out before him in case I felt like refilling it. "You know the first thing he'd ask me is where I got it, and then I'd have to say it was from you anyway, wouldn't I?"

Well, he naturally would. I didn't have an answer, but Cedric wasn't quite through. He pushed the cup a centimeter closer and said, "What about the union?"

I scowled at him. "What about it?"

"They've probably got somebody who could help you, don't you think? Did you ever read what it says on your card?" I never had, mostly because it was in Italian. Cedric translated it for me. " 'To do for you what you cannot do for yourself,' right? So let them do it."

What he was saying made sense—enough sense that I refilled his cup. Which he swallowed in no time, because the rain was stopping, and tourists were beginning to venture down the via again. By the time Cedric had scooted back to his own side of the road I had my first customers of the day, and the problem of what to do about the ring looked soluble.

Those customers were a pair of Danish blondes, whispering, no, mostly giggling to each other in their own impenetrable language, plus the pair of horny Italian youths following them who were what they were giggling about. English was difficult for all of them, but it didn't matter. The girls had no problem in understanding that the boys wanted to pick them up. The boys were quite clear on the ground rules, too. If they wanted that to happen they were going to have to beg for it. I understood them both. Well, I didn't have to understand any actual language, did I? I knew exactly what was going on without comprehending a single spoken word. And so did everybody else in sight.

When the boys came to the point when it was time to show what big sports they were they whispered to each other worriedly, then took the plunge. They ordered a couple of wines for the girls, who giggled but accepted them. When I filled their cups I decided the four of them were sufficiently interested in each other that they weren't going to care about anything I might do, and it was time I checked my dismal financial position again.

So I inched my cell out of its hiding place, wiped Mom's letter from the screen, and did a quick look up and down of the Via dell'Abbondanza. A gaggle of twenty or thirty Korean tourists marched briskly after their banner-carrying leader just east of us—not really in step, but not much out of it, either. To the west, between us and the Stabian Baths, were some smaller groups, some of them laughing and pointing at that virt litter with the virt Pompeiian whore, making its regular 11:47 AM appearance. It looked like I had a moment. I was already dialing up my money management program and had the cell in my hand when, all of a sudden, things changed. The virt litter queerly flickered and flowed and broke into a bright fog of quickly dissipating sparks of light.

And everything around me went weird at once.

What I mean by that is that everything in sight was melting and changing before my eyes. Façades of some buildings, second stories of others, bits of Roman statuary and odds and ends of wall plaques and ornamentation, they all flickered and disappeared, just as the litter had. All that were left were the bare, broken, virtless and two-thousand-year-old stone walls of the original Pompeii. The fake living Pompeii had become an authentic ruin again, and the little gasps of surprise from the customers turned quickly into a frightened babble. A fairly loud babble, that is, especially from the Korean group. A bunch of people yelling remarks at each other from one end of their caterpillar to the other made a lot more noise than a couple of Romanians or Papua New Guineans exchanging close-range expressions of worry with each other.

About five seconds later my cell along with the cells of the pimp across the street and the laundryman next door and everybody else around who worked for the Jubilee gave their five staccato emergency burps and began to yell at us: "All personnel! Hear this! There has been a power interruption! You must keep guests reassured and maintain order! Power will be restored as quickly as possible. Meanwhile, prevent panic!"

It didn't say how we were supposed to do that.

On the other hand, nobody in my part of the city actually seemed to be doing any panicking. By the look of most of the customers they found the event entertaining. It might have been worse if it had been night when the power died. It hadn't. The bright Italian sun didn't need any help from electricity to keep the world well lit. Even the remote *bleep-bleepbleep* of emergency vehicles—maybe Security, maybe UN, I couldn't tell—didn't scare anyone. Those noises weren't very close, anyway. They came from past the baths, maybe as far as the Civic Forum, I thought. Still—powered vehicles on Pompeii's two-thousand-year-old streets? I couldn't believe it had been allowed.

Anyway, for the next hour or so, until at last everything sparkled into its designed shape again, my biggest problem wasn't quelling panic. It was keeping up with orders for refills. My crowd of wine drinkers were laughing and telling each other what they'd been doing when the generators went out. I actually got rid of more wine in those couple of hours than I had in any full day before. Would have sold more than that, too, but by the time I went off duty every vat in my shop had been drunk dry. Even the hydromels.

When my shift was finally over everybody in the refectory was talking about it. Maury Tesch was the one with the most information. "It was a little black guy did it all," he proclaimed. "From Gabon, somebody said. He looked like any other regular tourist to me, except, you know, he got kind of roughed up when they took him away." But even Maury didn't know what the terrorist's grievances had been, or what organization he represented.

Nobody knew where Security had taken him, either, but a few people had caught enough of what the Security guys had been yelling back and forth to each other to be able to piece out some of what he had done. Somehow or other the man had managed to get into the main electronic complex that was buried in the caves under the Forum. He didn't seem to have been very well prepared for whatever it was he was planning to do, though. You'd think he would have carried enough explosives to blow the complex back into its two-thousand-year-old cindery rubble. He hadn't. All he carried was a fire ax he'd grabbed off some wall.

You had to hand it to him, though. He got a lot of mischief done with this primitive tool.

He and his ax had disrupted all the Jubilee's electronics. Not a single virt exhibit had been left functioning, all the way up to the Villa of the Mysteries, kilometers away from the city of Pompeii itself. That was the impressive part. The rest of what the poor a-hole did wasn't. When you added up all the actual physical damage he'd done you had to admit it was pretty trivial. Economic harm? The laugh was on him there, because business was better than ever. It wasn't just in my wineshop that the tourists decided to stick around. All over Pompeii, there were more customers in the city an hour after the shutdown than there had been before.

Of course a lot of the scheduled spectacles had suffered. The sacrificed bull for the Temple of Isis didn't roar out its virtual agony or spill its liters of virtual blood when they cut its virtual throat. Its throat didn't get cut at all, there being no even virtual throat there to be even virtually cut. My generally absent roommate, Jiri Kopthellen, was flat-out exhausted by the time the day was done. He had been working the amphitheater as a gladiator that day, and because the crowds kept coming the show had kept going on. They didn't have the large-animal virts of elephants and rhinos and bears to "kill" over and over. They didn't even have the virt "Christians" to be eaten by ravenous virt "lions," so all twelve of the flesh-and-blood gladiators on duty had had to work every show. It came to six pairs of mano-a-mano bouts in that one evening, one show right after the last, and Jiri was just about worn out.

When Gerda came by she planted a kiss on the top of my head. "It was unbelievable, hon! You wouldn't believe how many people showed up to look at the dirty mosaics—the beat-up old real ones, I mean, not the augmented ones we usually show—and the graffiti." Then she took off for her orientation class. Which, as I have mentioned, was not the same as mine.

While I was talking to Gerda, Maury Tesch came in. He threw me a kind of quick nod, and then sat himself down before one of the wall screens.

I wondered what was on his mind, so I walked up behind him to see which service had his attention. On the screen was a man in doctor's whites, in what looked like a hospital room. There was a bed behind him, and in it either a child or a really small grown-up, with a second doctor standing over him, or her, or whatever. The doctor the camera was on was being interviewed by a pretty Ethiopian girl, about what I could not say.

I made a logical, but wrong, assumption. "That guy really screwed up today, didn't he?" I said to the back of Maury's head.

When Maury turned to face me his expression was somber. "I guess you're talking about that clown from Gabon? Sure. He was a nuisance, all right. I had to check every damn flow meter in the Jubilee manually, just in case the power outage screwed up our telemetry. But that isn't what I was looking at. Have you ever heard of necrotizing fasciitis?"

I not only hadn't ever heard of it, I had no idea how to spell it. When I shook my head Maury said, "There's that little girl in Puteoli—you've been to Puteoli, right? And she and two of her schoolmates have come down with this really nasty disease. Did you get a good look at her?" He didn't wait for an answer, just zoomed the picture past the head of the doctor and right onto the figure in the hospital bed. Then I did get a—no, not what Maury had called a good look because there was nothing at all good about what I saw, but certainly a clearer one. The person in the bed was a young Italian girl, maybe ten or twelve years old. Both of her arms were totally bandaged. So was one leg. Unfortunately, the other was not. It was normal looking enough as far down as the knee, but below that it wasn't. Where there should have been a skinny little-girl calf instead was a pair of the second doctor's hands holding a sterile cloth, and in the cloth a chunk of raw and bloody meat.

"Holy crap," I said.

Maury nodded. "Yes," he said thoughtfully, "it's pretty ugly to look at." Then he snapped the picture off and gave me a big smile. I thought it didn't look very sincere. Was something troubling him? "So," he said, "want to get something to eat before class? We've got plenty of time."

What he said was true enough. But Maury's little display had pretty much canceled any appetite I might have had just then. Besides, I had an errand that needed running. "'Fraid not, Maury," I told him. "I've got to do something first." And I left him standing there.

I won't say I'd forgotten how that little girl's leg had looked, but it wasn't the kind of thing I tried hard to remember, either, and anyway I had to concentrate on trying to find the union headquarters.

To get there you had to duck under the tracks that led to the electric station and climb a slight hill. The office was in an old-fashioned office building, the shape of a truncated cone, five stories high, walls of pearly, translucent glass, with balconies at every level.

The union office didn't take up the whole building. Not even very much of it, actually, and in fact not even all of the third story. The suite of offices across from the elevator bank belonged to a firm of lawyers, and you had to pass three dentists and a podiatrist before you came to the door marked "Confederazione Sindacale Lavoratori del Giubileo di Pompeii." Once inside it got easy. The man I needed to see about returning misplaced Jubilee knickknacks was right down the hall and, the receptionist said, would be glad to see me at once.

Actually that turned out to be untrue. He wasn't glad at all.

His office was nice enough, with a window that looked out on the distant slopes of Mount Vesuvius, but the man who was just rising from his seat behind a desk, with the beginnings of a smile of greeting on his face and his right hand half extended to shake mine, wasn't a stranger. I'd met him before. He was old Vespasiano Gatti himself. And he was clearly not feeling any more cordial to me today than he had been the last time we met.

The handshake offer was retracted and the potential smile replaced by a scowl even before I got the ring out of my pocket to hand him. Then, for a moment, he almost did smile. "What's this?" he asked. "Why have you appropriated an item of property belonging to the Giubileo for yourself?"

I didn't care for the look on his face, but I thought maybe he had just jumped to some wrong conclusions, and all I needed to do was explain the facts.

That wasn't a maybe, it was plain wrong. Although I gave him a complete and quite truthful explanation of what had happened he didn't go for it. "You were evidently tempted by the ring," he mused. "Once having stolen it, however, you realized discovery was inevitable. So, naturally enough, you decided to turn it in."

"Hey," I said. "Stop right there. I didn't steal anything."

He looked honestly perplexed. "Are you thinking that your decision to return the ring canceled the theft? I doubt that a court will take that view."

He got me there. "Court? What court?"

"Well," he said meditatively, "I imagine a municipal police court first. Of course that's for the prosecutors to decide, isn't it? Excuse me."

There was more hostility coming from that man than I could handle. I didn't know what to do about it, especially when I saw that he was fingering his deskpad. "Hold it," I said. "What are you writing?"

It was obvious that I was annoying him, but he stopped writing long enough to read back what he'd already put down. " 'The accused, Bradley Wilson Sheridan, American nationality and Indentured, after removing the article in question from its proper custody, retained it for forty-eight hours before deciding to turn it in.' Anything wrong with that?"

"It's wrong as hell! The way you have it, I stole it and then changed my mind about keeping it because I was afraid I'd get caught."

"Yes? Are you claiming that's incorrect?"

"Of course it's incorrect! I didn't steal the damn thing, I just didn't get around to returning it."

"I see," he said. His fingers got busy on his pad again, and then he looked up. "I've added your claim. Now shall I print this up for your signature?"

By then I was gritting my teeth, which made him look more closely at me. "Is something wrong, Mr. Sheridan?"

I couldn't help it. "Yes," I said, hearing the way my voice was almost cracking with anger, unable to do anything about it. "One question. Why do you hate me? Is it just because I'm Indentured?"

For a moment I thought he hadn't heard me, because he took a long time to speak. Finally he said, "No, it's not that. I'm Indentured, too, did you not know that? What do you think I'm doing in these three imbecile jobs?" He didn't wait for an answer to that. He slammed the drawer shut and set its lock and said, quite conversationally, "I do hate you, and all your kind, Mr. Sheridan, but it is simply because you are an American. You people ruined my life."

Then he went on to tell me in detail just how his life had been ruined.

He hadn't been exaggerating. What had loused his family up was simply good old Yellowstone. At the time the super-volcano sneezed out all that rock and ash and dust his family, he told me bitterly, had just taken a great financial step. His father had sold everything they owned and borrowed all he could. What he did with the proceeds was to purchase twenty-six hectares of prime Lacryma Cristi vinyards, right on Vesuvius's lower slope—Gatti waved at the mountain, looming over the farmlands and villages past Pompeii. It had been a very sensible move, he told me. The crops had been reliably good. Their existing winemaking facilities could handle the entire harvest, new land and all. It was the obvious right thing to do, and the longer his father waited to do it the more expensive acquiring these new hectares would be. The time, then, was perfect.

Only it wasn't, because that's when Yellowstone did its thing.

Before they could pick their first crop Yellowstone's clouds of stinking dust and burning acid particles had darkened Italy's sky. Had darkened pretty much the whole world's skies, when you came right down to it, but it was only those twenty-six hectares of Vesuvian slopes that concerned him, because they were his family's.

Yellowstone hadn't doomed all the world's farmers, but it did cost many of them quite a lot of money—for extra fertilizers, extra irrigation to wash the acid off the plants, insecticides to hold the number of plant-eating bugs to a bearable minimum, anti-mold sprays of a dozen kinds. And at that particular moment money was what his family was fresh out of. Paying for the vineyard had bled them dry. Other grape growers dug deep and weathered the storm, but for his family there was nowhere left to dig.

"They thought it was funny, even those other victims," he said, morosely reminiscing. "They called my father Fungus-spore Vittorio." He paused there, his eyes on me. Looking for sympathy? I couldn't tell.

After a moment I said, "You know, you guys certainly got a lousy break, but it wasn't our fault. Americans got hurt a lot worse than you did."

He shrugged. "Do you think that should make a difference to me? It doesn't. What ruined our family came from America, so America has to pay."

He actually seemed cheerful about it as he skated a printout across the desk to me. "Don't forget your receipt for the ring, Mr. Sheridan. I do not know what action Security will take. Perhaps none; they are sometimes unnecessarily credulous, and they may choose to accept your excuses. But perhaps then there will be another time, in which the evidence against you will be more clear. And, Mr. Sheridan, if such a thing comes to my attention, I promise I will see that you receive everything due you."

So by the time I got to my Security briefing my head was so full of Gatti's injustice that I barely looked at the teacher's desk. Actually if I had been thinking about the briefing at all I imagine that I supposed all the old professor was going to do was talk about the day's inept terrorist.

The old professor didn't, though. He wasn't even there.

The person who replaced Bartolomeo Mazzini I recognized, with no pleasure at all, as Piranha Woman, the one who had handled my first Security interview.

What I had mostly hoped concerning her was that I would never have to see her again. So finding that she was my new teacher was that day's next big disappointment. The one—tiny—consolation was that she seemed to be having a conversation with whomever was on the other end of her opticle link, and thus perhaps hadn't noticed that I was late.

The nearest empty seat was next to the woman named Elfreda. Her last name, I was told, was Barcowicz. She was dark, slim, short, about as unlike Gerda as any woman could be, except that if Gerda hadn't been my girl I might very likely have tried sniffing after Elfreda. What might have made that more likely on this particular evening was that, unusual for Elfreda Barcowicz, she didn't seem to be attached to anyone. Of course, being plentifully supplied with Gerda I wasn't interested in additional female company. Still, I gave Elfreda a friendly smile. That could have been pushing my luck a little, because Elfreda might have considered herself a little out of my class. Elfreda was Indentured, just like me, but you'd never know it. Somebody said her debt was down under a thousand euros, which meant that before the end of summer she'd be a free agent.

Anyway, all Elfreda gave me back was a blank look. Then our instructor lost that faraway gaze that meant she was having a conversation with someone not physically present, pushed her opticle out of the way, made a note on her pad, gave me a glance that wasn't blank at all—or friendly—and began to talk.

"Tonight," Piranha Woman said, "we are going to try to understand what terrorists are motivated by, so that we can better work to defeat them. In my lecture I will occasionally ask a question. When the questions are rhetorical, no response is required from any of you. When the question is not rhetorical I will point to one of you for an answer—who will give it promptly and correctly, or will face consequences. Is that understood? Good. Now let us ask ourselves what terrorism is all about."

She pursed those narrow lips, looking around the room. If it had been the old guy talking, probably one of us might have answered that question. Piranha Woman wasn't pointing at any of us, though, and we had just heard her ground rules. So nobody spoke. Then, after a moment, she took a swallow of water from the pitcher on her lectern and began to talk. One by one she went over some of the most famous terrorist groups of those old Twentieth Century days when terrorism first began to be a major concern: the Red Army Faction and the Weathermen and Aum Shinrikyo and Baader-Meinhof and Al-Qaeda and Hamas and the Irgun and the Stern Gang and the Rajneeshees in the American state of Oregon and the RISE group in the American city of Chicago and the IRA and the one the Serbs called "Union or Death." Then she paused for a moment, and then she said, "The question is, what do they all have in common?"

She looked around the room, very much as though she wanted one of us to volunteer an answer. She didn't point, though, so none of us did.

Then she gave a swift, stern bob of the head and did point. And the person she pointed at was me.

"Stand up," she said. I stood up. "So tell me, Mr. Sheridan"—it did not improve the situation for me to discover that she remembered my name—"what is it that all those groups have in common?"

Unsurprisingly, I didn't know the answer to her question. That caused Piranha Woman to make it clear to me that, while it was bad enough to come late to the briefing, at least I could have come prepared. Then she asked for volunteers. Elfreda's hand shot up. "Because they were all trying to stop some great social change," she said. That was the right answer. Piranha Woman told her she could sit down, which I guess was Elfreda's reward for being right. Since I hadn't been right, I didn't get that reward, and in fact Piranha Woman left me standing there, with my bare face hanging out, for the whole rest of the briefing.

She didn't stop with the Twentieth Century, either. She gave us a synoptic of The Great Terrorist Atrocities of all time, from the Nuovi Risorgimenti who disabled Venice's flood protectors just when the spring tides were due to the Very Greens who dynamited the Atchafalaya dams so that the Mississippi River no longer flowed past the ghost town that had once been New Orleans. And she mentioned Brian Bossert, the legendary terrorist mastermind who finished his career by amputating the city of Toronto from Canada's economy for two full weeks one spring, using a staff of no more than five accomplices of whom four had no skill more complicated than the pulling of a trigger. ("At least there was one good thing about Toronto," Piranha Woman said, actually sounding quite pleased. "Bossert got himself killed in the explosion. It wasn't a bad trade.") And all the while the four walls of our room were showing examples of their master terrorist handiwork. We saw the lopped-off Empire State Building, and the Golden Gate Bridge approaches that no longer led to any bridge, and the long lines of empty caskets waiting to be filled from the hordes of shivering Muscovites when the power lines had been destroyed one January.

But it came to an end.

Piranha Woman turned out to be a stickler for everybody's punctuality, not just mine. At the thirtieth second of the sixtieth minute she clapped her hands and said, "You are finished for this evening. By the next session you are all required to have familiarized yourselves with the datafile on each of the individuals and groups I have named tonight."

And she turned and left the room without bothering to say good night.

Outside it was already dark, with a sky full of bright Italian stars overhead. I stretched and yawned. I had turned my opticle off so it wouldn't buzz at me during Piranha Woman's briefing. When I pulled it out of my bellybag to put it back on the little blue message flasher was blinking.

The funny thing is that I really didn't want to turn it back on to take that message. I can't say that I knew what it was going to be. I was just suddenly pretty sure I wasn't going to like it.

Sure enough, I didn't.

The face looking up at me was my Gerda's, and the look on her face told me the whole thing before she said one word. "Oh, hon," she said, tone sad, remorseful—and firm. "I can't tell you how sorry I am about this. You know my great-uncle Gerhart?" I didn't. "The rich one? The one with the dacha outside of Moscow?"

That began to register. I did recall that Gerda had once said something about a Russian summer home somewhere in the family. But then she went on with her news bulletin, and it was bad. "Sweetie, he died. Left the dacha to me, would you believe it? Only the thing is I have to get up there to take possession of it. There's a lot of legal stuff." She bit her lip, and I could almost see the beginnings of a tear in her eye. "Oh, hell. I hate having to go away from you like this, dear Brad. The good thing is, just imagine what kind of good times you and I are going to have in the dacha after I get all the law nonsense straightened away. And, hon, I give you my word, I'll be back just as soon as I can. A day or two. Three at the most. And then—"

Her expression changed. "Oh, damn it, there's the taxi, and if I'm going to make it to the zep I can't wait. See you soon!"

And that was the end of the message, and just about the end of all the good feelings that the city of Pompeii had for me.

9

WORLD WITHOUT GERDA

Well, it wasn't a day or two that she was gone. Naturally.

It wasn't four days, either, or five. It wasn't even six days, because when the seventh day came along she still hadn't come back. Hadn't even called. And there was a great big hole in my world where Gerda should have been, and wasn't.

I'd got used to having Gerda in my life. It wasn't as much fun without her. It wasn't even as interesting. The things that I would have treasured, and told Gerda about as soon as I saw her, and chuckled over with her— well, they had lost their savor and there was nothing about them to treasure now. Like the troop of Bengali Girl Scouts that came charging down the via looking for God knew what, only to be turned back by the virt Roman legions at the ropes. Or like the (I guess) gay lovers who were snapping at each other all the way down from the Stabian Baths, looked at my wine list and turned up their noses, paid Cedric for a tour of his make-believe whorehouse and came out looking appalled. And then went back toward the baths, now holding hands. Or like the Saudi nuns with burkas over the veils of their habits, or any of the couple of dozen other things that passed by my wineshop and that I certainly would have shared with Gerda. And the two of us would surely have talked over the fact that those sick Puteoli girls—there were seven of them now, and one was expected to die quite soon—had been visitors to the Jubilee. At their local Catholic junior high fifteen of them had baked cookies, mowed lawns, washed cars, baby-sat, and done just about everything they could think of to do to get money to pay for a bus charter to take them to the Jubilee. They'd had a great time (one of the uninfected ones wailed, dabbing the tears from her eyes). But they hadn't expected the additional bill to come due that they could pay only with gobbets of their flesh.

And Gerda wasn't there to share any of that with.

So I trudged along my dull and solitary life and I did my stupid job. And then, the seventh morning, I reported to the Bastard's dispatch room, wearing my slave smock and slave sandals because he'd said he wanted to inspect me before I went off to peddle my wine, and, hey, guess what, Maury Tesch was standing next to the Bastard's desk, wearing the exact same outfit as mine and almost looking as though he was enjoying it. "Right," the Bastard said, looking us over. "You'll do. What's the matter, Sheridan? Don't like your new partner? I thought Tesch was a pal of yours."

"Well, of course he is," I said, because why would I say anything else with him standing right there? "But what's he doing here? He works for the water department."

"What he's doing here is helping you out, Sheridan," the Bastard said, talking to me as though I were a somewhat handicapped four-year-old. "There're going to be crowds today, you know. Everybody that can be spared is on show duty today. Or have you forgotten what day it is?"

Indeed I had. Why shouldn't I? I didn't really care what day it was, for the same reason that I didn't care much about anything else, either. Still it did occur to me that taking a high-ranking waterworks technician like Maury and assigning him to help at a low-ranking job like mine must mean something special was happening. Maury came to my rescue. "It's the twenty-fourth, Brad," he said helpfully. "You know? The two thousandth anniversary of the death of Vespasian and the ascent of Titus to the throne? With a big celebration and fireworks and a sky show? Remember?"

. . .

By then I did remember, and by the time the wine bar had been open an hour I was glad to have Maury there. The Jubilee people had figured it right. Business was terrific. There were at least half a dozen customers busily lapping up my lousy wine all that morning, from the moment we opened. Throngs filled the via. There was even a waiting line in front of Cedric's whorehouse, for heaven's sake. And the promised sky show was as good as had been promised, and the best of it was repeated every hour on the hour, all day long.

I didn't really ever get a chance to watch the show straight through. Too many customers, too many interruptions. But by the third or fourth time it was on I had just about seen the whole thing, and it was worth looking at.

All that emplacing and fine-tuning the projectors had paid off. The show started with a flock of immense Roman gods—Jupiter, Venus, Mercury, the whole kit and caboodle of them—rolling across the sky in golden virt chariots, pulled by ten-meter-long white virt stallions. Five-meter-tall vestal virgins marched in procession from one horizon to the other—more virts, of course. Over the foothills to the north of the city a pyramid of immense logs erected itself, with wads of giant dried leaves and huge dead branches stuffed into the lowest tier for kindling. An immense human figure, silent, white-clad and majestic, lay in state on the topmost layer.

There weren't any subtitles. There didn't need to be. You didn't have to be told that what you were looking at was the Emperor Vespasian's funeral pyre.

Then torch-bearing arms reached out to the lowest level of wood. Flames danced up the sides. They merged. They grew. In a matter of moments towering masses of virt flames licked at the sun itself.

No heat came from those flames, of course. On the other hand, you couldn't look at them without rising a thirst . . . so, as I say, business was great.

The Bastard had been right. I had needed a helper that day. The two of us were kept busy filling the cups and taking the fake ancient Roman money and washing—well, rinsing, it was all we had time to do—the cups for the next customer.

I don't want to give the impression that I'd forgotten about Gerda. That never happened. It's true, though, that she wasn't really in the forefront of my mind on that particular day . . . and then, much sooner than I would have guessed, it was quitting time, and our relief wine sellers were waiting to take over and the supply slaves who had driven up in a three-wheeled cart were refilling our vats from the mule-driven cart.

"Well," Maury said, giving me a smile that was only a little bit tentative, "that wasn't so bad, was it?"

I cocked one eye at the head supply slave. He knew what I wanted to know. "Looks like about sixty, sixty-five liters gone," he called. "Pretty good day."

He could have made that a lot stronger. Sixty liters was nearly double what I sold on an average day, and I really had needed an extra pair of hands to deal with the customers. So I said, "Thanks, Maury," and the smile he gave me was twenty-four-karat happy.

And then there was a funny thing. He blinked, and the smile disappeared. He wasn't looking at me anymore, either. He looked as though there was something really nasty in his field of vision.

He was just standing there, so I thought it was only polite to say something. "Think we'll ever have another day this big?" I offered. "Like maybe on the anniversary of the actual eruption?"

His expression froze again, then he gave me a little laugh. "Who knows?" he asked. "How do we know if we'll even be alive then?" And then, when he saw the look on my face, he gave me a quick apology. "I don't mean to be a wet blanket, but I've had a lot of disappointments in my life. Makes me worry about the future. Anyway—" quick change of subject—"want to get something to eat now, Brad?" he said, all but lolling his tongue out and wagging his tail. So I said sure, and all the way to our changing rooms he was chattering away as though he had never had a somber thought in his life. We were sharing laughs at the expense of our morning's customers—the couple with the four kids, all of whom kept begging to go to some other place where they sold something besides wine, and the old Turkestani who had ordered one glass of each kind, set them in a row on the counter and worked his way through the varieties, one sip at a time. And the Taiwanese family who spoke no English or Italian or anything else either Maury or I could understand, but kept giving us taste verdicts on the wine by how tightly they held their noses.

So then we were dressed and trying to figure out where to go to eat lunch. "There's always the refectory," Maury said—back in the happy mood again. "Or, do you like Mexican? There's a new place outside the gate. Or there are lots of Italian places, only I know you don't like much garlic." He tipped me a wink, having touched on his usual garlic joke. "Which reminds me," he said. "My sausages are okay, right? Your room-mate hasn't been getting into them, has he?"

"Well," I said, "there's not much chance of that. He hasn't been here all week. Called in sick on, let me think, I guess it was Tuesday."

He stopped plugging his ear-cups into their proper places. He studied my face. "Sick?" he said considerately, more concerned than I would have expected. "Sick with what?"

I told him I had no idea, but he could check with the payroll machine. He nodded briskly at that, but his expression was abstracted again. "Good idea," he said. "Listen, come to think of it I'm not all that hungry right now. Give me a rain check?" And before I said I would he was gone.

I was only a little annoyed—hardly any, in fact, because I'd been getting tired of Maury's company, especially when the company I really desired wasn't around.

Then things looked up, and I forgot about Maury's changing moods.

I was just picking up a tray to get in line at the refectory when one of the cleanup people put her hand on my arm. "Don't do that," she said. "Go out in the kitchen, why don't you?"

I looked at her. "Why would I do that?"

"Oh, hell," she said impatiently, "why don't you just do it, and then you'll see why for yourself."

So I did, and there she was. Gerda. Sitting at a little table out of everybody's way, looking healthy and well rested as she picked at some fruit salad the kitchen staff had made up for her.

I didn't say a word. I just stopped short, staring at her. She didn't say anything right away, either, just jumped up and grabbed me in a monstrous hug. Then she stepped back, studying me. "Everything all right with you, Brad?" she asked, sounding anxious. "Want some pineapple?"

Since it was offered I took some. I chewed for a moment before I answered the question. "I'm fine, Gerda," I said. "A little confused, maybe, about why my girl takes off for a week without warning."

She nodded seriously. "Hon," she said, "sometimes you just can't help it. Want to go for a walk?"

That wouldn't have been my first choice. There were about a million things I wanted to say to her, or ask her—or, maybe, just yell at her—but of them all the one I picked to say out loud was, "Why not?"

"Fine," she said, standing up and flashing me an affectionate grin, "only I haven't checked in yet, so let's go by the Bastard's office first."

And again, rejecting all the other things I might have chosen to say, I said, "Why not?" She took my hand and gave it a fond squeeze, and held on to it as we walked, the very image of a loving couple, out of the refectory and past the building that held the changing rooms and the lockers and right up to the Welsh Bastard's office. Where I got to sit in the anteroom and listen to the shouting from inside when Gerda showed her face.

The shouting was pretty loud for a moment, but it didn't last. Then for a while I couldn't hear anything at all from inside. Then the door opened. Gerda was looking repentant. The Bastard was grinning a rueful grin. "Oh, hell," he said to her, "what's the use? You damn volunteers are more trouble than you're worth. Just make sure you show up for work tomorrow, okay?" And he gave her a friendly little pat on the behind and let her go.

We went for our walk.

See, what bothered me wasn't so much seeing the Bastard patting my girl's ass as though he had a right to. Naturally I didn't like it. Who would? And, naturally, it got me sort of wondering again about some things I had wondered quite a lot about before. For instance, one—how come the Bastard let Gerda get away with so much when he let hardly anybody else get away with anything at all?

Well, of course I didn't have to think real hard to think of a reason for that. All right, maybe he and Gerda had once had an affair. Why shouldn't they? Gerda certainly hadn't been a virgin when she and I got together, and what business of mine was it who she had slept with in the days before she was my girl? Answer: no business at all.

That was assuming that any such events had taken place before, but not during, the time when she was my girl.

I was, I had to admit to myself, getting pretty tangled up in the kind of suspicions I didn't really want to admit I had.

So I didn't talk much as we walked, still hand in hand. Gerda did the talking for both of us. "The dacha? Well, that's kind of a long story. But, hon, I have to say that that was a great trip. Those zeps are really something, and the places I saw were, wow, spectacular! Like Moscow, hon. You wouldn't believe it. It's like a whole damn city of statuary and monuments, only the monuments are the buildings people actually go to work in. And Prague—you've never been there, have you?—is like some really beautiful old cuckoo clock. And then there's that wonderful old city in what used to be Yugoslavia, Dubrovnik? And then, when you're heading for home and you're crossing the Adriatic Sea at night—"

"Sounds like you had a great time," I said, counting up in my head what a five-thousand-kilometer cruise in one of those enormous Chinese zeppelins would cost.

I guess I put more into my tone of voice than I had intended. Gerda gave me a look, then sighed and shook her head. "Oh, Brad," she said, "you need some hugs, don't you? Let's find a place where we can sit down with a drink."

We were both too wise to drink any of the pseudo-Roman cat urine from any of the Jubilee's wineshops. Even the higher-class ones around the Forums. Gerda had her own resources, though. We found some seats behind that never-finished Temple of Isis that the Pompeiians hadn't quite got built when Vesuvius finished things for them. She pulled out of her bellybag a couple of tiny bottles of a passably good brandy, obviously out of one of the zep's bars. They weren't the only ones she was carrying, either. By about the third bottle I was feeling quite a lot more relaxed, and the images inside my head began to slip and slide into new shapes. Well, sure, let's admit it. Into one particular new shape.

See, I hadn't forgotten how lousy the past week had been, or how pissed off at her I had every right to be.

But I kept seeing the Bastard's hand giving a friendly pat to a part of Gerda that I had wanted to think was all mine. So I opened my mouth to ask if it was true that the Bastard got paid in sack time for special favors to good-looking women. Only I didn't ask her if Maury Tesch had told me the truth. I said, "What I've been wondering about, why does everybody call him 'Bastard'?"

I didn't get the same answer as from Maury. What I got was a mildly annoyed look, as though I was giving her a kind of annoyance she hadn't expected and didn't much want, followed by a clear, consistent answer. "Because that's what he is. Didn't you know? His dad knocked his mother up and took off for calmer waters. What's the matter, he giving you trouble?"

That was a perfectly good answer, if not the one Maury Tesch had offered. I was inclined to accept it and change the subject because, all of a sudden, there was a growing pressure between my thighs. That, and the smell of her. And the fact that, well, hell, what I wanted most at that time wasn't conversation, it was just to get laid.

But there was one big thing in the way. I put my finger over Gerda's lips. "Honey," I said—without noticing the transition I was back to calling her "honey"—"I need to ask you a question. Are we in a monogamous relationship?"

She abandoned, in the middle of a sentence, her description of what eating was like on a zep—"Eight or nine different restaurants, Brad, plus if you call room service they'll make you pretty near anything you ever heard of—" and regarded me in silence for a moment. Then she sighed. "You know I have to get to class in about twenty minutes, don't you?"

Well, yes, I had known that that was the case, although her terrorism class schedule had been a long way from the principal subject on my mind. "Are we?" I asked.

"Oh, hell," she said. "Sometimes you ask really hard questions, Brad."

"So give me a hard answer."

"Well— Here's the thing," she said. "Don't rush me on this. It's a big step for me." She was silent for a moment, then, "There is one thing I can tell you, though. You're the very first man I've ever thought I might make that kind of promise to." And she gave me a quick kiss and was gone.

My own class, due to the Bastard's bastardly scheduling, was in the other direction from Gerda's and an hour and a half later. I spent the time in the refectory. For the first time in a week I had an appetite.

I got to the classroom in plenty of time to choose a seat—one that was right up front, because I was ready to be called on. Having had nothing better to do with my time I had used all the search engines in the library and I knew all the answers.

So what happened? Piranha Woman never brought the subject up at all. Instead, she said, "I presume you are all familiar with the case of the Puteoli children."

She paused, as though expecting a response. While most of the class was trying to figure out which of her ground rules applied, Elfreda took the chance. "You aren't telling us that their sickness involves terrorist activity, are you?"

"No such determination has been made. It is of interest, however, that the organism responsible for their symptoms has not been identified."

She stopped again, and Elfreda pushed her luck. "It sounds like you're saying that somebody's bred a new bug."

"I have not said that. Terrorist groups are generally quick to claim credit for an event of this magnitude, and perhaps the pathogen will be found to be known. However, there is one more bit of interesting information that has just been made public. Of the eleven young Puteoli women, eight have been found to have been present here at the Giubileo within the past nine or ten weeks."

That produced a sudden murmur from a couple dozen throats, including mine. Elfreda spoke right up again. "Has Pompeii become a terrorist target?" she demanded.

Piranha Woman shook her head. "I do not care to waste time on speculative questions. Actually I have prepared a practical project for us tonight which somewhat relates to that question and we will now begin it. For the purposes of this exercise each of you people are all now designated as members of terrorist groups. You have orders to strike the Giubileo in your next action. Start planning your attack now." She pointed a finger at Elfreda. "You."

From the look on Elfreda's face she would have preferred a little more lead time, but she dealt with it. By the time she was on her feet she was already speaking: "Well, what I wouldn't do is just mess up the virtuals like that clown that hit the central computers the other day."

That was as far as she got. "Sit," Piranha Woman teacher ordered. "I didn't ask for what you wouldn't do, I asked for what you would do. Tesch!"

The finger was aimed straight between Maury's eyes. He took his time getting up and didn't speak for a moment, pursing his lips. "Let's consider what would make the Giubileo an attractive target for terrorists," he began. "Two factors stand out. First, publicity. The Giubileo is news, and so is anything that happens here. Any terrorist action here would be reported in every news medium in every country in the world. Second, penetration. Chances are that nearly all of those countries would have people at the Giubileo on any given day, so it wouldn't just be news, it could be local news."

Piranha Woman didn't stop him, but she did say, "I asked for what, not why."

Maury gave her an earnest look. "But it's the why factors that determine the what. As Elfreda reasonably pointed out"—his "reasonably" had to be taken as a criticism of Piranha Woman, but Piranha Woman didn't change her expression—"turning off the virts for a couple of hours wasn't big enough to achieve anything. Really, it was just sort of comical. To make any action effective, people have to die."

Piranha Woman didn't nod, but her lips tightened a touch, as though the mention of death had interested her. "What number of deaths would be appropriate? What would kill them?"

"I'd recommend between twenty and fifty deaths as a minimum," Maury said. "For a relatively minor action, that is. Less wouldn't make enough of an impact, more would be unnecessary, that is, unless you choose to get up into the thousands. Or more," he added, looking suddenly pensive.

"How?" the teacher insisted.

"Poison," he answered at once. "You could use some sort of explosive if you chose, but that would unnecessarily damage unique historical sites. Worse, it would be a one-day story. However, poisoning, with careful selection of the poisoning agent, could be arranged to go on for weeks, with people dying all over the world every day. One scenario would be to put a slow-acting poison in the food at the refectory, perhaps in the wine or the water. Of course," he added, smirking a little, "that isn't going to happen to the water here. That's clean. We keep it that way, and to make sure we take samples every hour, day and night. When it's my turn to do it there's an armed Security guard escorting me and the sample all the way to Security's lab."

Piranha Woman had a comment. "It sounds as though you've given this a lot of thought."

He said simply, "It's my job."

The teacher made a small, possibly approving, sound in her throat. Then she said, "All right. Sit." And to the rest of class, "What other scenarios could be useful? You."

This time she was pointing at the Senegalese. He was ready for her with a quick and (I thought) pretty implausible idea about lacing the food at the Refectorium with radioisotopes. Then so was the Mongolian woman and so, thank God, was I when she got around to my side of the room, because each of us had by then had time to think it over.

Well, mine was pretty dumb—never mind what exactly, it had to do with releasing disease-carrying insects at the games, and that's all I'm going to say about it. But Piranha Woman hadn't specified that the plans had to be workable. All she was asking us to do was to invent some ways to kill, maim, or simply demoralize some large bunches of people, and, considered as a kind of party game, that wasn't hard at all. Actually it was kind of fun.

So Piranha Woman had successfully kept us from spending our session on speculations about the Puteoli Eleven. She hadn't made me forget about them, though, and as soon as I was out of the classroom door I had my opticle searching for details. There weren't many, but someone had dug up a little backgrounding.

By the time I got to Gerda's room she was sitting before her news wall, though what she was watching wasn't what I would call news—some modern dirty dancing, with music that hurt my ears. She gave me a peculiar look. "I'm sorry about the New York business," she said. "I just turned it off."

I was already sitting down at the little table where she'd set out one of Maury's wine bottles with a couple of glasses. Her tone wasn't romantic, though. "What do you mean?" I asked. "Piranha Woman didn't mention anything new about New York. Did something happen there?"

She came over, her expression still grave, to open the wine. "Damn right something did. It's still happening, too. And, sure, using stink bombs is kind of funny, but the ones that got killed aren't laughing much, are they?" And then, when she saw the look on my face, "Wait a minute, I'll go back to it." And switched her screen to the news menu. She selected New York City and in a minute we were looking at the old UN building on the East River.

Well, it wasn't Staten Island. My parents were not involved.

As to the UN building, it didn't look much different from the last time I saw it—which had been while guiding an elderly couple from Panama City, Florida, around some of the Big Apple's major tourist traps, until they were drunk enough to rob.

Then I took a closer look and I saw the little dots that were dropping down the sides of the building.

At first I couldn't figure out what those dots were—until, that is, I saw that they had arms and legs that were waving wildly as they fell.

Then Gerda finally thought to switch to the English-speaking voice. "—some kind of a super-skatole," the newsperson was saying, "so powerful that many of the victims on the upper stories broke their windows and jumped out to their deaths to get away from it."

I did some jumping of my own then. "Bastards," I snarled. "As if there were enough Lenni Lenapes left to occupy all these what they call ancestral lands."

All right, it was a bad guess, but this had caught me by surprise. Never mind the fact that I wasn't really all that crazy about my old fart parents. When I heard "New York" and saw what was on the screen the first thing I thought of was them.

But that wasn't where the action was. Dad and Mom were free to keep right on eking out their pointless days. And I had radically confused Gerda. "What do you mean, 'ancestral lands,'" she asked, and so I found out that, this time, it wasn't the same old Lenni Lenapes that were doing the terrorizing, it was a bunch I'd never heard of. Neither had the newscaster. However, she had backup to conceal her ignorance, and she read it right off the screen built into the surface of her desk. "They call themselves," she said, "something that I can't pronounce, but means they say something like 'Inguishi will rise.' The Inguishi, it appears, are somehow related to the Chechens, who have been trying to secede from the Russian Republic as long as there has been one. Apparently they're protesting the arrival of United Nations peacekeepers in their country after the recent violence."

Well, there was a lot more about the politics of that part of the world, but I stopped listening. I didn't care about that.

I did, however, care about what I saw on the wall screen.

The Inguishi hadn't stopped at the UN building. They stink-bombed several of the tallest buildings down around Wall Street, they did it to the new opera house in the Bloomberg Cultural Center, and they even stank up three or four of the old Times Square skyscrapers. Big ones. Ones where I had occasionally sneaked in to see if there was an unlocked office door, after most of the people who worked there had gone home.

These terrorists were fouling up my old home grounds. I didn't like it.

Gerda listened to the news with critical interest. "Good placement," she said judiciously. "Right in the heart of the city, with plenty of news channels all around to cover. But where do you suppose these wildbloods got hold of super-skatole? That's potent stuff. You can do all the containment and isolation in the world and it gets through anyway. And then half the people who make it get exposed, and then they've got to do hair removal and skin ablation baths for six months or so before they can live with themselves, and even then nobody else can live with them."

I wasn't listening to her. I was fixated by what I saw on the screen. Most of the places that were stricken were my old stomping ground—the buildings, the high-speed transit stations where we lay in wait for tourists, the Fifth Avenue porn shops where we took one variety of them, the theater district where we took others. And most of all what the screen was showing was that hourglass-shaped tract where Seventh Avenue crossed Broadway, what the tourists still called Times Square. Now it was filled with thousands of people in major distress, office workers fleeing from the stink, pedestrians trying to get away from the stinking office workers, the cops and parapolice trying to control the mob.

It had the makings of a first-class riot, so I knew what had to be coming next.

It came. The cameras changed views, and over the buildings a squadron of NYPD ultralights were fluttering down to their job of crowd control.

See, I knew exactly what being on the receiving end of that was like. I had been there myself. That was back in '71 or '72, when the mayor ordered the cops to chase all us refugee kids out of town and we wouldn't go. I remembered it all, the ultralights methodically cruising overhead as they sprayed us with that three-millimeter radiation. Three-millimeter is seriously hot. They say that 45°C is when the pain threshold begins, but they're wrong. By the time the microwaves get your skin up to even 40° it really hurts, whether it's theoretically supposed to or not. By the time it hits 45° you don't want to riot anymore. You just want to jump into something with a lot of ice cubes floating in it. Or, as a reasonable second-best choice, die.

That had been only a couple hundred of us that the cops were targeting, back in '71. This time the crowd was ten or twenty thousand. The good part, this time—the only good part—was that this time I was watching it on a news broadcast and not getting sprayed myself.

It took the joy out of the evening. When at last Gerda and I finally climbed into her big, warm bed I thought the opportunity was going to be wasted on me. I wasn't in the mood for sex, and stayed that way for at least ten minutes, maybe twenty. There were a lot of things on my mind. Even the way Gerda was spooned against my back, with both of her hands free to be friendly, didn't make me forget them. I realized I hadn't been keeping up on the news, and over my shoulder I asked her, "Anything happening today with those Puteoli kids?"

Her breath was coming into my ear, warm, soft, and sweet. "Oh, yes," she told me. "It's terrible. You know two of them died? And five or six new cases have turned up outside of Zagreb?"

I said, "Hell." What else was there to say? She didn't respond to that, though. She was doing other things. And, you know, when you're under the covers with a good-looking naked woman who is amusing herself with your body parts—well, then all those petty worries about things that are happening somewhere else, and to some other people, certainly do diminish.

Now I am happy (or in another sense heartbroken) to say we come to the best part of all. (The one, that is, that makes me feel worst of all because it is totally and irrevocably gone.)

I have to say that the next couple of weeks were pretty near the best time of my life ever. I know I've thought that kind of thing about other times before. Makes no difference. These were better.

Never mind the fact that—for example—the world news was getting lousier by the day. Within a week five more of the Puteoli girls had died, the Zagreb cluster looked like it was associated with a blimp excursion to the Jubilee—and more people around the world were beginning to call the disease the Pompeii Flu.

Of course, there was plenty of other unpleasing stuff. The Russians were rounding up Inguishi leaders—fairly brutally—to punish them for their New York action. Some bunch was firebombing department stores in Romania, some others kidnapping the families of policemen in Bangladesh. Truthfully, I didn't care. What I cared about was Gerda Fleming, and there she was for me, every day of those weeks. The Welsh Bastard was being uncharacteristically unbastardly, too, letting Gerda juggle her schedules to give us more time together than usual. Her job that week was being a Pompeiian matron guide for tourists wanting someone to show them around the city in the mornings, while I peddled my foul wine on the Via dell'Abbondanza, but then the afternoons were all ours. And so, God bless them, were the nights.

But then there was Maury.

He wasn't sharing our idyll. Something serious was bothering him, even totally ruining his disposition, if not indeed eating him up.

See, the principal reliable fact about Maury and me was that it was always Maury who came chasing after me in the refectory, or knocked on the door of my room to see if I was up for some chess or a machine game, or just hanging out. But that was then. Now wasn't the same. Now Maury not only had stopped hanging around me, he twice, on two different occasions, saw me walking down the street in his direction and turned around to go a different way.

And then there was that business with him and Gerda. I heard voices at my door and when I opened it there stood Gerda, looking amused, and halfway down the walk a view of Maury's back as he stalked away. Naturally I asked Gerda what the problem was. She made a face. "He's a pain in the ass," she told me. "Always looking for something to argue about."

That was unexpected. Actually I hadn't known that the two of them knew each other well enough to argue. When I tried to find out what the argument had been about she just shrugged and said she didn't want to discuss it.

I let it drop.

Figure it out for yourself. She's sitting right next to you, close enough for you to feel the warmth coming off her body and smell that unmistakable smell of her. She leans up against you and says, "Can we please not talk about it, hon?" And of course we definitely could do exactly that.

Sure, I could have pursued the matter, maybe gone looking for Maury the next day to ask him what the argument was about. Possibly he would have answered, though not necessarily truthfully. And possibly then he might not have died so soon.

But those aren't the things that actually happened.

What actually happened was that Gerda and I were spending more of our time together now. She had begun showing a new interest in exploring the countryside around Pompeii. I encouraged that. Local explorations were cheap. They were also kind of boring, though, because we had done almost all of them before. Back to Capri, this time to make the long uphill trudge to the cliff where the old Emperor Tiberius used to have people who pissed him off thrown to their deaths. ("Knew how to keep peace in the family, didn't he?" Gerda offered.) Out to Puteoli, not to check on the condition of those dying little girls but to gape at the roily, burny Phlegrean Fields. "Little volcanos that never grew up," Gerda called them. Back to Naples to stroll along the waterfront and peek at the weird little creatures in the aquarium. Back to Caserta—

Well, actually that was the weirdest trip of all, I thought at the time (though I didn't know at the time just what it meant). Once before we'd taken a rented three-wheeler down that stinky Naples–Caserta road because Gerda said she'd heard that the old king's palace was worth a visit. It wasn't, though. No towers, no battlements, no nothing that looked like a palace at all. What it most closely resembled when I got to look at it was one of those multistory housing developments that the American government put up for welfare families in the 1950s or so— and dynamited down by the 1990s, because nobody wanted to live in them. And the first thing that happened when we got there was that I lost Gerda. Lost myself, too, and wandered around all five or six stories of the huge old building, ducking in and out of corridors that were mostly roped off with big "Ingresso Proibita" signs everywhere; lost myself so thoroughly, in fact, that I couldn't even find where we'd parked the three-wheeler.

I never did find either Gerda or the car. I had just about given up, sitting on the rim of one of the fountains and wondering what the bus fare to Pompeii would be when I heard the shrill *peep-peep* of the three-wheeler's horn. When I looked up there she was. Barreling at seventy or eighty kilometers an hour down that gravel path that wasn't meant for any sort of car, not even a three-wheeler. Looking really mad, too. I wanted to say something about how strange it was to see her driving herself, but she was demanding to know where the hell I'd got to, because she'd been just about out of her mind looking for me.

It all worked out all right. The nice thing about a lovers' misunderstanding is that you can have such a good time making up when it's over.

Anyway, that had been the first time Gerda demanded we go to see the Caserta palace. I hadn't thought there would ever be a second, but there was.

I don't think I said what made the Naples–Caserta road stinky. It was patches of farmland, but what the Italians grew on those farms wasn't food. It was flax. The way you raised a crop of flax was to grow it and then, when it was ripe, you just left it in the field to rot. When it was good and rotten you could pull the flax fibers right out of the decaying greenery they had grown up in.

By the second time we made that trip the rotting had gone full compass. The stink was a little hard to describe, not anywhere near super-skatole strength but plenty unpleasant. You might say it was like your neighbor's garbage when he hasn't paid his sanitation bill and it's been decaying in the sun for a week or two. After about twenty minutes' exposure I expressed my feelings to Gerda. It only took one syllable: "Phew!"

She gave me a look that started out annoyed but ended apologetic. "Oh, hell, hon, I thought the harvest would be all over by now."

I was big about it. "Not to worry. We've only got a couple of kilometers to go."

She gave me a fond smile and blew me an air kiss. "I'll make it up to you," she promised. Then she rested one hand on my lap, by which I mean on the part of my lap where it could do the most good. So things were going well, except then we hit a particularly thick stretch of stink and Gerda took that hand away to hold her nose.

"Jesus," she said. And then, "Oh, something you mightn't know. Ever have grappa?" She didn't wait for an answer. "It's what drives the Italian government guys crazy. The farmers distill it out of homemade rotgut wine, and they don't pay taxes. And they put their stills in places like these, because with all that decay stink nobody can smell their stills. I bet you could go into any of those farmhouses and pick up a bottle of white lightning." Then she caught sight of a roadside sign—it said "Caserta 1.5 km"—and forgot about the smelly flax. "Almost there, hon," she informed me. "Let's hope there's a parking space we can find again."

Well, there was. Lots of spaces, right up by the main entrance. But we couldn't use any of them. Big signs warned that the best of them were for doctors and other medical personnel only, and for the second-best spots the signs said they were reserved for the families of patients in the medical center only. Because the king's palace wasn't a tourist spot anymore. When we weren't looking the palace had been requisitioned to become an emergency clinic for victims of the necrotizing illness people were calling Pompeii Flu, and ordinary civilians were no longer allowed entrance.

Never mind what Gerda said then—or, for that matter, what I said myself. It was mostly profanity anyway, except for the part where she said, "Move over, Brad." And, when I gave her an uncomprehending look, "Didn't you hear me? I'll drive."

The best way to deal with Gerda was not to argue but just to do as she said. I let her turn around and head for home without argument. I was patting her thigh as she jockeyed the three-wheeler through the gate to the highway, trying to console her for the loss of her excursion.

It turned out she didn't need much consoling, though. A couple of minutes after we were back on the road the grim look on her face abruptly lightened. "Hon," she said, "you know what? Remember what I said about the farmers bootlegging grappa? Well, I bet right there is one place where they do! Let's take a look at—that one. The one that looks the most like a plain old Italian flax farmer going broke because the Ethiopians can grow it for half his costs."

She didn't have to tell me which farmhouse she meant by "that one." She screeched the three-wheeler in a left turn to the underpass and up a driveway to a two-story house in serious need of fresh whitewash. I waited in the car. She was gone no more than a couple of minutes, and when she came out she patted her backpack, grinning. "Told you," she said. "Now let's go home."

So we did, me driving again and the trip made to seem a lot shorter by virtue of passing the grappa back and forth. It was vile stuff, all right, sort of what I imagined drinking cleaning fluid would be if it were mixed with lye. But it made us happy. Happy enough so that before we got on the Pompeii autostrada Gerda unwrapped a fresh pack of chewing gum and handed me a stick. "In case the *polizia* stop us," she said. "So we won't smell quite so drunk."

I laughed out loud. "You have to get over that morbid fear of police," I told her, having teased her once or twice about her being such an obsessively law-abiding driver.

She gave me a mild frown. "You wouldn't take that attitude if you if you knew why I had it," she said.

"Ah, but I do. You told me last time I said something about it," I began, because she had. The local *carabinieri* were famous for stopping pretty women driving alone.

But I stopped in the middle of the sentence, as she reached over and good-naturedly patted my leg. "We don't want anything keeping us from getting right home, do we? Because I haven't forgotten what I promised."

Well, neither had I.

What Gerda had promised was that she would make that trip up to me. She did, too. Very fully and enjoyably. Enough so that I would have done the whole thing over the next day, for the same reward.

There was one other thing about Gerda that seemed to have changed. That was her sudden appetite for news.

That was a surprise—Gerda hadn't seemed to take very much interest in what the world outside of Pompeii was up to—but it wasn't altogether a bad thing. Staying home in front of the event channels was a lot cheaper than hitting the casinos on Ischia or the Neapolitan bar scene. I was even able to send enough money to Staten Island, my mother wrote me, to let her go shopping for some new clothes.

I didn't share Gerda's interest in world events at least until the evening when I went out to get some more wine and, when I came back, there was something other than the inevitable Pompeii Flu stories. There were about a million rioters raising hell on the screen, I didn't immediately find out where, beating up on a couple thousand badly outnumbered cops, I never knew why. I thought at first that I might be seeing a reprise of New York City and the Inguishi, but it turned out to be Bulgaria, and the issue was something about local politics. The scenario wasn't all that different, though. The police ultralights were painted a different color, but they were right up there to make the rioters want to go home. They did a good job of it. The Bulgarian cops weren't bothering with the old infrareds. What they were firing into the mob was PEPs—pulsed energy projectiles. Those hurt more than anything else most police departments possessed, and the screaming that came out of the rioters as they hit you wouldn't believe.

Actually the world seemed to be returning to normal.

Then there was the day I stopped by my room to pick up some clean clothes. I had finished picking out the clean socks and underwear I had come for, when it occurred to me to look in the fridge.

Maury's sausages were gone.

A few crumbs of repellent-looking meat—or something—on the back of the shelf was all that was left of them. Well, the crumbs plus that unforgettable smell. Nothing more.

So I called Maury at his office right away. When he answered his expression was abstracted. "Oh, it's you," he said. "What do you want?"

His unfriendliness had been elevated a notch or two. I chose to overlook it. "It's Jiri," I told him. "He died yesterday. His widow just came by to pick up his stuff."

Maury looked mildly interested. "What did he die of?"

"She didn't know. But, listen, I checked the refrigerator and your wursts are gone."

"Oh," he said, looking not at all as stricken as I would have guessed he would be, "right." He was actually giving me an embarrassed grin. "I should've told you. I didn't like them being left alone, and anyway I've got my own rooms to myself now. Didn't I tell you? My roomie quit and went home. Said he didn't like Pompeii's climate. So day before yesterday I came by and picked the wursts up. Sorry if it worried you. I have to get back to work." And his picture shivered and was gone.

So one question was answered. It did, however, leave me with another.

Neither Jiri nor I had been present in the room when Maury said he'd been there, so how did he get in?

10

REMEMBERING UNCLE DEVIOUS AGAIN

When I say those weeks were great I don't mean there weren't any little worries here and there. In fact there was one quite large one, because I never quite relaxed. I did not forget that Gerda had left me before. Three times before, if you counted that first time right after we'd met. And I had no guarantee that she wouldn't do it again.

Apart from such grim thoughts, though, the days were great. It wasn't just the parts of them that we spent in bed, either, although those were untiringly fine. It was something else that made that time so happy I was consciously aware of how much happiness I was being blessed with, something that I'd never had before.

I think the right word for that condition is "friendship." In addition, I mean, to love. What that amounted to was getting to know each other, Gerda and me, in ways I had never known another person. Like, for instance, there was the night when Gerda had put out some wine and fruit and cheeses, which we had formed the habit of eating instead of a real meal so we could get to bed sooner. While we were eating I told her about Jiri's widow and Maury's grouchiness.

She didn't seem particularly interested in either. So later, after we made love, I must've drowsed off. When I woke up Gerda was sitting cross-legged on her couch, next to her shelves of tiny porcelain dolls and fanciful seashells and all the other little bits and pieces of what did you call them, bibelots or tchotchkes or maybe just junk, that she liked to have around her. I supposed she'd just come out of the shower, because her hair was wet. She was wearing a terrycloth robe and talking into her opticle. When she saw me looking at her she killed the connection and came over to give me a wakeup kiss. "Have a nice nap?" she asked.

I nodded, but what I said was, "Who were you talking to?"

"Just Jeremy Jones," she said. "To tell him I'd be a little late this morning. There's coffee." There was, too. American-style coffee, too. Definitely not the concentrated sludge that Mediterranean people preferred. When she brought the cups over and sat down next to me I was surprised to observe that her jaws were moving rhythmically.

"You shouldn't chew so much gum," I remarked. "Bad for your teeth." It wasn't meant as a criticism, just a comment, but she seemed to take it seriously.

"I brought it back from Russia. I think they get it from the Stans, but don't tell anybody. Look." She opened a drawer in the end table and pulled out what looked like a box of fancy, foil-wrapped chocolates. It wasn't, though. It was a selection of maybe half a dozen flavors of chewing gum, each in a wrapper colored to match its taste. "The strawberry's my favorite," she told me, "but the lime's good, too. And the cherry."

I accepted one of the bright red cherry-flavored ones, and her praise had been justified. It didn't taste like the kind of cough medicine my mother had forced on me when I was six. It tasted precisely like sweet fresh cherries, picked right off the tree, with the morning dew still on them. Not that I'd ever had any like that to remember so it was like I'd imagined from all those TV cooking shows and commercials. "So did I lie?" Gerda asked. When I admitted she hadn't, she said, "Oh, by the way. Nonno's—my uncle's—caretaker at the dacha—his name's Vassili something—said he remembered your Uncle DeVries."

That wasn't the most pleasing sentence I'd ever heard from her. "Did Uncle DeVries swindle him, too?" I asked cautiously.

"Well, yes," she conceded. "Not Nonno personally, but he pretty much cleaned out Nonno's brother. Nonno almost lost the dacha."

There was one particular thing I had got used to saying most of the, happily infrequent, times when Uncle Devious's name came up. I said it again. "I'm sorry."

She patted my hand. "It isn't your fault, Brad. Were you fond of your uncle?"

Well, in a way I had been, I admitted to her. As had almost everybody else Uncle Devious met. People liked him. That was the secret of his success as a confidence man. My mother wasn't the only one who had handed over substantial sums for his Goro Lama's Mercy Fund for Needy Tibetan Children. "It wasn't just the Goro Lama's name he used, either," I told her. "He had a scroll that he told everybody had been calligraphed by Sonam Gyatso himself. Know who Sonam Gyatso was? The Dalai Lama, that's who. I don't mean the current one, whoever he is. I mean the one centuries ago who went out among Genghis Khan's Mongols and converted them to Buddhism. Uncle Devious used to give copies of that scroll to high-end contributors, like my mom."

Gerda was wearing a doubtful look. "He must have had more going for him than just a nice personality?"

"Oh, sure," I said. "He had all the props, too." And I told her about his fancy office in downtown KC, with his primitive 2055-style virts of hungry but scrubbed and neatly dressed Tibetan children, in the schools his fund (he said) had provided for them. And his fifteen or twenty devoutly dedicated employees, handling the bookkeeping, liaising with the other funds Uncle Devious sat on the boards of, and sending out the thank-you scrolls to the mom-and-pop contributors too small for Uncle D to give his personal attention to. And especially his head employee, Merrilee Bournemouth, the knockout.

Gerda gave me a confident little grin. "Prettier than me, Brad?"

I gave her the right answer. "Of course not. But to a kid, she was plenty pretty enough. I would have given my right arm to kiss her just one time."

She gave me an acknowledging smile. "One thing I'm not so clear about. He wasn't your real uncle?"

"Well, technically, sure, he was real enough. He married my mother's sister, the old maid. The sick old maid, with the type-four leukemia that they couldn't do much about and the hard-core somadone habit. She had just three years of being Mrs. Rev. Delmore DeVries Maddingsley, and then she died. Leaving him everything she owned. Which he said he would never accept a penny of, so he donated the whole thing to the Goro Lama Fund. Which, of course," I said, "was really himself anyway, wasn't it? But nobody knew that at the time."

All this time Gerda was holding my hand and letting me just talk. Which I found easy, and kind of comforting, to do. It took my mind right off Jiri's death and Maury's bad mood, and all the other recent annoyances.

It had been a long time since I'd really talked to anybody about my Uncle Devious in a comfortable, that is to say noninterrogatory, way. So I told her everything I could remember, winding up with the day my uncle's head auditor from the fund office called, sounding pretty well terrified, to tell us that Uncle Devious hadn't come in that morning and none of the servants at his duplex on Heinlein Street had seen him since the previous afternoon, and did we have any idea?

We didn't. The next day the police showed up. And then the FBI. And then every law enforcement agency you could think of, from Security and Interpol on down. By then we had a pretty clear idea that Uncle Devious was actually a despicable swindler of widows and orphans. And of anybody else trusting enough to believe in his foundation for Tibetan kids.

Gerda shook her head commiseratingly, but she didn't say anything. What she did was get up and fetch a couple of glasses, along with a bottle of Maury's wine. "Here's to better times," she said, and I drank to it with goodwill. She was silent for a moment. Then she said, "He wasn't just an ordinary embezzler, though, was he?"

I drained my glass. Then I gave her the truthful answer. I told her about the day when Merrilee Bournemouth had come to our house. She didn't look like a video star then. She looked haggard, and she was begging for every clue we could give her that might help her figure out Uncle Devious's whereabouts.

Mom didn't want to tell the woman a thing. She suspected that Uncle D had been banging Merrilee all along—certainly since her sister's death, and most probably for quite a while before it. (He had, too.) But Dad hadn't been that suspicious, I guess. He told Merrilee all he knew, which was essentially everything we'd told the various law enforcers and not much help to anybody. And then a few days later the cops began to ask us if we knew where Merrilee Bournemouth had taken herself to.

We didn't know the answer to that. Neither did they. Not then. Not until later that year when the plan to blow up Inner Mongolia's city of Hohhot got ratted out by the ticked-off girlfriend of one of the terrorist explosive experts. In the subsequent ruckus they said Uncle D was killed and Merrilee got paralyzed by a couple of fletches in her lower spine, and the whole thing came out. What that whole thing had financed was three or four years of arsons and assassinations in Inner Mongolia and Outer, along with parts of Siberia and several of the neighboring Stans. And all the money that financed those goings-on had come right out of the very deep pockets of my charitable uncle.

"From the Tibetan orphans' fund," Gerda guessed.

"Sort of. Ultimately. But a lot of those funds had been siphoned out to the Dalai Lama's fund for indigent Mongolians—that was another of Uncle Devious's little charities. And then, through several cut-outs, dribbled to the terrorists as needed. To the other terrorists, I mean, because, you're right, that's what Uncle Devious had been all along."

Gerda was silent for a moment. "Interesting," she pronounced, "but I think that's about enough talk, don't you think? I'm sleepy," she added, nibbling at my ear, "but not too sleepy. So why don't we go back to bed?"

So we did. I was glad to change the subject. I guess I had been afraid that having a terrorist for an uncle would make her think less of me. It didn't, though.

The lesson I had long ago learned, but did my best not to think about, was that things that are too good to last don't last. And the proof of that came the next day when Gerda, looking sorrowful, came by the wineshop right at the peak of the tourist business. It was, of course, raining.

I braced myself. Whatever the news was going to be, I wasn't going to like it. I began to worry in earnest. It was bad enough that she was going to tell me something I was going to hate; I didn't want to hear it surrounded by my customers.

I had one possible way out. I looked pleadingly across the Via dell'Abbondanza to where Cedric the Pimp was lounging in his doorway, and sure enough he took the hint. "Go," he called, ambling across the narrow street toward me. "We aren't busy right now. I'll take care of your shop."

So I left Cedric dishing out wine for the thirsty crowd—and, of course, for himself—and I pulled Gerda down the street. "What?" I asked as soon as we had found a sheltered doorway to get into.

She shook her head mournfully. "It's my gram, Brad dear. They've put her in intensive care." She squeezed my hand. I didn't squeeze back. "But the worst part," she said, "is they don't really seem to know whether she's going to make it. Hon, I'm sorry, but I don't have any choice, do I? I hate it, but I just have to go."

Her eyes were actually misting.

I couldn't tell her not to do it, could I? Even if my telling her would have as much as slowed her down, which I was quite sure it wouldn't. I could have mentioned that her family seemed to be having a pretty lousy summer, but I didn't say that, either. So all I did was ask her where dear old Gram was dying, and when she said, "She's got that place up in Sirmione," I had to ask where Sirmione was. Up in the lake district, about as far as you could get in Italy before it turned into Switzerland, she said. And when I pointed out, trying to get the facts straight, that neither the

Chang Jang nor its sister ship, the *Haihe,* was expected back for days and probably wouldn't be heading that way if they were, she shook her head affectionately. "I wouldn't be going by zep, hon. Too slow. I'll just grab a superspeed rail out of Naples and I'll be there in two hours."

That sounded a little better to me. I ventured, "So you probably won't be gone that long."

But she was sorrowfully shaking her head again. "Oh, sweetie, well, you know you can't predict these things, can you? It might be just overnight. It might be, I don't know, a lot longer than that. But you know I'll try to get back when I can." And a kiss on the cheek and a quick half hug and Gerda was gone. Until when, not specified, and maybe, oh, shit, maybe until goddamn never.

It was turning out to be another really bad day.

I stumbled back through the drizzle to my hole in the wall. The wine drinkers gawked at me and Cedric the Pimp gave me a commiserating little shake of the head before retreating—with a full cup of wine that I was sure wasn't his first—to his own side of the via. It seemed our conversation hadn't been quite as quiet as I'd thought.

The rest of my shift that day seemed to last forever. And when it was over so did that whole night.

11

MY DEAR LOVE GONE, AGAIN

Among all the other things that were wrong with the world was that our whole part of the Italian peninsula went through another rainy patch just then. And attendance was down.

That didn't make sense to me. Sure, sometimes the weather cut down the number of people showing up on a given day. But not this much. Customers just weren't showing up the way they had been. The Bastard said we were down over 10 percent, and he said it to me the way he said most things, as though it was my fault.

Losing any customers at all was bad for me. It hurt my chances of making an honest as—all right, an as, never mind the honest part—out of my moneychanging or wine-recycling fiddles. On the other hand, the good part, or the not good at all but actually the worse part, the worst as hell part was that my outgoing cash flow had dwindled, too. The dwindling was good. The reason for the dwindling, though, was that Gerda wasn't around to use up all my spare euros on impetuous runs into Naples for a couple of drinks in the Galleria or taking rides in rental cars down the coast to gaze at the hot mud fountains that looked the way parts of Yellowstone must have looked before it went ape.

Gerda wasn't just not there. She didn't even call.

You know what was tough for me to understand?

Intellectually, I mean? The fact that I really missed her.

I hadn't ever really missed a human being before. It made me feel foolish. That didn't stop the missing pain, it just added one more way of feeling bad to the sufficient number of ways I already had. So to try to take my mind off all those things, what I found myself doing, more than ever, was checking, almost obsessively checking, the news pages. Some of the news, of course, was simply too lousy to make anybody feel better, except maybe some mega-misanthrope that wanted the whole human race horribly destroyed. That was what the Pompeii Flu news was like, and it got worse every day.

Actually, that helped a little. I didn't care much about purely local horrors. If fifty passengers were turned into well-done hamburgers when their railbugs plowed into a broken-down internal combustion truck on the same high-speed track—well, that wasn't really cheering me up any, no, but at least it reminded me that there were people in the world worse off than I was. And anyway, the particular railbug line where that had happened ran from Boston to the Maine coast, nowhere near the one Gerda would have been on.

If indeed she had taken the high-speed rail at all, of course.

There was a lot of that sort of thing on the news, too. Terrorism seemed to be having an uptick, and some of their actions were pretty spectacular. When the New Falangists set fire to the copy of Columbus's ship *Santa Maria* where it had been moored for the past century or so at the foot of Barcelona's Las Ramblas it was mildly interesting, although I'd never been in Barcelona, and didn't care much about Christopher Columbus. (It did get a little more interesting when a team of Barcelona firemen tried to put it out, and a delayed-action bomb killed them all.) Then the Flat Earth Society guys knocked the heads off the statues in Moscow's Cosmonaut Park on the grounds that space travel was a hoax . . . and the Hebrides Society bombed London's Albert Memorial to protest England's murder of Mary, Queen of Scots . . . and the Rock of Ages Purifiers swiped a couple of ultralights and dropped porno pictures over most of Salt Lake City. And like that, over and over again.

It seemed to me that there was too much of that sort of thing. No one else seemed to care, though. Cedric the Pimp listened patiently to me one rainy morning when nobody seemed to be wandering down our street, but all he said was, "Yeah, it's a shame," and scurried back across the via when a couple of figures strolled toward us. They didn't really matter. They were just virts. But it was obvious that he had taken the excuse to leave because the subject either bored or frightened him.

My best bet for someone to talk to, just as in old pre-Gerda days, was Maury Tesch. He was still pretty moody, but once again reliably up at almost any time for a quick game of CIA Against the Militants or Planning Nine Eleven All Over Again—or, more likely, chess, because he didn't really like the machine games. But then, once when he had checkmated me in a dozen moves and was setting the pieces up for the next game, I mentioned my notion that the terrorists were getting more active and he said wisely, "What's worrying you, Brad? Is it your idea that there's some big terror offensive going on?"

"Well, something like that, maybe," I admitted.

He shook his head. "Think about it, Brad. Remember what I said back at that briefing about this kind of thing?" I didn't. "Well," he said, sounding a little miffed, "let me spell it out for you. What've all these attacks got in common?" He didn't pause to give me a chance to guess. He went right on. "They're all local, do you see? Small groups. Limited objectives. If you just go by what you see on the news you have to think that the days of concerted attacks all over the place are done. And," he said earnestly, "there are good reasons why they might be. They're too damn big. They take so many people in so many places to work, and somebody's always going to rat them out. And then they'll all get bagged and spend the rest of their lives in some jail. Right?"

This time he did pause for a comment from me, but I didn't have one. He didn't seem to mind. "No, Brad," he went on, "you can forget that. If there are ever going to be more large-scale operations that cross national lines I guarantee there won't be more than a handful of people involved."

"Well," I said, "what about something like this Pompeii Flu?"

Now he was shaking his head sorrowfully. Evidently I had said something stupid. "Brad, have you heard of any terrorist group claiming credit for the Flu?" I gave him a head shake of my own. "Or make any demands? Or even show that they were hitting some specific target?"

"Well," I said, "the Jubilee?"

He shook his head harder than ever. "Be reasonable, Brad," he said. "Why would anybody hate the Jubilee that much?"

I was getting to be uncomfortable with the subject. "I guess no reason, Maury. Unless you could say it's the whole human race that's the target."

He said patiently, "And who would hate the whole human race that much?"

I had an answer for that. "Martians," I said wisely. "Once they get rid of us they can steal our women and our water."

That made him grin. Not right away, because Maury didn't have that much of a sense of humor. But then the grin did arrive, and, "Ah," he said, suddenly sunny again, "you're joking. So we agree, that's one thing we don't have to worry about? Good. Now you're white, so what's your first move?"

So I made one. And, of course, lost again, and after a while wandered back to my room to sleep.

You might think that Maury's positive kind of comments might have reassured me, a little, anyway. They didn't. They only made it easier for me to concentrate on my real and pressing womanless condition.

Which I did, that night and most of the next, right up to the time when Elfreda Barcowicz decided to become part of my life.

The way she did it, she plumped herself down beside me while I was having a solitary beer at one of those outside-the-wall sidewalk cafés and said, "Hi."

By then Elfreda had already paired up three times in the previous week or two, twice with tourists and once with my successor at the flour mill, none of those joinings lasting much more than a few days. I hadn't really kept tabs on her, but if asked I would have guessed that she was at present hooked up with the muscleman, Jamie Hardesty. She wasn't, though. "That rat Jamie," she told me right away, "is the reason so many good girls go gay. Talk about full of himself! Mind if I join you for a drink?"

I didn't, particularly. It wouldn't have mattered if I did because she'd already flagged down a waitress and ordered a grappa and lemon soda, and when it arrived she paid for it herself, so quickly that I wouldn't have had a chance to do it myself even if I'd wanted to. I have to say that, after Gerda's high-maintenance habits, that made a refreshing change. So, to be sociable, I asked, "Weren't you going with him?"

"Was, yes. Not now. What is it with you guys, you're all scared of making a commitment?"

"Commitment" was not a word I would have associated with Elfreda's track record. I made the mistake of asking her what kind of commitment she was talking about, because she told me. "I'm a healthy, normal woman, Brad," she explained. "What I want is good old-fashioned true long love. That's 'true.' And 'long.' You follow me? The kind of love where the two of you turn old and gray together, and when one of you finally dies the other one lasts maybe a month or two and then she's gone, too. Or he is; doesn't matter which goes first. They both die, and then the crematorium mixes their ashes in one big urn and then casts them into, I don't know, Lake Superior."

She was getting too somber for me, and besides what she was describing didn't sound like the Elfreda Barcowicz I had thought I knew. I couldn't help making a little joke. "That won't happen," I told her. "There's still too much of the Yellowstone ashes in Lake Superior already."

She gave me a withering look. "It doesn't matter where the hell they cast the ashes, does it? The Mississippi River. Waikiki Beach. They could do it anywhere."

I took it a step further. "Right here would be pretty good for ashes-dumping," I suggested. "The zeps will be back any day, right? So you could do the casting from one of them as soon as it's over the water. And, hey, there isn't much you could do to the Bay of Naples that hasn't been done already."

Elfreda put down her second drink—this time it was one of those toxic Italian brandies that they make out of God knows what—and gave me the most reproachful look yet. "I hate sons of bitches like you," she told me. "You take all the romance out of sex."

I had realized by then that I was doing comedy where her skin was unexpectedly thin, but I couldn't let that stand unchallenged. "Not true, Elfreda. I'm as romantic as anybody, honest. I'm all in favor of being in love with somebody, and having kids with her, and growing old with her, just like you said."

She gazed at me in silence for a while. "Yeah," she finally said, in a suddenly darker, more thoughtful mood. "You probably are. But not with me, right?" And she got up and walked away, leaving a centimeter of that poisonous brandy undrunk in her glass.

I could've sympathized a little with Elfreda. That was what she had been asking for. It wouldn't have been much trouble for me and there was nothing to stop me. At that very moment Gerda might well be doing some old friend, or for that matter some new one, up there in the Italian lakes. And even if she wasn't, she wouldn't really have any serious grounds for complaint if I had just happened to do a little flirting—or maybe even a little down-to-earth recreational sex—with somebody else while she was gone. With Elfreda, say. Who had been really *inviting it*, and happened to be friendly (maybe too friendly), and was definitely smart (smart enough to have landed the plum job of keyboarding the Giubileo's publicity in a nice air-conditioned office instead of sweating over a hot triclinum all day long) and that wasn't all. Put Elfreda's specs all together: slim waist, sweet hips, man's-hand-sized breasts, cute little brown-eyed, full-lipped face. Looked at objectively, by which I mean not with the besotted vision of someone hopelessly smitten, like me, she was at least as good-looking as Gerda. And her earlobes said heterosexual, active, open to a good approach.

Nothing wrong there, was there? And I'd let her walk away.

I was back in my room and tugging my blankets into some sort of usable condition in my unmade cot, when there was a tapping on my door.

I did the usual quick guessing game. It wouldn't have been Gerda; even if she had come back she wouldn't knock. I doubted it was Elfreda giving me a second chance. The only thing I could figure was that Jiri's wife had forgotten some of his goods. So I opened the door, and it wasn't Jiri's wife. Widow, I mean. What it was was a slim, slight Asian-looking man in formal shirt and shorts, with a bellybag and—remember, this was the middle of the night—wearing dark blue sunglasses.

He didn't wait to be invited in. He politely nudged me out of the way so he could get past me, shut the door behind him, and said, "Good evening, Mr. Bradley Sheridan. Do you remember me? I am Eustace Chi-Leong. We were introduced by my honored father, Dr. Basil Chi-Leong, when you were kind enough to let us photograph you at your place of business. How are you?"

By then I did recognize him. He didn't wait for me to get around to that, either. He rejected the unmade bed and the rickety old armchair I'd thrown my clothes on and seated himself on the straight-backed chair. Then he spoke right up. "Allow me to show you something," he said, pulling a package out of his bellybag.

Whatever it was, it was wrapped in purple fabric, and judging by the care with which he unwrapped it, pretty valuable. The thing that finally came out of the several layers of wrap looked to me like a pewter gravy boat, fifteen or twenty centimeters long. "Is it not beautiful?" he asked me with pride.

Well, I supposed it was. I don't know a lot about high-priced tableware, but the thing did have some pretty scenes of nymphs and centaurs engraved on it. If I'd discovered it in any hotel room I was robbing, back in the old days, I probably would have taken it along and tried to figure out how to fence it later. I said, "Looks expensive, anyway."

He waved that off. "This chalice," he said severely, "is made of platinum and is believed to have been made by Benvenuto Cellini. There is one like it in the papal treasury in Rome, not so good as this. That is all. There is no other anywhere in the world. The reason I have it now is that my esteemed father, Dr. Basil Chi-Leong, has purchased it as a gift for the collection of my grandmother, Madam Katey Chi-Leong, whom you have also met. He has asked me to invite you to help us get this chalice on the zeppelin, *Chang Jang*, which in some seventy-two hours will be moored over its repositioning depot along the shore of the bay. The zeppelin is then scheduled to depart for several destinations in North Africa, where arrangements can more easily be made to transport the chalice to our home in Singapore." He gave me an appraising look. "Of course," he added, "what we wish to do may not be considered entirely legal."

"I kind of guessed that," I told him.

He nodded. "For that reason," he said, "you will be quite well compensated for your assistance. The figure my father mentioned was two thousand euros."

He stopped, absentmindedly stroking the chalice in his lap, waiting for me to respond to the offer. But I knew better than to do that just then. I said, "Sounds like you're in a hurry."

He gave me an unfriendly look. "Is that so strange, with all the stories about disease vectors here at the Giubileo?" He paused. A moment later he nodded and said, "I will take it upon myself to increase the offer to five thousand. So can we count on your help, Mr. Sheridan?"

Well, when it came right down to it, they couldn't.

None of the guys I roamed the streets with back in the Apple would have believed it if anyone had told them about it, but I backed away from the offer.

Before I did that I listened to everything he had to say, though, and I could see that he had really thought the thing through. "Yes, Mr. Sheridan, it is true that only passengers and crew are allowed by the zeppelin's security to board it, but you must simply be more creative. After all, one need not pass through the established checkpoints. There are areas where their surveillance is somewhat lax, one of which being what is called the 'honey-bucket system.'"

As I say, he'd thought it through.

Actually I was pretty sure that his schemes could work. Like all zeps, the *Chang Jang* had to remain in as close to neutral buoyancy as it could.

So at every port of call, while the shoregoing passengers were doing their touristy things down below, the zep would make a quick trip to a pumping station on the ground. There the zep would settle down close to the surface. Mooring cables, along with three big hose pipes, then held it securely in place. One hose piped the zep's accumulated waste water and sewage down to the honey wagons waiting below, while one of the other two sucked up an appropriate weight of fuel for their tank and the last one pumped up fresh water to go into the ballast tanks and the swimming pool, which doubled as their water reserve. The fuel would be burned. Much of the water became the carrier for the new sewage at their next stop.

And, Chi-Leong said, hardly anybody bothered to check on the sewage system. All a person would have to do was put on a uniform, possibly one that was a little bit stained; stick some pipe wrenches in his utility belt, climb the ladder attached to the sewage hose, tapping and listening to it from time to time to add plausibility in case, against the odds, anyone happened to look in that direction. And that was it. At the top a nervous but well-paid room steward would be waiting to take the package off the climber's hands. Then he would be free to climb back down and live his life, five thousand euros richer.

Or, I considered, maybe ten thousand. Or more. Because if the kid could raise the price from two thousand to five, then probably the old man could be pushed a little higher, too.

But I still said no.

It wasn't that I was unwilling to break a law—assuming that the price was right, and this price wasn't bad at all. It was just that my personal situation didn't make it worthwhile. See, if Gerda had still been around she and I could have had a hell of a fine time with a few thousand extra euros. She wasn't.

The Antica people still were, though.

I clearly remembered what they had done to Abukar Abdu, the Somali from down the hall, for picking up a couple of mosaic tiles to sell to the tourists as souvenirs. This wasn't a matter of a few tiles. I could barely imagine what the Anticas might do to someone caught trying to smuggle a national treasure out of the country. The Krakow coal mines looked very near.

So I kept on saying no, even when Chi-Leong upped the ante again. He wagged his head at me. "My father, Dr. Basil Chi-Leong, expected a better answer from you, Bradley Sheridan. He will be extremely disappointed at your refusal. As am I."

He rewrapped the chalice in its purple cloths and made it disappear into his bellybag. At the door he paused. "You have made a very poor decision," he told me, and was gone.

Things didn't get better for me. They got worse.

Well, hell, everything else was getting worse, too. Every day the news became another degree more horrific, when I hadn't thought that was possible. Within a week over eighty thousand people were dead from this Pompeii Flu, all around the world, most of them having done their dying in excruciating pain and horrid disfigurement. Then there were at least another hundred thousand, probably more, presently going through the dying-in-disfigurement process, but with their lungs still pumping air and their hearts chugging along—for the time being, anyway. And then there were the ones who had been infected but hadn't found out yet.

The statistics didn't have anything like a firm number for those, but the assortment of guesses all had one thing in common. The low estimate might be any number at all, but the high-end one was always in the millions.

And for me personally . . .

Well, that wasn't great, either. The Welsh Bastard had finally begun to notice that my wine vats were still pretty full at the end of my shift, and was getting suspicious. "What the hell're you doing there, Sheridan? You insulting the customers? Let them catch you pissing in the wine? Torco and Molderman both do twice the business you do, and you got the good location." That part about the location was certainly untrue, but the heat was on. I temporarily had to cut down on the number of cups I recycled, and that made my cash flow even worse.

And then there was Maury Tesch's problem.

Before Jiri died Maury had carried the pieces of his nonkosher delicacy away to, I supposed, savor them in private. But then, a week or so after Gerda took off, Maury came knocking at the door, not grinning and not looking at all happy. He was waving something in my face, and I knew without looking what it was. The smell told me everything. "Brad," he said, voice tight and either seriously pissed off or pretty thoroughly scared, "somebody's been into my wurst. See? The wrapping's been torn."

I pushed his hand away. "For Christ's sake, Maury, get it out of my face! I didn't touch it. Maybe Jiri did before he got sick."

He stood. "Oh, hell," he said, and stopped there.

It struck me that he was now looking sick himself. "Hey," I said. "Sit down, why don't you? Can't you like send away for more of your—" And then, as the penny dropped, "Oh, Jesus! You think it was your stuff that made him sick?"

He didn't have to say yes. The way he looked as he sank into the chair said it all. I offered him a cup of tea or some of his own Israeli red, thinking hard. By the time he was finished turning down everything I had to offer I thought I had the answer for him. "There's nothing to worry about," I said. "Nobody knew about your stash but you and me and Jiri himself—and Gerda, but she's not around right now. Jiri could've told his wife, maybe. But I don't think she knew about them. She didn't say anything. So I don't think anybody's going to come after you for his death."

Maury's expression had changed again, and this time I couldn't read it at all. He just sat there, gazing at me—or maybe looking straight through me at God knows what.

Finally he sighed. "You think?" he asked.

I did think that. I told him so.

And then his whole look changed. He managed a kind of a smile. "Oh, Brad, Brad," he said, "you don't know what it means to me to have a friend like you." And many more repetitions of the same sentiment, until at last I pushed him out the door.

I was glad to see him go. As far as I was concerned Maury and his damn sausages were just another annoyance that kept me from concentrating on how much I was hating my present life. He wasn't even a big pain in the ass, just a little one.

But then the next thing that happened was big, all right, just about big enough for anybody.

12

THE BIG THING

I suppose that that next big thing was going to happen whatever I did. Maybe so. Still, if it hadn't been for the sky show they gave on the day before at least one thing would have been different. I wouldn't have been there to see it.

It happened when I was about two hours into my wine selling, the day already hot and my mental state pretty maximally depressed. Then the show began. First the sky overhead just rolled itself back, and then its summery blue turned into icy white. The spotty clouds vanished. When I looked up that blue sky had suddenly become a close-up of something that was unlike sky of any kind and had no business being there. The clouds became floating heads. That giant thing in the air was old Mount Vesuvius itself. In the proper world the mountain should have been squatting peacefully way over against the horizon, where it belonged, but now there it impossibly was, up there in the air and puffing out its plume of white steam as though it had every right to be there.

"Now what the hell?" muttered one of the customers.

The woman he was with answered him in a tone heavy with well-rehearsed sarcasm. "See, Gerald, you old fool, you just don't remember anything at all anymore, do you? This is the preview they talked about, what we're seeing now. Like what they're going to show on the anniversary itself, but only a short version of it, see? Like a coming attraction. For God's sake, Gerald! I read you all about it right off my opticle when we were still in Norway."

Gerald wasn't the only one who had forgotten. I was another, but the virt machines hadn't. They had been programmed to put on a commercial for the Jubilee's customers and that's what they did. What we were gaping at was a sky-wide virt version of that two-thousand-year-old eruption of Vesuvius that had put Pompeii out of business in the first place. It was spectacular. I don't mean just your usual wow-that's-a-beaut! spectacular, like you might have said about the Fourth of July fireworks they used to set off from the old Statue of Liberty. I mean it was knock-you-on-your-ass *wonderful*.

Cedric had wandered over in order to be with somebody else for the spectacle. "Remarkable what they do with virts," he informed me, as a gigantic, if unreal, cloud of flame-laced death billowed in our direction.

Remarkable it was. The best thing about the flame was that we didn't have to worry about it killing us because it wasn't real. I particularly appreciated that fact when, a moment later, a sudden hail of pumice particles fell out of the cloud. Back in the year AD 79 those same falling rocks had inflicted pain and death on thousands of Pompeiians as unsheltered as ourselves. Us they didn't harm at all. Like everything else going on above us the pumice pebbles were a collection of photons and nothing more. When a batch of them hit Cedric on the head they simply disappeared into his bushy hair. When spinning dust devils of smoky gases dropped down on us from the cloud they didn't hurt. Back in AD 79 those things had been hot enough to sear the flesh off the bones of any human being they touched. But this bunch, heatless and massless as they were, did us no harm at all.

Then it was over.

The gawkers who had been too busy staring at the virt show in the sky to think about visiting Cedric's brothel had turned back into being potential customers again, as had my wine drinkers.

The show was over, but it did have an effect on my life.

. . .

The next morning started out like any other. Sometimes my opticle woke me up, more often I just woke up by myself, long before I wanted to. I'm talking about before-dawn stuff here, maybe just happening because now there wasn't any nice, warm, Gerda-sized body sharing the cot with me, and my half-awake mind found that worrisome. (My fully awake mind just found it lousy.) Anyway, most days, after half an hour or so of convincing myself that I wasn't going to go back to sleep in the foreseeable future, I would give in, get up, get dressed. Then maybe I'd stop for a cup of coffee in the refectory kitchen, where the cooks would be starting to think about breakfast for the early shift. Probably I'd walk around for an hour or two. Maybe up the hill to take a look at the sunrise, maybe down to the Marine Gate to see if any of the concessionaires had fired up any calzone yet. Maybe anywhere at all, just because I had nothing better to do.

I know how that makes me sound.

I knew it then, too. I told myself that I should be ashamed of myself for acting like a lovesick high-schooler whose best girl has just been caught in the backseat of a convertible with some damn football player.

I reminded myself often that there wasn't any reason for me to act that way. I wasn't that kind of man.

The virt show had included scenes of what that AD 79 eruption had done to the old city itself, including a couple shots of the wrecking of the Forum—toppling the Apollo statue, crushing the upper stories of the buildings—and I guess that was what made me want to take another look at the Forum's unrestored, unvirted, fully demolished self. So that morning, having got up preposterously early for even my ridiculously early job, I went for a walk in the old Forum.

Not many people were around. That was no surprise. I didn't expect to see anybody, but then there really was a little bit of a surprise because I did. A woman. Halfway across the Forum, carrying something that looked like a pipe wrench, and then she was gone.

I hadn't really got a good look at her. It was still dark. I was waiting for the virt generators to come on, bank by bank, turning the old, time-destroyed structures into the pulsing, living, flower-bedecked, statuary-rich city of the Giubileo. While I can't say that doing this was a lot of fun, just then I settled for small amounts.

With the virts still turned off the Forum didn't look much like the busy, brightly colored square the tourists saw. The structures that once had their second stories given back to them by the Jubilee's virt engineers were beheaded again. The flesh-and-blood vendors of the Forum, the ones who sold actual clay pots and souvenir togas and anything else they could make an as from, were nowhere around, probably still in their beds.

Not everyone was, though. Without warning the quiet was violently shattered as the sound of a shot and then a sudden angry yelling came from somewhere between the Apollo temple and the basilica.

When I turned I saw that the screeches were coming from a woman wearing an Antica uniform, complete with boots and a backpack. Her fly-eye goggles were pulled up to the top of her head so she could do a better job of yelling at a tall, fair-skinned and uniformed woman in the blue helmet of the UN inspection team who had just fired a shot over her head.

That was surprising. What the UN was supposed to be doing in Pompeii was basically what it did in every place where there were large gatherings of strangers—that is, look for loonies who might be terrorists. The Antica woman didn't fit the profile. Her uniform meant that she wasn't a stranger. She was someone who had as much right to be there as the UN soldier, and I guess what she was doing was telling the soldier so. I couldn't be sure, though, because the UN soldier seemed to be speaking something like Swedish and the Antica woman mostly Italian, and neither language was intelligible to me. And the fingers of the soldier's right hand were playing over the metallic-thread keypad embroidery on her blouse. She was, I was pretty sure, calling her headquarters.

The Antica woman seemed to think so, too. She didn't like it. The yelling stopped short. She shrugged apologetically and, half-smiling, she turned away.

It seemed that something had suddenly changed for her. I couldn't see what. Then I did. From down the Via Stabiana I heard the sound of a car turbine. A UN troop carrier was racing toward us, with a dozen armed soldiers on board.

The soldier didn't let that distract her from watching the Antica woman, and that was a good thing. The Antica woman gave her another of those apologetic smiles as her hand reached up to touch something at the top of her backpack.

She never made it. The UN soldier didn't hesitate. I heard her yell something that sounded like the words "Bom! Atombom!" And then she lifted her sidearm and, just as the other troops were jumping out of their vehicle, shot the Antica woman point-blank in the throat.

Well, all right, I didn't really know what had been going on. Still I was pretty sure of what was supposed to happen next. The arriving troops would grab the shooter and drag her away, for—I don't know, for some kind of court-martial? Or whatever they did to UN soldiers who killed a civilian?

I was wrong about that. It didn't happen that way. The arriving soldiers didn't restrain the killer. They paid her no attention at all. All six of them leaped to the side of the fallen Antica woman, two of them grabbing her arms and holding them away from the backpack, just as though there were any chance that the woman was still alive. Two of the others were, with great care, unbuckling the backpack and carrying it to the vehicle. And while I was standing there, dumbfounded, mouth hanging open, somebody grabbed me from behind.

That person was the UN soldier herself. She was saying something I couldn't understand, probably because it was in that same might-have-been Swedish language. Then she tried English. "Is enough," she said. "You to go away." Then she put her fingers to her lips and, pointing to the dead woman, said, "You understand? Bad thing! A-bom-bom terrorista!"

Since I was the only witness to this bloodletting, I didn't think they were going to give me a hearty handshake and send me on my way.

They didn't. What they did for the next half hour or so was keep me sitting on the steps of the Jupiter temple while they tidied up. First they carried the corpse of the Antica woman away, along with the thing from her backpack that I guessed might have been the thing that might have been a bomb. Then a couple of cleaning machines rumbled up, spraying the blood off the stones and blowing them dry in the same pass. Then the soldiers stuck me on the back of a scooter on which I was carried to the door of the Welsh Bastard's dispatch room.

The Bastard wasn't there yet, of course. It was his practice to come in early, yes, but never as early as that. They left me there, sitting next to his desk, with the door locked from outside.

When at last the Bastard did show up he had two messages for me. One was that I was the biggest asshole he had ever seen. The other was to keep my mouth shut and stay out of trouble. Then he got into a deep conversation with one of the soldiers. When finally he came over to me I naturally tried to ask him for some kind of an explanation. Naturally the Bastard told me to shut up and mind my own business or he would mind it for me.

So I did shut up. Not just because the Bastard told me to but also because I didn't have much to say, since I had no real idea of what the hell was going on.

See, I had never imagined that I would even be a spectator to the murder of an Antica woman. Especially by a UN soldier. Especially when words like "atom bomb" and "terrorist" were being thrown around.

I was still trying to worry some sense out of the episode all the time the Bastard was yelling at me. I didn't really even hear him. I wasn't paying much attention to anything but the memories of the surprised look on the Antica woman's face as the soldier shot her, and the way all that blood came spilling out, and the scary words that the soldier had used.

Out of the window I could see that at last the virts had come on, restoring Pompeii to its resuscitated life. One moment the naked Apollo statue on his marble pedestal was its natural dirty-ashtray black, the next it was brightly gleaming polished bronze, and the bow that Vesuvius had struck from his hands two thousand years earlier had magicked itself back—of course only as a virt—and he was ready to puncture some hapless tourist with one of his restored arrows. I didn't take time to admire the view, because my head was busy with other things. I only really heard what the Bastard himself said, for that matter, when he was telling me—for, I think, the third or fourth time—to keep my goddamn mouth closed and get my goddamn ass to work. "And," he added, "what the hell were you doing there anyway?"

I told him the truth. "I couldn't sleep."

That got me a full-fledged sneer. "Couldn't sleep my Welsh ass. Do you know what kind of trouble you could get me in with Security? Now get the hell out of here, and, remember, not one damn word to anybody."

I couldn't do that. This was too big to be swept under the carpet. I said reasonably, "But didn't you hear what the soldier said? She said 'atom bomb' and 'terrorist'!"

The Bastard sighed. "Jesus, Sheridan," he said, "are you so dumb you don't know an exercise when you see it? That wasn't any real goddamn terrorist. Security was *practicing* for the way they would take a real nuclear terrorist out if one of them ever showed up around here."

I couldn't buy that. "That blood was about as real as—" I began.

The Bastard gave me a sneer. "Screw the blood! You imagined it! Don't you know what— Wait a minute."

He got the absent look of a man being spoken to on his private ear opticle, while his fingers played for a moment with the keys on his own blouse. Then he looked annoyed—at, as usual, the world, I thought at first. But then his eyes focused in my general direction, particularly at me. "You still here?" he demanded.

I tried reason. "The thing is, Bas— Jeremy, I mean, I actually saw that soldier shoot the other one in the throat. I saw the blood!"

"You saw the blood, you saw the blood! My God, Sheridan, how stupid are you? You've got virts all around you, and you don't know virt blood when you see it!"

That was a stopper. "Virt blood?" I said. "Really? But honestly—"

"Go!" he said, mean and loud. "One more word and I'm debiting your account a hundred euros for misconduct."

That was an injustice I couldn't accept, but when I opened my mouth to say so he didn't let me speak. "I said *go*," he told me. "Do you want me to make it five hundred? And listen, forget about this whole thing. That's an order. Watch your mouth. Don't go talking about what you thought you saw or you'll be getting something a whole lot worse than a fine."

And that ended the discussion.

Well, I didn't forget about it. I couldn't. But I did watch my mouth, at least a little bit.

I didn't *say* anything to anybody. I just *hinted*. Hinted to Maury Tesch when I saw him in the dressing room, with more than an hour still to spend before opening: "Maury? Did you hear anything about some weird stuff going on in the Forum this morning?"

Maury was speaking to me again, though just barely. "Of course I did," he said. "Everybody knows that there were two drunken UN soldiers shooting it out. They say one of them's not likely to live."

That made me swallow, but I didn't dispute Maury's version. I just said, "Wow," and went to my breakfast. And ten minutes later, feeding coins into the machines in the food court, I caught snatches of four or five other versions of the story, all different. And was no more than halfway through my creamed chipped beef-flavored tofu on toast, which I was eating pretty slowly because my mind was on other things, when someone sat down beside me. It was Elfreda Barcowicz, arriving with a coffee cup and an eager expression.

If she was still disappointed in me for carrying the torch for Gerda she was willing to overlook it for the sake of a good gossip. She wasted no time. "Did you hear? A bunch of UN guys got drunk and began shooting up the big amphitheater?"

I got cautious. "I thought it happened in the Forum."

"Oh, no. It was the big amphitheater, all right, the one they didn't fix up. And two of the UN guys died!" She added a heaping spoonful of sugar to her not much more than a spoonful of thick, black coffee. "Scary, isn't it?" she added conversationally. "Armed drunks shooting off their guns in the middle of the night? Makes you wonder if it's safe for us to be around here."

That wasn't what I was wondering about, though. What I was wondering about was whether all this was just the normal process of everybody getting things wrong, or somebody was manufacturing rumors in order to keep the truth obscured.

I looked her over more carefully than I usually did.

Elfreda didn't fit into my usual notion of what somebody I could talk to would look like. She wasn't—I mean, after I'd been spoiled by Gerda she wasn't—quite sexy-looking enough to inflame my male instincts, and she wasn't male enough to be a Maury Tesch kind of, well, pal. Though I don't think I had really got used to the idea of having a pal at all.

But I did quite badly need to talk to somebody, so I gave it a shot. "Elfreda," I said, "what would you say if I told you there was just one UN soldier involved, and what she did was shoot and kill an Antica woman because she thought the Antica woman was a terrorist who had a nuclear weapon . . . and the reason I know all this is because I was there and I saw it go down?"

It was Elfreda's turn to look me over more carefully. She did. Then she said, "This is what I would say, Brad. I'd either say, a. you're the damnedest liar I ever met, or b. you're the biggest fool for talking about it."

And she got up, leaving her undrunk coffee behind, and walked away.

Later on, when I was loading my breakfast dishes onto the conveyor belt the woman running it didn't answer my "How's it going?" And a couple of minutes later, when I saw one of my old gladiator acquaintances across the room and flipped him a good morning wave of the hand he turned and walked rapidly away. He wasn't even one of the ones I had accidentally stabbed, either.

There wasn't any doubt. I was back on the bad list. The word had gone out. I had been seen to be asking for trouble by spreading rumors the high-ups didn't want spread and therefore I wasn't popular. Everybody knows that trouble is more contagious than a head cold, and nobody wanted to catch my dose of trouble.

Well, I hadn't ever been really popular. But it hadn't been like now. Now I might just as well have been ringing a little silver bell and calling out, "Unclean! Unclean!" as I walked.

13

DOGHOUSE DAYS

What happened the next week or so? Nothing.

For a while I had the idea that the cash customers at the wineshop must have heard something. They were definitely scarcer than they had been. The tips were even slimmer than usual, and hardly anybody gave me any euros to change to sesterces.

That was something I could check out, though. I had observed Cedric the Pimp slouching just inside the entrance to his faux bordello. So I abandoned my customerless shop to hustle across the via for a good morning chat. "Pretty slow this morning," I observed experimentally, to see if he would take a chance on talking to me.

He glanced at me, then looked up and down the street to see if anyone was looking before he acknowledged what I had said. "You mean not so many customers? Oh, sure not. They're scared," he informed me.

"Of terrorists?" I said, and bit my tongue to keep from adding something about Antica women getting shot and UN soldiers going wild. He let me know right away that that wasn't what he was talking about, though. "Not terrorists," he said. "Pompeii Flu is what's scaring them off. They're afraid they might catch it if they come here. I can't say I blame them." Then he gave me an embarrassed grin before he did that even more embarrassed clearing of the throat that meant that the next thing was going to be the observation that a tiny little shot of Giubileo red would go down well right about then.

That happened. I didn't mind. Cedric was willing to pay for his wine in the currency of conversation, and there were things I wanted to know.

Although *I* hadn't really been paying attention it was true that I had noticed the crowds were smaller, and my guesses at the reason hadn't made a lot of sense. But as soon as Cedric said the words it became obvious. Sure, there were all those news stories about people turning up sick after they'd been to the Jubilee, so who could blame your average tourist for thinking that this was the place to visit if you wanted to come down with Pompeii Flu, but not otherwise.

Well, I didn't really mind that, either. The people who owned stock in the Giubileo might lose some dividends from customers' nervousness. For me it just meant more time to stare into space and wish my life would get better.

Of course. If I'd thought it through it would have occurred to me that anything that cost me earnings was going to cost Mr. and Mrs. Daniel Sheridan of Molly Pitcher Redeployment Village back on Staten Island even more.

When I thought of that I did care, a little. Just a little, though. There was only one thing I really cared about, and that was the fact Gerda wasn't around and there was nothing I could do about that.

So that's the way the picture was. The crowds were down, Maury seemed to be avoiding me, and Gerda was absent. There wasn't much that was good about the next few days.

The closest we came to excitement was when the authorities reran their teaser virts to build up a crowd for the big show. They showed the coming attractions scenes four or five times a day, and that had been sort of interesting. At least it was the first couple of dozen times they did it.

The only other thing I paid much attention to was the news. I won't say I enjoyed it—I wasn't really in the enjoyment business—but it did hold my interest most of the time, especially when the news they were talking about wasn't related to the Pompeii Flu.

Of course, about their only other area of interest was some new outburst of terrorism. That sort of thing didn't exactly make me feel better but at least those stories didn't have Pompeii's name on them and weren't usually about anything nearby. For instance there was the Goan ferry captain who drove his little boat right into a cluster of half-submerged rocks, killing everybody aboard, including himself. He'd found out that most of his passengers were Christian missionaries on their way to bring Jesus to the part of Goa's that were still heathens. And a train bombing in Kiev, and a sniper with a long-range rifle in the hills around Monte Cassino, picking off truck drivers on the Naples–Rome *soprastrada*. . . . And, oh, well, enough others to remind me how many terminally unhappy people there were in the world. Which did, sometimes and for a little while, take my mind off what an outstandingly crappy life I was having.

Of course there was one thing I could do. I could walk away from the whole situation.

There wasn't really any way anybody could stop me. All I had to do was to walk out the Marina Gate and get on the electric to Naples and not come back.

Why not? After all, when I was still a punk teenager I had been able to survive on the mean streets of New York City, hadn't I? How much harder could it be to do the same thing in Rome or Milan or, who knows, Tbilisi or Beijjng?

Well, yes, I had to admit that it would be somewhat harder, at least. There were big differences between then and now: a. I wasn't fourteen anymore, b. I didn't have my parents' slum to hide out in if things got dicey, and more than that, c. when I was fourteen I hadn't had the Krakow coal mines to look forward to if the cops caught me running out on my Indenture money.

And of course none of those was the real reason anyhow. Which was d. the one big misery that made all the others unimportant. Walking away from my life meant permanently and irretrievably walking away from whatever chance I had of a better life, which is to say a life with Gerda coming back. That far I was not yet prepared to go.

Put all those things together and you can see why I was not a happy camper. If asked I would have said that the situation could not get much worse. Which goes to show you how hopelessly, totally wrong I can always somehow manage to be.

After a few days things did begin to pick up, crowd-wise, a little bit at the Jubilee. Maybe some of the accelerating bad news that was coming in from the rest of the world relieved some of the Flu worries about visiting Pompeii. Whatever the reason, the customers did begin to come back. It was kids first, of course. On the Thursday a couple pairs of teenaged boys showed up, uneasily trotting along the Via dell'Abbondanza and paying no attention to any of the attractions, as though they had dared each other to make the visit and wished it were the hell over. None of them bought any wine from me, although that was the age group that had produced some of my best customers. None of them visited Cedric's brothel, either, although their cohort had often provided the only customers he had. Then, Friday, there were more of those show-off teenage boys in somewhat larger groups. By Saturday the groups began to include a few girls, looking scared—or at least looking the way they elected to look, in order to make the boys they were with feel brave. And by the next weekend the crowds were pretty much back to normal quantities.

I don't suppose the populace at large had become any less afraid of the Pompeii Flu, only that they had come to realize that there wasn't any safety from it anywhere, because the news stories were beginning to show that you could catch it from any person who was infected, even if not yet showing symptoms, at any place in the world and any time.

Oh, yes. There was one interesting thing. Early one morning, when there was hardly anyone else around, Elfreda Barcowicz came by. She ordered a glass of my best Falernian, touched it to her lips, made a face and never touched it again. And said, in the tone of an inquisitor, "Listen, Brad, I've been worrying about you. Can I ask you something?"

I said she could, and so she came right out with it. "That story you were telling, the one about the shooting in the Forum. Tell me again what happened."

This was, remember, the woman who had told me never to mention that subject to anybody ever again. I elected to be difficult. "I never said it happened," I reminded her. "I just said suppose it happened."

She sighed and tried again, this time sweetly. "Fine, I agree that's what you said. So now I'm going to suppose that you're in the Forum and it's before start-up time, and you notice a woman from the Antica who's also there."

I decided not to be difficult anymore. "And there was a UN soldier, too," I said. "And they got into an argument and the soldier shot the woman in the neck." And then I added, "I thought."

Elfreda pounced on that. "You *thought?*"

"We're just supposing," I reminded her.

She gave me an unfriendly look. "All right, Brad," she said, all the honey having long since seeped out of her voice and her expression. "Go ahead. Be a son of a bitch if you want to, but I'm asking you for help. I know that something happened there. I know it must've been important, because Piranha Woman is threatening to call the Indenture loan from anybody who spreads rumors about it. So I believe that you really did see something. Sure you won't be a reasonable guy and tell me about it? Not even if I promise not to drop the word about your deal with the Singaporeans?"

Now, that was a totally unexpected body blow. I heard myself gasp, I temporized. "Hell, Elfreda, I turned their deal down!"

She nodded morosely. "Sure you did. But is Piranha Woman going to believe you when you say it?" Then she sighed, surrendering. She stood up to go. "I guess I'd be cautious if I were you. Think it over, Brad. If you decide to trust me, remember that I can be a good friend."

She didn't wait for an answer. She just went, leaving me to meditate on the fact that, although there seemed to be a lot of secrets being kept around the Giubileo, my own secrets weren't among them.

There was one other thing that made those hot summer days kind of interesting. It was another little terrorist attack on the Jubilee, this one taking place right there on my own Via dell'Abbondanza.

It wasn't much of a threat. It was just three elderly women from some little town in South Carolina, and what they did was throw paint on some of Cedric's dirty murals. They didn't accomplish much, though. They had made the mistake of using that you-can-change-your-mind-if-you-want-to wall paint meant for the chronically undecided. It worked just as advertised. The Jubilee's maintenance people got it all washed off before it set.

Truly unimportant. I might not even have remembered it at all if it hadn't come right before that funny business with Maury Tesch.

14

THAT UNFUNNY FUNNY BUSINESS
WITH MAURY TESCH

I was in the changing room after another lousy day of selling lousy wine to people who, by and large, I would just as soon have seen dead. Somebody called my name, and it was Maury.

He looked like hell. "What's the matter?" I asked him.

He didn't answer that. He just said, "Have you got anything special on for tonight?"

That was so improbable that it almost made me laugh. I didn't, though. I just said, "What have you got in mind?"

He didn't seem to have a ready answer for that. He thought for a few moments before he came up with any answer at all. "Anything you want, Brad," he said beseechingly. "You've never been to my place, have you? Maybe you could come up there? I've got all kinds of vid stuff, or maybe just have a drink? Or, if you wanted some, like pills, I could get—"

I shook my head at the word "pills," so he stopped there, with an expression like a puppy caught in a misdeed in his toilet training. He looked imploring. "Would you do it, please, Brad?" he coaxed. "I don't want to be alone."

Naturally I asked him why that was, but that seemed to be too hard a question for him. He mulled it over for a bit and then shook his head. "I can't tell you that," he said, and then again, "Please?"

If I had had the sense God gave a termite I would have told him, I don't know, maybe something like I couldn't do it because I had a date with one the local whores, I mean the freelance ones who hung around the Marina Gate, and I couldn't get out of it because I'd paid a deposit when I reserved her services. I wasn't smart enough to do that. I did what I was pretty sure I probably would regret doing later on. I said, "Oh, I guess so," and finished dressing and followed him out the door.

Understand me here. I'm not saying that I particularly cared if Maury Tesch was suffering from the lonesome blues or not. I didn't feel I owed him consideration as a friend, either, because I had long since decided that he wasn't one, really. If I had a reason at all, I guess it was contemplating the possibility that Maury's troubles might be real and hearing them might cheer me up.

It became evident that he was going to some pains to make the evening pleasant for me. I had assumed that we were going to have to climb the hill on foot in order to get to the support staff quarters. We didn't, though. Maury had another three-wheeler and driver waiting for us. It took less than ten minutes before we pulled up in front of that dormitory building I had already seen on the way to the pine forest. It was at least twice as nice as Gerda's, and in a whole other space-time continuum than my own. And when we got inside Maury's rooms it was even more so. I didn't know what to expect, though certainly I wasn't expecting his actual four-room, two-bedroom suite, with little railed balconies outside the windows of the bedrooms and a personal steamcuzzi in the bath. Two of the rooms were made up as bedrooms, but only one seemed to be in use. In the other the bed—the double-width bed with its double-length pillows—had been stripped, and there were no personal items in the furnishings. "That was Walt Fossett's room," Maury said from behind me. "New Zealander. He got homesick so he quit. What would you like to drink?"

I said I'd like to be surprised. I was, too. When he opened the mirror over his personal wet bar what was behind it was a liquor cabinet. I had known, what every Indentured knew, that the plumbers and electricians and carpenters and computer geeks got paid more and got treated better than we did, but I hadn't known just how very much better. I didn't even know the names on some of those bottles.

So I said arbitrarily, "Is that tequila on the bottom shelf? I've never had any, and I've always wondered what it would be like."

He had it, all right. Dipped the rim of a glass in a saucer of salt that was hiding behind the bottles, cut a slice off a lime plucked from a bowl of fruit, and served. When I tried the tequila I didn't think it was bad. I wouldn't have minded if my evening's drinking had been limited to a couple more of the same. But Maury had other ideas.

Actually I didn't think the imported Russian vodka he gave me to try next was bad, either. Or the Japanese rice wine that came after that, and somewhere around then I began to lose count. Maury was drinking some himself, though I wasn't really keeping track of what or how much. He was talking, too, and at considerable length. Early on I tried to pay attention to what he was saying because the weird way he was acting had made me a little curious about what his specific troubles were, but after about my third or fourth drink he hadn't got very lucid and I gave up trying.

Actually the kind of thing Maury was talking about wasn't at all what I had expected from him. He wasn't reciting a list of personal grievances. He wasn't really talking about himself at all. Some of what he was saying had to do with how wrong it was for people who possessed power to do harm to people who didn't have any power of their own—I think something like that, anyway. Later on I wished I had paid closer attention. But later on what Maury wanted didn't much matter anymore.

Then a little of his rambling seemed to be about Gerda, and then I did prick up my ears. Or tried to, the best I could with all that alcohol swirling around inside me. But all he was saying was how Gerda and he used to be good friends but they weren't anymore. And some of it was just nonsense, like some kind of story about the Antica woman, the one that the UN soldier had shot right in front of me, and why she had been there to get shot in the first place. But by the time he got to that I was way too full of his liquor to try to follow what he was trying to say.

"Wanted to join," I think he said—without ever saying join what, "but she wouldn't have her." Without ever saying who "she" was, either.

Take it all in all, and it was one of the most bizarre evenings of my life, and it had an even more bizarre, and nastier, ending.

What do I mean by bizarre?

Well, consider this. By about my fifth sampling of the inexhaustible contents of Maury's liquor cabinet—or maybe it could have been the sixth or seventh—Maury suddenly up-ended his glass and swallowed right down the centimeter or so of Scotch that he had been nursing. He gave me a cold-sober look. "Do you want to know something? I lied to you about knowing Maris Morchan."

"Knowing who?" I asked, because I was losing him again. It took a moment for me to connect the dots and get straight that Maris Morchan was the Antica woman I had seen the soldier blow away. When that had clarified itself in my head I said. "Oh, her. Sure. Say, I didn't know you knew her."

He gave me a look I can only call disgusted, though what he had to be disgusted about when it was his damn booze that was tangling up my thought processes I couldn't say. He said, "Of course you didn't. That's what I'm trying to tell you. But listen, Brad, I never wanted to know her real well in the first place, because she was too crazy. Do you know what it was that she was carrying?"

"The soldier said it was an atom bomb," I said, pleased to have remembered the answer.

The look he gave me then was definitely disgusted. "Atom bomb, my ass. Just killing her like that might have made some sense if that was what she had, but the grunt got it wrong. What Maris was carrying was a little glass tube full of anthrax bacteria. Are you hearing what I'm saying? *Bacillus anthracis*, that is, and I'm not talking about spores. I'm talking about the actual damn bacteria." He paused to study his empty glass, then poured himself a refill. "You want to know how many ways that was stupid? One, the spores are about a hundred times as communicable as the bacteria. Two, they're about forty times as lethal. Three, you know what she was going to try to do with her lousy bacteria? She was hoping to get them into the Giubileo water supply. My water supply! As if we wouldn't have detected it in the first ten seconds!"

He hadn't been paying attention to his hostly duties, so I cleared my throat to call attention to the fact that I was holding an empty glass— God knows why, because I surely didn't need any more drink. While he was recharging my glass I asked, to keep the conversation going, "Who's 'we'?"

This time the look he gave me was just irritated. "What?"

"You said we would have detected it. Who's the we?"

"Me and my water-handling team, of course. The ones that handle all the hydrology for the Jubilee. What did you think they pay me for? To make sure nothing bad gets into the water here, that's why. It's my job."

By then he had swallowed his last refill. While he was helping himself to another he gave me an odd sort of sidelong glance. "Anyway," he said, "that isn't what I wanted to talk to you about."

Whatever that other subject was, he didn't seem to be in any hurry to get to it. He took a tiny sip of his freshened drink, pursing his lips as though to taste it better. I thought he was going to speak when he finished rolling it around in his mouth, but that didn't happen. He just took another sip, just as tiny.

I said, "Well?"

He shook his head reprovingly. "Don't rush me, Brad. This is hard for me." And then he was silent for a while longer, frowning as though he was thinking hard about something.

He didn't tell me what, though, and that wasn't cheering me up. I was beginning to feel really nervous—feeling drunk, too, of course, but still woozily worried. It was beginning to seem to me that it was time to get out of there. I cleared my throat, getting ready to say something like, "Gee, look at the time."

I didn't say it. Maury came out of his reverie long enough to say, "I told you, don't rush me." And he said it with enough anger that I decided to give him a little more time.

Only it was a lot more time. Several minutes, anyway. Then he said, "Did you ever happen to think if you wanted to hide something small and kind of flat—like one of those sestertius coins, you know?—a good place could just make a little incision and slide it under your skin?"

Drunk or sober, I knew what to say to that. "Hide what?" And knew pretty well that he was going to say he couldn't tell me that. And then, just as I was making my mind up to just get out of my chair and go out through the door, he sighed. A long, deep sigh. But then he turned to me and gave me a real smile, apologetic and good-natured at the same time. "You wouldn't want to do that, would you?"

He had lost me. Then I backtracked in my woozy mind to what he had just said. "Oh, you mean about hiding something under my skin, you mean? No, I don't think I could do that."

He gave me another sigh, a really sad-sounding one. "I was afraid that was what you would say," he told me. Then his expression brightened. "Say, you look like you're getting ready to leave," he observed.

I didn't either confirm or deny, just gave back as close a copy of Maury's own smile as I could manage, and he nodded. "I guess all good things come to an end. Listen, I'm sorry if I've been giving you a hard time, but I was sort of thinking I would ask you for a favor, and then I realized I couldn't do that." He didn't say what the favor was. What he did say, getting out of his own chair, was, "So let me fix you a stirrup cup, and I'll call the car to pick you up." He was already at his bar, back to me, mixing up something I really didn't need.

But took. And swallowed. And that was when things really got weird.

How weird? you ask.

Well, the next thing I knew I was waking up—I hadn't realized I had gone to sleep—and I was in a ditch halfway down the hill to old Pompeii.

That wasn't all of it. I was also hurting like hell in several parts of my body. It started with my head, starting with what I was pretty sure was an earthquake-sized hangover.

And somebody was blinding me by shining a laser light in my eyes.

I could see a little if I squinted, and what I saw was a big uniformed Security guard holding the light, and he was talking to his just-as-big partner. They weren't talking in English, but I understood them all right. The one with the light was pointing out that I stank of vomit, and I had probably been in a fight, and now they were going to have the rotten job of carrying me off to the lockup, and were probably going to get their nice clean uniforms all messed up with my throw-up, not to mention whatever else I might contaminate them with.

They didn't like the prospect. I liked it even less.

15

MY LIFE AS A MURDER SUSPECT

The goons took me to what turned out to be a corner lockup, furnished with one (empty) jail cell along with one bored sergeant and two half-asleep patrolmen.

The sergeant took over. The first thing he did was send one of the uniforms off to Maury's place in order to get his side of the story. That meant I had to stay in the lockup until she ran her errand and came back to report. (I didn't mind that. I stretched out on one of the desks and went back to sleep. I guess I was still somewhat drunk.)

When she did get back she reported only partial success. She'd looked around his place and, yes, she found a lot of liquor there, but what she didn't find was Maury himself. He was gone. When questioned the concierge said she hadn't seen him leave—or seen me go, either—but admitted she might've been catching forty winks when traffic got slow.

The other thing she didn't find was anything that clarified just what had gone on in Maury's place after that final stirrup-cup drink.

The way it ended, after some telephoning to headquarters, the sergeant said I didn't seem to have broken any serious laws, and he was pretty sure that I wasn't the one who had beaten myself up, so after I filled out the incident report I could go home. The uniformed Security goon who had checked Maury's place out—actually she was, you might say, a gooness, but she was as big and tough-looking as the males— took me back to my room, saw me inside, let me close the door on her.

It was broad daylight by then. I can't say I was in great pain anymore. The sergeant had given me a couple of pills and they were doing a really good job of preventing my brain from finding out what my body's pain receptors were doing their best to tell it.

As soon as the uniform was gone I collapsed onto my cot—dirty and pukey as I was; I thought briefly that I probably ought to get into the shower, but I was asleep before I even got as far as thinking the time to do it was right then, before I filthied up my bed linens. When I opened my eyes again it was once more dark.

Then I did drag myself to the shower. Then I sat on the edge of my cot, staring into space and pondering.

I did that for quite a while, but it didn't help. I didn't know what had happened, or why Maury had done whatever it had been that he did. I didn't have any idea what these latest insane developments in my basically worthless life were all about, so I gave up. Then I got back into my cot, fastidiously trying to avoid the most messed-up parts, closed my eyes, and waited for sleep.

It came pretty quickly. I appreciated that, because while I was awake I kept asking myself questions for which I didn't have any answers, and that just made me even more depressed.

I managed to sleep the clock all the way around, waking up just before daybreak the next morning. I should have been grateful for that, because it meant there were all those hours, maybe twelve or fourteen of them, in which I hadn't been conscious and so hadn't been torturing myself with questions and worries and regrets. That didn't make me feel any better, though, and nothing else about that day did, either. It was a rough one.

It began about as badly as a day could, with my opticle waking me up and reminding me that missing a day's work wasn't good, but it wasn't nearly as bad as missing two days would be. So I got up and got dressed in my Roman slave shift and went off to my day job as a purveyor of fine wines. Well, of wines.

Don't ask me what happened on that shift. It passed. That's all I can tell you. I talked to people now and then—talked to the cooks at breakfast, talked to Cedric the Pimp when he came over, all curiosity and thirst to find out what had been going on with me—I don't remember what I said to him but I'm pretty sure he went away unsatisfied in both departments. And of course I talked to the customers. I poured wine, and lied to them about how good it was, and I suppose I rinsed cups and made change, too. I might even—I couldn't have been that far out of it—have wondered from time to time about Maury's strange behavior, but of that I remember nothing at all.

It did end, finally. When it was over I grabbed some food, God knows what, and ingested it on my way back to my welcoming cot. (I did, this time, strip the dirty bedclothes and throw on a couple of clean sheets. I guess that meant I was beginning to come out of my shock.) Then I kicked off my sandals and shed most of my slave garments and hit my cot. I tried to find the faint aroma of Gerda that by rights should still be clinging to the pillows. I couldn't find it, and then I was off to dreamland anyway. (Oh, I did dream, all right. I know I dreamed, but I don't remember what any of those dreams were about. Which is probably just as well.)

The next day was the rough one.

It began about as badly as a day could. What I mean by that is that in the middle of the night some noises outside woke me just in time to see my door fly open and some really bright lights flash on, all of them directed at my face. "Maury?" I hazarded—remember, I was still pretty much asleep. I propped myself up on an elbow and tried to see past the laser torches people were aiming at me.

Turned out it wasn't my old chess and drinking partner Maury Tesch, though. It was a woman's voice that answered, and it was one I had heard before. "No," Piranha Woman said—snarled, maybe. "I'm not your pal Tesch, who, as you probably know better than anybody, is certainly not going to be coming to visit you anymore, ever. Screw the small talk, Sheridan. Get your ass out of bed. We want to ask you some questions."

16

BACK IN THE HANDS OF SECURITY, ALAS

It was definitely Piranha Woman, and she wasn't alone. Two of those hulking Security knee-breakers were right there with her and they weren't being amiable. If they cared about my beat-up condition they didn't let it interfere with business. They didn't even give me time to get dressed, just to pull on a pair of pants to go with the work shirt I seemed to have been sleeping in. No shoes. And it was the middle of the night, and those damn Pompeiian street stones were cold.

I expected them to drag me to the place where I'd been interviewed the first time. That didn't happen. They pushed me into a three-wheeled truck and we bounced past the Vesuvius Gate and up the hill. And when the truck stopped it was at the clump of old cottages where the volunteers slept. Where Gerda slept, when she was home. Wouldn't be likely ever to sleep there again, though, because when they shoved me into her place— the door wide open, a Security bruiser standing guard—the first thing I saw was somebody lying sprawled and unmoving on the floor.

For one scary, lump-in-the-throat moment I thought it might be Gerda. It wasn't. It was a man, and one I recognized. Specifically it was my sausage-hoarding buddy, Maury Tesch. He was crumpled. He was bloody. And he was definitely dead.

I stood up as straight as I could. "Hell," I said, making sure I got the exculpatory facts out as fast as possible, "I hope you're not thinking I did this so I could, I don't know, get even with him for what he did to me. Because I didn't. It's true Gerda gave me a key to her place but I didn't use it today. I stayed right in my room. I'm afraid I have no way of proving that because there wasn't anybody in the room but me, but—"

Piranha Woman raised her hand. "Sheridan," she said, "shut up. We know you didn't leave your room. Sergeant DiMoralis left a man outside your door in case whoever beat you up came back. Who's that?"

I didn't try to answer that one because I had no idea what she was asking this time. But actually the reason for that was that the person she was asking wasn't me. It was another Security man, standing in the window alcove, and next to him another man I almost recognized as another volunteer from one of the cottages nearby.

The Security man was pointing at the other volunteer. "He saw the whole thing." The man wasn't asked to testify, though. The Security man did it for him. "He was taking out the trash when this Gerda Fleming person came in the back way," he said. "Then a little later he heard a lot of yelling coming from her room."

Piranha Woman snorted. "I don't doubt he did," she said. "Tesch probably made a lot of noise while he was being murdered." Then she scowled. "Do you want something else?"

"Yes, Major. I want to take Gatti here to make his statement."

"Go," she said impatiently, and turned back to me. But I wasn't looking at her. I was goggling at the man in the shadows, who came out now and, oh, my God, yes, that was the one all right, the one who had promised to get me next chance he got, and now had got it. Oh, I was in the deep stuff, for sure.

So what did I do? I did the only things I could do. I told Piranha Woman that this witness was a congenital liar who blamed me for Yellowstone and the ruin of his family's fortunes.

It didn't do any good. The major wasn't interested. "Yes, of course you can try to deny it all when you get to your hearing, but right now what I want to know is what Fleming was up to. So tell me, Sheridan. Why did she do it? Was she punishing him for what he did to you, like you say? Or was it a lovers' quarrel? Or what?"

Well, of course I didn't know why Gerda had done it—if in fact Gerda had actually come back from dear, dying Grandma's on Lake Garda (if that truly was where she had gone) and killed Maury for—for what? For getting me drunk and beating the crap out of me, as Piranha Woman would have it? It didn't seem like an adequate motive to me.

That didn't stop Piranha Woman. She kept on asking, endlessly and not a bit courteously, about that and about everything else I knew about Gerda Fleming, and about everything I had ever suspected or guessed or imagined about her. Then, when she was willing to accept for the moment that she had sucked every last Gerda datum out of my brain, the same about the late Maury Tesch. (Well, I wasn't entirely candid with her about that. I told her about the drinking and all that, all right, but I was too hazy about some of the other stuff—like his plan to make me hide something under my skin—to want to get into it with her.) Then finally she was asking about anything else I might have known, heard, or dreamed that might bear on this matter. "Like what?" I asked at last. I was beginning to get over the shock and transition into the anger—at Major Yvonne Piranha Woman Feliciano, and at everybody around her, too.

She didn't answer that. She didn't believe in answers, only questions. But finally she ran out of those. She didn't announce that fact to me, though. She didn't say anything to me at all, just jerked her head at one of the Security goons, who got a firm grip on my arm and marched me out of the apartment and into the waiting Security van.

As we drove away he explained the rules: 1. Don't leave Pompeii; 2. Keep my nose clean; 3. Keep my mouth shut. They weren't hard to remember. They were pretty much what everybody had been ordering me to do for some time. He wasn't entirely heartless, though. When he noticed I was having trouble sitting up straight he asked if my bruises were bothering me. When I said they were he nodded, perhaps sympathetically.

Didn't do anything about it, of course. But did nod.

He didn't tell me where we were going, but I recognized the signs. When we got to the Indentureds' hostel building that contained my room he made martyr-like mumbles to himself about how many steps he had to climb to my floor. He climbed them all, though. He didn't ask for a key to my door. He opened it with a key of his own, and looked around suspiciously before letting me in.

Nothing had changed. My bed was still as unmade as I had left it, the mess of odds and ends dropped wherever I had left them was the same. Clearly my housekeeping did not come up to his standards, but he just grunted, turned around, and started to leave.

Aches, pains, lack of sleep, my girl not only no longer apparently willing to work at it but now accused of being a murderess as well—I was a little light-headed and, I guess, had every reason to be. I can't think of any other reason why, without conscious intent, I opened my mouth and said, "Too bad he took his sausages. They might've been some kind of clue."

He paused. "What sausages?" So I told him what Maury had kept in my refrigerator, and that got his full attention. Out of my fridge he pulled my two cans of beer I'd brought back from my day's labors, some wax paper Jiri had left behind—and how I had missed it when I was scrounging for anything that might have been considered edible I can't say—and a couple of crumbs of meat, though nothing that resembled a whole sausage.

"What sausages are you talking about?" he asked me, without any affection at all in his voice.

"I guess that's what's left of them," I said. The crumbs didn't look to me appetizing enough to justify Maury's devotion, but the Security man treated them as though they were emeralds. He sniffed at one crumb, then at another. He held the first one up to the light and sniffed it again—longer this time, a deep inhale with his nostrils almost touching the thing. Then he zipped them into his bag and gave me an accusing look. "Any other evidence you're concealing?"

He wasn't quite as fear-inspiring as Piranha Woman, so I took a chance on giving him a little lip. "I haven't concealed any evidence. I'm the one who told you about the sausages in the first place. And anyway, there isn't anything else— Oh, wait," I said, remembering. "They aren't exactly Maury's anymore, but he did give me those bottles of dessert wine in the closet. They're mine now, though."

They weren't, though. Not anymore. They had become the property of Security before I could blink, and the man lectured me at some length on the desirability of giving full cooperation to the authorities, concealing nothing, telling everything. He finished with his Three Commandments—Mouth Shut, Not Leaving, and, oh, yes, Nose Clean. Then he left. Taking the wine with him in one hand, what was left of the repulsive sausages in the other, leaving no hand for him to close the door.

I did it myself. After which there was nothing to keep me from swallowing a couple more pain pills before getting onto that rumpled cot and trying to finish out my night's sleep. That is, nothing but the fact that my whole world had just blown up in my face, and there was nothing I could do about it.

Was it possible, was it by any extreme stretch of the imagination remotely *possible*, that my Gerda had, for what reason I could not begin to guess, actually murdered Maury?

I couldn't believe it. Couldn't deny the possibility, either, and so I stayed sitting on the edge of my bed, unable to figure out what to do and even less able to stop trying, until it was time to get in the shower and get dressed to go to work. I looked like hell. The liquid-bandage stuff camouflaged my wounds well enough, helped by the fact that my slave smock covered the worst of the others. I stopped at the infirmary to wheedle some more of the antipain stuff from the medics and was ready to go to work. Or as ready as I was ever going to be.

Which I did, wondering what unplanned and devastating disaster was going to strike me next.

· · ·

Actually, when it arrived it didn't appear to be that much of a disaster. It was just Elfreda Barcowicz. She showed up that afternoon, close to quitting time. Clearly she was once again intending to ask me a lot more of her annoying questions.

This time it wasn't about—what was her name? Maris Morchan?—the murder victim in the Forum. (Which was good, because then I didn't feel I wanted to tell her that Maury had known the woman before she got herself murdered.) This time Elfreda went straight for the heart. "I never cared much for Gerda Fleming," she informed me, setting the coffee container she'd brought down on my counter and not even pretending to buy any of my wine, "but I wouldn't have guessed she was a killer."

I didn't have an answer for that, and didn't try. All I said was, "Go away, Elfreda."

She shook her head at that. "We need to talk"—and as I started to point at the four or five wine-drinking customers, all interestedly listening to what she had to say—"no, not here, of course. But your shift's up, and here's your relief coming down the street, and let's go somewhere quiet so we can have a nice little chat."

So we did.

I guess I was pretty easy to talk into pretty much anything around then. My afternoon relief, Gianmarco di Maio, looked curious about Elfreda but didn't say anything, and I followed her meekly away.

Well, all right. I might as well admit it. Things hadn't been going all that well for me, and I must have been hungry for a kind word, especially from a female. Elfreda was no Gerda Fleming, but she was good-looking, and solicitous, and deeply, deeply interested in every word I had to say.

So I said a lot of them.

Never mind how I hadn't wanted to mention some of the things Maury had said and done because I hadn't wanted to get involved. All right. I still didn't want to get involved. But the place Elfreda took me to was one of the fully restored villas used for those nine-person, five-hour dinners, and the "slave" watchman seemed to know her. At least all he did was turn around and look the other way when she led me inside, right past the "*Chiuso. Non Entrare*" sign on the door. We sat in the villa's beautiful little courtyard, with its reflecting pool and all those sweet-smelling and meticulously tended flowers—real, not virt—in its garden all around us, and I guess I did, after all, get involved.

And when Elfreda decided she had got out of me everything that was worth the trouble of getting she leaned forward and planted a non-lustful sisterly kiss on my forehead. "Poor bastard," she said. "Life hasn't been treating you very well, has it?"

And was gone.

Oddly my little one-on-one with Elfreda had made me feel a little better. Not cheerful, of course. But not suicidal at least, and I stayed that way through my boring dinner at the staff mess hall, and all the while I watched the mostly unpleasant news on my opticle, right up to the time I got back to my room and sprawled across my cot and went instantly to sleep. So nothing specially upsetting had happened that day. It was the day after that that the sewage hit the aerator.

That day didn't begin well. I set my opticle for a news channel to wake me up. That wasn't really because I was so hot for newscasts. That had always been more Gerda's thing than mine. But maybe it was one of those sub-aware things that the shrinks used to accuse me of, like, well, like some under-the-radar attempt to get some part of Gerda back. Anyway, what ended my (inadequate) night's sleep was the opticle talking about terror-ists. Particularly nasty terrorists, their specific cause not mentioned, who had taken over an air traffic control center in Luxembourg and flown three supersonics into three separate tourist zeppelins in three widely separated parts of Europe. The death toll was more than seventeen hun-dred, and that didn't count the casualties on the ground. (The *Chang Jang* wasn't among the three zeps named, so I supposed Chi-Leong's little smuggling project was still on track.)

Then, as a follow-up, there was also a story about a gang of ten or twelve other terrorists (these having something to do with Inuit people and whales) who had died that day, when the nuke warheads they were trying to salvage from a sunken Gulf War Three submarine went off unexpectedly. So all the losses weren't all on the same side. It didn't seem like a fair trade, though, especially if you counted out the probable local casualties from nuke fallout. Then, as soon as I got out of the shower, there was a note on my cell from dear old Mom, subject matter very much like the other dozen or so that had been accumulating that month. New York's summer was miserably hot. Dad was depressed. The weather statement said another darn hurricane might be coming up the coast. The Conklins down the hall weren't doing their share of keeping the bathroom tidy. And, oh, yes, Dad's dentures got chipped when he slammed the nightstand drawer on them and the insurance wouldn't cover the bill for new ones. Which was my mother's way of reminding me that there hadn't been much money coming in from Pompeii lately.

Add to that that I couldn't find a clean topshirt to wear.

All depressing, right? And, as usual, then things got worse. As I was pulling on the least armpitty of the shirts in my laundry bag there was a knock on my door. No. Not a knock. A *lot* of knocks, thunderously impatient ones, and when I opened it there was Piranha Woman with two of her goons flanking her. The bigger of the two already had his fist clenched for more and louder knocks, but Piranha Woman stopped him. "You, Sheridan, you haven't been honest with us," she called. "You better come along now."

I didn't ask where. The goons discouraged questioning. We rode in silence, at least until the car took a sharp turn and, out the window, I caught sight of something whale-shaped and huge, way off on the horizon. "Is that the *Chang Jang?*" I asked. "With all those police blimpets and choppers all around it?"

The bigger of the two at least looked where I had been looking. He must have seen what I had seen: the air-whale shape of a giant zep—I guessed the *Chang Jang*—no more than three or four kilometers down the coast, and around it clouds of aircraft and smaller airships, like flies around a horse dropping. He didn't say anything, though, and the smaller one didn't even give it a glance. Perhaps because he was aware of the steely gaze Piranha Woman had fixed on him.

So I was left wondering, and then the car stopped. I wasn't at all surprised that the place where we wound up was the place I well remembered from a couple of nights before, Piranha Woman's private interrogation chamber. It didn't look a bit more welcoming than it had the last time.

I didn't expect that this interrogation would be any better than my previous ones. It wasn't. It was a lot worse. For one thing, I went through it naked; they made me strip and they carried everything I had taken off away, for what kind of laboratory inspection I could only guess. This time they didn't skip the cavity searches, either. For them my modesty was not a concern.

Then they stretched me out on a thing like a massage table, and one of the Security guards, this one in white scrubs, was rubbing something greasy over my naked body while another had one hand on my shoulder to remind me not to object.

Did I mention that this whole procedure was being done in the presence of a fair-sized audience? There was Piranha Woman herself, her male partner from that long-ago first meeting, the two uniforms who had brought me there with a few of their buddies, a pretty young uniformed woman wearing a data monocle and a dictation mike and, surprise, old Professor Mazzini, spryly perched on a gurney against one wall of the room, the one who'd taught our orientation classes before Piranha Woman took over. It was a pretty full house. It would've been nice if I could have sold tickets.

Then another goon in white, this one apparently female, approached me. She was holding something roughly the size and shape of a flashlight, but with a shiny, five-centimeter freely spinning metal ball where a bulb and reflector should have been. Which she employed, I had no idea why, to roll around over my exposed skin. All of it. And along with everybody else in the room—Professor, Piranha Woman, guards, and all—she was watching some kind of a colorful, shape-changing display on a wall screen that I could barely see out of the corner of my eye. Then, having thoroughly explored all my back surfaces, the two goons turned me over to get at my front and I had a better view. Of what exactly I could not say; the images on the screen made no sense to me, although I did observe that every time she moved her roller ball on my body the colors and shapes jerked and flowed.

Outside of the screen, and me, there wasn't much to look at in the room. Against one wall was a table with the crumbs of Maury's sausage and the two bottles of wine they'd commandeered. It was chilly in the room, too. For their comfort more than mine, I'm sure, they had the air-conditioning turned way up. I had goose bumps on my arms before they started the rub-a-dub-dub on my body, and well before they got through I was definitely shivering. Not that any of them cared. Not that I cared much myself, because what they were doing took my mind off my personal comfort.

Do you know how many square centimeters of skin it takes to enclose an average human body? Let's just say there are a lot, and the woman with the rollerball rubbed it over every last one of them. Then, when she was through, she put the gadget down and looked toward the woman with the dictation mike. That one had been muttering into her mike throughout the examination. Now she spoke up. "That is it, sir," she said, to my surprise addressing Professor Mazzini rather than Piranha Woman. "There is no evidence of a recent contact. Do you want me for anything else?"

He shook his head. "You can go," he said. Obediently she and the woman with the rollerball left. As they exited the door the wall screen's psychedelic picture of my insides blinked out.

They had taken with them all their portable equipment except for a stack of towels. It could have been that they were leaving them for my convenience, I suppose. I didn't think so, but I kept my eye on them because they might come in handy.

Piranha Woman, however, had her own agenda. Before the door had quite closed on the rollerball team she was standing over me. "Let us now clarify some points," she began.

The professor reined her in. "At least let the poor son of a bitch put his pants on," he said.

This particular poor son of a bitch didn't just pull his pants up without argument. I took my time. I put on every article of clothing I had come there with, and before I put on any I raided the stack of towels to wipe off as much as I could of the lubricant they had smeared on my skin. The professor hadn't said I could. He might, of course, have stopped me at any time. He didn't. He was busily studying his opticle, and the look on his face might have had the beginnings of a smile.

Piranha Woman had no such look. There was a major scowl on her face. She didn't say anything until I was almost finished buttoning my overshirt. Then she gave Professor Mazzini a fed-up look and pounced on me. "Now, Sheridan," she said angrily, "let's have some truth out of you. I want to know everything that Tesch said to you or you to him. Honestly. Every word."

She asked for every word; I did my best to give her what she asked for. I took my time about it, too.

First I told her about how much trouble Maury had gone to to get me up to his rooms, and about the amazing scope of his wet bar, and as close as I could remember the very words of our chatter. And then, as an afterthought, "Oh, wait, I don't know if I mentioned this before. Did I tell you he said that at one time he had known Maris Morchan?"

Then I yawned, making it clear I didn't believe that anybody would care about the fact that Maury Tesch had once known a disease-carrying terrorist named Maris Morchan, but as I was politely covering my mouth I kept a watch on the expressions on their faces. The professor's displayed forthright astonishment. Piranha Woman's look was all of that, plus a generous helping of fury. "Why did you not tell us this before?" she demanded, her voice suddenly shrill.

She had asked for honest answers; I gave her what she had asked for.

"Because I knew you'd have a cat fit about it." And that was probably a mistake, because then the yelling started all over again.

That is, her yelling. The professor didn't seem to care to be involved; he was talking to his opticle and paying little attention to Piranha Woman's screeches. They started loud, and got louder, but I couldn't tell her much more than I already had. That didn't stop her. She kept asking the same handful of questions in a dozen different ways, differing mostly in the amount of invective they contained, until finally the professor put a hand to his opticle and called, "Major! There is some new evidence. We must talk."

And talk they did, the two of them, at considerable length though never loudly enough for me to hear. Whatever it was he was telling her she seemed to enjoy it, her expression ranging from startlement to pure pleasure, with grace notes of anger mixed with joy.

Finally she asked something, as though requesting some kind of permission and he nodded, granting it and she turned back to me.

Then I really began to worry. I could tell by the look on her face that whatever they had been discussing I wasn't going to like it.

She gave me what I can only describe as a now-you're-going-to-get-it look, then turned and walked to the table against the wall. "Have you noticed this cup?" she asked me, but as usual didn't wait for an answer. It was simply an inverted plastic cup and she was already lifting it. What was under it was a pink, gooey lump that did look familiar, though what it was doing there I couldn't guess.

I didn't give her the satisfaction of showing my surprise. "Looks like some of Gerda's chewing gum. So what? Probably it's been there for weeks."

Piranha Woman was shaking her head, looking pleased with herself. "Not this piece, no. We gave it to the lab for DNA and they've just given the colonel the results. It's fresh, all right."

For a moment my heart skipped a beat. "Gerda's back?" I demanded.

But I knew that wasn't likely, and anyway Piranha Woman didn't bother to answer it. "The results were a bit of a surprise," she informed me. "Looks like there were three males in her apartment. One of them, of course, was the late Mr. Tesch. We didn't find any of you on the gum—but that doesn't mean you weren't there—but there was DNA on the gum that came from an unidentified male."

"Well, hell, it could've come from anybody. I chewed some of her gum myself now and then—"

She was clearly enjoying herself now. "Oh, it's not your DNA, Sheridan. It was from some other male." The gloating look slid from her face for a moment, and actually she seemed almost embarrassed. "Well, sure," she said. "It took a while to identify him. The lab didn't make the connection right away because he wasn't in the active file. He was listed as dead, in fact. His name—the name he was known by in the case files—was Brian Bossert. That mean anything to you?"

It took me a minute to recognize it. "Oh, sure," I said. "You were talking about him in class. The terrorist. The Toronto guy. Blew himself up when his ship exploded."

But she was shaking her head. "That's what was thought, yes," she admitted. "Apparently we were wrong."

The professor took pity on her obvious suffering. "Everyone thought that, Yvonne," he told her. "The evidence seemed clear."

"And wrong," she snapped. "I am going to recommend an investigative commission to see why we were so wrong."

It would have been smart of me to stay out of it, but I was puzzled. "So then what's your problem?" I asked. "This Bossert's the guy you should be looking for, right?"

"Oh," Piranha Woman said, the expression on her face returning to the now-I've-got-you look that I hated, "we'll be looking for him, all right. The only thing is, he isn't a him anymore."

That got to me. "What the hell are you talking about?" I asked angrily, though I wasn't at all sure I wanted to hear the answer.

She was smiling now. "See, the lab checked everything in her room. Even her dirty laundry. And off two pairs of her smelly panties we got traces of, well, secretions. So naturally the lab DNA'ed them, too, and guess what? The DNA was the same. They were male. And they were Brian Bossert's, just like the gum." She gave me a moment for that to sink in, then delivered the coup de grâce. "So where does that leave you, Sheridan? Do you feel bad because now you know that the woman you've been banging all these weeks started out as a man?"

17

THE VERY WORST BLOW EVER

I can't tell you how I felt after that.

Well, I can, sort of. I hurt in places where I didn't even think I had a pain nerve. I had never before felt anything like this.

The closest I can come was way back when I was a kid. Had to be no more than nine, because that was the year we spent in the transit camps in Knoxville, Tennesee. I had the hots for a twelve-year-old girl named Edna Hollander, and that didn't work out very well, either.

Actually "hots" may be the wrong word. I wasn't yearning to have sexual intercourse with her. I didn't know exactly how that was done, for one thing. But I did, definitely, want her to let me put my hand down the front of her dress so I could caress her bra. Her bra, remember. Not even her naked breast, because that far I did not aspire.

Edna was a little older than me, and a little taller. And, yes, she actually did have breasts, or at least the beginnings of them. And she was alleged to have her mother's permission to use a little lipstick, powder, and perfume. She did smell definitely better than any of the other girls, and the big thing was that she acted as though she liked me. A couple of times at lunch she gave me part of her ham or tuna salad, so much better than the prefabricated mystery meat the transit camp kitchens provided for the likes of me.

Anyway, I knew where she lived. So sometimes, after whatever miserable stew we were given for supper at the transit camp, I would hike over to her neighborhood—it wasn't more than a kilometer or so each way—just so I could skulk in the shrubbery to see if I could catch a glimpse of her diving into her pool or rocking herself on their verandah, or sitting, usually with a friend, in the little summer house on their back lawn.

Doing that last part wasn't always a lot of fun for me, though. All too often the friend she was sitting with was that bastardly high school senior, Randy Doberman. And one night, just after dark, they were talking low-voiced in the summer house, and I was desperate to know if they were just talking, or if they were doing some kind of non-talking activity that I didn't even want to think about. I thought that, with a little luck, I could sneak up into earshot without being seen. It turned out that I could. I did.

Nobody ever has to tell me what a dumb move that was. I even knew at the time—what was the thing my mother used to say? Eavesdroppers never hear anything good of themselves? I did it anyway, and my mother's old saying was right.

Most of what I heard at first was from Randy, how he had scored not one but four goals at soccer and, from Edna, how wonderful he was. I couldn't hear all they said, but what I heard was too much. It went like this:

> Randy: —pisses me off when—(inaudible, inaudible)—you can't tell me you like the little prick.
> Edna: (inaudible, inaudible, and how I wished it wasn't)
> Randy: (inaudible, inaudible)
> Edna: (sounds of her settling herself closer to Randy) Well, what am I going to do? Reverend Burford says we have to be nice to them and Mom thinks every word Reverend Burford says comes right out of God's mouth. And anyway—

And from then on it was pretty much inaudible from him, except for some kind of grunting sounds, and pretty much inaudible, inaudible, inaudible from her, until I heard him say, kind of out of breath, "And do you do this for that little prick, too?"

She didn't answer, and I was pretty sure why. It spoiled my sleep for months, even after we'd moved up to Allentown for the next stop after Knoxville, and what these goddamn Security shits were telling me now in Pompeii was having exactly the same effect on me.

So what I did for the Security shits, I sat there and took it while Piranha Woman had her fun with the situation. She was trying to hurt me, of course. If she wasn't succeeding that was only because I was already hurt a lot worse than she could possibly do.

So she asked all her questions about our specific sexual practices, and about the physical description of Gerda's private parts, and about a million or so other things that were absolutely none of her damned business . . . and, more often or not, were often a lot like the kind of questions one part of my head was throwing at another part. And getting no satisfactory answers, of course. But then, I didn't have any answers to give Piranha Woman, either.

It was quite a painful hour or so, until the professor said something to a guard, who at once trotted over to Piranha Woman to mutter at her. Looking startled, she turned to the professor: "But there is much more I want to question him about." He shrugged. "We haven't even told him about the Flu!" she finished, puzzling me a bit. What was there to tell me about the Flu that the news channels hadn't already told the world, with pictures?

"All the same, Yvonne," he said, "let's end this session, please."

He had phrased it as a polite request, but it was an order, and one she didn't like. She pursed her lips and narrowed her eyes, and turned to march out of the room. That appeared to be a cue for the rest of my audience, too, because they almost all followed. Even the professor. He did give me a sort of apologetic shake of the head as he left. I couldn't guess why.

The only person now in the room with me was a very wide-awake female Security guard. She wasn't conversational. She was at least human, though, because when I explained a growing problem to her she escorted me, one hand on her gun, to a toilet down the hall. Ordinarily I'm not crazy about having a strange female standing not fifty centimeters away while I'm using a urinal. The need, however, was great.

She even answered me when I asked what time it was. Eighteen hours fifteen, she said, which meant I'd been answering questions or asleep for the short balance of one night, all of the following day, and almost into the next night.

When we got back to the interrogation room she took her position at the door and I sat on the edge of the examination couch, trying not to think about anything anybody had said to me for the last day or two. That didn't work very well until it occurred to me to stretch out on the couch. Which I did, and the next thing I knew, or didn't know, was that I was asleep.

That was a successful way of dealing with the questions, but only a temporary one. When I woke up the questions were all still there in my head.

I opened my eyes. Old Professor Mazzini was sitting with his hands clasped and occasionally covering a small yawn—probably because he'd been asleep, but not long enough to completely satisfy his ancient bones. To the guard he said, "You can leave us, Agnes." To me: "I imagine you're hungry, Bradley. I brought a few sandwiches."

He was right. I was hungry enough to consider that they were probably the best sandwiches I'd ever had, too. And when I had finished the professor leaned back, and stared at me, and shook his head. Then he said, "Aw, Bradley, do you have any idea what you've got yourself into this time?"

I did not care for his tone. Oddly enough, that was a disappointment. I had come to think of him as—not as a friend, to be sure, but at least as something a lot closer to a human being than any other employee of Security I had ever run across.

Anyway, I didn't know the answer to his question. The professor knew it himself, though, and, surprisingly, he seemed willing to talk about it without blaming it all on me—another difference between him and the rest of Security.

He hesitated for a moment, then said, "May I ask you a quite personal question?"

I almost laughed out loud. "You mean there's one that Piranha Woman forgot to ask?"

He didn't respond to that, but he asked the question anyway. "Tell me, weren't you ever suspicious that Ms. Fleming was concealing something from you?"

He was getting me pissed off all over again. "Hell, yes. She had plenty of secrets. I knew that. But if you mean about being, what do you call it? transsexual?, no. Never. I don't care what you say. She was a *woman*, totally. Trust me on this. I've checked every damn centimeter of her body, a dozen times over."

He was shaking his head again, in that damn terrorist-briefing-class way he had. "That doesn't actually prove anything, Bradley. If you've got the money and you know the right doctor and you don't mind the pain, you can change the sex for anybody in the world, male or female. It's not quick or easy, of course," he said, the professorial lecturing tone stronger than ever. "It takes months just to do all the carving up you have to go through, and you can't do it in a single session because there needs to be a significant amount of healing time between the stages. Then you have to clone some of the parts and grow them to maturity and so on. Then there's a year or two to flush out the last of the old hormones and bring in the new. But no, Bradley," he said, with a nod of satisfaction, "you're wrong. When your Gerda was born she was a boy, all right. Came fully equipped with the penis and the testicles and all the other plumbing you have. She just traded all that stuff in to acquire the new parts that you liked so well. We think she had it done in the Stans because they have some pretty fine facilities there and no government interference. And they don't keep any records, or at least none they share with us. And there it is."

. . .

What can I say? As far as the medical details were concerned the professor wasn't telling me anything I hadn't known about what a plastic surgeon could do, even outside of the Stans—look what they'd done to my Uncle Devious.

Well, yes, there are things I can say. One of them is that my life, already about as bad as I thought it could be, was rapidly getting worse. Invasively worse. I couldn't think of anything else, not even simple housekeeping things like "my arm's tired" or "I'm going to need to pee again pretty soon" without ugly, undesired pictures spilling into my mind from the professor's news. I'm not going to say what those pictures were like. There are a lot of things in my life that I don't care to talk about, but there are only a few that can actually turn my stomach, and those details were at the top of the list.

Professor Mazzini was silent, occasionally glancing at his book as though he really wished he could get back to reading it. I wished that too. I didn't want to be told anything else, by anybody, about anything at all.

That was not to be. The professor cleared his throat. "There are a couple of other things," he informed me. "Major Feliciano felt it would be interesting to get your reaction to some other evidence our people have turned up."

I said, not intending it to sound like a compliment—and it didn't, "Your people have been pretty damn busy."

"Yes," he agreed. "It's what we do. Given something to work on, we work fast. So let's talk about the things we want to ask you."

He started some long thing about the "biochemical assay" of the late Maury Tesch and the "anomalous antibodies" they'd detected in his blood. Then he said something about how that had "alerted" them to a fuller investigation of Maury's background, including his work for the Jubilee, and that woke me up.

"Hey," I said. "Back up. You were suspicious of Maury?"

He looked surprised and maybe disappointed in me for not paying attention. "Oh, very. According to the bio data he had been infected with the Flu but was cured. We didn't think the cure was spontaneous."

I was close behind him by then. "You think Maury had some kind of a cure for the Flu? Maybe he was helping to spread it?"

He nodded. "They took those sausage crumbs he'd left in your refrigerator and cultured them, and sure enough they share many genetic markers with the Flu organism. Some of our people think he may have used them as a growth medium for samples of the infectious material itself. Or, more likely, for something sharing genetic markers, but for what purpose no one can say." He looked self-reproachful. "And it seems likely that from time to time he used his position to contaminate Pompeii's water system with the organism."

I was surprised. "Shouldn't you have tested the water?"

"Of course we did. But, you see, it was Tesch who scheduled the tests."

He stopped there, I supposed for a little more self-recrimination. I said, "Wait a minute! If he had a cure— That thing he wanted to ask me to do for him but decided he couldn't—"

He produced a wan smile. A student had come up with the right answer. "Exactly, Bradley. We think that he may have been talking about something involving you and some kind of a cure. Maybe a sample of a vaccine? A biochemical analysis? So now you know why we're so anxious to know every word he said. If there is something we need to find it. Because people are dying in very large numbers."

I don't know if the professor thought that all this explaining would motivate me to do more to help him. Perhaps it might have if I'd had any idea of anything I could have done for him. I didn't.

He was looking at me expectantly, so I said, "That's all a little hard to take in. Do you have any more surprises for me?"

"I don't think so— Well, there is one thing that I'd like to tell you but can't. It's very tightly classified. Pity, because I think you'd like to hear it. Might even make you, let's say, feel better about yourself."

I looked at him in surprise. If there was anything around that could do that I would have been glad to hear it. He wasn't going any further, though. Now he stood up. He said, "I need to talk to Major Feliciano again, Bradley. Perhaps you'd like to get a little more rest. I'll send someone in to keep you company."

I didn't answer that, but I did as I was told, climbed back up on the examination table and closed my eyes while he left and another guard came in to keep an eye on me.

What was on my mind was a logical deduction that I didn't want to make. It seemed clear that Maury was part of a murderous terrorist conspiracy to kill thousands or millions of people. I supposed that explained some of his odd behavior. The question on my mind was, did the same thing explain some of Gerda's?

18

COFFEE WITH THE COLONEL

I think I did sleep for a while, and if I had any dreams I'm really glad I don't remember them. When I woke up Mazzini was back in the chair, looking a lot more alert, and the corporal was serving him coffee.

He saw me sitting up. "I'm waiting for a call," he said. "Want some coffee? Agnes, give Mr. Sheridan a cup."

She did. It was black and strong, and very hot. I sipped at it cautiously, waiting to see if the unexpected "mister" meant anything. The professor seemed oddly cheerful. And actually chatty.

"You might remember the Purity Action Society bombings," he was ruminating, taking a sip of the coffee. "Firebombing drugstores if they sold condoms? Before your time, maybe, but I was the one who infiltrated those buggers, Sheridan. By the time I was through every last one of them was rounded up and in the pen, and I got a commendation. And the Daughters of Manifest Destiny? I don't guess anybody's really forgotten about them, have they?" And he was right, nobody had. At least I hadn't, or anyway not entirely. I did remember my dad complaining to my mom about the Daughters because he said that you couldn't even kid a waitress in a diner anymore without her calling the cops. Or even bombing your neighborhood bar, if they knew where it was, and that was back before Yellowstone.

My attention wandered. I knew that now he was explaining to me why I shouldn't judge Piranha Woman too harshly—"born in the slums of Brazil, father took off when she was three, it's a marvel what she's made of her life. Joined Security as a trainee, and last year they made her a major!" He paused, moodily refilling his glass. "Half my age," he sighed. "Oh, there are times when I could wish she was a little less aggressive, but, by and large, it's best to give her her head. Don't you agree?"

I didn't care one way or another. I hadn't really been listening. But it was simpler to agree. "Sure," I said.

He nodded. "Especially now," he reminded me. "That business with the zeps—probably you saw the *Chang Jang* moored down by the refueling station? All of them are ground-moored tonight. Every zep in the world is grounded, while they try to make the air traffic control stations secure enough so it won't happen again. They claim that job's done and they'll let them go tomorrow, but what's next?"

"You bet," I said, still not listening. I guess it was the wrong answer because he gave me a funny look, but it didn't stop him.

And then there was a distant, faint chiming sound—I recognized it, it was the "Ode to Joy" from that old Beethoven symphony, but in this case it was the professor's opticle ringing for his attention. He blinked the other eye eagerly, listened for a second and then grinned at me. "They've accepted my recommendation, Bradley. No charges have been filed against you. You can go home at any time."

That woke me all the way up. I took a big hit of the coffee, careless of the way it was scalding my mouth. All I could think of to say was, "Really?"

"Yes, really," he said, gently mocking me. "If you want to wait for a bit I'll wake up my driver to take you home. Or the door guard will call you a cab. Have you got any money? Wait a minute." He was fumbling in his wallet, then taking something out of it and stuffing it into my breast pocket. It looked like a fifty.

He was waiting for an answer. I gave him one, sort of. I said, "Well . . ."

But I was stalling, and the reason for that was that pictures were flashing through my mind. They were pictures of Piranha Woman crashing into my room one more time with her little posse of brutes right behind her when they changed their mind back again.

I didn't want to sit around and wait for that to happen.

But I happened to know that there was a pretty good place to get away to that wasn't all that distant. If Chi-Leong hadn't lied to me, the *Chang Jang* should right now be floating over its refueling base no more than a kilometer or two from where I stood. And, thanks to Chi-Leong and his proposal of high pay for some easy smuggling work, I had a pretty good idea of an inconspicuous way of how to get to it.

19

THE BIGGEST ZEP IN THE WORLD

Unlike every single other thing in my life, escaping from Security went without a hitch. I just told the guard on duty, lurking outside the interrogation room, that I preferred to walk because it was such a nice night. It wasn't, but he didn't seem to care. I walked briskly in the general direction of where I lived until I was out of sight, then doubled back toward the refueling station.

And what do you think I was thinking about on that long, lonely walk? That's not hard to guess. I was thinking about the same thing I had been thinking of all along, with at least that small fraction of my mind that wasn't taken up with how the dickens I was going to get out of all the messes that were multiplying in my life, namely Gerda. Or, more accurately, those terrible and unbelievable things everybody had been saying about her . . . or, no, not really unbelievable, were they? Because willy-nilly, like it or not, I was sort of, very tentatively, beginning to almost believe them. I didn't think the professor would have lied to me about that. And the way I knew that was happening was that I was beginning to wonder just what kind of a man my dear, dear woman had been when a man was what she was.

Compared to dealing with that kind of thinking, being questioned by Security was easy.

Well, it had been easy, as a matter of fact. So easy, in fact, that as we were almost to the dump my reveries about Gerda were interrupted and I began having sudden flashes of discontented reality. It was all too easy! It was almost like some old vid comedy. It didn't feel like a real escape. What it felt like was some kind of a farce.

But that, I told myself, was silly, and the brisk walk through dark and mostly deserted streets had abolished such worries by the time I was actually standing under that immense airborne whale that was the *Chang Jang*.

My luck held. Getting onto the zep was just about as easy as Chi-Leong had promised. The honey truck was still there, sucking out the old liquids to carry off to the settling tanks, while another set of hoses was pumping up the new fluids for the next departure—whenever that might be. There wasn't a living soul in sight.

The part of the scheme that had been most worrisome to me was climbing the hoses. That had looked like hard labor, but I discovered that there was a ladder hanging off the pipe. Climbing it made me sweat, all right—lifting my own body weight fifty meters wasn't really easy—but no special skills were required, just the sweat. Well, quite a lot of sweat.

It wasn't until I had swung myself over the stinking downlink hose that I got my first real scare. I had expected to be alone. I wasn't. A uniformed crewman was drowsing against a wall of the pump gondola, but when he opened his eyes and saw me there he woke right up. He said something sharp and scared—not in English, and not really addressed to me. Then he turned and bolted, banging a door shut behind him. When I got to the door and opened it again all I saw was an empty short corridor ending in a flight of steps. The crewman was out of sight.

What I didn't know was where he was running to. To alert the ship's crew that a stranger had sneaked aboard? There was another possibility, and one I liked better: He just might be the man Chi-Leong had said would be there to receive that old platinum gravy boat. In which case things might not be so bad, because anybody who worked for Chi-Leong would have good reason to keep quiet about the whole matter.

When the man didn't come right back with armed guards that possibility began to look more likely. I didn't hear any approaching shouting, either. I began to breathe a little easier.

And then, when I was safely aboard the zep and I had had a chance to look around at what I'd got myself into now, I have to say it almost took my mind off my troubles. I was really impressed.

In my life I had been in some places that I thought were pretty nice, like some of the upscale New York hotels I solicitously helped my drunken tour guide customers to get back to, before I robbed them.

I had been wrong about that, though. Compared to the *Chang Jang* zeppelin, even the fanciest of them was a slum. The zep was an airborne treasure house, beautifully furnished with plenty of good taste and vast amounts of money.

True, not everything on the zep was what it seemed. The oil paintings on the hallway walls weren't really oil paintings. The statuary wasn't statuary, either. That wasn't because the decorators had been trying to save the odd euro by fobbing the passengers off with cheap simulations, though. It was a matter of weight. Virts were made up of photons, and photons weighed a lot less than thick old canvases and massive old marble nymphs and satyrs.

The other thing about that art was that I suddenly realized I could use it to give myself some cover. All I had to do was pause consideringly before every piece of it. I wouldn't be admiring the artist's technique, of course. I simply didn't have any better place to go.

See, I knew that I didn't look like a zep passenger. What I looked like was a bum who'd just been unexpectedly turned loose by the cops, but that was a matter of attitude more than physical circumstances. After a little cogitation I thought of some help for that.

I had seen, outside some of the stateroom doors, abandoned room-service trays that sat waiting to be collected—or, usefully, for me to add to my camouflage. So I grabbed a cup and saucer from one of them. Thereafter when the occasional person hove into view I at once became both fascinated and thirsty. All they saw of me was my undistinguished back as I faced whatever art object was handy. Sipping from the coffee cup pretty well covered my face, too. Put them all together and I was just another passenger who wasn't sleeping very well, and so was passing the time until breakfast by wandering the halls and admiring the artworks that lined them.

That wasn't all that improbable, you know. Under other circumstances, like if I had taken up Chi-Leong's offer, I might have been doing just that—especially if Gerda had been along to instruct me in what those particular kinds of art were all about. (I turned that thought off as soon as I could.) Art of any kind wasn't one of my good subjects. Still, they had had some courses in it at NYA&M naturally enough, because they were as totally useless to us as most of the other subjects we were taught. I had taken one or two, but I can't say they had meant much to me. All the same, I recognized ancient- (and valuable-) looking Japanese scrolls, and paintings—portraits, landscapes, bowls of fruit on a table—that looked like things I had seen on some TV program or other, usually described as having been borrowed from some famous museum. There was one painting of a woman who looked like she had a mild toothache that I was pretty sure came from the Louvre in Paris, and there were several statues in niches that looked like they had been copied from places like the Hermitage in St. Petersburg or New York's Met.

I wasn't actually concentrating on art appreciation, of course. All I was doing was to pause in front of almost every piece of art along the hallways, occasionally pretending to sip from my coffee cup.

Well, there was one other thing I was doing—doing a lot of, actually. That was worry. My idle-tourist ruse was not going to be a permanent disguise.

At least I wasn't at the Giubileo anymore, which meant I was thereby out of the hands of Piranha Woman and her pals. That was good. However, it was just about all there was on the plus side. The list of the bad parts of my situation was a lot longer:

One, somebody a little higher up the food chain than a hall sweeper—say, a ship's officer—might at any moment show up and ask me who the hell I was. I wouldn't have any good answer for that.

Two, sooner or later my performance as itinerant art connoisseur was going to wear out, and what was I going to do then?—do about, for instance, sleeping that night? I could see how to manage all the other necessities, at least for a day or two—toilets all over the zep, food 24-7 in at least a dozen restaurants. The zep did not, however, provide casual beds.

Then, three, the hard one: Assuming that I somehow managed to avoid capture until the *Chang Jang* reached some other port—maybe Casablanca, or Malta, or, for all I knew, maybe Trenton, New Jersey—how was I going to get ashore? And where was I going to go when I did? And what was I going to use for money to buy whatever it was I would have to be buying just to stay alive?

Those were hard questions, all right. And all the time there were increasing numbers of people beginning to appear as the early risers passed on their way to breakfast, and I wished all over again that I had never met the late Maury Tesch.

Astonishingly, I managed to stay alive and unimprisoned that way for as much as an hour and a half. Then the whole plan began to fall apart. The problem was this white-uniformed man with stripes on his sleeve who appeared around a corner, striding in my direction and talking on his opticle. His free eye was idly focused toward me.

I didn't know what to do about him. As a kind of reflex action I gave the man a cursory bob of the head, the way any passenger might to any ship's officer as they passed in a corridor, raised my hand to my mouth, yawned and turned away, not hurriedly but carefully not doing it too fast, either.

Then I turned the first corner I came to, wishing I could believe he wasn't going to follow.

I was heading toward the latticed steps that led up and down to other decks, thinking that I might head up toward the dining areas. Unfortunately a quick, and when I thought about it probably ill-advised, glance behind me revealed that the officer had turned after me. He didn't seem particularly agitated about me, just a little curious, maybe, and with nothing more pressing on his mind than satisfying that curiosity.

I didn't think it had become quite a hopeless situation, yet. But I couldn't see any direction it might be heading to other than worse. And then a familiar voice called, "Hey, sweetie, where the hell have you been? We've been waiting for you and we're starving."

It was Elfreda Barcowicz.

She was standing, arms-around-waist, waiting for the elevator, and the person whose waist her arm was around was young Eustace Chi-Leong, the gentleman from Singapore who had told me about the informal way to board the zep. When he saw me he winced as though he had just been given a punch in the ribs. He looked irritably at Elfreda, and then, with some comprehension, at me. "Oh," he said, "right. I see what is happening. So come on, for heaven's sake. Look, here is the lift."

It was, and the two of them swept me into it. The door closed on the ship's officer, who gave us one mildly perplexed glance before turning away, and there we were.

Blessedly there was no one else in the elevator. Chi-Leong was looking annoyed anyway. "What in the hell are you doing here, Mr. Sheridan?" he asked as though it were a personal offense.

Elfreda shook her head at him. "What do you think he's doing, Eustace? Security picked him up because they thought he had something to do with Tesch getting killed. You knew that because I told you myself. And now he's getting the hell away from them as fast as he can. Wouldn't you do the same thing?"

Chi-Leong didn't answer that right away. I could see that he was thinking in high gear, no doubt ruminating over such questions as: Would I be gentleman enough to avoid implicating him if I was caught? What was the actual risk exposure I would leave him stuck with if I wasn't? And, most of all, was this going to interfere with whatever new plan he had made to get his precious gravy boat out of Italian jurisdiction?

Then he gave me a scowl, but when he spoke it was to Elfreda. "What then do you wish me to do, Barcowicz? Hide him in some fashion? I do not know how to do that. For you it has not been a problem, as a certain amount of bed-hopping is expected on a cruise ship of this kind, but with another man it is quite a different matter."

She looked pained. "What I want from you," she said, sounding just as pained, "is for you not to be any more of a horse's ass than you absolutely have to. Brad needs to get somewhere where every cop on the corner isn't looking for him. So think it through now. It will be better for you if he does get away, won't it? Because how do you know what they'll make him confess to if he's caught? So what is there to think about?"

She gave him a short, decisive nod and then informed him what his decision would have to be. "We'll help him get away, right? And then everybody will be happy."

20

RUNNING AWAY, FIRST CLASS

A luxury cruise zep, a category of transportation of which *Chang Jang* was definitely a member, has all sorts of entertainments for the paying passenger. (Or even for stowaways like me, as long as we remained uncaught.) To start, there were the heroic-sized swimming pools—two of them, actually, one for fooling around and one to swim laps in for the energetically inclined. There were cold rooms and warm rooms. There was a sauna that was warmer still. There were bingo halls. There were restaurants and bars. There were casinos—and not just one of those, either, in fact not even two of them, but a total of five fully equipped gambling hells, one on each of the *Chang Jang*'s passenger decks. "So you see," Elfreda murmured in my ear as we passed a room called "Library," which did indeed have shelves of book disks all around the walls—and also had three apparently taken-down drunk middle-aged male passengers, eyes closed and gently snoring at three of the library's six carrels. "So you see there's not really much of a problem— What?" she added, sounding impatient.

I was holding back, peering into the library. "Do you suppose they have recent history coils?" I asked.

"Of course," she said, sounding peevish. "Why do you want to know?"

I said, "Oh, I wondered." And let myself be pulled away.

She gave me another of those looks. "Well, it might not be a bad place to hole up. Don't fall asleep like those guys, though. Sooner or later somebody's going to wake them up." In the event, what decided our next move wasn't actually a thought-out concealment plan. It was just Chi-Leong sulkily complaining that he was hungry. As far as I could see we were quite satisfactorily inconspicuous in the eatery we wound up in—it was called General Lao's Gumbo and Quesadilla Heaven, but the menu was American Mall Eclectic. I had bacon and eggs and a mound of corned beef hash with plenty of ketchup. Eustace had something called eggs Benedetto, which was basically the eggs Benedict I'd seen people breakfast on in the New York hotels I burgled, only these had chopped black olives sprinkled on their tops. Elfreda had dry toast and black coffee and fresh-squeezed orange juice—by which I mean *fresh*-squeezed, squeezed right at the table by a pretty little Cambodian with a clever little Korean squeezer. And also with a microskirt that I would have paid a lot more attention to if I hadn't been doing my best to forget about women—or, well, especially about formerly male approximations of women—forever.

As I was chewing, there was a little lurch of our table, startling me. Elfreda gave me a little smile and put her hand momentarily over mine. "We're taking off," she said. "I guess they've canceled the embargo."

That sounded like a good guess to me, but it raised a question that I really hadn't thought about: "Where are we going, exactly?"

I didn't get a chance to ask it just then, though, because Elfreda had a question of her own—well, the same question, really. "So," she said socially, chewing away at her toast, "where were you going to run to?"

I gave her an honest answer. "I don't know. I just wanted to run."

"Why, Brad? You weren't actually accused of anything, were you?"

I didn't really want to discuss it, so I just shrugged. Elfreda sighed, but seemed willing to let it drop, at least for the moment. Eustace wasn't. "See here, Sheridan," he said. "If you expect us to help you you must at least be candid when we ask you a question."

For an answer I glanced pointedly around the noisy room. "I really don't like talking here," I said. "Can't we at least get out of this place?"

They humored me. Well, Elfreda humored me, and Eustace at least recognized the wisdom of getting away from all those ears. We didn't seem to have a really good place to go to, though. Eustace's suite was the logical candidate but the maids had been coming in for cleanup as he and Elfreda left. So what then? Another art gallery stroll?

No one came up with a better idea. At least, I reminded myself, I had been fed. The three of us then wandered along a passage lined with tropical flowers, past the third-deck wedding chapel and the medium-intensity gym to the third deck's casino. That immediately struck me as a good place to hole up. "Can we?" I asked, pointing.

Chi-Leong looked reluctant, but Elfreda sighed consent and he disgruntledly led the way. Once inside, and after being well nudged by Elfreda, Chi-Leong fronted me a roll of quarter-euro coins. Then Elfreda ordered him off to see if their room had been made up yet, so they could light the *"No Molestar"* sign on the door and talk—or, my own idea, get some real sleep. Then she went off to join a few early risers around the one active craps table, where she could keep an eye on me without being obvious about it.

The handiest virt slots were labeled "Futbol." They did not look a bit like the football game we kids had played in the villages, and I had no idea of the rules. I didn't really have to. The computers in the machine would pay off every time I won anything, whether I knew I'd won or not.

Actually, I didn't care whether I won or not. I just sat there, feeding quarter euros into the slot and saw, without really seeing, the tiny virt figures running like crazy around their virt playing field. My mind was full of other things that weren't virt at all. Maury's murder. Gerda's false, but entirely operational, female body, young Chi-Leong's damn gravy boat, Piranha Woman's probable pissed-offness at my having got away (and what she was probably trying very hard to do about it), my parents' upcoming financial ruin, since I wasn't employed anywhere anymore and wouldn't any time soon be in a position to resume sending them their pittance.

And again—over and over again—Gerda. It always kept coming back to Gerda. I wanted her back with me, no matter what.

At the same time I really hated her/his/whatever's lousy guts for being what she/he/it was. And on top of all that, I was more mad at myself than I had ever been before, in what I would have to say was an entire lifetime of never liking myself particularly well anyway. What a *fool* I had been about Gerda! I had never before let any human being of any imaginable gender get this far under my skin. For one time in my life—just one time—I had let myself care more about another person than I did about myself, and look what it got me.

The virt footballers on the screen of my slot suddenly began making little virtual soprano-mousy shrieks of excitement to tell me I was suddenly a winner, and the payoff gate began ka-chinging out euro coins. I counted as they fell into my tray. There were eight hundred and fifty of them.

It was my lucky day—in a sense. Actually I didn't feel lucky at all.

When Chi-Leong announced that the maids had finished with their room is when I at last got the nap I had been needing. It wasn't that either Eustace or Elfreda liked that plan better than simply proceeding with the questioning of me. It was only that by then I was getting so close to falling-down exhausted that they didn't really have much choice. Then, waking, I got a shower, hot, drenching, and long. Finally I even got to put on some clean, and very touristy, clothes that Elfreda had gone out to buy for me in one of the zep's many boutiques. The shorts were iridescent, the sandals were bright green, and the shirt bore an image of an alp with the legend "Welcome to Beautiful Bavaria." Nevertheless they all more or less fit me, and I had no other choices anyway. I discovered that the deep pockets of the shorts easily held all the bills I had changed my chips into before I left the casino, too, which made their preposterous color scheme suddenly look less ridiculous in my eyes.

Chi-Leong had treated himself to an outside suite on the *Chang Jang*, but I didn't think he'd got his money's worth. There were picture windows, all right, but there wasn't much to see through them but endless, featureless water. Chugging along at its steady fifty knots, the zep had by then left Pompeii far behind, and a wide stretch of the Tyrrhenian Sea as well. By straining I could catch a glimpse of something a long way to our stern that might have been one of those mountains of southwest Sicily. That was all. Nearer to us there was nothing but some kind of surface cargo ship steaming along across our course, and no other hint of any land anywhere.

When Elfreda came out of the suite's bedroom wearing shorty pajamas and a recently showered look I asked her, "By the way, where are we going?"

She gave me a confidential smile. "You really don't know?" When I shook my head she looked dubious but turned on the coffee machine. "You didn't fool me, Brad. I figured you just ran on impulse all along, right? So, then where would you like to go?" she asked. When I shrugged she gave a little sigh, but then keyed the wall screen to display the cruise itinerary. "Take your pick," she said amiably.

The list looked like a reasonable way for a multimillionaire to get rid of a month he didn't need, along with a lot of unnecessary money. Elfreda gave me a chance to memorize it before she asked brightly, "So which one would you prefer?"

Since I had no idea I picked the farthest one, thus giving myself as much time as possible to invent a real plan. "Abu Simbel," I said. "Up by Lake Nasser."

That produced a quizzical look from Elfreda and an unamused growl from Chi-Leong. "You did not say he would be with us for eleven days," he complained.

She turned a frown on him, but it was to me that she spoke. "Really, hon?" she asked. "Abu Simbel? But there's nothing up there but the dam and some old statues." I shrugged, attempting to show a fondness for old statues. She persisted, "Isn't there something before that?"

"Oh, hell," I said. "As long as I'm on the run one place is as good as another. Tell you what. You pick. Where would you like me to leave the zep?"

"Island of Malta," Chi-Leong said at once.

Elfreda gave him a far more punitive frown this time. She turned to me. "Where we want you to get off is where you want to be, Brad. If you aren't comfortable telling us that yet we'll wait until you are."

"Well, thanks," I said, and, "Is there any more coffee?"

Obviously she wanted to continue the discussion. I didn't, and I settled the matter by turning my back on her to watch the wall screen. Over the next hour I caught up on all the news, which of course was mostly about the Pompeii Flu.

I didn't have to pretend interest. After a while Elfreda sighed and switched it to the "Caution: May Be Offensive to Some" channel, the basically all-Flu one that recommended a strong stomach and no children in the room.

I would have preferred to stay with the regular news, but I didn't turn away, although it was hard to take. Lysing is not pretty to look at. Pustulent sores on a little girl's belly are bad enough, but the tiny baby whose right leg and hip joint had simply rotted off him was more than I cared to see.

I kept my eyes fastened on the scene, though. I had thinking to do.

Elfreda's curiosity about my choice of destinations had finally triggered an unexpected suspicion. It was possible that some half-formed suspicions that were beginning to float around in my brain had been right and I was caught in the middle of another of those complex, multiperson charades, apparently designed to find out where I would run to if allowed to run.

So perhaps my escape had not been just a bit of amazingly good luck. In fact, as long as I was being guarded (if I was) by Elfreda and Chi-Leong, it wasn't even an escape.

What made all that more probable still was Elfreda's behavior. She was watching me intently out of the side of her eye, while doing her best not to look as though she was watching me at all. When she saw that I was looking at her she produced a new subject. "What we all need," she announced, "is a decent dinner. It better be room service, so we can talk without other people listening in. Shall I order for all of us?"

She did.

You know, spending time on something like the *Chang Jang* could get addictive. I found that out when I listened to Elfreda ordering dinner— wild boar ham and fried Peruvian black potatoes and whatever assorted (she told the person taking the order over the phone) vegetables the chefs might recommend, plus salads with three or four different kinds of dressings. Plus breads, and both coffee and tea—US of America tea, she told the woman, none of this Chinese dishwater—and a selection of cheeses and sweets for dessert.

A part of my mind that wasn't involved in figuring out how to get free of this new kind of captivity was now—metaphorically—salivating. But most of it was just going around in circles of worry.

Anyway, when the food came both Chi-Leong and I were banished to the suite's luxurious bathroom, with the door closed, while Elfreda supervised the placement of the dining table and the bringing in of the meal. Chi-Leong didn't talk to me when we were alone there. He sat on the padded rim of the hot tub, watching one of the bathroom's screens, and he didn't look happy. I fiddled with the steam chamber, the bidet, and the aroma dispensers, with one eye on him. I was trying to figure out what his part was in this little game. I conjectured that Elfreda had been undercover for quite a while, no doubt picking up crumbs of intelligence for Security from her endless succession of boyfriends. That didn't seem likely for Chi-Leong.

But a spot of Security blackmail, involving looking the other way from his grandma's gravy boat, pretty well did.

When the servitors were gone, the door locked and the "Do Not Disturb" sign lighted, Eustace and I were let out. The table setting was for only two persons, but there was plenty of food. "Enough for the three of us," Elfreda said, but the way it looked to me it was enough for at least six. It wasn't just plentiful, either. It was about the most expensive meal I had ever had, including a few with Gerda that had pretty nearly busted my budget for a week.

When we had finished eating a major fraction of what the waiters had brought Elfreda disappeared into the bedroom, leaving Eustace and me to make sparse and unfriendly small talk about whether the boeuf en croute had been properly seasoned or not. When she returned she had changed into a monokini and a basically transparent modesty smock. "In case we want to go in for a dip," she explained, and when I pointed out that I didn't have a bathing suit she opened her little carryall and showed us the suit of Eustace's she had borrowed for me. "It's just a thong, so it should fit you. They fit anybody, don't they? And, Eustace, hon, why don't you take a nap or something while Brad and I check the zep out."

"For what?" he asked.

"For I don't know what," she said patiently. "To see if there's anything we need to know about, and, hon, after we've left why don't you call the steward and have these dishes taken away?"

He sighed and surrendered—not, I mean, without displaying his annoyance, as seemed so often to be the case when Elfreda was pulling the strings. "Oh, very well," he said, and that was all he said. What he didn't say was, "Be careful," but then I didn't think he was very good at playing his part. Even Security had to work with whatever people it could get.

But what there was, once I had the wit to look for it, was a wall screen that—once I found where the control pad was hidden—was fed by the zep's main communications links. Since Elfreda and Chi-Leong were presumably asleep in the next room I kept the sound down to a whisper—

And in a moment there he was. Brian Bossert. Not very tall, not particularly good-looking, and not in any respect that I could see resembling the person he was, namely the love of my life. He was a rather ordinary-looking young man, but definitely a man. A man who, to be sure, had murdered at least 13,351 people in his terrorist activities, or perhaps as many as 55,000 or even 150,000 if you included the ones who died of traffic accidents or simple overexertion in New York when he shut down the subways and Las Vegas when he cut off electric power and so on. It was a large number, anyway—though pretty trivial when you compared it with what he, now she, was doing every day.

I went to sleep, wondering at the strange world I was living in.

. . .

And the next morning, now that I didn't have to pretend to be interested in looking at *Chang Jang*'s corridor art, I discovered I was.

There was plenty of it. Right at the bottom of a three-story atrium just down the hall from Chi-Leong's suite there was about the ugliest three-legged statue I had ever seen. Elfreda read from the plaque at its base. "They call it the Toad God of Wealth. Think it'll make us rich?"

I said, "I wish," just to be sociable. The thing was big enough, four meters tall at the least. If it had really been carved ivory, as it looked, it would certainly have weighed a couple of hundred kilos—far more mass than the zep's designers would have permitted. It wasn't real, of course, but just another virt.

We weren't the only passengers patrolling the zep's corridors, in the search for additional ways to get rid of their surplus cash. Actually, it was kind of interesting. Up until then I hadn't really known what people with excessive money actually did with their time. I discovered that they weren't idle. In fact, they were often frantically busy, just not busy in any way that produced anything of value. On the Yellow River deck groups of twenty or thirty practiced ancient dance rituals like the Twist and the Charleston, under the tutelage of skilled instructors and to the tune of appropriate music from virt instrumentalists. Non-virt servitors stood by to offer definitely non-virt champagne to the overexerted. Up on the sun deck scantily, even negligibly, clad passengers stretched out on deck chairs, in pursuit of a golden tan. They weren't going to get it from the actual sun in the actual sky, of course. The whole bulk of the zep's lift ballonets were between them and it.

The tanning rays for the passengers came from halogen tubes, and they wouldn't burn any passenger skin because the hard, carcinogenic frequencies were left out. When we peeped into the dining room at the forward end of the uppermost deck, a couple of artists with mini-chainsaws were putting the final touches to an ice statue of a bride in a flowing snow-white dress. I might have wondered what they were doing that for, but not for long. One of the wedding chapels was just down the passage.

For a moment I was puzzled by the thought of loading the zep with all this extra mass, not less than four or five hundred kilos, I was sure. The sculpture wasn't a virt. It couldn't be. We were feeling the proof of that, because we got a steady trickle of ice particles flying off the saw. But (Elfreda told me, amused at my ignorance) there was a difference between the toad sculpture and the ice bride. Water was water, whether in a frozen state or not, and however much frozen water the ice sculptors used simply became part of the ship's ballast when it melted back.

There was a burst of music as the chapel door opened and ten or twelve people spilled out. I could tell which ones were the bride and the groom. They were the drunkest of the lot.

That was another puzzle. See, every passenger on the *Chang Jang* had news screens in their cabins. Some of them must at least have sometimes glanced at them. They could not be totally ignorant of the hell that was eating up the human race. But if those stomach-turning scenes of dissolving flesh had made them afraid for their own lives there was no sign of it in the way they scarfed down the zep's edibles and intoxicants.

Elfreda was observing them with the benevolently critical smile of a woman who had never been married, but might not reject a reasonable offer out of hand. It seemed like a good time to try to get a straight answer from her. . . .

But I didn't, and the moment passed, and it didn't return. I lost my best chance of it in the middle of that night. Chi-Leong had reasserted his privileges, so I had been assigned the couch in his sitting room, while he and Elfreda tucked in on his vast, air-cushioned bed.

I wasn't jealous, you know. Morose, maybe. I didn't begrudge Chi-Leong a romp with Elfreda, I just resented the fact that the world in general was better off than I in just about every aspect I could imagine.

Well, except for the people who were actually dying of that unwished gift Maury and Gerda seemed to have given to the world.

Those live but doomed people weren't better off than anybody. They weren't getting your tactful and unhurried old-man's-death passing, where you just go to sleep and don't wake up again, and who could ask for a nicer croaking than that? No. These particular dying people did not go gently into that good night. They were all wide awake when it happened, and the reason they were awake was that the agony of having their flesh rot and dissolve on their bodies kept them from any hope of being sound asleep ever again. Along with the particular nastiness they called necrotizing fasciitis the victims got a breakbone fever that had them sobbing or whimpering, or sometimes screaming out loud, before the poisons in their flesh interrupted the communication of cell to cell, and the overtaxed heart failed, and then they did die, usually—mercifully!—within a few hours of the beginning of their body rot.

And time passed.

Time passed, and the *Chang Jang* faithfully followed its published itinerary, and I did nothing.

Nothing but enjoy the *Chang Jang's* multitudinous creature comforts, anyway. Under the right circumstances I could see that that would be enough—defining the right circumstances as, say, if I had a Gerda with me to enjoy them. But those circumstances didn't obtain. The ones that did included quite a long and unpleasant list—

1. Maury's murder.
2. The strong possibility that Gerda was the one who murdered him.
3. Old Dan and Marilyn Sheridan, often in my mind as I thought of them hopefully watching the mail machine every morning for the remittance that wasn't going to come anymore.
4. The mighty force with which Security was leaning on me, which was what led me to escape in the first place.
5. The fact that, as I was now convinced, that whole escape was a Security setup, which meant I was in even worse trouble than I'd thought, because the stakes had evidently become higher.

And 6, 7, 8, all the way up to the highest number I could think of. That was the lack of Gerda—plus the horrid knowledge that Gerda wasn't really much of a Gerda, insofar as that name denotes gender, at all.

That's a funny thing, isn't it? If a fraction of what I knew or suspected about Gerda were true I wasn't going to want her back, was I? But it sure as hell felt like I did.

So the days passed, and each hour of *Chang Jang*'s cruising brought me an hour closer to wherever it was I was going.

The identity of that place, however, was slow to appear. I didn't get off at the zep's first stop, which was the island of Malta. Elfreda did, for a short visit—would never get another chance to see where a tattered handful of European knight-crusaders could fight off ten or twenty thousand infidels, she said. (But I thought maybe she was just going to look for a secure line to talk back to Security HQ.) Anyway she made sure that Eustace Chi-Leong stayed aboard to keep an eye on me. Which he did by setting us up in the ship's library, me at one carrel, him at another between mine and the door. I used the opportunity for checking out every place on the zep's schedule, hoping that one would reveal itself as the ideal place for me to sneak away and be finally really free of Security.

None did.

I didn't try to jump ship at the second place, either. That was Lepus Magnus, too small for me to hide in. Then Petra: even smaller, not to mention with no useful way to get out of there except another zep.

The next stop on the tour was good old Cairo.

I woke up early and headed for a window as the zep was gliding toward its mooring place outside of the city. The captain had taken the long way around, and we were coming in right over the Sphinx itself, all bright red and gold and green when the virt replays of its appearance were switched on, the familiar sandblasted ruin when reality was allowed to show. And then from behind me someone cried—screamed—"Oh, my sweet Jesus God!"

It was Elfreda, looking scared. No, terrified. She was standing in the bedroom doorway, and a trickle of sound from behind her showed that she'd been listening to news. She was wearing a kind of baby-doll nightie that she hadn't bothered to pull anything over, and hadn't been wearing anything under, either. "Did you hear?" she yelled. "Christ, we're really in it now."

I looked at her in surprise. No doubt the Flu was scary, but I hadn't thought that even the death in agony of a few million people would get her that upset. I said, "Yes, it's a pretty serious epidemic, all right, but—"

"Oh, Brad," she groaned, "who's talking about the goddamn epidemic? It's the *quarantine*. The zep isn't going on to Aswan! It's grounded here in goddamn Cairo, because somebody else has been shooting holes in zeps and nobody's going anywhere until they make it stop!"

Behind her Chi-Leong had appeared, standing in the bedroom doorway and glowering. He wasn't wearing whatever he usually wore to bed, if that was anything at all. He had put on a kind of Cossack cavalry officer's leisure robe—I guess—and he had taken the time to button all the score or so of buttons before exposing himself to my eyes. He said, in a tone of deep indignation, "That is extremely troublesome for me, Sheridan." He didn't say why, but I could figure that out easily enough by myself. He didn't say why he looked like he was blaming me, either, but that was almost as easy: He was blaming me for everything he didn't like.

I stopped paying attention to him as soon as I got the wall screen on. Then I knew what Elfreda was talking about, and I could see why she was scared. From a small boat in the Gulf of Finland somebody had shot down a Russian aerozep dirigible with an incendiary missile on its run from St. Petersburg to Helsinki. Everybody on board was dead, and every passenger zep in the world's skies was ordered grounded while Security figured this new thing out.

The others were listening, too, Elfreda with the back of her hand pressed against her mouth, Eustace shaking his head, "Dr. Basil Chi-Leong, my father, will be extremely displeased," he informed me.

Well, I was pretty displeased myself. Set down? Made to leave the ship, as all the others had been in the last attack? And in Cairo? Cairo, Egypt? Egypt, where there was a really good chance that some cop's villain-scanner might pick up my face out of a crowd and identify it as the man who'd been thrown out of the country a few months before?

Of all the stops on the *Chang Jang*'s tour Cairo was the last one I would have picked. But I didn't have the luxury of a free choice anymore.

Chi-Leong had decided to be our group's alpha male. He looked over his shoulder at Elfreda. "Kindly dress yourself," he ordered.

Elfreda looked surprised, then rebellious, then resigned. "That makes sense," she conceded, "because we might have to move pretty fast. You guys, too, you know."

Chi-Leong gave her a nod, the kind that could have meant he agreed with her point or that he just wanted her to get on with following his orders. She bit her lip, but left the room. When she had closed the bedroom door behind her he turned to me and lowered his voice. "You should go, Mr. Sheridan. Now. Before she finishes dressing."

He was getting under my skin. "Chi-Leong," I said, "that would probably be good for you. The thing is, I'm more interested in what would be good for me. How would I get off this damn zep without documents?"

He was losing patience with me. "Are you not aware that I have a considerable supply of the best documents of all, namely euro notes? The person who guarded the uplink will get you past whoever is guarding the ship's boarding elevators."

I was getting impatient, too. "You make it sound easy. Suppose I do get down to the ground, what then?"

"That," he said, "is of course your problem, Mr. Sheridan. I hope you will avoid capture—it is for my sake that I hope this, not yours. Now," he added, lifting his bellybag to his lap and opening it, "you may need some money. Fortunately I have actual physical currency notes, as you would be unable to use my joystick without my ID. This"—he pulled out five

five-euro notes and handed them to me—"should help." I tried not to laugh. It would, of course, not have been a laughing matter if I hadn't had the professor's fifty as well as the wad of ten-euro notes I'd won in the ship's casino. He went on, "I have sent for my man Miguel. He will help you. Now hurry—no. Wait."

Elfreda was coming out, dressed and unaware of anything we had been saying, just as we felt the *Chang Jang* slowing and stopping. The three of us went out onto the viewwalks and gazed down at the hundred or so square kilometers of the town . . . and the much larger communities that flanked it, bustling Gizeh on one side and colossal Cairo on the other. Elfreda didn't say a word, not even good-bye, when she hurried off to keep a date for a drink with one of the ship's assistant pursers—who, she hoped, might tell her enough about the ship's buoyancy system to suggest a place where I might hide.

And thirty seconds after that there was a knock on the door, and a crewman slipped Chi-Leong a package before scurrying away. I recognized the man. I had seen him in the pipeway when I sneaked on board the zep. When Chi-Leong shook out the contents of the package I recognized them, too: a white shirt and a pair of white shorts like the ones worn by the zep's crewmen. They were pretty tight, and the badge on my breast described me as someone named John Smith. I was about to complain that no one got away with calling himself John Smith until I realized that in this part of the world "John Smith" was probably as foreign and exotic a name as it needed to be to be ignored.

"So, Sheridan," Chi-Leong said, inspecting me with mild distaste, "shall we get on with it?"

We should. We did. I changed clothes, packing my own laundered stuff into the bag, and left, heading for the part of the zep all the noise of getting ready for disembarkation was coming from, and I didn't say good-bye, either.

I don't know how good Chi-Leong's suborned helper, Miguel, was at his regular job. I didn't have any idea what that job was, for that matter. At the work of finding unlawful ways on and off a zep, however, he was just fine.

When I got to the disembarkation lounge all four of the zep's ship-to-surface gondolas were going busily up and down. Going up they were filled with Egyptian medics, carrying ominous-looking kits of supplies, and soldiers wearing expressions of pop-eyed delight at finding themselves in such unimagined luxury. Going down the gondolas were all but empty. When I was staring at one and wondering how in the world I might board it Miguel appeared behind me at the last minute, shouting "Captain's orders!" to the zep crewwoman supervising the event. She looked confused, but didn't attempt to argue with him. Neither did anyone else, as good old Miguel, shouting in a language that wasn't English and may indeed have been pure gibberish, because no one else seemed to understand it, either—as Miguel, that is, tugged me onto a gondola and slammed the door behind me. Four minutes later I stepped out onto the soil, or at least onto the landing platform, of one of Cairo's infinite supply of suburbs.

So here I was, finally fully escaped (I supposed) from even the longest-range of Security's oversight.

But escaped to what?

I didn't have an answer to that, so I did the next best thing. I just stopped thinking about it.

21

CAIRO AGAIN

Were things going my way at last?

It almost seemed so. There was a squalid little café on the edge of the square, and as soon as I was out of my new best friend's sight I headed for it. I sat down at a table the size of a quarter-euro coin to think things over, screened from most of the soldiers by a couple of pots of very nearly dead palms.

It was not the most secure place I had ever been in, surrounded by crowds of strangers whose language was impenetrable to me, whose skin color was different from mine—so much so that in this one city, of all the cities I might have been in, there was no hope of vanishing by blending in. And finally also, I was pretty sure, a place that had no friendly feelings toward me at all.

Cars and buses were rolling into an inadequate-looking parking area, controlled by half a dozen sweating and surly cops. I could see three or four bright-red police cruisers parked nearby, but I was hidden by the palms.

This suburb was not one of the metropolises that every traveler wants to visit. I doubt that many travelers had ever heard of it. On the other hand none of its locals, now engaged in gaping up at the *Chang Jang* as she tugged against her tethers overhead, were ever going to become world travelers themselves, and thus they were unlikely to recognize me. I should be able to get out of here intact. What I needed was simply a place where I could hole up indefinitely, or at least until Security stopped looking for me.

It was at that moment that my luck really did change, because I remembered.

What I remembered was the wonderful fact that such a place might well exist—really had existed, just a few months ago, and quite possibly existed still. Patty Hopper had owned a shabby old apartment that she used mostly as a storeroom for her stock of fake antiquities to sell to the tourists. She hadn't had time to clear it out before her trial, and the cops hadn't confiscated it, because they hadn't known it existed. It would still be there. I was sure of it. All I had to do was get to it.

And then the latest van to roll into the parking lot supplied a way for me to do it. The legend on its side proclaimed that it belonged to "University of Cairo, Department of Agricultural Statistics." A middle-aged woman was bustling toward it as fast as her stumpy little legs would carry her, crying, "Abdul! Here I am! Thank heaven you found me!"

And Abdul was leaning out of his window, grinning and saying, "Yes, Dr. Stubb! Is I indeed! Come get in and I will take you at once to university!" And then he saw me, trotting toward him and agitatedly waving, and my luck had changed as far as it was going to go.

When Abdul heard that I was one of the specialists invited to a secret Pompeii Flu seminar, and that the world-famous Professor Heisenstadt—*the* Professor Heisenstadt! From Gottingen! Truly a name to conjure with, in spite of the fact that I had just made it up—was supposed to send someone to pick me up, but at the main terminal, and now I had no way to get to the university unless Abdul and Dr. Stubb would—

They would. They did. The magic words were "Pompeii Flu." Neither of them could refuse anything to somebody who might have a way of coping with the biggest, dangerousest, breathtakingly worryingest terrorist action in human history. And best of all was the word "secret," because it kept them from asking questions I couldn't handle.

Cairo traffic was, as always, hopeless, but Abdul was inspired. He found shortcuts I could hardly believe existed, and in not much more than half an hour we were rolling onto the campus. He had just turned around to ask me what building I wanted when I caught sight of the big Metro sign. "Right here!" I commanded. "I see Dr. Leshinsky! He'll get me to the symposium!"

And the rest was easy, since I was at the door of Cairo's subway system. The Cairo Metro was hardly confusing at all, and I clearly remembered the route. Take a westbound on what they called the Japanese—I guess because Japanese engineers had built it—line to the Sabat station, change north one stop to Nasser, then northbound again to Zamalek station, and I was there.

Well, no, I wasn't. Patty's hideaway wasn't really close to the Metro station. Wasn't all that far, either—she used to take a taxi from that Metro station and was at her hideaway in five minutes. No taxis for me, though. I didn't want to leave any more of a trail than I had to, so I walked.

It was farther than I remembered, but finally I got there. An abandoned furniture store took up the ground floor. Patty's pied-à-terre was on the second. The key was still under the stand-alone, and never emptied, hall ashtray—and by "key" what I mean is a piece of metal one edge of which was scalloped in an irregular shape; my new home was preelectronic. But when I twisted that actual key in an actual keyhole on the apartment door it worked.

And there it was: large room, unmade bed against one wall, sofa, couple of chairs, other unimpressive bits of furniture, walls hung with religious paintings of some kind, stacks of cartons which turned out to contain ancient Egyptian vases, all chipped and cracked and every one chipped and cracked in the same way. Those, of course, had been Patty's stock in trade. The bathroom was still there, with its toilet and its claw-footed tub for bathing, although I did not think there would be any hot water. There wasn't, though—great good fortune!—the toilet did reluctantly flush.

I went to the window and looked out, careful to hide most of my body behind the dusty curtain. No one seemed to be looking up at me. No one, I was pretty sure, knew where I had gone.

What all of this added up to was that, at last, I myself was master of my fate and captain of my soul and if any terrible blunders were going to be committed at least I was going to have the privilege of committing them myself.

Good news, right?

It did not, however, feel absolutely good. What it suddenly felt like, as I stood at that filthy window and gazed out at the desolate street, was lonesome.

22

MY HOME FROM HOME

The room was not in any sense luxurious, but it did seem to have everything I might need for a few days. The window was nearly opaque with the filth of years, but when I looked out on its narrow street I could keep an eye on everything that moved there, and even more that didn't—the burned-out wreck of a school bus at one corner, some of the largest potholes I'd ever seen at another. Most of all I saw the shabby little store at the corner, with its half-dozen loafers sitting or slouching around the door. At least there I could actually buy food as I needed it—being, naturally, careful to see that I was as close to unseen as possible.

Just to make sure, I waited until dark before I crossed the street. By then the loafers were gone, no doubt to their homes and dinners, but it was almost a mistake. By the time I showed up at her door the old woman whom I had seen sweeping a fraction of the filth off the sidewalk was already getting ready to crank down the metal chain-link curtain that would cover the shop window. She wasn't really interested in selling me anything. For that matter, she didn't have all that much that I was willing to buy, but I finally pulled out four or five cans of soup and a couple of boxes of crackers.

Then the real trouble started. She looked at my twenty-euro note and began to shriek—presumably for help. Which arrived.

The man who came pushing through the curtains at the back of the store was fatter than the woman and just as old and, when she had explained the situation to him, even louder.

My best first guess—the only thing that made any sense at all—was that they thought I was trying to pass a counterfeit bill on them. That wasn't it, though, because when I pulled another twenty out of my stash to offer them it didn't help. Then the man paused long enough to say something in a different tone to the woman. She answered him, then pressed a key on their old cash register. It said something I couldn't understand—I suppose, the Egyptian equivalent of "no sale"—and slid its cash drawer open. The woman, now screeching in my direction again, pointed at the coins and greasy bills in the drawer.

And comprehension came to me at last. "Oh, hell," I said. "You mean you can't make change for the twenty."

We finally reached a solution to that, though it took their total cash reserve, and then I had to make four trips to carry up to my room the remainder of twenty euros' worth of selections from the stock of their little shop. Still, when it was all stacked against one wall I was glad enough to have it, particularly the two-liter boxes of drinking water; I hadn't really had much confidence in what might come out of the place's plumbing system. I did find it interesting to sample some of their previously unexperienced assortment of canned and dried fruits, vegetables, and stews. And the other good thing about having done a week's shopping in one night was that I didn't have to go back to the store the next day.

Or the next.

Or the one after that, either. The trouble with that, though, was that it had taken a lot less than seventy-two hours to get really tired of Patty's former apartment. Not to mention that by then I was getting pretty bored with my cold meals, since nothing I could do would make the little stove work. So as soon as it got dark and the store loafers had gone home I crossed the street one more time. There was, I remembered, a tiny section of fresh produce—unfamiliar tubers, tiny tomatoes, heads of what looked like some kind of cabbage, fuzzy little globular fruits that were probably something like peaches or apricots.

However, when I was actually looking at the selection the problems began to occur to me. Nothing that required cooking was of any use to me. As to the other thing—well, if I suspected that tap water might be unsafe, what about the raw fruits and vegetables? With what inexpensive and readily available material, for example, were the local farmers likely to be fertilizing their crops?

I didn't know the answer for sure, but I had my suspicions. I finally settled on a melon and a hand of stubby little bananas, all of which would be peeled before I ate them. The shop lady was a lot friendlier now. While I was paying for the fruit out of the Egyptian change she'd given me the first time she was jabbering amiably away. I didn't understand her, of course, but then I didn't really have to. The melon was a disappointment when I got it upstairs—opaque white flesh that looked like chalk and didn't taste much different. I ate it, regardless. I was glad to trade every gourmet item in the *Chang Jang*'s ample larder for the absence of Elfreda's watchful stare. And I tried to figure out what I was going to do.

First question: How long could I hole up here in Patty's little nest?

Answer: Well, probably as long as I wanted to, I guessed. A few days. Maybe a week or two. As long as it might take for the heat to dwindle. After all, there wasn't anybody I wanted to get back to . . .

Which, of course, brought my thoughts, never far away, back to Gerda.

I don't mean I was thinking of her in every minute. There were times when I could pretty nearly put her out of my mind, with the aid of the fact that there were so many unignorable other things that competed with her memory. But then I would slip. In my mind's eye I would see her— smiling, so cheerful it hurt to look at her; so loving, with her arm tucked into mine and, once or twice, her face upturned for a kiss. . . . Well, at those times she was not at all out of my mind. She filled it to the brim.

No one needs to tell me that was stupid. I knew it. It wasn't just dumb, either. It was worse. It was simply pathetic for a healthy young man like me to yearn so for another human being. (Of course, healthy young men like me have done just that over and over in human affairs. It is what three-quarters of all literature is about.)

The fact that she was not only the woman I loved but also a merciless mass killer somewhat dampened my ardor. Didn't dispell it, though. Didn't change the fact that I ardently wanted her back.

By the second or third day I had managed to deal with that paralyzing longing, by which I mean that when it smote me I just let it smite and waited for it to go away. Anyway, I had plenty of other things to think about. For example, the nagging question of had I really done sensible things in running away—repeatedly—from Security's supervision? And, once I had managed to set that aside as at the moment unanswerable, what should I do with this unexpected freedom?

There at least I had come to a few conclusions. The fact that I had no plan for the future that made any sense at all meant that where I sat was as good a place to be as any other. Perforce I then began thinking not in terms of days but of months.

This meant that the winnings from *Chang Jang*'s casino would run out, so I needed a source of income. Short of trying to burgle a home or rob a bank only one possibility presented itself: the endlessly gullible Western tourist.

I could, for instance, sell some of Patty's stock in trade. She wouldn't be needing it for some time. But her fake little antiquities were junk; I'd have to sell dozens of them each week just for eating money, and what Cairo cop wouldn't notice somebody toting a backpack full of fake vases?

Alternatively there was the little racket I had been planning to try the last time I was here, and never got around to. I'm talking about manufacturing fake papyrus copies of The Book of the Dead, every ancient Egyptian's only hope of an eternal afterlife, and every tourist's first choice of something to hang on a living room wall. That wouldn't be hard to set up. I would need a supply of imitation papyrus, but there was plenty of that in every art supply store. If I took a camera into any museum I could copy some version or other of the text. Then I'd want access to a decent copy-ing machine, and then, for the aging process to make them look authentic, I needed only matches, a little bit of animal fat and some time.

There was one big drawback to that plan. It meant that I would have to go where the tourists were. For that I would have to disguise myself.

Perhaps I could grow a beard, and maybe see if the shoplady across the street had some suitably black and greasy hair dye, and at least a pair of dark glasses to hide the fact that my eyes were very non-Egyptianly blue.

All those things were possible . . .

Or, I told myself, what was also possible was that something would come along to make all of that unnecessary . . . and, you know, that very night something did.

I was at the window, once again trying to figure out what the future might hold for me while simultaneously doing a before-retiring check on the outside world. Apart from the store window, its lights already out, and a single elderly man limping home after a long workday, there wasn't much to see . . . until there was.

What appeared was a red police four-wheeler cruising slowly down the street.

I pulled back from the window. I wasn't sure that the police in the car were looking for somebody, but nothing about them gave any other impression. And if they were looking for someone, the odds were pretty good that that someone was likely to be me.

Then all those thoughts were driven out of my mind, because the police car turned a corner, and I saw her.

Gerda Fleming.

It was Gerda, all right. She looked harried and more unkempt than I had ever seen her before, but it was definitely Gerda, walking down the dusty street all by herself. Stopping to talk to nobody and, all right, having al-most nobody else on the street to talk to since pretty nearly everybody else had gone home. The one scruffy little three-wheeled truck on the street was turning off it. Even the loafers who usually sat or leaned in front of the dirty little store were now sitting or leaning somewhere else. And I was thunderstruck. Gerda? Here? Where I could ask her for explanations . . . or for instructions on what I was supposed to do about all this . . . or, most of all, for simply being where I could put my arms around her?

I didn't trouble myself with incredulity, or wonder that she might so suddenly come back into my life. I didn't stop to think at all.

I was out of the door and hurrying down the stairs and out onto the dead grass beside the sidewalk and after her. By then I was flat-out running, the hot air I was sucking into my lungs burning them, gasping. And yelling—"Gerda! Hold up! It's me!"—as well as I could yell with my lungs on fire.

She didn't answer. She certainly didn't turn around to look at me. At the corner where the burned-out bus blocked the sidewalk she made the left turn, still not looking back. I was right behind her. When I'd got past the bus she was no more than a dozen meters ahead of me, approaching a red police van that was parked, its motor idling, maybe another ten or a dozen meters farther along.

That made me hesitate. The last people I wanted to see were police. But there was Gerda . . .

Then she did stop. She didn't turn around. She didn't seem to do anything at all, just stopped and stood there.

And a moment later her red hair blossomed into a bright blue-white flame, and her arms and legs turned into fire, and all of my Gerda that I'd lost and found and who I'd loved and hated and altogether missed— all of her—

Evaporated into a blaze of sparks and fire—

And then wasn't there at all.

Those flames hadn't scorched the sidewalk. There was no pile of ash. There was nothing. I had been chasing after a virt.

And not just any old virt, either, but a virt which the cops had probably been deploying all over the parts of Cairo where I might be hiding. Trolling for me, that is. Hoping that I would be dumb enough to leap out of my safe concealment and take the bait, like any other stupid fish. Just as I had.

The van door was opening. A Security man came out, head turned back so that he could finish a conversation with whoever was still inside. Not hurrying. Planning, I judged from the unlit cigarette in his hand, to catch a quick smoke before heading back to base to report that that wily Brad Sheridan had eluded them again.

He hadn't seen me.

That meant that I had an option. I could turn and get away, and with any luck at all they wouldn't notice.

But I didn't do that, though, because all of a sudden I was fed up. Tired of acting guilty when, as far as I could see, I wasn't guilty of anything at all, and even more tired of asking myself just what the hell I thought it was that I was accomplishing with all this running away and hiding.

Since I wasn't accomplishing anything, wasn't it about time for me to turn decision-making back to those who wanted to do it? Even to monsters like the Piranha Woman or old fools like the professor?

So I took a deep breath and kept on walking. As the Security man finished exiting the van and turned his head more or less in my direction I called, "Hello? Listen, I'm Brad Sheridan. I think you're looking for me."

23

HOME AGAIN, JIGGETY-JIG

Security goons were not my favorite people, but I have to admit that those two weren't particularly rough with me. They weren't particularly solicitous, either, and they sure weren't taking any chances in letting me get away again. Stick-tight wrist cuffs bound my hands behind my back and a sticky collar was around my neck with a leash attached. A leash! And the guy at the other end of it never let go.

But they didn't hurt me. Helped me, actually, or maybe you could say pushed me, into the van, offered me food when we got to an airstrip I hadn't seen before—not only food but a shot of genuine Scotch and a trip to the toilet, too—and then untied me completely when we were airborne. They even answered my questions—well, some of my questions. How had they known where to deploy their Gerda virt? Simple. They had a picture of me leaving the Metro station. You might wonder how that was possible, considering how many tens of millions of riders took the Metro every day. I did. But they explained that. There were those unnoticed crowd-control cameras all over the Metro, they said, and the Naples office had sent them pictures of me. Of course it would have been impossible for human beings to pick mine out of all those other faces. So they didn't bother with human beings. They had pattern-recognition programs that were more accurate and far faster than any flesh-and-blood person, and they found me leaving the station with no difficulty. Then it was only a matter of playing the Gerda virt everywhere within walking distance. With a lot of pressure on them to make it work—especially, the plumper one said, grinning, from Civilian Informer Barcowicz, burning up the circuits in tears as she pleaded with them to make it work because Major Feliciano, the one I knew better as Piranha Woman, was promising to do her great bodily harm if I wasn't recaptured right away. They even told me what kind of a plane we were in. We were in a SCRAM. The kind of high-speed aircraft that the security agencies used, and a couple of high-government officials, and hardly anybody else. It got you where you were going, fast.

It got us where we were going so fast, in fact, that when they ordered me back into the seat restraints I thought I must have done something that displeased them. Only when I heard the sound of the SCRAM's engines change as we moved into lower, thicker air did I figure out that we were landing. "Oh," I said. "We've arrived. I thought you guys were mad at me."

The one binding my ankles gave me a frown. "Welcome to Capodichino Airport, Naples," he said. "Now shut up."

When he frowned it was aimed at his partner, not me. "Lighten up, Brian," he said reprovingly. "Think about what we've got here. Think about those twenty million euros."

"Oh, hell," Brian said. "You're dreaming. They'd never give us the whole reward just for bringing him in."

"And if they give us any part of it, what's wrong with that?" He shook his head. "Now sit down and belt yourself in; we're landing."

And so we were; and then we taxied a bit; and then someone opened the door of our hardwing and I got a look at who was waiting for me. Security, all of them. One was holding the handles of a wheelchair, a couple were standing there with weapons drawn, and the last one was female and recognizable to me and looking quite pleased for a change. She had one hand on the waiting wheelchair and she looked almost happy, an expression I had never seen before on the face of Major Yvonne Feliciano.

. . .

Whatever interior joy Piranha Woman was experiencing, she wasn't offering to share any of it with me. "Yes," she said—not to me but to my
own personal Rosencrantz and Guildenstern Security guards, "that's
Sheridan, all right. I identify him. Bring him right in for the deep penetration." She did the thing she was good at doing—giving orders—and
then turned around and left the room. She didn't even look at me again.

It had an effect on my captors, though. Both of them were now scowl-
ing and even looking sort of worried—not for themselves. surely, since
Piranha Woman hadn't told them they were degenerate incompetents.
So it had to be for me.

I cleared my throat. "Guys?" I asked. "What's deep penetration?"

The only answer I got was from the plumper one, and it wasn't helpful. It
was just, "Shut up." And then they hustled me into the wheelchair, hooking
my ankles to the chair's footrests and locking a seatbelt around my waist.
Then they slapped a heavy blindfold on my eyes and we started to move.

It was a longish trip. It took us through several doors that whined
themselves open before us, and then whined closed again when we were
through, and at least two elevators. I heard a familiar voice registering
displeasure, and then we stopped and someone removed my blindfold.

The place they had taken me to was shiny white and flooded with sun-
bright lighting. Two women were facing off at the other side of the room,
next to a big and shiny tubular thing that looked like a cross between a late
Twentieth Century MRI scanner and a medieval torture rack. One of the
women was Major Piranha Woman, her mouth still open because we
seemed to have caught her in mid-screech. The other was young and
chocolate brown. She was wearing a medical gown and an obstinate expression, and I had never seen her before. She turned toward us and spoke
to my captors. "Take the cuffs off him," she said, "and then you can go."

Piranha Woman, however, was quick to correct the order. "You can
release him," she told the guards, "but then stay here to watch him. This
is a dangerous man. You're authorized to shoot him if necessary but do
your best not to make it a mortal wound. We need his testimony."

Then, as she returned to the other woman and my captors began to release my ankle cuffs and belt chain, not looking happy about staying there, she resumed screech mode. "You may not refuse a direct order from a superior officer, Lieutenant! This man has information we must have!"

To set the record straight I called, "I don't."

No one was listening to me, though. Not even my two guards, who finished taking my restraints off and then went over to stand with their backs against the wall. I stayed by my wheelchair, listening to the argument and gazing around, without much pleasure, at this unpleasantly surgical-looking place, with its imitation tank of virt fish at one end of the room and quarreling women at the other.

The lieutenant, though well outranked, was standing her ground. She didn't look like a fighter, with her uniform concealed by her medical gown. She looked more like a junior orderly assigned to bedpan detail, but I heard her say, "The regulations are specific, Major Feliciano. Civilians may not be required to undergo deep penetration without the permission of a field-grade officer. I've messaged Colonel Mazzini but he has not replied."

That stopped Piranha Woman at least for the moment. "You did what?"

"I messaged Colonel Mazzini to tell him you were requesting deep penetration for a civilian and asking for orders," the lieutenant said. "As required by regulations."

Piranha Woman closed her eyes for a moment, then shook her head. "You have overstepped your authority. Sheridan isn't a civilian. He's a criminal in custody and not protected by the regulations."

The lieutenant clearly felt herself losing ground but she wasn't giving up the fight. "I am not aware that Mr. Sheridan has been convicted of a crime."

Piranha Woman was smiling now. Over her shoulder she called, "Sheridan! Did you stow away on the cruise zeppelin *Chang Jang* and jump ship in Egypt?"

I had been listening with interest to the squabble, but I hadn't expected to have to take part in it. It took a moment for me to answer. "Yes, Major Feliciano," I said, "I did."

"And did you pay the cruise line for your transportation?"

That was an easy one, and I didn't try to drag it out. I just said, "No."

Piranha Woman gave a little nod. She had never taken her eyes off the lieutenant; now she said, "You have heard Sheridan confess to two serious crimes, which means he has lost his civilian status. Prep the subject. I'll be back in ten minutes to observe the penetration." And she left. She still didn't bother even to look in my direction. But she did look pleased with herself.

The lieutenant didn't look that way at all as she fiddled with a keypad attached to that worrisome-looking cylindrical thing. Then she pressed a button and, as a door behind the shiny machine began to open, dismissed my guards and turned to me. "I'm sorry we put you through this squabbling, Mr. Sheridan—or may I call you Brad?" She didn't wait for an answer but turned to that far door, where a couple of other white-gowned women were coming in. "These are my assistants." And then to the newcomers, "Bring him over and sit him down, Shao-pin."

To me that sounded fairly peremptory, by which I mean very much like what everybody else had been saying to me for the last while. They didn't act that way, though. The one I supposed was Shao-pin—because she looked Asian, while the other seemed more or less Italian—even brushed off the seat of my chair before she helped me into it.

"I'm First Lieutenant Amy Everard," the one at the desk told me. "I'll be conducting this DP, as ordered by Major Feliciano. I suppose you know that a deep penetration is similar to a lie detector."

I was easing myself into the chair before her, and that almost amused me. "What, again? Your guys did that to me already."

"Ah," she said, "but that was a different kind of machine, Brad. It was noninvasive. Do you know what that means?"

I was suddenly beginning to be afraid that I did. "You mean what you're going to do is different?"

"Very different. Deep penetration isn't noninvasive. For that reason, among others, the kind of interrogation we need to do with you now is not entirely lawful, under international agreements. We are only allowed to use it in cases of great emergency, and we have to get special permission each time from the global HQ. But it is very useful."

"Because it can tell if I'm lying? But why do you think I'd lie to you anyway?"

"It's not exactly a question of lying, Brad," she said. "It can actually tell us the truth about things you did with Fleming that you may not even know you know."

I held up my hand. "Wait a minute. What are you doing to my head?" When I wasn't looking the Italian-looking one had moved behind me, and she was rubbing my skull with something that buzzed alarmingly. And suddenly there was a stabbing pain at the base of my neck.

Lieutenant Everard patted my arm. "It's nothing serious, Brad. The scalp needs to be shaved, that's all. Were you going to ask me something?"

I was indeed. "You said this thing you want to do is what you call 'invasive'?"

She looked apologetic. "I'm afraid so, Brad. Definitely so. Which means, I'm afraid, that it is likely to hurt you quite a lot."

"But you're giving me something for the pain?" I asked, clutching at straws.

"That injection you just had? No, Brad. We need you to be awake. That needle Nola gave you wasn't an analgesic, it was just to keep you from moving. While you still can, would you put your forearms on the arms of your chair, please?"

I said what anybody would say. I said, "What for?" But actually I was already doing what she'd told me to do, and I found out what for pretty fast. Memory-metal bands popped out of the chair arms and secured my wrists. So did the bands that secured my neck, waist, and thighs.

"That isn't too tight, is it?" she asked politely. "It's just to keep you still while the aldehyde kicks in."

"The what?"

"It's just a pharmaceutical. What it will do is help us examine your hippocampus."

"My—?"

She said obligingly, "I'll show you. Sometimes it seems to work better if the subject knows what's going on." Her fingers were busy with the keypad again. In the tank along the wall the virt fish flashed and disappeared. In their place the tank displayed a slowly rotating chunk of grayish, wrinkled meat.

"Oh, Christ," I said. "Is that my brain?"

She nodded. "It's already mapped, so let me show you what we're looking at." The virt image in the tank shed a chunk of its outer layers. What I was looking at then was some inner section, the same unpleasant pinky gray color, the details meaningless to me.

But not to the lieutenant. "That," she said, "is your hippocampus. That's where most of your explicit, long-term memories reside, sort of distributed among the dentate gyrus, the subiculum, and—well, you don't really want an anatomy lesson, do you? Nola," she called, turning away from me, "is the tray ready?"

"All ready," the Italian-looking one told her. While I wasn't looking she had pushed over a wheeled table bearing an assortment of oddities. One looked like a football helmet; the others I didn't really want to identify, because they looked a lot like surgical tools. The lieutenant turned back to me. "How are your toes?" she asked.

I hadn't expected that question. I tried wriggling them and the funny thing was they wouldn't wriggle. I got no sensation from them at all. "I don't know what the matter is," I told her, "but I don't feel a thing."

"Good," she said. "Then I think we can begin."

Everard hadn't lied about the pain. Pain isn't all there was, either. The part that hurt the most—physically, anyway—was right at the beginning. That was when they put the helmet on my head and the inside of it began sprouting little needles, needles of a kind that I couldn't see but surely could feel as they prodded here on the surface of my shaven skull, prodded there, sought the exact right place to get to my poor, unresisting brain. And then found it.

I knew from a lot of hours of watching hospital shows on the wall screens that the brain itself doesn't feel pain. But if there isn't any anesthesia the skin of the scalp certainly feels enough of it to provide all the pain a person really needs. My scalp did that, and didn't stop feeling it. The helmet was lined with a plentiful supply of those agile and untiring needles, and now, one batch after another, they were busily inserting themselves right through my skull into the unresisting meat of my brain.

If what they were doing was looking for buried memories, they found them, so many of them that I couldn't keep track. I didn't just see or hear things, either. I felt them—I mean *really* felt them—at one moment shuddering with cold, then sweating, then the muscles of my thighs burning with the lactic acid of overexertion and my bladder almost bursting with an urgent need to relieve itself. And pain. Serious pain, like the sudden, violated hurt revisited for me from one sultry summer New York day when I'd been going into the city to hustle a few illegal dollars. Now it was back, as agonizing as it had been on that long-ago day when I'd fallen off the car I'd been hanging onto, and took off thirty square centimeters of skin on the concrete floor of the tunnel.

Then there were the quick flashes, coming and fading, so fast that it was only later that I could remember what they were associated with. There were bellyaches and headaches, and there were overwhelming sexual sensations: massive erections and massive ejaculations. None of them were imaginary. Each one was a kind of snapshot of some one real thing that had actually happened—yes, had truly happened, and had happened with Gerda. Those were the ones where she was with me in all the places we had been together. Sometimes she was naked and sprawled sleeping across that dingy cot in my dingy room, sometimes chewing happily on a high-priced meal at one of those high-priced clubs and casinos that she loved so well. Or in the dress of an ancient Pompeiian matron at a triclinum dinner. Or beside me on the seat of a three-wheeler, perhaps on the way to the Caserta palace or the Amalfi shore.

But mostly she was naked, and the smell of her was there, and the touch of her skin and her always talented fingers and tongue. I guessed—no, actually I was quite sure—that these were not accidental, that really those deeply penetrating people were deliberately driving their machine through the parts of my past life that involved Gerda. Put the memories all together, and they were a sort of taped record of every last thing she and I had ever done together, from that first moment when I'd met her outside the refectory at the Giubileo to the hour when she kissed me good-bye and left to join her grandmother at her place on Lake Garda.

You'd think I would have been paralyzed with embarrassment, lying there and knowing that these medical investigators and Security hangers-on were all watching these same private, not to say outright porno-graphic, sexual experiments Gerda and I had performed. Well, I was somewhat, when I thought of it. But it tells you something about the way I was feeling, about all the different ways I was feeling at once, about my dearest transsexual love, that the most hurtful feeling I had was the agonizing, overriding miserable sense of loss.

Oh, I did wish all those strangers weren't there, all right. But if they hadn't been there, if I weren't having the most painful and private parts of me exposed, I wouldn't be having this one, final and machine-generated repeat of my Gerda time. And I could try to reassure myself that all these unwanted onlookers must have seen this same sort of thing so many times already that it meant nothing to them.

I never quite succeeded in persuading myself of that.

I did know, of course, that all this was not happening in real time. In real time all of these things had taken much of a real summer, so I would've been stuck in that machine for weeks, at least. But even in the hyped-up tempo of the machine it took a long time—not to say forever—before the kaleidoscope turned itself off and I heard someone say, "Anything use-ful?"

There was a silence, and then a new voice—no, a familiar one, the voice of Professor-Colonel Mazzini now in the room—sounding fretful. "Not what we need," he said, and then, to me, "Sorry, Bradley. I didn't want this done to you unless it was our absolute last resort, but I wasn't here."

Someone helped me to sit partway up, and I had a partial look at his blurry face. He didn't look the way he had the last time I'd seen him, though. He didn't look at all befuddled or ditsy, and what he was wearing was some kind of surgical smock.

He was looking regretful, too, and certainly sounding that way, so I tried my luck. "So can you get this thing off me?" I asked, reaching, but failing because my hands still did not want to do what my brain was ordering, no doubt because of that pestilential helmet.

"Ah, no, we can't do that," he apologized. "See, it's all right, though. It doesn't matter as much now, because if you're going to have a bad reaction to the penetration it's probably on its way. Sorry. If I'd been here in time I would have forbidden it. I wasn't. And we do need to find Brian—or whatever you want to call—"

I interrupted him. "I know. People are dying."

His voice changed. "They are indeed. Lie down now, please." He did say please, but that wasn't his tone anymore. So I did. And the next hour or two of my life was devoted to my encounters with Mr. Maurice Tesch. At one moment he was strolling with me across the Forum, then warning me against eating his horrid sausage. Explaining the Giubileo's underground hydraulics. Commiserating with me on Gerda's desertion. Sharing some of his crappy Israeli wine . . .

And then sharing some more, a lot more, of the contents of his marvelous wet bar.

These Maury-flashes weren't much like the ones of time shared with Gerda—mainly because there was no sex—but they were just as immediate, as detailed, and as real. When we got to that prolonged drinking binge, in fact the getting totally drunk binge, the last time I saw him—the last time, that is, before he'd somehow got himself murdered and dumped me right in the septic tank.

All the surrounding sounds and stinks of that long drunken night were there. I was sweating, because it was really warm in the room—I believe that for some reason the professor had turned the AC off—and I was getting that garlicky smell on Maury's breath . . . or maybe on his fingers, maybe from having handled his repulsive sausages. And most of all I felt the sensations that the professor's magic memory machine were reviving for me. First being mildly buzzed from the first glass or two of Maury's liquor. Then a lot more than mildly, not to say really, bombed, and then—

Then everything went truly weird at once.

Long ago, when I was a kid and way too young and too dumb to fight back, some louse of a teenager got tired of setting stray cats and dogs on fire so he and his posse decided to get some fun by slipping some innocent little kid a hit of old-fashioned acid. The lucky little kid was me. And now what came next was a kind of a scary montage of those impossibly unreal scenes of my childhood acid trip. . . .

And then suddenly, without warning, it hurt.

It hurt like hell. I got a glimpse of Maury, who now was straddling my legs to keep me from moving. My pants were off, and I didn't know when that had happened. He had a sharp knife in one hand, and something that glittered in the other, and what was hurting was that he was sawing away at my butt. The me that this was happening to was struggling, but weakly, and moaning a bit, too, but was way too submerged in alcohol to do anything effective about it. But the me who was experiencing this reprise wasn't too drunk to respond, and that me was yelling.

Then, all of a sudden, I wasn't the only one who was yelling. I heard someone call, "There's nothing there!" I opened my eyes.

The professor was there in his surgical scrubs, and now bossier than ever. "Stay the hell put, Brad," he ordered. "It won't take more than a minute. Won't hurt, either—for this we can let you have an analgesic, anyway. So come on, Brigitta. He's all yours."

Those are not the cheeriest words a person might ever hear, especially when he's paralyzed and just getting over that helmet experience, and pretty woozy, besides. It wasn't that bad, though. The person apparently named Brigitta stuck my leg with something that immediately numbed it, and somebody else was kind enough to pull the helmet, its needles now obligingly retracted, off my head and, hey! I could see! And what I saw was someone else in scrubs, some female person I had not previously seen, bending over my numb thigh with something sharp in her hand.

That was damn good anesthesia. I didn't feel a thing. I just saw the woman with the scalpel triumphantly lift high something bloody but crystally metallic under the blood it was drenched in. And the professor was looking pleased with himself. He was nodding to everyone else in the room, looking as though he was accepting shouted congratulations from a boisterous crowd of well-wishers. Which I guess he sort of was.

"Wh—" I began, and again, "Wh—" Meaning, that is, to ask what was to be, but the tongue wouldn't move the way I wanted it to and the words wouldn't come out. And then all of them were gabbling together— all but me and a pale young man who was busy stitching up the gash in my thigh and mopping up my blood. They all seemed pretty happy.

Well, so was I. Or would have been, now that they had stopped quarrying private images from my mind, if only I had been able to make my mouth form intelligible words. Finally the professor took a break from congratulating himself and glanced in my direction again. "Ah, Bradley," he said, sounding more maternal than military, "you're trying to say something, aren't you? And your musculature is still paralyzed and isn't letting you do it? Don't worry. Deep penetration does sometimes have that effect, among others. A good night's sleep clears them up most of the time." He patted my arm. "But you can nod your head, can't you? So are you all right?"

The thing is, "all right" was much too upbeat an expression to describe the way I was. I did try to nod. The professor sighed, and gave me another pat, and swung into action. Which was trying to make everybody in sight do the best he could to make things at least a little bit all righter than they had been. They lifted me onto a gurney, where six or eight of the reinforcements went over every centimeter of my head with new-skin spray to stop the oozing of blood from the thousands and thousands of little holes they had poked into my scalp.

So things seemed to be improving, apart from that central vacancy in my life where the woman I loved used to be. They took me back to that room that looked so much like a jail cell. Shao-pin and Nola did. And they tucked me into that reasonably comfortable bed. Then I asked them to leave me alone and they did.

And I had what I had been longing for! The opportunity to find out what kind of a person Gerda had been before she was Gerda! And what did I do about it? The day had worn me out. I turned over, closed my eyes, and drifted off to sleep.

I didn't think that all the problems were solved. I was sure plenty of really urgent problems were left. I just didn't think that the worst of them were mine anymore.

24

GETTING TO KNOW THE MAN WHO
WAS THE WOMAN I LOVE

When I woke up it was still dark. I didn't care—not about that and not about the fact that my body still resented what I had put it through the day before. I got on the phone and ordered a pot of coffee, not really sure I was allowed to do that, and turned on the wall screen. By the time I was being given choices to make, the coffee was there, and Nola was carrying it, looking as fresh as a teenager on her way to a picnic with the new boy on the block. I supposed she and Shao-pin were taking turns to sleep. I also supposed that they were watching me 24-7, and didn't care. When she asked if I wanted some real breakfast I said, "Sure. Whatever you think I'd like, and then if you don't mind there's some stuff I'd like to do."

"Fine," she said. "I'll bring you something to eat and then we won't bother you unless the colonel needs to talk to you." And was gone, closing the door behind her.

By then I had discovered that there was a vast collection of files about Brian Bossert, but I got lucky. One of them was a formerly best-selling book called *He Held the World to Ransom* and although whoever curated that particular library had posted a prim little note to say that some of the statements in the file had been questioned by other investigators it sounded just right to me. It started with Bossert's beginnings, a cop's son in Ponca City, Oklahoma, the cop being one known for his exceptional generosity to his only son. It sounded like an idyllic childhood except that when Bossert was eight years old his father was killed in a bank robbery gone bad. It had an unusual payoff: When they stripped the masks off the dead robber's face it turned out that the robber had been Timothy R. Bossert, supplementing his pay from the Ponca City police force with the occasional bank stickup.

With the head of the house deceased, the little Bossert family were on hard times. Brian's mother had to go to work, Brian himself had to sell his virt games and his electric bike. He began, the author of the book said, hanging out with kids older than himself and with criminal records. Brian himself helped them in their getaways by opening a hydrant on the year's coldest day, which turned a stretch of highway into a skating rink—and, once, jamming a raw potato on the exhaust of a police car lurking by the side of the road for the miscreants' car to drive past.

Interesting, I thought, but not very.

By then the breakfast that Nola had brought me was getting cold, so I dealt with the oatmeal and the crisp bacon and the sliced kiwis, leaving the wall screen going. As I chewed on some crunchy, if cold, buttered toast I was thinking about what I had just watched. This person who had just taken the lives of a number of innocent human beings, I reminded myself, was in some sense the same person I loved with all my heart. I got up and stared out the window, trying to make sense of those two irreconcilable facts. That person did not resemble the Gerda Fleming I knew.

On the other hand, neither did the person who had loosed the Pompeii Flu on the world.

25

THE LIMITATIONS OF DEEP PENETRATION

When Shao-pin came in with my four o'clock tea and cookies—what she called biscuits, because she'd done ninety days in the London office before coming to Italy—I was more or less back to normal. That is, I was trying to figure out how Bossert had got the motorman on that West Side train to Brooklyn to sit still while he arranged the timer and the shaped charge and everything else just the way he wanted them. Shao-pin picked up one of my scribbled cards from where I'd put it on top of a book by a screen speaker who'd written about being one of the first to reach the drowned train when they finally began pumping the subway tunnels dry. She held the card up to show me. It was too far away for me to read, but I knew what it said: *Wh m = man not keep B fm settgup?* "I can tell you that," she said. "Bossert shot him. Shot everybody in the car and barred the doors to the next car. They found the slugs in the motorman's head at the autopsy."

"Huh," I said. "You read the book."

She gave me a faintly worried look. "I didn't think you'd mind," she said, and, although I hadn't known she'd been doing that, of course I didn't. Shao-pin or Nola or the professor—or anybody else—was welcome to snoop through anything in my room when I wasn't there because there was only one thing I was hiding and that never left my person. I said, "What?"

The worry went out of her look. "I said, do you have any other questions?"

"No, I don't think so," I told her, taking a nibble off the edge of one of the cookies—ginger, all right. "So just leave the tea things and— Oh, wait a minute. There was one thing I meant to ask you. Did the people in the farmhouse turn out to be bootleggers? Gerda said there was a lot of that going on along the strada because of all the decaying flax in the farms. Covered up the smell of the brewers' mash."

She was paying more attention to the folding of my napkin than to what I was saying. "How would I know that?"

"Weren't you going over the follow-up on those tests on my brain?"

She said, "The deep penetration, right. I hope you don't mind? I was just checking to see if the teams had found anything useful."

"And had they?" I asked, hoping to get to my soup before it got cold.

"No, Brad. Especially not about that farmhouse. Did you forget you didn't go there?"

She was almost annoying. I decided to set her straight. "I didn't, no, but Gerda did."

"Well," she said, "that explains it, doesn't it? They didn't have enough interview teams to send out to every place that came up in your DP so on the first run they're only talking to people in places you visited together. Is it important?"

I shrugged. "The only thing is there was this other time we went to Caserta and she disappeared for a couple hours. I wondered if she went to the same place. It's probably nothing."

"Probably," she agreed, "but I'd better report it." And that she did, and played her report to me while I was working on the soup, and I had nothing to add.

That lasted all the way through the afternoon and dinner, during which I decided the New York subway system was really lucky that it had Park Slope on one side of the river and Murray Hill on the other, because if the tunnels hadn't had to climb those hills where they did it looked to me as though they could've flooded a lot more of the system than they had. I watched most of a soccer game while I was eating dinner and got myself into the shower afterward. Then I stretched out in my bed, not particularly sleepy, looking for some sort of wall program that wasn't about the Pompeii Flu or sports.

I didn't get it. I didn't get any entertainment app at all. What I got on my wall was an override picture of Piranha Woman, not looking particularly glad to see me. "What are you doing in bed, Sheridan?" she demanded. "Get dressed! Colonel Mazzini's having you picked up in ten minutes. For what? What do you mean, for what? We think we know where your girlfriend's hiding out and the colonel thinks you're going to want to see her captured. Up! Are you listening to me? Get the hell up!"

That was the end of her message. Her preempted image froze on the wall and then broke up, quickly replaced by a remote from Ulan Bator, where the mayor had just announced that because of the number of people either turning up sick or taking care of those who had, the city's working departments would be operating only between ten in the morning and two thirty in the afternoon until further notice.

26

ONE LAST KISS

I had just gotten myself into a pair of pants when there was a rap on my door. I opened it and there was the professor, Piranha Woman hot on his heels and wearing a scowl even deeper than usual. The professor wasn't scowling. He in fact was looking quite pleased about something, and when he spoke he sounded that way, too. "Get dressed, Bradley," he ordered.

Well, I was doing that already, but I paused in slipping into my shirt to tell him so.

He just said, "Do it faster. We've got a job to do."

He didn't look evil, the professor never did that, but I was taking no chances. I stopped with my head just ready to slip into the shirt collar. "What job?" I demanded.

He opened his mouth to give me an answer but Piranha Woman got there first. She spoke to him, not even looking at me, "I say once more, Colonel, you are making a serious mistake."

That was when the old man stopped looking jolly. "I say once more, Major, shut up," he said. She cringed a little, bit her lip a little, but did as she was ordered as, back to good-natured, the colonel turned again to me.

"Why, Brad," he said, "what we're going to do, we're going to pay a call on that farmhouse outside of Caserta. I think Gerda may be holed up there."

I took a chance. "Because of what I told Shao-pin?"

"Yes, partly," he said. "We knew she had a place somewhere around here and the other possibilities got eliminated quickly. Your lead may eliminate, too, but at the moment it's the only one we've got." He sat down on the edge of my cot, watching me pull on a pair of socks. "Bradley, I'm not wrong about this, am I?" he asked. "You do want to be there when we take her, even if—even if she resists."

"You're not wrong," I said, pulling on my sandals. "Even if anything."

He said, "Yes. In fact I think she's more likely to be peaceful if you're there." He rose. "Though we can't be sure of how she will react," he added. "Now we're out of time. The column will be waiting."

He was right about that, too. I could hear the engines as soon as we left the room, more than a dozen vehicles, and as soon as we got into the command car that was waiting at the curbside, doors open, our driver slipped us into what looked like a space right after what seemed to be the fourth or fifth vehicle in line. I noticed that all the vehicles ahead of ours had machine-gun emplacements on the roofs.

As our driver slipped us into place the whole column began to move, bright lights began blinking on every car, and we accelerated into the stream of traffic, Piranha Woman in the front seat next to the driver, me sharing the rear with Colonel Mazzini, who was already looking out the window with one eye and keeping data flow from his opticle for the other, and we were barreling down the autostrada at something over a hundred kilometers an hour. From the backseat I couldn't tell how much over, but I could hear the faint *eepeepeepeep* that informed the driver he was in violation of the posted speed limits.

We weren't alone, of course. It was well past rush hour but the autostrada carried the usual autostrada's 24-7 worth of traffic, buses and tandem trucks and farm pickups and about a million private cars, all unwillingly shoehorning themselves over to the slow lane when the strobes and ultrasounds of our lead high-speeds warned them that a chunk of

Security was on the move. I couldn't see exactly how many Security vehicles were in the posse that the professor had summoned out of nothing. More than a dozen, counting the personnel carriers behind us that I couldn't see most of the time, and the ambulance and the two fire trucks that were only visible when the road was making one of its gentle curves. With all the pulsing strobes and the shuddering of the ultrasounds and the *heehaw* of the clear-the-way signals it looked and sounded like many more.

And there I was in the middle of it, racing like a bat out of hell to join Security in the hunt—the ultimately fatal hunt, no doubt how it would turn out, for my dearest, dearest love.

Once we were well on the way Colonel Mazzini pushed his opticle to one side and turned to look at me. "We've got a few minutes," he told me. "No doubt you have questions."

I surely did. I didn't have to ask any of them, though. The professor knew what they were, and economized on time by answering them all without waiting for me. It was that silly trip to Caserta, the one when Gerda got lost, that did it. Only she hadn't been lost at all. After I got out of the three-wheeler? Gerda had waited just long enough for me to be out of sight. Then she drove off on an errand of her own.

So the professor said. And how did he know this? Simple. It was satellite surveillance that gave him his answer.

There was very little that happened on the surface of the Earth, or at least the inhabited part of it, that one spy satellite or another was not watching.

So it was no trouble for the computers to locate Gerda's car in the palace parking lot, just where, and when, I'd got out of it. When it pulled back out of the lot they did briefly lose it in the overpasses and underpasses that went to the autostrada. That wasn't much of a problem, though. By then the same search programs that had picked me out of the Cairo subway mob knew what the three-wheeler looked like from overhead. They widened the search a little, and there she was, tootling up the farm road to the place where she had scored the grappa.

Where we were heading, me and Piranha Woman and the professor and all those heavily armed Security grunts.

Before anything began to look too familiar the professor ordered all the bells and whistles off. "We don't want to tell them we're coming," he told me. I hadn't asked for an explanation. I didn't ask for one when I observed that all the other autostrada traffic had been stopped on the shoulders, so that nothing moved on the highway but our Security cavalcade, nor even when I felt our car slow from its 120 kph or so to maybe 70. I didn't need to be told that the reason we were slowing was that we were getting close, and the reason for halting the other traffic was that the professor suspected there was going to be shooting, and didn't want any of it to kill civilians. Then, tardily, I recognized the dingy old warehouse on a hill, and the dirt road to the farmhouse where Gerda had scored her half-liter of grappa.

We were there.

Our car slowed and pulled as far as possible to the right, fifty or sixty meters short of the farm road, so the personnel carriers could slide past. A three-wheeler with a machine gun mounted on the right was already chugging up the hill. It stopped halfway there. The machine gunner sighted in on every visible door and window—most of them shuttered— while the driver scanned the house with field glasses.

What their next step would have been I never found out. They didn't get to take it. On one of the windows the shutters flew back.

I had no doubt of what it was that flew out of it, incandescent red and fiery yellow, drawing through the air a shallow arc that ended in the face of the machine guuner. He didn't stand bemused, waiting to be turned into bloody, crispy shrapnel. He responded as he was trained to, fingers seeking the machine gun's trigger, the barrel swinging toward the opened window. He was fast, yes, but not as fast as the rocket from the handheld launcher inside.

The missile did not only pulverize the upper body of the machine gunner, it caught the driver and flung his racked and burning body onto the nearest row of rotting vegetation. But by then the next Security vehicle had opened fire on that window, and then two more behind it; violent explosions flared inside, and then a dozen square meters of outer wall peeled away and toppled to the ground. The missile shooter had to be inside, along with his weapon, but all I could see was flame. What I didn't know was whether the shooter had sensibly got out of there right after firing that one shot, or stayed around in the hope of another. If he had he was no longer alive.

Or she was.

By then every vehicle in the Security line was bouncing up that road. From the front seat Piranha Woman turned to the professor, her face a mixture of eagerness and joy. The professor was shaking his head. "No," he said. "Let the grunts do their work. They'll fetch whoever's in there out for us."

Well, that was sensible enough for someone commanding an assault force. It didn't appeal to me, but then Gerda was involved and about her I had never been sensible. "Can't we at least get a little closer?" I asked. Or begged, or maybe even whined.

I don't know what the professor thought of me at that point. He glanced at me without any recognizable expression at all. Then he raised his voice. "Move us up to the turnoff," he ordered the driver.

As we began to move the file of Security vehicles was just beginning to bounce off the road to get around what was left of the destroyed three-wheeler. The room the missile had come out of was blazing merrily. There was no sign of life from anywhere else in the farmhouse. . . .

And then, as we entered the farm road, there was.

It didn't come from any of the doors or windows we could see. There was at least one door on the far side of the farmhouse, though, because something came roaring out of it, heading across the planted fields.

What it was (we found out later) was a four-wheel-drive farm jitney, meant for cruising plowed fields. It did its job. It bounced across the rows of rotting flax, headed for the Caserta-bound highway. Piranha Woman had the glasses on it. "I think it's her!" she screeched. "I can't see the face, but it's a woman! Don't let her get away!"

If anyone was going to catch her it had to be us; all the rest of our posse was tangled along the side of the road, bypassing the ruin of the three-wheeler. "Do it!" shouted the professor, but even before he spoke the driver was backing us bumpily onto the empty autostrada. Our car was at least twice as fast as the escaping Gerda's could ever be, but backing onto the highway slowed us down. As we began accelerating down the highway Gerda's crop-jumper was a hundred meters away and already climbing the autostrada's embankment. And Piranha Woman had opened her window, with a rapid-fire gun poking out and ready.

She wasn't firing, yet. She was looking back over her shoulder at the professor, waiting for his order. But if Gerda showed any sign of getting away from us I had no doubt that that order would come.

There was not going to be a happy ending for my love. Dead or captured: there were no other apparent possible outcomes.

What that estimate didn't figure on, of course, was Gerda's—or maybe I should say Brian Bossert's—track record. He (that is, she) had been in plenty of tight places before, and survived, by doing what was not expected.

She didn't try to run away from us along the empty autostrada lanes heading toward Caserta. She cut right across the paved lanes and kept going, bumping across the parkway strip and right into the lanes that led to Naples.

The professor had stopped the eastbound traffic. Westbound it was sailing right along, 100-plus kph, maybe a little slower than usual as the Naples-bound drivers tried to figure out why the Caserta lanes had become suddenly empty, but still chugging along.

I saw what Gerda was up to. If she could just get through that cross traffic there was a chance—maybe not a good chance, but a lot better than no chance at all—that we couldn't follow.

Oh, it wasn't a wonderful plan. What it was was just the only one open to her and, hey, it might have worked.

It didn't, though.

.   .   .

It was an intercity hydrobus that hit Gerda's farm jitney, but of course the smashing and crashing didn't stop there. I don't know the final total of fender benders that were lined up on the shoulder, the drivers yelling accusations at the other drivers and at the carabinieri. The carabinieri didn't yell back, just went on with the job of getting all the warm bodies at least a dozen meters away from the hydrobus, all that is but my busted-up beloved, stuck irretrievably behind the little engine, which had taken up residence in her lap.

It hadn't been an equal match. The intercity bus outmassed Gerda's little cart at least a dozen to one. It was efficiently crumpled, and the released hydrogen in the bus's fuel chamber could not be prevented from flaring up. Fortunately the system was designed as a release-as-needed fuel provider. If it had all gone up at once there wouldn't have been any survivors at all. As it was even Gerda survived for a little while. Long enough to talk to me. As soon as the flare died down I pushed the carbinieri away and ran to her. I took her in my arms, calling her name. She said, "Brad? Is that you?" I don't think she could see, but she was pressing something into my hand and whispering, "Take it. Hide it! Don't let them get it." Then the others were getting there, trying to make me release her.

At first I wouldn't let them, because she was still talking. "Brad," she said, "was I wrong?" But then she did stop, and I let them take her, because I had felt her die.

27

MY CAREER AS AN EVIDENCE THIEF

"Hide it," Gerda had said. So I did exactly as I had been commanded by the dying wish of the woman I loved with all my heart. That is, I hid it. I wrapped my fist around it, which was not hard to do because it wasn't much bigger than an American quarter, and I didn't unwrap it until I was slipping it into my hip pocket.

You see, I had a very high opinion of Security's spy cameras. The chance was slim that they had such things bearing on this patch of super-highway between Naples and Caserta, but slim is not the same as none, and Gerda had wanted it hidden.

It stayed hidden all the way back to the Security complex in Naples, where they drove me into a built-in garage. I was well inside the build-ing before I stepped out into one of those bare Security rooms, where they got me to make a statement for their records before they let me say good-bye to Gerda.

Well, actually they were fairly nice about that part. They had cleaned her corpse up a little and covered most of her with a white cloth. She lay on a gurney with her eyes and mouth closed, and they left me alone in the room with her for a bit.

I didn't protract it. She was gone. I just kissed her cold lips, and whispered into her unhearing ear, never mind what, and I went out and closed the door behind me, and never again saw that body that I had once so thoroughly enjoyed.

The professor came by while I was eating something Nola had brought for me. He asked if I needed anything. I said no. He asked if I had any questions. I said no to that, too, although that wasn't true. I had great big and seriously worrisome questions about that object in my right hip pocket.

But he was not a person I could ask.

He studied me in silence for a moment. I didn't say anything, either, but I was beginning to feel exhausted. I didn't dare fall asleep, though. What if someone found a bed to put me in, and undressed me and, very naturally, checked my pockets? I suppose my weariness showed, because the professor stirred. "We'll get you out of here pretty quick," he said, standing up. "But there's one thing I want to say to you." He put his hand on the doorknob, looking a little—well, bewildered, I thought, as though unsure of what message he wanted to give me. And then he said, "Thanks," and looked as though he had something more to say, but didn't say it. Then he opened the door and was gone.

Getting me home took some doing. First they gave me a prisoner's jacket to pull on over my own clothes. They put me in a police van, along with six or seven petty criminals shackled to their own seats. There were cars full of reporters circling around all the entrances to Security's building. All the people in them looked us over with microscopic care and some took pictures. But the Security people had pasted a quite plausible-looking mustache under my nose and put bifocal glasses on top of it and none of the watchers looked any harder at me than at any other of the felons. And when we got to the transient jail there were half a dozen ways out, with Nola sitting waiting in a three-wheeler in one of them. Off came the mustache, on went a jail guard's cap, and I drove us carefully home, avoiding temptations to speed or to rush a traffic light. When we got to the barracks for Indentureds like me I turned the three-wheeler over to Nola to park and for the first time in—had it really been not much more than one full day?—let myself in to my own dingy little room, with its own narrow and lumpy cot that I no longer had anyone to share with me. I pulled the covers into something like order and checked the wall screens to make sure they still worked. They did, of course, but I had no interest in hearing some hastily assembled experts tell their audience who Gerda and the Welsh Bastard had really been, so I turned it off again.

At least they didn't mention me.

Nola tapped on the door about then, to tell me the three-wheeler was being driven away and if I wanted anything, anything at all—food, drink, whatever—I had but to name it and she would deliver it. "Thanks," I told her, "but not right now. I'm going to try to get a little sleep." When she was gone I kicked off my shoes, turned off all the lights except for one bright one near the head of the cot and, fully dressed, slid into bed. I looked up at the remaining bright light that I couldn't quite reach and scowled in irritation. The irritation was theater, if anyone was bothering to perceive me just then, directed at myself for failing to turn the light off.

Then I petulantly pulled a quilt over my eyes. After a while I let my breathing get light and regular, changing position two or three times as though responding to the lumpiness of the cot. And then very slowly, timing each move to go with my breathing, I gradually slid out of my hip pocket the thing that Gerda, with almost her last breath, had asked me to hide.

All that was also theater, meant to make whoever was manning the spy cameras (if any) on my room lose interest in the sleeping me.

For a wonder—no, for what I was thinking of as practically a once-in-a-lifetime miracle—my planning was working out just as I wanted. I was quite sure that my room was bugged for Security, but I considered it very unlikely that they had stuck a camera in among my bedclothes. And when I held the blanket just so then plenty of light from that "forgotten" fixture leaked into where my clenched fist was holding the object Gerda had entrusted to me.

It was what I had thought it would be, a data coil. It was smaller than the ones I was used to. It wasn't the usual colorless plastic, either. It was ruby red, and it had printing on it that wasn't in English. The letters looked Russian to me, in the quick glance I gave it before carefully repeating the process in reverse to tuck it away again. That made me think Stans. And then I began to think about that very large question that lay before me.

First, what was the thing?

It could after all just be another data coil, but of some foreign manufacture. That was a quite likely answer to the specific question, but, like most easy answers, it just raised harder questions. All of them centered around the question of what kind of data did the data coil hold?

That was a biggie.

Suppose, just suppose, what Gerda had been carrying around with her had been nothing less than the secret way of curing Pompeii Flu. That was quite possible, was it not? And what medium would she carry it on, if not a coil? And she had recently been in the Stans where there was still a strong Russian influence left over from Cold War days, so a Cyrillic alphabet was quite possible.

And there was a suspicion that was taking up more and more room in my more and more worried brain. If it was right, then I was carrying a heavier load of responsibility on my quite self-centered shoulders than I had ever supposed possible.

I didn't know how to answer those questions. But then, fortunately, I was spared the pain of that particular attack of indecision, because pretending to be asleep carried its own consequences, and next thing I knew—or didn't know—I actually was.

28

ANOTHER UNDESERVED REPRIEVE

Sometimes fate is a lot kinder to me than I deserve.

What woke me up was riotous noise in the hallways. People were tramping up and down, talking loudly, once or twice actually singing. When I got out of bed and began turning lights on it was only moments before Shao-pin was tapping at my door. She was wearing a party hat and carrying a party glass of what I thought was champagne, which she carefully set down before throwing her arms around me. "Oh, Brad!" she cried, pausing only to kiss me again. "She had it! They found it! The cure!"

And it was true. When Security did their professionally methodical search of my beloved's French-fried and julienned body they found that special coil, the coil of a recording with all the specs for the cure that saved the human race, or at least way the most part of it. They found the coil in a little pouch around her neck that looked like leather but wasn't. It had kept the fire out and the coil was unharmed. Maury hadn't been wrong about it. He had just lost out to my very dear Gerda.

So the world was now safe?

Well, that was going a step too far. A lot of things had to happen before the dying stopped. Knowing what the solution to a problem is isn't quite the same as having actually solved it. When there's a deadly disease threatening your dearest you may have all the complete printed directions for making a serum in your hand, but you can't inject printed directions into a dying four-year-old. You have to manufacture the stuff the directions are all about before it can do her any good, and by the time you finish doing that the four-year-old is probably dead.

We were luckier. With the data on the coil it took only three weeks and two days (I counted) for laboratories all over the world, all the millions of them, to start churning out the magic little pale yellow capsules that stopped the disease in its tracks. No one not already infected would get it. And even some of those already rotting away did not get worse . . . Well, they didn't get better either. The tissues that were gone stayed gone.

I was not surprised that some of them preferred not to keep on living in their present fragmentary state.

But I am getting ahead of myself. For those twenty-three days people were still getting infected and things were happening. Most of my personally interesting news came from Nola and Shao-pin. When I was ordered to the labs for another round of testing it was Nola who shepherded me from examining room to examining room, each one a little different, with their doctors or sometimes nurses who poked me and listened to my heart, my breathing, and the faint rumblings from my belly. And it was Lieutenant Nola who told the testers, most of whom were at least captains and majors, how much trouble they would be in if they overtired me and what the colonel would say when she reported to him.

People were being nice to me, too. Especially female people like Nola and Shao-pin.

Probably that was orders from the colonel, I thought, although I don't believe his orders included hinting to me that sex wasn't out of the question. The way Nola put it was that she would undress me and give me a nice hot bath before tucking me in. That didn't sound bad, but I didn't want her going through my pockets before I found a good hiding place for the stolen coil. Elfreda Barcowicz didn't hint about what she offered. She invited me to check out her lavish new suite—with, she said, "a really comfy double bed." And then when I told her I couldn't because I was still in love with Gerda Fleming, she got all misty-eyed and a day or two later she called me into her new office—the place that used to be the Welsh Bastard's dispatch room—and gave me back my job as a purveyor of fine, or not so fine, wines. The Bastard wouldn't be using that room anymore. He had been the one in the window with the rocket launcher, and Elfreda inherited his job—and the pay and the deluxe housing that went with it. I supposed that Security wanted somebody they could trust supervising personnel, and who better than one of their own snakes?

When the professor did finally show up at my winebar in full uniform, the onlookers were the first things he noticed. "Who are all these people?" he demanded. When I told him that I didn't know but just wished they would go away, he scowled. "Somebody has outed you, Bradley. I don't know where the leak came from. Not from anyone in Security, of course, but there were all those witnesses on the autostrada." He shook his head, then looked around at the gapers and settled on Cedric, gazing unhappily out of the door of his establishment. "You!" the professor called. "We need your premises for a bit. You can relieve Bradley at his shop."

That was a man wearing the uniform of a Security colonel who spoke. Cedric jumped to obey. (Of course he also instantly realized what being left in charge of the wineshop implied.) He put the "Chiuso" sign on the bordello door for us and scampered back across the street.

Inside the building, the professor gave our surroundings a dismissive glance. I didn't think they were that easy to dismiss. Over every door was a mural displaying what specialties were on offer inside, and inside the tiny rooms virt teams were doing them. I couldn't take my eyes off them—not because I liked looking at dirty pictures so much as that sometimes they made me think of something Gerda and I had done, and never would do again.

The professor poked at things in the control panel by the door until all the virts fizzled and disappeared at once, then looked around for a place for us to sit. Since the brothel had had little use for chairs, the professor settled for patting one end of a stone slab—in the old days no doubt the workstation for one of the whores—and sat himself on the other.

"Bradley," he said, "I'm worried about you."

I thought I was for once ahead of him. "Because your tests showed you what was wrong with me?" I guessed.

He was shaking his head. "No, Bradley," he said. "They didn't. We don't have a lot of experience with people who have gone through a deep penetration, and we're even scantier on people who were given a Stans love shot. We do have some theoretical projections on what should be happening with you now." He turned to look at me more closely. "Worst case," he said, "you should have killed yourself by now. You haven't. You haven't even tried."

"You don't know that," I told him.

"Oh, hell, Bradley, of course we do. Do you think I haven't had you watched? I could tell you what the projections show, but it gets pretty technical," he said.

"Go ahead," I said, and it did. It wasn't just full of high-tech psychobabble; it was simply all wrong. The important thing was not at all descriptive of the heartfelt, the almost holy love that I felt for my permanently beloved, if absent, sweetheart.

Well, I listened to all of it, or at least pretended to. I don't think I fooled the professor. When he had finished he looked at me in silence for a moment, curled around on that unforgiving stone slab, and then he sighed.

I thought it was my turn to speak, so I said, "I understand what you're telling me. So what do I do now? More tests?"

He made a face. "Of course you're going to do more tests, but for our sake, not yours. All your test results'll be in the literature for a hundred years. For you, all you have to do is go on living your life, avoiding stress as much as you can."

I had been observing the lines of worry and weariness on his face. "You ought to do that yourself," I told him. "You look like hell."

That almost made him laugh, or at least produce a kind of raspy chuckle. "I'm a little tired," he admitted. "Shao-pin's been after me to take naps and that's probably a good idea. Have you got any questions?"

At that point I swallowed hard. It was the first good chance I had had to unload a second question that was keeping me awake at night. "Actually I do," I said. "It's about Gerda. Why do you think she did it?"

The professor had been standing up to go, but now he sat back down again, looking at me with something like resentment. "I said questions," he remarked. "I didn't say hard ones. How do I answer that? When she was Brian Bossert she killed innocent bystanders and that didn't seem to bother her. You could even say she was sanctimonious about it."

"Not millions and millions," I said.

He sighed. "Point taken. That does make a difference, doesn't it?" He was silent for a moment. Then he said, "I wasn't going to tell you, at least not just yet, but one of the things we found in the farmhouse was stuff Gerda was working on. What she was doing seems to have been giving a lot of thought to that exact question. We found a lot of—I guess you'd call it research—on the subject. Of course," he added, "it's all classified. Security would classify the used paper in the toilets if they could figure a way to get it out of the bowl."

I could feel my mouth opening to ask him a question—it was going to start with the word "please"—but he was shaking his head. "I was thinking when I was going over it that you'd really like to see this stuff. I don't know, maybe you even have a right to it. Anyway if I can find a way to get some of it to you I will." Then he was standing up again. "Enough for now. Let's get out of this fake whorehouse."

At the door he paused, regarding me. "But you know, Bradley, we need to do something about these gapers outside. They're more stress on you, and it's going to get worse."

I didn't like the sound of that. "Does it have to? Couldn't I just, like, change my name and move away?"

Then he really did laugh. "Bradley," he said, "you have no idea how much trouble people are going to go to to get a look at you." He stared at me for a moment and then sort of half-laughed again. "Yes," he said, "I think it would work for you if you're willing. Did you ever hear of Lola Montez?"

I probed my available memory. Some European floozy who had been in some sort of scandal? "Not really," I told him. "Why?"

He opened the door a crack and peered out. The gapers had, if anything, multiplied. "Let me think some more, Bradley. I'll get back to you. Right now I'm going to have Barcowicz send someone to take over your duties here and take you to some more private place for a while."

The more private place was the not-a-real-jail-cell that I had occupied before. It was handy for the new job Elfreda had found for me, and both it and the job site were well out of the public eye.

That new job was back at the live-action gladiatorial arena where I once had performed, briefly and poorly. Now my job was supervising some of the actual non-virt living combatants, which mostly meant seeing that they weren't too drunk or stoned to perform. It didn't take much of my time. Neither did the tests the professor kept ordering, so I had plenty of hours in each day for my principal occupation, not to say career, which was namely mourning for my lost love, Gerda Fleming. Because you must not think that, just because I haven't mentioned it in every sentence, I wasn't always, always doing that. I was. Painfully. Obsessively. Endlessly.

I was getting overinformed in some ways—the wall screens were full of stories about the cure for the Flu—and information-starved in others, because neither Shao-pin nor Elfreda could, or would, tell me what the professor meant by his mention of this Lola Montez. For a day or two after I started my new job I worked the wall screens to find out what he was talking about, but all they seemed to want to say about his mystery woman was that she had been the bedmate for some old arch-duke.

I gave it up. He could explain when he liked, but meanwhile I had another mystery going on. A pair of carpenters showed up one day and began sawing and hammering together a great big chair, followed by a couple of painters and upholsterers. When they had finished, what their creation looked most like was the kind of throne big stores used to put up every year for Santa Claus to sit on so kids could climb up onto his lap and whisper their yearnings into the microphone in his ear that delivered every word of what they wanted for Christmas to the shopping counselors in the next room.

When the professor did at last call on me, I had a new sorrow to add to all the sadnesses I already had. The professor was sick. And I knew what the blood tests had to have shown.

He wasn't visually shedding pieces of anatomy—not yet. Nothing showed. But the reason for that was artifice, and it was denied by the pain in his expression and the fatigue in his eyes. When he said, "Good morning, Bradley. Please don't tell me how well I look," his voice gave it away. He rasped, and sometimes he squeaked. The Flu was eating away at his vocal cords.

I did what he told me. "I'm glad to see you, Colonel," I said.

He didn't respond to that. "You'll want to know about your tests. Nothing has changed. You've given us a lot of data about what the effects of that damn deep penetration are on the chemistry of that stuff Bossert gave you, for which all my successors will be indebted to you, but it doesn't help your case. But there are some things we need to talk about while I can still talk at all. One"—he raised a forefinger—"you're not going to want to spend the rest of your life in hiding. I don't suppose you want to let the plastic surgeons remodel you. So what I'm thinking is we can turn the problem into a solution. Do you remember I mentioned Lola Montez?"

"I do. The Irish girl—she wasn't even Spanish—that shacked up with the archduke of Bavaria."

"Good for you, Bradley. I respect a man who does his homework. But Montez's story didn't end there. Toward the end of her life for a while she's supposed to have been penniless and alone, so she joined a circus."

I began to feel that I was frowning—not in anger—not yet. But in puzzlement. I couldn't see what he was driving at.

Then he explained. "What Montez's circus act was was simply answering questions from the audience about what it was like to be the archduke's mistress. All kinds of questions. What the archduke was like. Whether she really loved him. Did she regret the kind of life she had led? She let them ask whatever they wanted, but you wouldn't have to—"

That's when I began to see what he was driving at. "I—?"

"Yes, Bradley, you. Did you ever wonder what they were building in the arena? That's where you will sit, and it will all be in good taste."

That's when I exploded. "Good taste?"

He smiled—I guess it was a smile. "I thought you'd take it that way, Bradley. But what else do you have? While I'm here, I can protect you a little, but I'm afraid that situation won't last much longer. And then your case is likely to be turned over to Major Piranha."

He didn't dwell on what that implied. He didn't have to. "For a while," he went on, "I thought I might have a different solution. There was a reward for whoever found a cure for the Flu. I thought you had a good claim for it and money can buy you privacy. But Brussels said no, so you'll have to earn the money yourself."

He paused, squinting as though in pain. "Well, Bradley? What do you say?"

I said it was ridiculous and offensive, and I kept on talking in similar vein after that, but not for very long. I really had no choice, did I? The convincer was that he had mentioned that I could be turned over to Piranha Woman. "All right," I said finally.

He said, sounding rueful, "I wish I had had a better solution." Then he grimaced. "A couple of other things. Shao-pin is willing to take early retirement to be your manager. The lawyers are drawing up a contract for you to sign. She'll protect you. She gets ten percent of whatever you earn, if that's all right with you."

It didn't sound like enough to me. I said so.

The professor said, "Oh, I think it will be. Now one last thing. These are for you."

He took a couple of coils out of his briefcase and set them in front of me. They all had printing on them, most of which I couldn't read at that distance. But there was one word, large, bold type, the same on each coil, that I had no trouble at all reading. It said "SECRET."

I looked at them but didn't touch. The professor said impatiently, "Put them in your pocket. Don't let anybody see them, not even Shao-pin. When you've seen all you want give them back to me."

I did as ordered, but I couldn't help saying, "Shao-pin would never rat you out."

He looked annoyed. "What are you talking about? The point is we're dealing with felonies here, Bradley. There's no reason to expose her. Or Nola. Now, I've given you two coils. One is the research sort of thing Fleming was working on; you'll have to make what you can out of it. Anything I said about it would just be a guess. The other's different. The agency is trying to put together a record of what Fleming was doing, those years in the Stans. It's nowhere near complete, and I can't tell you how they got some of it, and that's one of the reasons why that 'secret' classification has to be taken seriously. But I thought you should see what they've got."

He had taken my breath away. "See Gerda? Living those years? What she was doing? Where she lived? Who—?"

He cut me off. "Yes, that sort of thing, though only to a sort of first approximation right now."

I couldn't help it. It was totally unexpected, like the finest Christmas present anyone had ever found under a tree. I jumped up and grabbed his hand. "Thank you! Thanks more than I can say—"

He pulled his hand away, looking almost apologetic, shaking his head. "Don't say that, Bradley. After you've screened it, you may not be grateful. You may hate my guts."

29

GERDA IN THE STANS

It turned out that he was right about that. For a while there I did hate his guts—I'll come to why later on. But that wasn't the first thing. If he gave me a ton of pain when he gave me that coil, which he did, it was also true that first the coil also gave me a ton of joy.

I couldn't display the coils on the wall screen because I couldn't know who might take a notion to turn on the spy cameras, so I had to play them into my opticle. When I slid the first coil into the reader and the image of my dearest beloved swam into shape before me, the joy came first. I would not have believed so much of that was possible. There she was, seated on a gold hassock very like the pink one from her sitting room that, I remembered, we had put to good use more than once in those happier days. And, looking just as I remembered her, she began to speak.

"The next place I want to show," she was saying, "was called Rapa Nui by the islanders who lived there. What the captain of an English ship called it when he, by accident, came across it on Easter Sunday was Easter Island." But Gerda had disappeared from my opticle, and I was now looking at a not very interesting island, with Gerda's voice as her only presence. I tried to get her back, but for the next few minutes of the coil the pictures seemed to be of just the island and all there was of Gerda was the voice. I jumped the coil ahead at random and got Gerda's voice again, though now accompanying a picture of a little park with some kind of a monument in it, surrounded by tacky-looking high-rise apartments. "—outside of Kiev," her voice was saying. "It was called Babi Yar and—"

I ejected the coil, having figured out what I was doing wrong. I was looking at the wrong recording.

When I put the other coil in I could tell right away that it was definitely the one I expected, but that doesn't mean it was anything I wanted to see. What it showed was a man lying on an operating table, naked except for a few mostly see-through bandages, his head shaved bald, one eye bandaged shut, much of his skin covered with a sort of coffee-colored cream. Oh, and his right arm was apparently immobile, and his front teeth were missing.

I knew him right away. Apart from those alterations it was Brian Bossert. So whatever that bit of coil was about it was probably something I would want to know about . . . but, I told myself, not just then. At that moment in time what I wanted to see, what I hungered for, was more of my beloved.

And, happily, there really was more, much, much more, though quite a lot of it gave me no pleasure at all.

The ones that did, though, gave me plenty. These were pictures of the love of my life, and as I looked at them I was pretty close to blubbering. All my hopeless love and unbearable sorrow was coming to the surface at once. If the professor had been present just then I would have put my arms around him and told him that, far from hating his guts, I would have kissed him if he let me. But that was before I had watched the coil all the way through.

What I was seeing at the beginning of the coil was puzzling, because I didn't know what was going on, but it wasn't upsetting. There was a voice, no doubt doing some explaining, but as it wasn't in English it didn't help. But at the top of each frame were characters in the Cyrillic alphabet. It took long sessions of puzzling over the disk for me to realize that that was a name—something, when transliterated, like Vassarian Ilyitch Nevirovski, followed by a number of initials.

Once I had that much many secrets were unlocked. Then I could look the name up in the reference books in the public library. When I did things became more clear, because V. I. Nevirovski was the name of a famous surgeon, known to be practicing in the Stans. And it seemed that Dr. Nevirovski was careful to record every stage of Gerda's make-over because unmistakably that was what I was looking at.

I don't intend to tell all about every stage of what was on the coil. There was too much of it, and it went on too long.

Oh, when I sat there that day the first time seeing all those pictures I did study every one of them in detail, don't mistake me about that. But the refabrication of my true love into the shapes and textures I loved so much took a long, long time. There's no reason anyone needs to hear about the whole thing. It's often boring. A lot of the time Gerda herself was spared because she was in a chemically induced coma to spare her the pain and indignity—and the tedium—of what Dr. Nevirovski and his helpers were doing to her. I wasn't. Old Vassarian Ilyitch was wedded to his photojournalism. His operating-room cameras recorded every slice and stitch that he and his gang perpetrated on her. So I got to see pretty much everything that happened to those fifty-odd kilos of raw meat that were the person I so hopelessly—yes, even then—adored. Watched every moment of it, I did, all two years' worth of moments, no matter how much the subject came to look like the Sunday roast for some very large family dinner. Or, no, it didn't look that good, but more like the leftovers of a large freshman anatomy class that poverty had compelled to share a single cadaver.

As the stages began to approach the final it got even worse than that. You see, it moved.

Vassarian Ilyitch was too good a doctor to let what was left of Brian's, now Gerda's, musculature deteriorate still more through the effects of lying still in bed for so many weeks and months on end. To prevent that, his nurses and assistants festooned her body with clips and needles connected to timed power sources. These ticklers made the unused muscles twitch and contract to forestall the decay of inanition as she lay there.

It looked— Well, it looked obscene, or worse.

There was a word from childhood that came to mind as I played the coil of all this. The word was "yucky." And yes, I went right on loving that heaving, twitching mass of yuck.

But, thank something, those very yuckiest times did come to an end. And then there came the time when Dr. Nevirovski at last began to show some actual improvements coming from his work.

Gerda began looking a bit better, then a little later quite a lot better, as new physical structures settled in place and old ones began to heal. The studded muscle-ticklers vanished as Gerda began to be able to exercise herself. Vestiges of makeup appeared on her face.

I won't say she suddenly turned into the rather pretty woman I had first seen, but she had certainly become not really repulsive, especially when the lighting was controlled. Dr. N adjudged her ambulatory, and she again had the freedom of his mansion.

She used it, too, especially the gardens, the gym (cautiously), and the library.

I was interested in the library part of Gerda's expeditions because my love had never really struck me as a bookish person. (That's not a criticism; I wasn't one myself.) What I knew of the subjects that interested her came through Dr. Nevirovski's always available cameras, constantly snapping single shots of Gerda, I guess to study how her limbs moved as she performed various tasks. Since the doctor had no particular interest in her intellectual development his pictures did not include much of the subject matter she was viewing, so I often had to stop-motion and enlarge to learn what she was reading about. I wasn't surprised that the first things she read were accounts of her successful but costly Toronto exploit; and then, one after another, the accounts of all her other "actions," as she liked to call them. Well, even an aging Broadway star likes to browse through her old reviews.

But she didn't stay among her old press notices. She spent long afternoons in the surgeon's collections of historical works, with what seemed particular attention to the ecological crimes of the human race. The extermination of creatures like the Indian elephant and the passenger pigeons whose flocks once filled the skies of America from horizon to horizon. And the near duplication of that feat on the buffalo herds of the plains, shot by the tens of thousands and their tongues cut out for the luxury trade and the rest of them left to rot. And nearly all the anthropoids, and dozens and even hundreds of other species. And slaughters of that other always endangered species, the human race. And, of course, histories of slavery in America, of the subjugation of women in the Afghan state, of the peonage of the poor everywhere. I might have imagined that she was lining up targets for future actions, in case she ever got back in the terrorism business again, because it was evil treatment of whole classes of human beings that seemed to interest her the most here. But these crimes were almost all ancient ones. It was a little late to reprise John Brown at Harper's Ferry, or the Mau Mau in Kenya.

Gerda didn't get a lot of Nevirovski's attention just then. There was no longer a lot of delicate surgery involved, mostly just healing. What little sharp-edged work needed to be done was trivial stuff like digging out any surviving hair follicles in Gerda's chest, limbs, and face so she wouldn't become a sideshow bearded lady, and minor chores like reshaping a left earlobe that didn't quite match the right. That sort of trivial stuff was turned over to Nevirovski's principal assistant, a young black surgeon known to Gerda as Rollo, though when I checked the medical directories in the library I found that his last name was something else and he seemed to be related to some kind of African king. Nevirovski's own skills were reserved for those who really needed them. And, of course, for those who could pay the considerable price. When Gerda used the household TV links to look in on the hospital wing she saw two sad fourteen-year-old girls being readied for harlotry service as a favor for the pimp who was Nevirovski's oldest customer, a handful of rich but no longer young patients who wished to conceal that fact and—oh, look at that!—the naked frame of an old and very sick but very rich man, diagnosed by other authorities as possessed of an incurable and very soon terminal cancer, who had come to Nevirovski for a miracle and looked like he was getting it.

But that sort of patient never got the run of the mansion. Gerda did.

I've told this as though it was like some summer afternoon's idle viewing. Well, it wasn't really like that at all. To get this far filled up long days of opticle-using, and it was as little as that only because I skipped through as much as I could.

But when I got to the point where Gerda began to appear relatively decent I stopped for a time. There was more, much more, on the coil and from that point on, I was sure, Gerda would be looking more and more rewardingly like Gerda. But it would have to wait. By the time I was that far my opticle eye was sore and blurry and my head was pounding.

On the good side it had kept me from worrying about unanswerable questions, and even almost stopped the brooding about dead beloveds. Of course I hadn't forgotten that my beloved was dead, and that I was responsible for it. But with these startling new pictures to look at it only occasionally lanced through my heart and wasn't still a permanent agonizingly bitter pain.

And I certainly hadn't given a thought to the other coil the professor had given me, or to the new career as a Twenty-first Century Lola Montez that he wanted me to start.

30

PRESENTING MY GERDA

The lawyers showed up with their papers and I signed them. Now Shao-pin was my attorney in fact, which meant that she was authorized to receive and disburse and invest funds and otherwise transact necessary business, including the negotiation and payment of all appropriate taxes, of all my receipts whether in the form of cash, of shares of stock, or of commercial paper in any form. I shook my head as I signed them and passed them back to her. "I hope you know what all that means, because I don't," I told her.

She smiled. "All Greek to me," she said, "but that's what we've got accountants for."

I blinked at her. "We do?"

This time she laughed out loud. "The colonel said a lot of this was going to worry you. 'Tell him it's your department and you'll take care of it,' he said to me. I will, too, and yes, I've hired accountants and lawyers. Next week I'll be interviewing investment advisors," she finished, and kissed the top of my head and was gone.

I took a quick shower, slipped into the slacks with the deep pockets—patting them to make sure my increasing quantity of contraband was still safely stowed, and was almost out the door when I remembered that

I had another coil in that pocket that I hadn't really looked at, the one the professor had given me. I popped the coil into the earpiece, and suddenly I seemed to be slowly flying over a ruined city as a voice said, "—was the city scheduled for dropping the second bomb. But weather conditions there ruled out the primary target." The name of the city, or former city, seemed to be Nagasaki. I recognized it as something that I was pretty sure was Japanese, one of the first cities to get creamed by a nuclear weapon—a relatively feeble one, of course, because that had been back in the mid-Twentieth Century, though as I looked at the ruination below I couldn't think of it as weak.

I tried again and got another ruined cityscape, but one that had no features I recognized, and the soundtrack was in a language I didn't know. The third try was a forest. It seemed to be springtime, the leaves on the trees fairly small, and one or two trees—of the hundreds visible—were bearing blossoms. The trees looked healthy enough, but the ground was dug up in shallow pits as far as the eye could see, and the commentary, accompanied by mournful music, was in a language I couldn't understand. But as I puzzled over it there was one word, said with great, sad emphasis, that sounded like "cat in," and when I fed it to my opticle's search program they came up with a Polish forest where a lot of Polish army officers had been murdered and buried in unmarked graves. It apparently had happened around the same middle of that bloody Twentieth Century, but I didn't stay with the search long enough to find out exactly when, or why.

In fact it seemed that nearly everything on this coil had to do with substantial numbers of people getting killed. There had been, I remembered, a certain amount of that sort of thing in Gerda's notes earlier, but not anywhere nearly as many examples or reported in as much detail as here.

But I was tiring of scenes of mass death. I was entitled to something pleasant, not to say delightful, and what could be more so than just a few minutes of looking at the love of my life? Especially when the surgeons had finished with their work of making her even more attractive.

When I found the right time frame it was exactly what I had hoped for.

When old Vassarian and his teams of anesthesiologists and surgery nurses and organ donors got through revising Gerda she looked pretty good. She wasn't really beautiful, no, but she was definitely nice enough looking to interest any normal man. And she was something else. She was young.

Vassarian hadn't preserved her appropriate status of maturity. That is, he didn't make her thirty-something-ish, as the former Brian Bossert had rightfully been, he made her a barely legal eighteen-year-old, almost jailbait—that is, he made her the vintage of human female that nearly every human male would like to find dropped in his bed some lucky Christmas Eve. Especially, I believe, if that male human himself is pushing seventy but pumped full of goatish androgens. Like Vassarian Nevirovski. So, she said in a note on the coil, when all the scars had healed, and she was beginning to get good at acting the part of her new role, Vassarian showed up one evening at the door of her tiny room after dinner with a spray of roses and a bottle of wine and asked, politely enough, if she would care to give her new plumbing a test hop.

She did it.

Why not? She was curious, too. Maybe she thought it would be interesting to find out what it had been like for the various women that the unaltered Brian Bossert had tried out over the years as opportunities occurred. So she sniffed the roses, and took a good hit of the wine, and then let him do her.

It wasn't bad for her, she said, even that very first time. On the other hand, it wasn't particularly great, either, because Vassarian, the dedicated and compulsive artist that he was, had gone to the trouble of capping off her private parts with a working hymen, along with all her other bits and pieces of femaleness. She wasn't grateful for that final touch of artistry. When he gave himself the pleasure of busting it open that night, it hurt.

Later on, it didn't hurt anymore, though, and—why should I lie when Gerda didn't?—it got to be fun for her, too. For a man of at least seventy (who could know how often he'd rejuvenated himself?) old Nevirovski was pretty spry.

That was the beginning of a new life for Gerda.

What kind of a life was that? Well, I don't know what Gerda called it, but I had heard my own mother use a descriptive term—about someone else, of course—when I was no more than ten years old. It had required the questioning of all the kids I knew and the piecing together of all their scraps of information to find its meaning. Gerda Fleming, once the nightmarish terror of evildoers everywhere, had become a Kept Woman.

How did I feel about this development?

Oh, I hated it. But, to tell the truth, I didn't hate it all that much. What I was seeing had happened a long, long time ago. Gerda wasn't two-timing me. Gerda didn't know I existed, and if she had magically seen some kind of picture of me at that time, what would she have seen?

A little kid, that's what she would have seen, because that's what I was in the year when Brian Bossert finished being turned into a woman. Actually, I have to say that what Gerda was putting herself through at that time was really kind of touching. It was not just the lopping off of unwanted anatomy bits and their replacement with other varieties that made her so utterly female. Quite a lot of learning was involved. After watching some people at a party having a good time the cameras caught her complaining to Rollo Mbwirda, the surgeon's main assistant, "Oh, my God, I think I'm going to have to learn to dance backward, like a girl!" In fact, her long hours spent on the tricky business of learning to be girlish were kind of sweet. I think I played those parts of her coil more often than any others, especially when missing her got particularly painful. Things the cameras caught her doing, or telling someone like Rollo what she had been doing, tongue clasped between her teeth, working at the tricky business of putting on a little lip gloss to make her mouth look sexier and shaving her armpits to make the rest of her body look nakeder and, oh, all kinds of things. Like pretending she was having a menstrual period now and then. Not to mention doing weird personal things that no man would ever do, like using a tissue to dab herself dry after peeing.

Indeed, she was getting good enough at being a woman that Nevirovski began letting her join his other guests now and then for those dinner parties. And what she hadn't expected—and neither had I—was that she was beginning to enjoy it.

In the real world—not in the planet of bliss that I had had with Gerda, nor yet in the world of love and pain evoked by Gerda's coil—people were still dying of the Flu. Nevertheless the death rate was dropping every day. So the world had begun to celebrate. Some hundreds of its people, at noon, three, and six PM each day, chose to do it by attending the freak show in the arena, which consisted of me.

I hadn't thought I was going to like being the Lola Montez of the late Twenty-first Century. I got that right. I didn't.

That first session had been a nightmare. It was a good thing I had taken the professor's advice and signed Shao-pin on as my manager, because she had written the contract for my services. It wasn't just the money, though the amount of it was astonishing. I had the right to refuse to answer any questions that were too explicitly intimate. Which a large proportion of them were. It astonished me that so many people wanted me to describe Gerda's sexual organs, breasts, nipples, and pubic hair.

Of course I could have done that. I knew all those answers. Those were the sorts of memories I played back in my mind every night as I was waiting for the pills that Shao-pin gave me to put me to sleep. But I deeply, truly hated being asked such things in front of a crowd. I often refused to answer. Then I found a better way to handle it. Asked about some feature of Gerda's anatomy, I would pick out a woman in the first row to point to and say, "Probably a lot like hers."

All this might sound as though things were in some ways going well for me. In an objective sense, maybe they were. Certainly, the money was— what was that word I used—astonishing.

Paragraph one of the contract Shao-pin had written and made the Giubileo sign obligated them to pay my Indenture off and provide me with a €100,000 advance before I spoke a single public word. That was a pretty nice thing for my parents, back in the refugee housing in Staten Island. I gave the money to them. I didn't check the rate of exchange, but it had to give them at least a million or two of those feeble American dollars—perhaps enough to make up for the time when their screeching, giggling neighbor had banged on their door and summoned them to the newscast on their shared screen so they could see what their rotten son had been doing over in Pompeii.

So I gave the crowds what they had paid for, and then every day I retired to my lonely room—make that rooms, as many as I wanted, and furnished in whatever I wanted—to play the coils again and wish again that I was dead.

Brian was still in his teens by the time he began going after bigger game.

His first grown-up action was in, or against, New York City, to punish the city for its sins, whatever they were. Sixteen-year-old Brian stole a liquefied natural gas tanker truck in New Jersey, drove it halfway across the George Washington Bridge, and abandoned it there for a motorcycle the panicked rider had deserted—having first opened all the valves that released the gas. Then, safely on the New York side, he found a McDonald's with a good view of the bridge. There he enjoyed an Egg McMuffin and a couple of cups of coffee while he waited for the fairly large number of police who had flocked to the scene to try to figure out a good solution.

They never did.

When the blast did at last blow, it took with it the lives of six firemen, four civilians who had deserted their stuck cars for a better view, and two policemen. It made all the newscasts, too.

After that Gerda kept on running through her long list of other crimes, nearly all of them before my time, or even before I was born. Some of them I had heard of, like the bomb that blew up the New York subway tunnel under the middle of the East River. Others were news to me.

And then, of course, there was the big one. The one that, at least temporarily ended his (her!) terrorist career.

Toronto.

Toronto had happened well before my concern about general world events, but by the time I reached the age of fascination with horrible news I began hearing about it. Gerda showed us the web stories about it.

The Toronto thing happened when four men and one woman, led by the notorious terrorist Brian Bossert, overpowered the crew and drove the domestic heating oil tanker *Jewel of Ipanema* at its maximum speed of twenty-six knots directly onto the Toronto shoreline. Both the inner and outer hulls were breached by the impact. More than fifteen thousand tons of light oil spilled out onto the buildings of the shore and into the lake itself. It was quickly set afire by the collision. All of the terrorists were trapped in the fire (the news stories said) and their bodies were never found. Since Lake Ontario was Toronto's only source for its domestic water system, the city was immediately paralyzed. Its inhabitants were evacuated, and the city was deserted for more than fifty days until the bulk of the spill was siphoned away and the rest largely dissipated though natural processes. Torontonians bought more than 160,000 copies of a T-shirt that said, "Why Us? It Should Have Been Detroit."

What the books said was,

> They deprived Toronto of its only source of water for weeks. There really isn't much worse you can do to a city than take its water away. It's not just that then the people don't have a drink when they want it. They can't take a bath, they can't flush their toilets, they can't make a cup of tea or boil a pot of potatoes—in short they can't live. And if it's bad for the citizens, it's even worse for the businesses, from car washes to breweries and every other kind of business in between that employs human beings. It is one of the most effective things a hardworking terrorist can do. It doesn't just mess one city up, it screws up the finances of a whole nation.

Of course, all that would've been impossible if they hadn't had Mary Elaine Whitecrow on their team—someone who was both beautiful enough and smart enough, as well as willing enough, to do a good enough job of seducing a tanker captain to get him to lower his guard a bit. Enough so anyway, for her to sneak their roughnecks onto the ship to take it over. For that purpose, Mary Elaine was just about perfect.

What I hadn't known was that Mary Elaine Whitecrow was also Brian Bossert's wife. Somehow the news media had obtained a photograph of her, and that was the part that spoiled my day, because I had seen that photograph before. I had even asked Gerda about it, and she had said it was some aunt or cousin, or something.

I don't know which was worse, finding that my dear, almost, sort of, wife had once had a really truly dear wife of her own. Or discovering that even when Gerda was mine she kept that once-upon-a-time wife's picture by her bed.

After the Treaty of Spitzbergen defanged the Stan menace I didn't think much about those duck-and-cover days at Mme. Printemp's school for the kids of the wealthy, or that the Stans were where Aunt Carrie's somadone had come from, but that was history.

The Stans had more formal names than that. If you looked in an atlas, they'd be called Kazakhstan and Uzbekistan and Kyrgyzstan and Tajikistan and Turkmenistan, but nobody bothered with those names. What those places actually amounted to was nothing but the useless little chunks of real estate that were littering up the maps after that preposterously gigantic old Union of Soviet Socialist Republics did the right thing and took its own life. That was way back, what was it, oh, somewhere toward the last decades of that messy Twentieth Century. Up until that time those Stans had been pretty much a collection of little model Soviet states. It wasn't that the Stans people really wanted that. It was just that they didn't have a choice. Crotchety old Joe Stalin was running that part of the world just then and he had a system for refocusing the minds of any Stanian who didn't share his views. To such people he gave a quick one-way trip to the gulag and a new career in mining gold with their bare hands in the frigid Arctic. The Soviet-Stanian people whom those former dissidents left behind had learned a great moral lesson from this. They learned to do what Uncle Joe wanted, and keep their mouths shut about it.

Of course, once the Soviet Union had gone away the people in charge of the Stans still weren't the natives. There were some Germans and some Chinese and a lot of ethnic Russians who weren't getting along with their own governments, but were rich enough or somehow powerful enough to become a ruling class in the Stans. What they wanted most of all was to be left alone. So the Stans were where outsiders weren't welcome, and where they had retained all those great installations of nuclear and biochemical and everything-else-ical kind of technology that the Soviets had set up in that part of their empire in their (not very successful) attempt to transform those pre-Industrial Revolution Buddhists into technologically brilliant and fanatically atheist imitation Russians.

The other thing about that part of the world in present times was that it also had no extradition treaties. It was where Gerda-Brian's banks were located. And, what was most important for the fugitive and hurting Brian (because he had picked up some pretty deep burns in the blast), a surgeon, Vassarian Ilyitch Nemirovski, lived there, and he could turn him into something no cop would ever recognize as the desperately wanted terrorist Brian Bossert, namely into a woman.

Although I didn't know it at the time, from this name alone you could figure out two interesting things about him. From his middle name, which was the version of his father's that is called a patronymic, that he was an old-fashioned aristocrat, or wanted to be taken for one, and from the last name that that would never happen in Russia because he was a Jew. In the Stans, though, he did just fine. He was one hell of a surgeon. For that reason he had been able to rapidly become rich.

Nemirovski had got his start manufacturing sideshow freaks for some of the African countries that were beginning to get rich but not civilized. Young boys with ears the size of lily pads and penises like a stallion's, for instance. Nemirovski was known to be able to transform almost any variety of human being into almost any other variety you could think of. All it took was a large allocation of time, and an even larger one of money. Brian, who had taken the precaution of hijacking a Brinks-Renmin truck in Vancouver for getaway money a few weeks before Toronto, possessed enough of both. Though he had arrived in a state of ruination he could be repaired and transformed.

But it took time.

After an unpleasant few days in the beginning—devoted by the surgical staff to trying to stabilize the various damaged parts of their patient in order to keep him alive long enough to begin the transformation—the remains of Brian Bossert had a couple weeks of waiting while tests were made and new cloned parts were begun to be grown to make replacements for glands and nerve clusters and organs that the new Gerda Fleming would need.

But, thank something, I didn't have to keep on loving it at its very yuckiest. Gerda had no choice but to live through those unbearable months of tortured repair, though blessedly unconscious through some of the worst of them. I did not. I only had to view the bits and pieces Gerda herself had elected to preserve on her coil.

His patients didn't keep the surgeon terribly busy. He didn't let them, because he insisted on leaving time for his very active social life.

Which, as a special treat, he sometimes let Gerda share in, at least as a spectator on his TV net, on the occasions when he was entertaining at home. Mostly dinner parties, that was—local political people, visitors from Outside, almost all rich men, but with a decorative frieze of quite good-looking women. A couple of the men showed up so often on the clips Gerda incorporated in that diary-like coil I came to recognize them as regulars, particularly a tall, well-built but elderly Chinese named Bu Deng, who seemed to be to biochemistry what Nevirovski was to cutting and patching the flesh of human beings.

Gerda spent a lot of time in the doctor's pools and gym, keeping all those new and old muscles working, now that the little shock-stimulators were gone, and most of all in the library.

That was where Gerda had begun to put in longer and longer hours of her time. The professor had warned me that she seemed to have an insatiable appetite for records of the endless list of all the ways man had been violently brutal to other men.

My sweetheart was showing a previously unsuspected thirst for knowledge, perhaps because she had had so little time for education in her previous life. Being, you see, so very busy killing people and blowing things up.

So, you ask, how was it for me?

Oh, quite normal. I hated every minute.

Actually parts of what my love was going through were touching, and sometimes puzzling. One of Nevirovski's guests looked improbably familiar, and for several weeks I tried to understand how and where I might have encountered this figure from ten thousand kilometers away and nearly thirty years in the past. And then, in another appearance, it turned out that he had studied hydrology, and it all fell into place. Oh, sure! He was my old (dead) buddy, Maury Tesch! Or an earlier edition of him, when he still had a full head of hair. What this young Maury was doing in the Stans was hiding out from international charges of piracy on the high seas. He and the rest of a famous and feared eco-pirate crew had been torpedoing fishing vessels to protect the last of the world's schools of bluefin tuna, but their luck had run out. A satellite had located their submarine when it surfaced, and relayed the information to a Chilean pocket battleship cruising nearby. Ten minutes later the pirate submarine had been blown out of the water, killing every one of the crew except for Maury himself. And he didn't know what to do with himself, now that he no longer had a head pirate to tell him.

What he did have was a lot of money, because what he had been sent to do while the rest of the pirate crew was lobbing over-the-horizon torpedoes at a Chinese factory ship and the Chilean warship had caught them at it was shopping for a new submarine to replace their old Polish one. The new one wasn't really exactly new. It was serving with the Moroccan navy, but the Moroccan admirals were embarrassed to have a fission-atomic vessel in their fleet when all the other navies in the area were fusion-powered so it was about to be released from the Moroccan navy. They were close to a deal, and he was carrying euro letters of credit for the full purchase price in case the last technicalities got straightened out.

He still had the money. There was no one else alive to claim it.

31

THE SURGEON'S TROPHY HO

The thing about Gerda's new life was that I thought it should have been a constant humiliation to her. It wasn't. She seemed to be enjoying it.

There to help her with the enjoying was Nevirovski's junior surgeon, the one who called himself Rollo. Because the surgeon began letting her appear in public she needed a more elaborate wardrobe. Nevirovski cheerfully paid the bills, Rollo escorted Gerda to the appropriate shops.

She wasn't yet Gerda. The name she was going by, which she didn't much care for, had been given to her by Nevirovski himself, "Lolita Karenina." It seemed to be some complicated Russian kind of a joke, and between shops they had been amusing themselves trying to think of alternative names, as well as to invent a backstory to offer casual acquaintances—perhaps a childhood in Catasaqua, Pennsylvania, college at Pennsylvania State University, and now present in the Stans because she had fled the outside world with an embezzler who had then run out on her.

She was enjoying the make-believe, and enjoying the company of Rollo as well, not to mention the pleasures of spending large amounts of money on clothes and entertainments. Gerda hadn't had much of that kind of fun in her life. She was also drinking more, enjoying her various entertainments more, even liking her bed sports with Nevirovski more. And spending time thinking about the future not at all more, but quite a lot less. And the long sessions in Vassarian's library seemed to be slowing down.

It even sounded as though some of the other men she was spending time with were beginning to look sexually interesting to her.

That was getting into dangerous waters. The surgeon kept close tabs on her. Funnily, Nevirovski seemed not to worry about his second in command, Rollo, or about the big Chinese biochemist.

So one day when she was out with Rollo to buy some sport clothes, because Nevirovski had decreed that she needed more exercise, she asked him about it. He laughed and fingered the little amulet he wore around his neck. "You've noticed my jewelry? It's got a little radio inside it. The boss can hear what's going on around me any time he pushes a switch."

"All right, then what about this Bu Deng? Nevirovski lets me go out with him, even to his own house to see the orchards. Is he just somebody the boss trusts? Or maybe too old?"

He was laughing again. "It's true that Bu and the boss were in business together way back—back before the Stans were really independent from the rest of the world—but 'trust' is not a word his highness associates with women. As far as Bu is concerned, he is definitely not too old. But he's got a lover already. He's faithful to him, too, even when he's off somewhere on a trip. The lover's a man, hon. Bu's gay."

That was all he wanted to say on that subject, which sent her back to Nevirovski's own library.

Finding out what she wanted to know took time and labor. Nevertheless, she had not lost the skills that had let her learn exactly how many miners' explosive caps it would take to blow a hole through the roof of a New York subway tunnel or how one would pilot an oil tanker into the perfect spot on the Toronto shore. And she found the answers she sought.

The business venture the two multimillionaires had shared in—there was no other way to put it—was the enslavement of the native Stannian peoples. Oh, not all of them. Just the ones their occupiers had picked out to do particular jobs for their welfare and comfort. The beauty of the plan was that the mechanism of their enslavement didn't involve guns and chains. All it took was the same thing that had enslaved my own aunt Carrie, and, like her, they enjoyed it. Whatever tasks and duties they were assigned they did gladly, because part of the payday was in somadone.

That was Bu's share of the plan, but there was another part. What Bu supplied was the carrot, but there was also a stick.

That was provided by Vassarian Ilyitch Nevirovski. Before he had decided that brain surgery was too much trouble for its mangy cash returns he had tracked down some research on a couple of the human sensory centers. One was for the sense of taste, the other, nearby, for the sense of smell.

They turned out to be quite easy to reach with electric probes.

Nevirovski reached them. With his little needles he had a way to deprive any rebellious local of the use of some of his senses. For a first offense the sentence was the loss of smell, for the second, of taste. If you can't smell anything you're anosmic. If you can't taste you're ageusic. If you still offended the people who had taken control of the Stans you lost both. That was the worst of all. You couldn't tell whether you were eating a kosher hot dog with mustard or a dog turd with a streak of pus on top.

There was no need for Stalin's brutal firing squads or gulag archipelagos in the Stans. Between them, Bu and the surgeon had solved the Stannian labor problem permanently.

And what was happening in my own actual life was quite the opposite of Gerda's, and, really, rather nice. The money was rolling in.

It turned out that two shows a day in the arena weren't enough, so the Jubilee people begged—really all but got down on their knees and begged Shao-pin—for the right to do a third, which she allowed but made them pay lavishly for. Then, when they asked for a fourth, she turned them down, but for some additional money, actually quite a lot of it, allowed them to send in the virt cameras. Thereafter the virts of me, answering some of the most hated questions they asked that day, filled one of Naples's grandest halls ten times a day. Then they filled Rome's halls. Then Paris's and Beijing's and then Everywhere's.

I had never seen so much money.

Of course, I had no use for such vast sums. Mom and Pop did, though. So I took a little time off, set up a trust fund for them, large enough so that they would never again have to share a bathroom or live in a resettlement for the rest of their lives. I thought for a bit of having them move closer to me than Staten Island, New York. Shao-pin had chosen and staffed a very comfortable town house for me in the fashionable part of Naples called the Vomero. I could easily have picked up another one just like it for the two of them.

I didn't, though. I didn't really want them that close.

Oh, and listen. I did make another real estate investment. I bought the building Gerda's quarters had been in from the Giubileo corporation. Since the corporation didn't really want to sell I had to seriously overpay for it, but what did that matter to me? I made it easier for the corporation, anyway, by contracting with them to keep right on running the buildings as they always had. All I really wanted, you see, was to change the locks on Gerda's suite in order to keep everybody else out, so that now and then I could sleep a night there, alone in our old bed.

Well, it did have a practical use. There was a cubbyhole in the wall, just over a tall dish closet, that Gerda had used to hide some of her more private possessions. I used it for the same purpose. Things of mine like the very few notes in Gerda's scratchy handwriting that I had saved. And like—well, all right—like some of her underwear that Security hadn't already confiscated.

Gerda's old rooms were a convenient place to keep things I wanted out of circulation, but I would be lying if I said they were the biggest reason I wanted to own them. No, that reason was simply that they once had been Gerda's.

Sound obsessive to you? Sure it does. You've never been really in love, have you?

Oh, and by the way.

Outside of that kind of thing I haven't mentioned Gerda much lately. That doesn't mean I was forgetting her—that will never happen. And right about then I was being reminded of her more frequently. And more forcibly, too.

32

A VOICE FROM THE PAST

The thing is, I had discovered that the more I tried to do things that Gerda would have wanted to do herself or wanted me to do if she couldn't, the less agonizing was that terrible sense of loss that disturbed so much of my sleep. My latest effort had been to keep an eye out for peoples jailed for terrorism, and maybe if at some point they were released—if they ever were—give them a little helping hand. So I kept an eye on ex-terrorist ex-cons as they served their sentences and were paroled. Worked pretty well for a while, too. I still dreamed of Gerda almost every night, but they were frequently happy dreams, even very sexual dreams, sometimes in fact being the best part of my day. But that kind of thing gets pretty old pretty fast. And lately when I dreamed about Gerda, like as not, she was sad. Or even angry.

Then one day, idly checking the recent convict releases, I came across a name I thought I had heard before. On the list of felons released from the Alaska rehab center was one Arthur Daniel Mason, formerly of the Molly Pitcher Redeployment Village in Staten Island, and I did know him. He was the kid who had tried to recruit me for some junior terrorist thing a long, long time ago.

I paid a fair extra tab for the backgrounding service. When consulted it gave me some interesting data. Artie had been sentenced to the rehab center, but one day he got away. Found an Inuit fisherman who agreed to take him across the strait to Siberia. Spent the next ten years in the Stans, but then his father died back in New York. Artie took a chance on sneaking home for the funeral. That was a bad idea. Security picked him up. And he was just now released.

I thought about it for a long, long time. Then, the next time Shao-pin stopped by my house, I gave her a welcoming kiss, told her she was looking even prettier than usual, and mentioned that I was thinking of going to New York City to visit an old friend, and asked if she'd like to come along and see some shows.

She accepted right away. I don't know if she really cared about Broadway shows, especially the ones that were financed by the city to keep some sort of tourist business going, but I had been pretty sure she'd come along to make sure I didn't get into trouble.

We took a hardwing from Naples all the way across the Atlantic Ocean to New York. It cost the Earth. I didn't mind. I didn't want to be gone too long, either.

Of course, no one knew who I was. Security had introduced me to a group of theatrical makeup people, and they had turned me into a well-to-do elderly Chinese gentleman, apparently taking his pretty granddaughter to see some famous old sights. The hotel I picked was one where I had been quite seriously roughed up by a New York cop who thought I was planning to rob some of their guests (I was). But it was recently spruced up and, the travel agent promised, quite comfortable, and when we got there the two off-duty New York cops I'd hired for bodyguards were waiting for us in the lobby. I sent Shao-pin with one of the cops to inspect our suites, making sure they were both comfortable and defensible.

Then I asked the cop who stayed with me, "I wonder if you can do me a favor. I'm looking for a friend of mine who got in trouble with the law. They just let him out of that Alaska correctional center, but I don't know where he's living. His name's Artie Mason. Do you guys keep track of people like him?"

They did, as I had been pretty sure they did, but I had to listen to five minutes of advice before he admitted it. He hated to see me waste my time. Them terrorist gangs took kids and, you know, kind of brainwashed them? And you'd never get them to straighten out and be good God-fearing Americans again? And—

I finally stopped him. I told him that Artie had been the son of my late mother's best friend and I was just trying to do for him what my mother would have done if she had lived. And I mentioned that it seemed to me that it might take him an extra hour or even two to do that for me and he should make sure that was on the bill when I paid him.

He mentioned that he might be able to get it faster than that. I said that if so that would be his good luck, because I was willing to pay the extra thousand—that's $500 an hour times two hours—for the favor. Sounds high, sure, but it was in American money, and it cheered him right up. So when Shao-pin and the other cop came back he disappeared into one of the spare rooms in my suite and when he came back he handed me a slip of paper with two addresses on it, one geographical, the other electronic.

Then I wrote two notes to Artie saying I might be able to help him and inviting him to dinner the next night, got a hotel messenger for the hard copy, filed the electronic one on the net, and took Shao-pin—along of course, with the two cops—out to what was said to be New York's best restaurant for dinner.

I've had better, but it wasn't bad. The cops were ecstatic.

The meal the next night, with Artie Mason, was just as good although it was from the hotel's room service. (But Shao-pin had paid a visit to the hotel's kitchens to talk to the head chef, and money had changed hands.) Artie was certainly impressed.

The other thing he obviously was was suspicious. He was perfectly willing to tell me about life in the joint, and about the umiak voyage to a frozen beach in Siberia. Not as much about how he got through that huge and empty Russian province to its border with one of the Stans, and he wouldn't even say which Stan. And about his own life in the Stans after he got there a fair amount, but in an account significantly low on names.

I listened with pleasure as Artie worked his way through the lobster bisque, the salad, the amuse-bouche that followed, and the perfectly grilled, perfectly marbled steaks that followed that. I was enjoying his story on its merits—my God, what a virt play it could make!—but what I enjoyed even more was the way he had told it without incriminating any other person.

When Artie couldn't face the Tahitian prawns that followed the steaks he put down his fork and turned to me helplessly. I chuckled. "Full up, are you? Well, let's talk for a bit. Then we can eat some more, or the chefs will be glad to wrap the rest of the food up for you to take home. I said that I might be able to help you out with some of your money needs, didn't I? Let me show you what I was talking about." I reached into the pocket of my silk jacket and pulled out the little ruby-colored coil Gerda had entrusted to me. "This comes from the Stans. It seems to have something to do with a Belorussian bank there, and it may give access to something like a safe-deposit box they have. What I need is for someone to go there and find out what's going on. For that I'm willing to pay at least fifty thousand euros—I said euros, Artie, not dollars—plus expenses. That's for just doing the job. If you find answers to some of the natural questions there'll be bonuses. Oh, and if you agree to do it I'll start paying the fifty thousand, at the rate of one thousand a month, beginning tomorrow." He was giving me a cold, if attentive, stare. I added, "One other thing. As far as I know, none of this gets you into legal trouble. I don't think anything you will do in America violates any American law. If you want to check this out for yourself you can go to any lawyer you like and ask him and I'll pay his bill. What do you say?"

He was silent for a moment. Then he said, "Let me think for a bit. And while I'm doing that why don't we have those prawns?"

He didn't say yes right away. But he did ultimately say yes, between the baked Alaska (I thought that would amuse him, and I guess it did) and the brandies that came with the coffee. And when I dreamed that night Gerda was as loving and as sweet as she had ever been.

33

WAITING FOR ARTIE

Artie Mason had taken me up on my offer, all of it. I really hadn't had much doubt that he would—what other options did the poor slob have? And anyway when he said he'd do it I on the spot handed him the first thousand euros I'd promised to start paying, so he left the hotel that night with a smile on his face and the most money he'd seen in decades, or maybe ever, in his pocket—as well as a brand-new tendency to avoid alleys and doorways that might hold a mugger. (Though any mugger who would select somebody who looked as certifiably penniless as Artie Mason to attack clearly had no aptitude for the work.) I couldn't help asking him how long he thought it would be before he could give me at least a preliminary report. Dumb question. There was no way Artie could answer it until he was on the scene, but he was polite enough to say, "That's hard to estimate, but I'd guess at least a couple of weeks." And I had to be satisfied with that—

Well, with that and the welcome attentions of the Gerda of my dreams that night. She might be only the phantasm of a dream, but she surely knew how to show appreciation.

There was a little new problem, though, that I hadn't expected. Those dreams of Gerda were extremely nice, but they had one serious flaw.

That is, that's what they were. Dreams. They weren't real. And physically speaking I was a healthy male in my twenties, which is to say at the peak of my sexual curve, and while I was getting ready to fall asleep I couldn't help thinking that just a few dozen meters away, in the bedroom of the suite next door, was an equally healthy and sexually peaking female who had made it clear she would do pretty much anything I ever asked her to.

I wasn't planning to do anything about it in any practical sense. Still, I couldn't help reflecting that there were possibilities there that I wasn't exploiting. It wasn't even that I thought Dream Gerda would be jealous. Real Gerda certainly wouldn't have been, I was sure. Under those circumstances she would have cheered me on.

The two weeks Artie had mentioned went by, and two weeks more before I heard from him. And then it was just one of those electronic greeting cards, with room for a few words. Artie didn't need many. His message was just "Doing fine, more later." And then nothing at all for another few weeks.

Of course there was nothing I could do about it but rehearse patience. My stock of patience continued to get help from Dream Gerda, which I took to mean she appreciated that I was doing the best I could for her plans, whatever they were. . . .

Well, no. Wait a minute. That's not exactly right.

I wasn't brought up to be superstitious, and I didn't really think that Gerda was making that long, dreary trip back from the grave every night just to give me my jollies so I'd stay vigorous in her cause.

If anyone had asked me to explain it I guess I would have replied with more of that psychoanalytic babble that I hated so much when somebody tried it on me. You know, my id can open up as a whole other person. Or some other piece of my personality can disguise itself as Dream Gerda. Or whatever—that sort of thing.

That sort of analysis didn't mean that I was enjoying those dreams any less, of course.

But, also of course, there were some objective facts at work here. One of them was, as I've said, that I was a healthy male in my twenties for whom wet dreams weren't quite enough. And I noticed that I had begun looking at Shao-pin in quite a different way.

While I was waiting for Artie to get on with the job I was paying him to do—and while, I admit, I was sometimes beginning to have the unworthy suspicion that he was taking my money and laughing himself sick over my gullibility in some Stans gin mill—I tried to keep myself busy with attention to my own affairs.

One of those affairs was my own astonishing prosperity.

With all its faults, the human race had one trait that was of considerable benefit to me. They were all insatiably curious to get an in-the-flesh look at the guy who not only had banged the head Flu terrorist, but had ratted her out to her death.

That was weird. In a creepy way I felt that it was almost flattering to me. It was also immensely profitable. Remember I once worried that Shao-pin's 10 percent might not pay for her trouble? Actually it had already made her a multimillionaire. In euros. How much money it had earned for me I don't know. I didn't even have to show up for performances to earn it anymore. From the virts of the ones I had already done the techs had put together three or four docudramas—with me talking and varied shots of Gerda and everyone else involved sprinkled in. A lot of the stuff about Gerda was pretty racy. They had taken every intimate thing I ever said about her and slanted them to make them look more intimate still. I didn't mind, though. Why should I care what they think? And Gerda didn't mind, either, because she was too dead to have an opinion one way or the other.

Then there were the things I was discovering in those coils the professor had given me. For example, at some point Bu Deng's (male) true love had come back into his life. That didn't directly affect me, except that the man was large in all dimensions, almost the same size as Bu himself, and he looked vaguely familiar. I puzzled over that from time to time, replaying bits from all over those coils, until one day when Shao-pin was in the house, checking her ledgers against the ones my household accounts kept for her and I had retired to my bedroom to get out of her way. I was playing bits from the coils to give myself something to do. I had reached one episode where the stranger and Bu were the principal figures (I'll tell you about it later) when, for the first time, I caught a fragment of conversation between a man and a woman also present. I had to play that little fragment four or five times before (my excitement mounting) I was sure what they said, but then I was:

> Woman: I thought he was never going to quit until he offed old Harry.
> Man: I guess those royal guards were just too much for him. Anyway he says he's giving it up.

That was it! "Old Harry." "Royal guards." They had to be talking about the ancient and decrepit king of England, Henry IX. And that meant that Bu's lover was in fact a much younger version of the man I had known as that hater of the British royal family, Jeremy Jonathan Jones, otherwise known as the Bastard who ran all the behind-the-scenes operations at the Jubilee.

It was a revelation. The colonel had told me to keep the coil secret, but this was too good to keep to myself, and how fortunate it was that Shao-pin was only a couple of corridors away. When I asked her on the house intercom to come and join me she didn't ask why. She was there in minutes, and when she heard what I had just discovered she was even more excited than I was. "But this is wonderful!" she cried. "It puts Gerda and this Jones person together earlier than anyone knew!"

"Not to mention Maury Tesch," I pointed out.

"No, Tesch, too," she agreed. "All three of them together! Oh, Brad, I have to report this right away!"

That wasn't the kind of response I had expected, but I could see that for Shao-pin it was inevitable. I cleared my throat. "And if they want to know where I got those coils?"

For a moment she looked stricken, but then brightened. "I'll report it to the colonel and let him handle it. Excuse me for a moment—" But of course I wouldn't do that until she told me that, yes, the colonel was indeed still alive and, yes, he had had a confirmed case of the Flu, and now his life was no longer in danger but he had suffered some disfigurement.

She left me then, withdrawing to my dressing room to make her call, leaving me to think about exactly what that word "disfigurement" might mean. When she came back I was quick to offer her some wine, some coffee, just about anything she wanted, because I suddenly didn't want her to leave. She put up a little resistance, but when I offered to show her the exact point at which Gerda first began to believe that the enemy was the entire human race she gave in.

I could tell that she was wondering why I was so reluctant to let her leave.

The curious thing is that at that point so was I.

34

THE PHONE CALL

As I was running the coil to the exact spot I wanted I had to explain to Shao-pin that Gerda was allowed to attend an occasional luncheon with that dealer in potions and spells, Bu Deng. In this one they were at the luncheon table in his grapevine arbor with six or eight of the other good-looking young women that were Bu's favorite guests. Gerda was seated on Bu's right hand and was busily trying to get Bu to get specific about what militarized disease organisms he had, and would he ever show her how they worked? He wouldn't. He got a touch testy about it once or twice, too. At that point Gerda immediately backed off and began to tell him how much she appreciated being asked to join him for the meal and how beautiful everything was.

Well, that was easy conversation for her to manufacture. Beautiful was what everything was in Bu's mansion. Bu himself was a very Westernized Chinese, whose favorite apparel was knee-length plaid shorts, open-toed sandals, and the kind of huge fly-eye goggles that the Antica people chose to wear. He liked to have his luncheons, six or eight female guests at a time, within one of the dozen or so grape arbors on his estate, surrounded by the vines to dilute the heat of the sun, with Bu's expensive stingless bees doing what bees did so well on flowering plants and Bu's personal

Stannish manservant bringing them small increments of delicious foods. It was clear that Gerda wanted to get back to her questions about the militarized disease organisms Bu might have created to give the Stans a bargaining chip in dealing with the outside world. Bu was being indulgent enough to let her come titillatingly close. There was a minute or two of lighthearted chatter among the lunchers—

And then Bu's phone went off.

Half a minute later so did Gerda's, and of course, so did most of the other phones in the world because they were from some people trying to tell some other people some horrid news. Gerda's call was from the junior surgeon, Rollo. "Are you still at Bu's," he asked—had to ask, because she had turned off her vision circuits.

"Where else would I be?" she asked. "Is something the matter?"

"It surely is, heavenly bod," he said. "Get yourself to the nearest news screen! A big piece of America is blowing itself up."

It quickly became obvious that what Rollo was trying to tell Gerda about, of course, was Yellowstone, the super-volcano that changed everybody's life when it blew in 2062. My own life included.

For everybody Yellowstone was scary. It gave some really bad dreams to just about every human being on Earth in just the same way. But for Gerda it was worse. It threatened her very sense of purpose.

Now I'm going to skip over quite a long stretch of Gerda's life, five or six years at least. What it showed was that Gerda's principal occupation in those years became sex. Lacking any real purpose, she tried to give some meaning to her life with drinking and partying. And the way the drinks and the parties wound up was often in bed with someone, very likely a perfect stranger, or even several of them.

Her master, the surgeon Vassarian Nevirovski, must have known what she was doing. Nevirovski himself gave up using her for his personal sex partner, but he didn't interfere with her other affairs, just kept her around as, as Gerda said, "his trophy ho."

Ethnically speaking the people who ran the affairs of the Stans were mostly descendants of Russians from a few generations past, sent there by higher authority to run those mighty technological establishments. Or sometimes they were Russians who had moved there for reasons of health. (Careers bloomed faster in Moscow, but the more distance you could put between you and the Kremlin, the less likely you were to get caught up in some purge.) And then there were also the research guys who had immigrated to the Stans well after the breakup of the USSR, the ones who had come to the Stans for their unparalleled research opportunities.

Gerda was in a good position to have a great time as Nevirovski's companion with all these people. Unfortunately I could see that she wasn't happy. Even more unfortunately, so could Nevirovski. His cheerful trophy ho . . . wasn't. So at last a day of reckoning came and Rollo knocked on the door of her suite, looking regretful.

"It's his highness," he said when she answered. "He gave me a message for you. You're cured, so now you can leave any time."

Gerda got the message, the real one that was imperfectly hidden in the subtext. She was being evicted.

She didn't waste time in either complaining or pleading. She just said practically, "His bills wiped out my bank account. Where am I supposed to go?"

Rollo looked embarrassed. "Well," he said, "I could put you up until you got straightened out."

She knew what strings that offer came with, but she just said, "And wouldn't Vassarian object to that?"

Rollo looked even more embarrassed. "Well, no. He said it would be all right."

And so she became the trophy ho of Rollo Mbwirda. And after Rollo there was, well, everybody.

Those mean years must have been interminable for Gerda, living her threadbare and unhappy life. The unhappy part was not simply because so much of it was threadbare. It cut deeper than that. The great blast had made her question what her own life had been about. Was she the unfailing nemesis of evildoers anywhere in the country? Well, sure, sort of. But Yellowstone, you see, had created more abject misery in a few weeks than everything she had ever managed to do to punish the wicked had amounted to in her whole lifetime. And it had done even more, and worse, to millions upon millions of innocents, as well.

It broke my heart to watch those sections of the data coil. Gerda of course was still the woman I loved with all my heart. Now she was drinking, depressed, and bouncing from man to man, and I could do nothing about it.

Of course what I was seeing on the coil was ancient history, no more reversible by me than the murder of Abe Lincoln or the drowning of those who went down with the *Titanic*; yet I yearned to save her.

And, although that was quite impossible for me, someone else came along to do it for me. Astonishingly, that someone was the person I had known as Maury Tesch. I had not guessed that Maury's occasional glimpse of Gerda on some other man's arm had inspired him to want to possess her himself. But I think that must be the way to read it.

As to Gerda I know exactly what led her to grab Maury's offer so rapidly. It was certainly not sexiness on his part; she told him quite openly what an uninspiring bed partner he was. But there was also all that money left over from the aborted purchase of a nuclear submarine. She had not forgotten that Maury had once been a kind of terrorist himself and, although he told her many times that he had no wish to take another single human life, Gerda clung to the hope that he might someday change his mind and go back to the days of punishing evil with fire and blood. And meanwhile there were all the pleasurable things that life in the Stans had to offer to those who could afford them, for which Maury didn't mind spending the money. One might suppose that Gerda might also have felt gratitude for his kindness, but my darling never mentioned that.

It would not have been a bad life for Gerda, except that she was becoming increasingly aware that she couldn't think of any reason for going on living it.

In the old days (that is, when she had still been a he) she had had many motivating purposes—which is to say, many evils to avenge. Even before Brian-Gerda got into such large-scale actions as attacking whole cities he had causes like the way the cattle herds were treated in New Mexico, the coal miners in West Virginia, and with that the ruined West Virginia landscape, too. The minke whales. The fur seal pups.

Wherever the weak were being exploited, Brian showed up. He didn't always get the victims made whole, no, but he certainly made their exploiters wish they hadn't done whatever they did.

And he could not help but notice that all the villains had one conspicuous trait in common. They were all human beings.

Wherever Gerda turned in her obsessive quarrying of the history texts she found fresh atrocities to horrify her. Some were lacking precise quantification. The Fourth Century Emperor Theodosius executed seven thousand in Macedonia for rioting over the murder of one of his generals, or the Eleventh Century when England's King Ethelred the Unready ordered the murder of all the Danes living in England—a bad move, because then the Danish king invaded his lands, taking out Ethelred himself. Or, some decades later, when Moorish mobs in Granada killed their Jewish citizens—to the surprise of the Jews, because their people had lived peaceably in Muslim lands for centuries until then. Or Richard the Lion-Hearted, lion-heartedly dragging out three thousand bound and helpless Saracen prisoners and one by one putting them to the sword.

I haven't talked yet about the biggest one—which I think was probably in the early Twentieth Century—when the sultan of Turkey ordered the massacre of all the Armenian people—men, women, and kids—and actually killed about a million. And there were a lot, with names I sort of recognized—My Lai, the Israeli Olympic team in Munich—that had piddling little death tolls of hardly a hundred, or even less. Shoshone Indians plundering an emigrant wagon train in the Utah Territory, no doubt a horrible time for the victims, but only six dead; the employees and customers of a Browns Chicken during a robbery in a place called Palatine, Illinois—just seven killed there, curiously the same number as the much more famous gangland St. Valentine's Day massacre in Chicago.

But for sheer numbers nobody outdid the two Twentieth Century titans of bloodshed, Nazi Germany's Adolf Hitler and the USSR's Josef Stalin. They didn't deal in small numbers, and it was only fair that a good many of their decimations were done to each other.

All that seemed to make Gerda just more depressed. Maury spent a lot of his time trying to cheer her up. But that didn't happen.

35

COMING BACK TO PRESENT TIME

So once again I'm getting ahead—way ahead—of myself. For example, I haven't told about what news Artie Mason had for me from the Stans when I saw him again.

The reason for that is that I'm not going to tell that ever—or, at least, not all of it. I'm willing to say that the poor slob had done a first-rate job for me. The Pompeii Flu had come from Bu Deng's laboratories. There wasn't much left of those. After Bu's death the government seized them, located everything that could be militarized, and destroyed it. (Or said they did. Some people retained doubts.) What was left was mostly fragrances and flavors, and that was allowed to continue to exist. But Artie had managed to find a few people who had been part of the laboratories' glory days, and they had had a lot to say about what they called the "revolution." What they meant by that was the time when Bu Deng mysteriously died and his marriage partner and heir, J. J. Jones, impetuously made a lot of changes in Bu's labs. One was to destroy most of the carefully hoarded stores of militarized disease organisms because, J. J. had said in his most sanctimonious tones, he didn't want to benefit from the possession of what he quaintly called "weapons of mass destruction." That wasn't all he destroyed, either. He gave orders that the grapevines in Bu's favorite dining spot, the arbor he had been lunching in with Gerda when the news of Yellowstone arrived, be cut down and burned—because, he just as sanctimoniously said, he couldn't bear to be reminded of the person he had loved with all his heart every time he passed by.

Artie kept talking. I kept listening, too. I don't want you to think I didn't hear and understand everything he said. I know that he thought that—or maybe just thought that I was out of my mind, because when he was describing some things that these old-timers could do if paid to do them—I burst out laughing.

That stopped Artie in mid-flow. It took him a while to get back to what he'd been talking about—that is, the unimaginable horrors that he thought these old men and women would visit on the hapless human race if I chose to pay them enough money to do it—enough money, that is, to anesthetize what was left of their tiny, feeble consciences.

But at the same time another part of my mind had been processing a separate line of thought, starting with J. J.'s pitiful need to burn Bu's grapevines for sentimental reasons. You see, I knew Jeremy Jonathan Jones. I didn't think he was that sentimental. Which meant that I was trying to think of some other reason. And that corner of my mind, working with memories of how Bu's death had puzzled some observers because, after exhaustive post-mortem studies, they couldn't find a poisonous agent that could have done it. Oh, there were such poisons, but Bu ate nothing that had not passed through the hands of his private cook—who was also a doctoral-degree chemist who would have detected even the undetectable.

But—that corner of my mind began to shout, momentarily drowning out Artie's words, as the thought reached me—there were things that Bu ate that his chef never inspected: the grapes in his arbor.

J. J. had murdered the one person in his life that he had, he had said, "loved with all his heart!" And finally I understood why Gerda and Maury had referred to him as "the Bastard."

.   .   .

It took me a while to get Artie to continue with his line of thought. Even so, at first he was hesitant and frowning, but the majesty of the evil these old men and women could achieve took over, and he became almost lyrical. And, he said, they would do it if I would put up the money.

I would. I don't think I want to be specific about the details.

Artie warned me that what he thought possible would not only cost a lot of money—by which, he said, he meant a *lot* of money—but would take quite a lot of time. I said neither the money nor the time worried me, and he said, then so let it be.

I had noticed that he was a lot better dressed than he had been. When he left I saw that he, too, had employed a pair of off-duty New York cops for bodyguards—one on the jump seat in the back of the limousine with him, the other in the front seat with the driver and a machine gun.

I had wondered why his expense vouchers had been so high, but I didn't begrudge him a dime of it.

Oh, and one other thing.

When Shao-pin and I watched that portion of the coil together we sat together in what I believe is called a loveseat—a sort of two-person abbreviated sofa. It had been part of some decorator's plan, and I found the extra space useful for setting down my coffee cup or drinks tray or whatever, but never before to hold the handsome hips of a pretty guest.

It was better that way.

When Shao-pin shared the loveseat with me I was feeling quite upbeat—mostly, I think, because I could tell myself that I was doing what Gerda would have wanted me to do. So it was only natural that we held hands. Then it was just as natural that we got closer and finally, when the coil clip was over, got closer still in that huge bed that, with Gerda gone, I had never expected to put to a recreational use.

In the event, though, it worked fine.

I did wonder—though not until the heavy-breathing part was over and Shao-pin was softly purring her sleep sounds in the curl of my arm—just what Dream Gerda would make of this new development.

I needn't have worried. Once I drifted off to sleep myself it all became clear that she had no objection. I should add that that was the first time I had ever dreamed of a threesome.

36

SHARING A BED AGAIN

Now that Shao-pin had a new status in my household, sleeping over with me almost as often as she went back to her own sweet little villa, I began letting her in on selected previously withheld fractions of my own life. I showed her, for instance, more of the relationship between Gerda and Bu Deng. That was when I discovered that she really had no good idea who Bu Deng was, and I had to fill her in, starting with Bu's early job as a biochemist on the faculty of a Sichuan university until some of the students got political in unapproved ways. The students got themselves expelled. The professors who were thought to have encouraged them got downgraded, and where Bu wound up was at the Chengdu panda breeding station.

The pandas had been dying in record numbers, and Bu's new assignment was to develop microorganisms that would predate on the microorganisms that made the pandas sick. He did it, too. He went farther. He developed a shot that made the boy pandas and the girl pandas more interested in sex, which they hadn't much been before.

At that point Shao-pin gave me a startled look. "You mean like— I mean, something like the stuff—"

I took pity on her. "Yes, it's related to something like the stuff the colonel says is responsible for my feelings about Gerda. Mine was special. The product they made for general human consumption—the dealers called it Stannish fly, back when I was a boy—is related to what he did for the pandas, but what Gerda did, or is said to have done"—I saw the way her eyes narrowed, so I didn't press that point—"was a superstrong variation on the regular fly."

"Oh," she said, but she didn't press it either. So I told her how the production of baby pandas had nearly doubled after the adults got Bu's joy juice, and as a result of all that good work, the Chinese government gave him an exit visa so he could sharpen his skills at a French university.

Bu didn't go to France. He went to the Stans. Where he prospered, and before you knew it had a whole lavish lab of his own, with the finest state-of-the-art equipment building on what the Soviets had left behind, and the biddablest of graduate students to do the heavy lifting. And like the surgeon who re-created Gerda, just kept getting richer and richer.

"So he had it made," Shao-pin commented.

"Sure did," I said, "up to a point, anyway. Want to see what his place looked like?" And I showed her Bu's mansion, and then the surgeon's, and a few more of their parties, and when it was over I caught her looking around my own far from humble accommodations with a more judgmental eye. So I let her add on some improvements, because I wanted her to be happy and I still had more money than I was ever going to need—a hothouse that she filled with flowering plants and a dressing room of her own off the bedroom we shared and a few other niceties, and a lap pool in the backyard. Put it all together and she was as happy as a pig in ordure, and because she was happy so was I.

Well, because of that and perhaps because of one other thing: Artie Mason was turning out to be a treasure, diligently doing everything I had hoped he could, which was a lot. In fact, so much was involved that it took all of eight years to get it all done. During that time Artie located people who had worked for Bu in the old days, and—making some heavy inroads into my money—set them up in a lab of their own, where they made ingenious variations on some of Bu's old proprietaries. This had the happy effect of making quite a lot of money itself, which enabled him to give his new friends significant incomes of their own while considerably reducing the amounts he needed from me. And then he put them to work on the purpose of the whole project, which was to manufacture some of the stuff described on that ruby-red coil.

None of that went quickly. By the time Artie was able to hand me the transparent, multiply cushioned box that contained ten little black marbles full of Bu's secret weapon eight years had gone by.

I had become even richer with the endless flow of euros that came from the show the world never seemed to tire of. And I was thinking of asking her to marry me.

Getting around to that point had used up several of those years. There were a lot of stumbling blocks in the way. My own complicated feelings about the late Gerda Fleming, for one thing. But even after I had persuaded myself that that was all right there remained one major problem. Shao-pin didn't particularly seem to want to get married to me.

From time to time I had turned the conversation in that general direction, but she was too swift for me. She either ignored what I was saying or swiftly turned it away again. Her attitude was almost annoying—well, would perhaps have been if she hadn't been so great in every other way.

The other thing that was going on between me and Shao-pin was that I was teaching her all about Gerda.

The two of them had never met. Shao-pin's ideas about her were—well, I guess the best words for them is "confused." Working for Security Shao-pin had been affected by that pervasive Security doctrine that terrorists were pond scum to begin with, and the more effective they were the more evil. That, of course, was in conflict with the fact that I was smitten. Probably, Shao-pin must have supposed, the party line that all my love for Gerda came out of a test tube was the right way to look at it. But my feelings were unchallengeably still there.

Anyway, I wanted her to understand, so I was making it my business to watch bits and pieces of Gerda's coils, sitting side by side with Shao-pin in what Shao-pin herself once called Ex-Girlfriend 101.

I didn't force it on her. If she looked unenthusiastic when I suggested we watch a bit of the story of Gerda I changed the subject. But I didn't have to do that often. Gerda's life was definitely an interesting story. I started Shao-pin with bits from the days when Gerda had been young Brian Bossert—the George Washington Bridge, the subway tunnel under the East River, all those well publicized exploits right up to the disaster at Toronto. Then the interminable years of reconstructive surgery, and her subsequent career as Nevirovski's trophy concubine, then Rollo's, then that of maybe fifteen or twenty other men, some of whose names I had never learned. (And in truth sometimes wondered if Gerda herself had known all of them.) And I'd sat with Shao-pin as we watched that terrible day in Bu Deng's arbor when she got the news that Yellowstone had changed everything for everybody. And I had spaced all those segments out with bits and pieces of Gerda's researches into the total rottenness of the human race. And then, one evening after a pleasant dinner and a couple of brandies on the balcony off our bedroom, watching the setting of the huge Italian sun, I said, "There's one clip I've been saving for you. It's the last I have before they went secret. Would you like to see it now?"

She would, of course—I think that word "last" had sounded grateful in her ear—so we adjourned to the loveseat again. I threaded the coil into the player for the wall screen while she made a mild highball for herself and a slightly less mild one for me.

"All right," I said, "here's where we are. You saw that the Bastard—Bu's lover, I mean, had given up his plan to wipe out the House of Windsor and came back to the Stans. Gerda and Maury were having a drink in one of their favorite bars, Maury trying to jolly her out of her fairly chronic state of depression, when Bu and J.J. tracked them down. They had news."

. . .

So I sat her down in that well-used loveseat and blanked the wall pictures for the moment. "Maury had taken Gerda to one of her favorite gin mills, I guess to try to cheer her up," I told her, "and Bu and the Bastard tracked them down. It was less than a month after he came back." I started the coil bit, and there they were, two big men with news so big that it made them stammer and do their best to blush as they told their friends that they were going to get married.

"Because this is the real thing," the Bastard said, and Bu Deng, one big paw wrapped around the Bastard's equally big one, nodded, grinning.

I had never seen Bu with that particular expression before. On the wall images it appeared that Gerda never had, either. She looked startled, then demanded, "When?"

Bu answered for both of them. "You mean when will the wedding be? We haven't decided. We just made up our minds to do it today." His expression became almost comically defensive. "You see, I've never felt this way before. Never wanted to make this kind of a commitment. And we haven't yet got around to the arrangements."

"Then," Gerda said, getting up from her place at the bar and suddenly looking both younger and less gloom-stricken, "let us do it for you. Don't worry about a thing. We'll take care of all of it."

And so they did. The place for the wedding would be the very saloon they had heard the announcement in, with an open bar that Bu would underwrite. The date would be that weekend, three days away. Maury and Gerda became respectively their best man and maid (!) of honor, Gerda doubling as the producer of the event and the person who made all the arrangements.

There wasn't any problem caused by the fact that it was a same-sex marriage, not in the Stans, but they had a little difficulty figuring out who would perform it. Neither Jeremy nor Bu was religious. Still they wanted their union to be as formally binding as possible, which Gerda took to mean godly. There was a native sweeper in Bu's laboratory who was known to perform religious services for the aboriginal Stannish population, or anyway for those few of them who took an interest in such matters, and a barman from New Jersey who claimed he had once been a Catholic priest. Gerda rounded them both up and coached them to conduct the rite in tandem.

It all began well. Beside me, Shao-pin made little clucks of appreciation as the couple approached the altar—well, the free-lunch table, but for this day it bore flowers instead of cold cuts. Neither Bu nor J.J. had a veil, but they both wore gorgeous arm corsages. They spoke right up with their I do's and I will's. They drank champagne out of each other's patent leather shoes, and a pretty good hit of champagne it was, since Bu was a size twelve and J.J. an eleven. And then they got to their two-meter tall wedding cake that Gerda had ordered on her way in to the bar and was still hot enough from the oven that some of its icing melted and ran together. They didn't mind. They fed each other slices, while the eighty or ninety assorted people in the audience cheered. That was a pretty good turnout, although the happy couple didn't know most of them. Gerda had simply let it be known that there would be a party with Bu picking up the check.

The amusing thing about the icing was that Maury and Gerda had loaded it with one of the items from Bu's lab, and indeed one that was a variety of something I knew well, the aphrodisiac called "Stannish fly." So about ten minutes after they finished the cake, the newlyweds, all flushed and happy, excused themselves to find a room.

By the time they came back, nearly all the guests were gone, having eaten their own helpings of the cake to its last crumb. Gerda and Maury hadn't. They were having a final drink in the now empty bar.

When Shao-pin, by my side on the loveseat, pointed out that Gerda was drinking neat whiskeys now I explained, "What you're seeing is what the junior surgeon, Rollo, called Gerda's post-party depression, the feeling she got when something had been fun and then was over. That isn't the most important part, though."

She gave me a mildly suspicious look. "It isn't?"

I was busy resetting the coil. "Wait a minute. Here. This is a few hours later. Gerda and Maury are still in the bar, although it's past closing time, and Bu and the Bastard come back."

The newlyweds looked a good deal more relaxed than they had before, not least because they had got out of the formal clothing Gerda had demanded they wear—green and yellow striped shorts for the Bastard, the kilt that was one of his sartorial affectations for Bu. Bu ordered a couple of brandies from the weary lapsed-priest barman who was all that was left of the party's serving staff. Then he and the Bastard sat sipping the whiskey and smirking at each other as if those were the most delightfully enjoyable things anybody could ever do.

Maury was looking at them with affectionate tolerance, bobbing his head and grinning. Gerda wasn't. That soul-sick depression was settling over her until she couldn't help it. She burst out, "What is there to be so happy about?"

All three of them turned to stare at her as if she had just broken wind in public. Maury shook his head reproachfully. She had punctured that bubble of happiness the newlyweds had brought in with them. Looking at them, Maury said, "Don't mind Gerda, she's just having her period."

That was a joke, of course, and not the first time Maury had made it. Usually that started a fight between them. It might have done it this time, too, except that Bu was too full of just-married happiness to let anyone rain on his parade. He reached over and patted Gerda's knee. "Don't be out of sorts, dear Gerda," he said. "It's not such a bad life you have here, is it?"

She was in no mood to be jollied. "For you it isn't," she said. "Maybe it isn't even for me sometimes, but what about him?"—jabbing her thumb toward the barman, wiping glasses at the end of the bar and conspicuously not hearing a word the customers said.

"Why do you say that?" Bu said. "Our abos are quite well treated. Their standard of living is at least double what it was before—"

"Before you people stole their lands?" she interrupted.

That made the room's temperature drop. "For Christ's sake, Gerda,"

Maury exploded, and "Please," J.J. coaxed, and Bu said, "Gerda, you're American, aren't you? Americans aren't in any position to criticize other people for stealing their lands from natives. At least we didn't slaughter them."

He was pushing her a little too far. "No," she agreed. "You didn't, at least not right away."

She had seriously offended Bu. He sighed and pushed his chair back.

"Time to get to bed," he said, not even looking at her. "I have to get up early. Coming, hon?" he asked J.J.

Who surprised Gerda. "You go on, dear," he told his loving bride, or perhaps groom. "I think I'd like a nightcap before I go."

Now that had been a surprise to me, too. I wouldn't have thought that even the Bastard would send his dearly beloved off to sleep alone on their wedding night. I didn't have to ask him why, though. Maury did it for me. "What's the matter?" he demanded. "Trouble in paradise already?"

J.J. gave him a small smile. "God, no! We're as happy as we can get. Bu is everything I ever dreamed of—smart, gentle, kind—he's perfect. It's just that there are a few things we don't agree on."

It seemed that Bu had insisted on keeping the wall screen news on as they dressed for the wedding. What was showing was a new terrorist outbreak in Western Europe. Little gangs of local loonies protesting no-nudity beach laws or new property taxes just wasn't exciting.

J.J. said so. "That's all penny-ante stuff," he complained. "Supermarket stink bombs, for God's sake. Couldn't they at least derail a commuter train?" And then, perhaps because he was feeling a little guilty about pigging it in the Stans instead of wiping out the House of Windsor, he confessed, "I don't know who I am anymore."

He was looking as though something nearby smelled really bad. I was looking him over pretty carefully by then, which is probably why I hadn't noticed that something was changing the expression on Maury's face until he spoke up. "Who would you want to be?" he asked.

J.J.'s own face collapsed. "I don't know. Someone who has a purpose for living. But I don't know what that would be."

Maury nodded. "Maybe Gerda knows," he said. "She's been dropping hints for weeks. Let's talk about it, but not here." Then he said, as though it were the most natural thing in the world, "Why don't we go over to my place and have a little talk?"

So that was the end of the clip. Shao-pin turned a puzzled face to me. "What just happened?" she asked. "What did they do? You can't leave me up in the air like that."

"I don't have any choice. Right around then is when Gerda stopped making records of what they did. Of all her researches, too. I'm sorry, but I hate it as much as you do. Just when I wanted to know every last thing that every last one of them said and did, the three of them walked out of the gin mill where the wedding had taken place—that is, the place where all the massed automatic camera batteries had captured every sound and movement of every body there—and headed for Maury's place, where there might be plenty of recording equipment, too. Gerda would have seen to that—but it was all turned off. And it stayed turned off all that night, and all the next night, and all the day after that. And when there was a new recording it was time-stamped several days later, and no one I knew was in it. What was showing was a bunch of clips Gerda had made in the library. And what every one of them was about was more of the excruciatingly bad things that people had done, mostly along the lines of killing other people, and all that there was of Gerda on that part of the coil was her voice, sourcing some of the clips."

Shao-pin was looking incredulous. "And you can't tell me what they were doing?"

I gave her a smile. "Oh, I didn't say that. I knew what the three of them were doing, all right. They were conspiring. All I had to do was look ahead a few days on the coil, and then I could see, from what they were doing then, what it was that they had been conspiring about."

She was beginning to look less incredulous than irritated. "And that was what?"

"The decision to go ahead with the Pompeii Flu, and figuring out how to do it. It can't have been anything else."

37

THE EDUCATION OF SHAO-PIN

If Shao-pin had ever resented my attempts to make her understand Gerda Fleming she had never shown any ill feeling about it. Now, however, she was eager for more and more. I gave her freedom to read both coils whenever she chose, and there were many mornings when I woke up after her and heard the muttering of many voices from one of the sitting rooms near our bed, and there was Shao-pin, a cooling cup of that dishwater Chinese tea beside her, running through a repeated view of Gerda's stages of surgery, or a new catalog of slaughters. There was a mass murder in Amritsar, India, of ordinary Indians, peaceably gathered until a detachment of the British army opened fire on them, shooting until all their ammunition was used up and killing not quite four hundred. So it wasn't a particular kind of murdering that was interesting Gerda. It was simply the subject of mass killing of people by people, of which there seemed to have been a lot.

Her gleanings went on and on: Civilians in the city of Nanking, 1937, when it was taken by the Japanese army, somewhere between two hundred thousand and four hundred thousand dead; no count available on rapes and beatings. Drogheda, Ireland, 1649, thirty-five hundred people massacred by troops of Oliver Cromwell. Afghanistan, 1842, sixteen thousand Britons killed by Afghan tribesmen.

Had enough? Oh, but we're just getting started. We haven't done justice to the Germans. Once Herr Hitler put it into their heads they became so proficient in the killing of Jews (and Gypsies and other persons that they didn't care to have moving into the neighborhood), murdering them a few hundred at a time—but doing it many, many times—in their proudest invention, the gas chamber. With that in operation they didn't usually have to bother with the drudgery of all that machine gunning. Well, except now and then, as with some captured American soldiers at a place called Malmedy in 1944. No, they were the champions, although, to be fair, we must admit that Josef Stalin's USSR was coming up fast with 21,857 dead Poles (how methodically they conducted a census) in 1940 and about a hundred thousand (ah, sometimes the counts did get sloppy) in the Baltic states in 1941 and nobody knows how many hundreds of thousands or millions in that celebrated Gulag Archipelago of work-them-to-death camps.

And, listen, the religious institutions were not that far behind. Mostly they did their work a few at a time, hanging or burning at stake, though sometimes a few devout Muslim jihadists could take out a few thousand infidels at once when a tempting skyscraper just begged to be crushed and burned to the ground.

Well, enough of European, Asian, American, and Australian butcheries, and I don't want to get into African ones. Thirteen-year-old boys in uniform systematically chopping off the hands of thirteen-year-old boys in tattered shorts and tears? The males in one house trading places at sundown with the males in the house next door, because they know that when the soldiers came in the middle of the night they would amuse themselves by making all the males in each house have sex with all the females, and the householders wanted to avoid incest? No. Africa would make a cow weep.

Oh, humans do have their moments. Sometimes they are kind, and entertaining and even good, but then along comes a Hitler or a jihad-preaching mullah or a Ku Klux Klan kleagle and then they show their true selves. Not to mention that there are just too many of them for our one little planet.

So that was the problem that Gerda wanted to repair. I knew what tool the three of them were planning to use for the job—what they called the Pompeii Flu—because, along with all the rest of the world, I had seen it at work.

38

WHAT TO DO WITH MY PRIZE

From time to time, when Shao-pin was out of the house and I could send the servants away on made-up errands, I would take my ten little trophies out of their hiding place to look at them.

That was a reasonably safe thing to do. Those ten marbles that had cost me a decade and a fortune were quite secure as long as their shiny black shells were intact. That's what Artie Mason had told me, it being what the people who made them had told him. I had no reason to doubt it. All the same I was really careful to keep them in their padded packaging, in their heavily immobile safe in my rescue room.

Yes, I said "rescue room." A lot of people don't know what a rescue room is anymore, but there was a time when any family rich enough to own a big house probably had one of them. You could identify a rescue room because it had steel bars laced into all its walls, and no windows, and a steel door with steel tongue-and-groove locks and the most pick-proof locks that money could buy. The idea was that if your house got over-run with terrorists—or with house-robbing ordinary criminals, for that matter—you scuttled into the rescue room and locked the door. Then you just waited for the cops, or somebody, to show up to rescue you.

That is, that's what you did, anyway, if you hadn't made the mistake of seriously antagonizing the marauders, because if you did that they might just set fire to the whole house and burn it down around you. This was not a desirable outcome for anyone. Especially for you and your now crispy critters family.

That breed of marauders was no longer common, but the room was still there, and I had recognized it as a first-rate place to hide those ten little black marbles.

On one particular day, after Shao-pin had been a resident with me for a couple of months, I took that heavy, three-pronged key out of the secret pocket in my knock-about vest and went up to the end of the hall on the second floor to open the safe and look at them. Shao-pin was out of the house, gone to see her doctor for one of those regular checkups that she wanted me to copy. (I was resisting that idea. What was the point of safeguarding my health when I was intending to be dead before long?) I twirled the combination, opened the safe, and took out the box of marbles. Then—holding it quite securely—I lifted one of the marbles off its cushioned pad and closed my eyes and imagined dropping it on the floor and grinding it under my heel, the door wide open and the air-conditioning set high so there was a detectable little breeze carrying the rescue room air out to mix with the ambient air outside.

I thought about that for several minutes, unmoving, the plague pill wrapped in my right fist. Then I opened my eyes, restored the little globe to its nest, and gently pushed the safe's door closed.

I felt myself smiling. Actually it was kind of funny. I seemed to be unwilling to take the action I thought I had been preparing to do for years. I had invested a whole hell of a lot of money and effort to get the damn things, and now that I had them I couldn't make up my mind to use them.

It wasn't that I had turned in revulsion from the whole idea of slaughtering humanity. I hadn't. I was convinced that Gerda had made a pretty good case for wiping the species out. I simply wasn't quite ready to be the one who did it.

That did not make a lot of sense to me. What was wrong with performing an action that I was convinced was a proper one to do? And then as I sat in that bleak room, my elbows on that bare table and my chin in my hands, I realized there was one element that was wrong.

I hadn't given the other side a chance to be heard.

What I needed was some intelligent, kindly, well-informed person who was likely to love humanity more than I did to take the conventional side of that argument, and the more I thought about it the more eager I was for her to get back from her doctor's appointment so we could talk.

39

COMING CLEAN WITH THE
OTHER WOMAN I LOVED

When Shao-pin got back to the house she looked in on me in our calisthenics room, where I was exercising under the guidance of a good-looking virt female wearing hardly any clothes at all. "Glad you're taking care of yourself, Brad," she said.

I didn't respond to that. I just said, "I need to talk to you, Shao-pin."

That made her look faintly surprised, but what she said was, "Sounds like a good idea. Dinner'll be in about an hour: before?"

"Why not? Come into the shower room with me and we'll get started while I dress."

She nodded. "Meet you there," she said, and was gone into the hallway. Since I took the inner way I was there before her. I showered barely long enough to get wet all over, and was pulling up a pair of shorts when she arrived.

"So what are we going to talk about?" she asked, taking a seat on one of the chairs meant for tired athletes.

I pulled on a shirt and sat down next to her. "Listen, maybe we should order something to eat before we start."

Shao-pin picked up the towel I had dropped on the floor and hung it over the back of a chair. "I called the kitchen already. Alison said we shouldn't spoil our appetites so soon before dinner, and she'd send up some tea and coffee. What'd you want to talk about?"

There being no help for it I sat down across a tiny table from her, took a deep breath and started in. "What I have to tell you isn't happy, Shao-pin. It may make you think less of me, but I have to tell you it anyway. When Gerda was dying from that car crash near Caserta she gave me something to hide. It was a funny-looking foreign coil, and I took it. I hid it, too. No one saw it, no one knew I had anything from her. Then, when I had it in my room that night, I began to worry. I couldn't read it.

"I didn't know what it was. I began imagining bad things. What if what I had in my pocket was a cure for the Pompeii Flu? What if because I was hiding it I was condemning a lot of other people to catch the disease and be mutilated by it and die from it? I didn't know what to do. . . . Oh, here's the coffee."

I had been watching Shao-pin's face attentively while I spoke. At first what she displayed was concern. When I mentioned hiding something Gerda had given me it was pure shock. Then, when I talked about my fears that I might be causing unnecessary sickness and death it was revulsion. She got up to let the coffee bearer in. Over her shoulder she said, "You mean nobody searched you?"

"Not a soul."

She was scowling now, but when I started to say something she shook her head warningly, with a glance in the direction of Alison's grandson, learning to be a chef like his grandmother by starting as a gofer. When he was gone she said, "That's against all Security procedure, but I guess it's too late to worry about that. Please go on."

So I did. I told her how relieved I was when the actual cure was found on a different coil in Gerda's bag, and how I'd dithered about for that long, long time before I connected with Artie Mason, and what Artie had done. And I finished by telling her about those little black marbles in the safe in the rescue room. And then I stopped and gazed at her, waiting for a reaction. The whole story, all those worrisome years of doubts and delays, had taken less than twenty minutes to tell, and through it all Shao-pin had sat listening politely, with an occasional half nod to show that she was grasping what I had to say or an appreciative sip of her cooling tea, and hadn't said another word.

For a couple of minutes she didn't say anything now, either, just stared into space, or down into her teacup and hardly at all at me. Then she shook herself and said, "And these little helpings of extermination that you've got in the rescue room, are they anything like the Flu?"

"Worse," I said. "Or maybe in some ways better. Better because they're not agonizing. But just as fatal, and there's no cure with the pills."

She nodded. "And you've saved them because you're planning to turn them loose sometime soon and exterminate the human race?"

That was a hard one. "Planning" was way too strong a word for my muddled thinking on the subject. I said, "You've seen a lot of the stuff Gerda collected. Don't you think the species that does that sort of thing should be put out of its misery?"

She wasn't going to let me get away with that. "You're the one who has the stuff to make it happen, so you're the one whose opinion matters, not mine."

"Yes, damn it, I know that," I said, suddenly surly because she was touching me exactly where it hurt. "But you've seen Gerda's evidence, and what do you think?"

She pursed her lips. "Well . . . All right. Gerda makes a pretty good case. But there's something to be said on the other side, too." She had begun fumbling in her bag, pulling out a large envelope. "This," she said, taking a photograph out of the envelope, "is your daughter." She made me take it, but it didn't really look like anything I would call a daughter, more like a sloppily prepared scrambled egg, with a part of it circled in a grease pencil. "Yes, I'm pregnant, Brad. Dr. di Milo gave me this sonogram this morning. I call her Sasha, although so far she's only a six-week fetus. But, Brad—dear Brad—I don't want her to die."

40

MY DAUGHTER

There is a point at which questions of logic and justice and retribution just do not matter anymore, isn't there? I don't think that simply seeing that splotch of matter in the X-ray picture took me to that point, but something did. The fact that that cluster of cells was energetically dividing in order to become a child? The look on Shao-pin's face when she told me it had a name? The quick twist in my abdomen when I heard the words "your daughter"? Well, something did. And before we finished our delayed lunch I had promised that I wouldn't do anything with the little pills that could end a race for a good, long time. Until Sasha was six months old? Shao-pin bargained. And I agreed.

I probably would have agreed to postpone a decision until Sasha was old enough to vote, if Shao-pin had proposed it, because I was in shock. But the actual length of time, once Sasha had got herself born, didn't matter. This serious-minded little creature, determinedly attempting to wrap her insignificant fingers around my bony thumb, made her own case. Witless, often noisy, frequently smelly little lump of humanity that she was, she had her way of establishing the fact that she had a right to live. At any cost. Including, I was pretty sure, the cost of my own life.

So on Sasha's six-month birthday we tucked her in and went down to the rescue room with a half bottle of Lacryma Christi wine, and when Shao-pin had poured us each a glass she looked up at me and said, "Well?"

"Oh, hell," I said, "let the bastards live. Maybe they'll get better."

And so the next day we got in our limo, with instructions to our driver, Olivia, to not hit any bumps at all, took off for the funeral home of Terranozza I Guarnio, with me gingerly carrying the black velvet jewelry bag I had filled from Artie Mason's expensive trophies.

We had long since abandoned the idea of dumping the poison pills into a vat of some molten noble metal like platinum. Such vats were not easy to come by on the Vomero, and so we had taken expert opinion, judiciously asked for, on alternative 100 percent guaranteed disposals. The one we liked best, or anyway disliked least, was the process called resomation, originally developed to dispose of the used-up cadavers from medical schools. A few funeral homes offered it as an alternative to burial or cremation, and one of them turned out to be less than twenty minutes from our house.

Resomation involved simmering the no-longer-wanted stuff in a bath of potassium hydroxide for a few hours, after which, our informants assured us, no complex molecule would survive in what would have become a layer of snow-white ash at the bottom of the sealed vessel it had cooked in. There would be a few centimeters of a chemically sterile liquid atop the ash, which could be poured away into the household disposal system, since it was now totally sterile. As was the snowy ash.

So we drove into the parking area, where Signore Guarnio was waiting for us, and he conducted us to their resomation chamber. I was glad to note that it didn't smell of anything. A little acrid, maybe, but nothing like organic decay.

We had rehearsed Signore Guarnio carefully. He lifted the top of the vat of hot chemical, I gently placed the black bag of black marbles in it, he closed the top again and sealed it. And then we were through. "Come back if you wish in three hours and thirty," he said, "and you can see us disposing the remains."

But we said no, thanks, and drove back home, much more rapidly, to see if Sasha was still awake.

I haven't regretted what I did. I don't think I will in the future, either. But I don't think that I want Shao-pin to know that we only resomationed nine of those little death eggs, I having removed one when she wasn't around, just in case.

Oh, I don't think that that in case will ever be the case. But, you see, things don't always happen the way I think, and expect, they're going to.

And in the remote and improbable event that fate goes in the wrong, in some terribly wrong, direction, I would like to have the option of changing my mind.

ABOUT THE AUTHOR

FREDERIK POHL has written science fiction for more than seventy years. His novel *Gateway* won the Hugo, Nebula, and John W. Campbell Memorial awards for Best Science Fiction Novel. *Man Plus* won the Nebula Award, and altogether he has won seven Hugo Awards and two Nebula Awards for his fiction, among his many kudos.

In addition to his solo fiction, Pohl has published collaborations with other writers, including C. M. Kornbluth, Lester del Rey, and Jack Williamson. One Pohl/Kornbluth collaboration, *The Space Merchants*, is a bestselling classic of satiric science fiction. *The Starchild Trilogy* with Williamson is one of the more notable collaborations in the field.

Pohl became a magazine editor when still a teenager. In the 1960s he piloted *Worlds of If* to three successive Hugos for Best Magazine. He has edited original-story anthologies, notably the seminal Star Science Fiction series of the early 1950s. Among his other activities in the field, he has been a literary agent, has edited lines of science fiction books, and has been president of the Science Fiction Writers of America. Most recently, he won the Hugo Award for Best Fan Writer for his blog, www.theway thefutureblogs.com. He and his wife, Elizabeth Anne Hull, an editor and an academic active in the Science Fiction Research Association, live in Palatine, Illinois.